Praise for the novels of

'Read on, adventure fans.'

NEW YORK TIMES

'A rich, compelling look back in time [to]
when history and myth intermingled.'

SAN FRANCISCO CHRONICLE

'Only a handful of 20th century writers tantalize
our senses as well as Smith. A rare author who
wields a razor-sharp sword of craftsmanship.'

TULSA WORLD

'He paces his tale as swiftly as he can with
swordplay aplenty and killing strokes that come
like lightning out of a sunny blue sky.'

KIRKUS REVIEWS

'Best Historical Novelist – I say Wilbur Smith, with his
swashbuckling novels of Africa. The bodices rip and the
blood flows. You can get lost in Wilbur Smith and
misplace all of August.'

STEPHEN KING

'Action is the name of Wilbur Smith's game
and he is the master.'

WASHINGTON POST

'Smith manages to serve up adventure, history
and melodrama in one thrilling package that
will be eagerly devoured by series fans.'

Wilbur Smith was born in Central Africa in 1933. He became a full-time writer in 1964 following the success of *When the Lion Feeds*, and has since published over fifty global bestsellers, including the Courtney Series, the Ballantyne Series, the Egyptian Series, the Hector Cross Series and many successful standalone novels, all meticulously researched on his numerous expeditions worldwide. An international phenomenon, his readership built up over fifty-five years of writing, establishing him as one of the most successful and impressive brand authors in the world.

The establishment of the Wilbur & Niso Smith Foundation in 2015 cemented Wilbur's passion for empowering writers, promoting literacy and advancing adventure writing as a genre. The foundation's flagship programme is the Wilbur Smith Adventure Writing Prize.

Wilbur Smith passed away peacefully at home in 2021 with his wife, Niso, by his side, leaving behind him a rich treasure-trove of novels and stories that will delight readers for years to come.

For all the latest information on Wilbur Smith's writing visit www.wilbursmithbooks.com or facebook.com/WilburSmith.

Imogen Robertson has been shortlisted for the CWA Historical Dagger three times and is the author of The Crowther and Westerman crime series and *The Paris Winter*. You can find her online at www.imogenrobertson.com or on X @RobertsonImogen.

Also by Wilbur Smith

Non-Fiction

On Leopard Rock: A Life of
Adventures

The Courtney Series

When the Lion Feeds
The Sound of Thunder
A Sparrow Falls
The Burning Shore
Power of the Sword
Rage
A Time to Die
Golden Fox
Birds of Prey
Monsoon
Blue Horizon
The Triumph of the Sun
Assegai
Golden Lion
War Cry
The Tiger's Prey
Courtney's War
King of Kings
Ghost Fire
Legacy of War
Storm Tide
Nemesis
Warrior King

The Ballantyne Series

A Falcon Flies
Men of Men
The Angels Weep

The Leopard Hunts in Darkness
The Triumph of the Sun
King of Kings
Call of the Raven

The Egyptian Series

River God
The Seventh Scroll
Warlock
The Quest
Desert God
Pharaoh
The New Kingdom
Titans of War
Testament

Hector Cross

Those in Peril
Vicious Circle
Predator

Standalones

The Dark of the Sun
Shout at the Devil
Gold Mine
The Diamond Hunters
The Sunbird
Eagle in the Sky
The Eye of the Tiger
Cry Wolf
Hungry as the Sea
Wild Justice
Elephant Song

WILBUR SMITH

SMITH

FIRE ON THE HORIZON

WITH IMOGEN ROBERTSON

ZAFFRE

First published in the United States of America in 2024 by Zaffre, an imprint
of Zaffre Publishing Group, a Bonnier Books UK company
an imprint of Bonnier Books UK

Typeset by IDSUK (Data Connection) Ltd
Printed in the USA

10 9 8 7 6 5 4 3 2 1

Hardcover ISBN: 978-1-8387-7974-0
Canadian paperback ISBN: 978-1-8387-7975-7
Digital ISBN: 978-1-8387-7976-4

For information, contact
251 Park Avenue South, Floor 12, New York, New York 10010
www.bonnierbooks.co.uk

This book is for my wife, Mokhiniso.
Beautiful, loving, loyal and true,
There is no one in the world like you.

THE
COURTNEY
FAMILY
IN
FIRE ON THE HORIZON

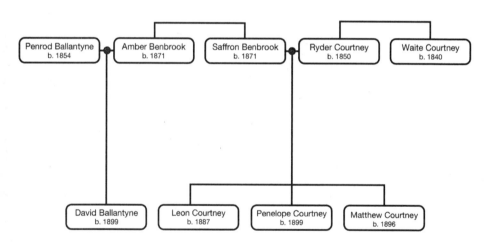

Penrod Ballantyne
b. 1854

Amber Benbrook
b. 1871

Saffron Benbrook
b. 1871

Ryder Courtney
b. 1850

Waite Courtney
b. 1840

David Ballantyne
b. 1899

Leon Courtney
b. 1887

Penelope Courtney
b. 1899

Matthew Courtney
b. 1896

Find out more about the Courtneys and see the Courtney family tree in full at www.wilbursmithbooks.com/courtney-family-tree

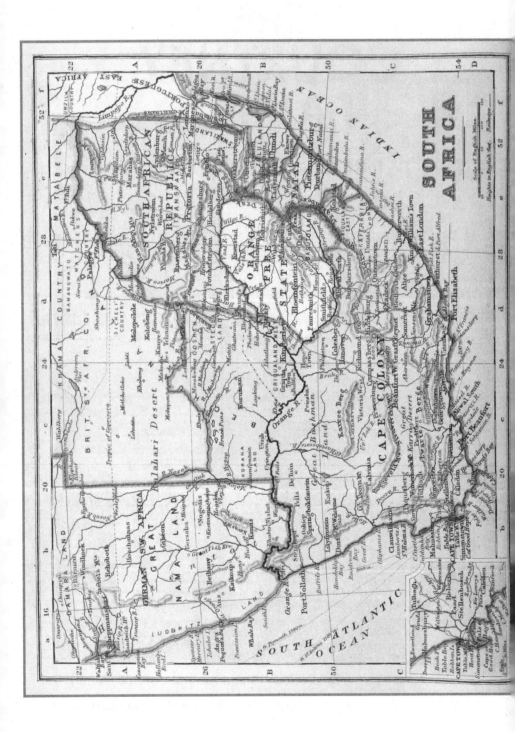

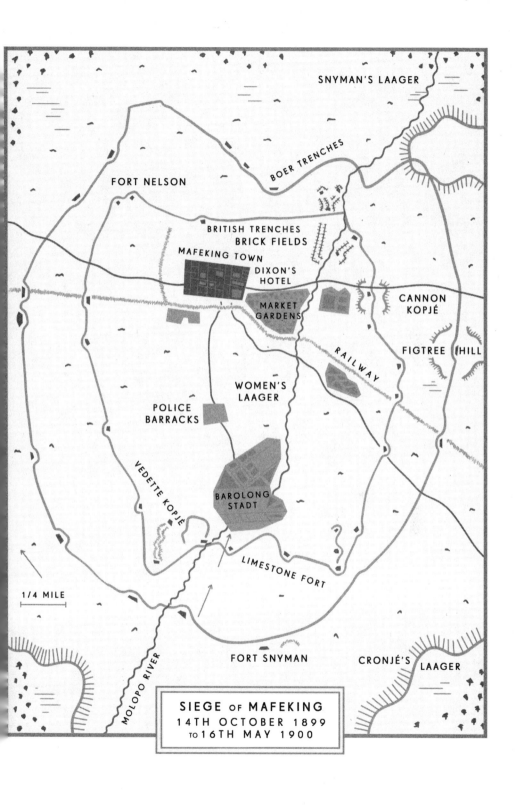

SNYMAN'S LAAGER

BOER TRENCHES

FORT NELSON

BRITISH TRENCHES
BRICK FIELDS
MAFEKING TOWN
DIXON'S
HOTEL

CANNON
KOPJÉ

MARKET
GARDENS

RAILWAY

FIGTREE HILL

WOMEN'S
LAAGER

POLICE
BARRACKS

VEDETTE KOPJÉ

BAROLONG
STADT

LIMESTONE FORT

1/4 MILE

MOLOPO RIVER

FORT SNYMAN

CRONJÉ'S LAAGER

SIEGE OF MAFEKING
14TH OCTOBER 1899
TO 16TH MAY 1900

Part I

1899

Colonel Penrod Ballantyne, hero of Abu Klea and Omdurman, pulled his wide-brimmed hat low over his forehead and pretended to doze, while the train rattled north across the open veld towards Johannesburg. In the winter sunshine of early June, the great plains unrolled to a far horizon. Pale grasses and low thorn bushes, desperate for rain under the vast blue sky, shook in the breeze as the train passed. There was no sign of a human hand other than the narrow train tracks reaching into the distance.

Penrod, dressed in the loose, hard-wearing clothes of a working man, his skin tanned to the colour of polished teak by the African sun, paid no attention to the view. Through half-closed eyes, he was watching the two other occupants of the carriage. The man, dressed in a formal black suit, stared out of the window, frowning, his fingers gripping the bowl of his unlit pipe. Next to him was a girl, thirteen perhaps, wearing a long dress of forget-me-not blue and a cream bonnet, the colours emphasising her fair skin, the cut drawing attention to her high cheekbones and long, graceful neck. She was reading her Bible.

The man was Gerrit Vintner. He was returning home with his daughter after the failed talks with the British over the future governance of the Transvaal in Bloemfontein. He was a man of means and reputation, with farms and a thriving business empire in the Transvaal. In his younger days, he had ridden with General Nicholaas Smit and delivered the British humiliating defeats at Ingogo and MaJabu Hill. Now in his fifties, he was still strong and vigorous, his thick beard shot through with grey.

Penrod had been travelling through the Transvaal for some weeks now. He had left his wife and son in Cairo, working his way down the east coast of Africa – Mombasa, Stone Town, Dar es Salaam, Beira – before arriving in Lourenço Marques, the capital of Portuguese East Africa, in the guise of John Quinn, exiled Irish patriot, occasional farmhand and mine worker, a man deeply sympathetic to the Boer struggle against British Imperialism. After a night at the Carlton Hotel, the newly completed railway – the pride of the Transvaal – had taken him from the wide, tree-lined streets of Lourenço Marques, the dhows riding at anchor in the turquoise water of the harbour, up to the yellow dust of the highveld, through Komatipoort and Nelspruit, to Pretoria and Bloemfontein.

While in Bloemfontein, Penrod had kept several prominent Boers under observation – Vintner being one of them. Then, two nights ago, he had overheard a muttered conference about his man, which had decided him on this journey and this carriage.

The rear door opened suddenly. A blast of noise, the thundering churn of the wheels on the track shattering the peace of the almost-empty carriage.

'Here, boys! More room to spread out in first class.'

The man who had spoken strutted into the carriage. His clothes, dirty and badly patched, hung loose on his tall, stringy body, and under different circumstances Penrod would have taken him for a vagrant. But the rifle he had slung over his shoulder was a Mauser, and he wore a knife and a gun at his belt. He was followed by two companions, dusty and unkempt but heavier. One with a dusting of freckles across his face, the other with a scar running from his temple down into his sparse beard. Their eyes were dull and brutish and the stink of the previous night's cheap alcohol followed them in a cloud. Penrod remained motionless, observing the new arrival and his friends from under the brim of his hat. He had been expecting them.

The first man grinned like a dog baring its teeth, then nodded to his freckled friend. The man slid along the bench behind Penrod, unsheathing his hunting knife, and placing it against Penrod's throat with such alacrity that even Penrod was surprised by the speed of his movement.

'My name's Alfred,' he said in a foul-smelling whisper. 'And this is no business of yours.' Penrod felt the pressure of the blade against his windpipe increase slightly. 'So, you and me are going to sit here nicely, like good friends, while Cecil and Barney there conclude our business with the fat farmer and his girl. Nod to show me that you mean to be a sensible fellow.'

Penrod nodded slightly, feeling the blade sharp against his neck. He had known many thieves and cut-throats. Some – the cowards, who took what they could from those weaker or slower than they were – had become his informants during his work as an intelligence officer for the British Army. Others – men of violence – revelled in their power, and whatever they stole was a bonus. Penrod had heard this trio plotting this robbery and judged them to be the latter.

Hester looked up as the two men approached her, then she saw the man holding a knife to Penrod's throat.

'Oh, Pa!' She clutched her father's arm.

'Be still, Hester,' he said sharply, taking her hand and returning it to her lap.

The leader slid his rifle from his shoulder and set it down on the bench across from Vintner and his daughter, then stared at the girl, his head on one side.

'A good morning to you, pear drop! Did your pa get you up early to catch the train? I'll tell you a secret. I haven't been to bed all night.' He rested his hand on the end of the bench. 'Not to sleep, anyway.'

The girl wrinkled her nose and looked away.

'On your way, boy,' Vintner said, his voice heavy with disgust.

The man's eyes flicked to him then back to Hester.

'Your old man's not very friendly, is he? My name's Cecil.' He leaned towards her. 'What's your name?'

He spoke slowly and deliberately as if talking to someone of weak understanding. His rat-faced friend, the one called Barney, giggled.

Vintner stood, bracing himself against the rocking of the carriage. 'I said, on your way,' he growled.

'Maybe I will, maybe I won't, *maan,*' Cecil said with a sly grin, mocking Vintner's accent. 'I happen to know you're carrying a good sum of cash on you, old timer. Hand it over quietly, without any fuss – we'll call it a fine for your rudeness to me and my friends – and we'll leave you and your daughter to your Bible study at the next halt.'

Most men would have been concerned in Penrod's position, sitting in the rocking carriage with a knife to his throat, but Penrod Ballantyne was not most men. He was merely curious to see how the Boer would react.

'Unless you'd like to come with us, pear drop? Spend Daddy's gold on some fun? I'll buy you a nice frock, make you my girl if you're good enough.' Cecil reached forward and touched her chin with a dirty finger. Hester flinched.

Penrod's wife, Amber, would have broken Cecil's hand, but Hester had none of Amber's fire.

Vintner shoved Cecil forcefully in the chest, pushing him away from his daughter, then delivered a back-handed slap to his cheek. The sound echoed off the wooden walls.

Cecil grunted and stumbled backwards. His rat-faced friend, Barney, unholstered a revolver and pointed it at Vintner, but Cecil regained his balance at once and pulled out his knife.

'Hand the money over, old man!' he roared. 'Or I'll take it from your body! And the girl with it, too.'

'You'll have neither,' Vintner spat back.

Penrod could tell from the smooth lines of his black suit that Vintner was unarmed. Penrod had his own revolver in his pack, and a sheathed blade under his canvas jacket in the small of his back. Neither was any use to him with Alfred's knife pressing on his neck. He readied himself.

Cecil pounced, slashing at the left side of Vintner's neck with his knife. The older man reacted fast, leaning away so the blade arced and hissed through the empty air an inch from his face, then he threw his weight forward and punched Cecil in his midriff. The blow staggered the younger man, but he stayed on his feet.

'Kill him! Stab his eyes out!' Alfred shouted from his place behind Penrod.

Now! The second Penrod felt the pressure of the blade slacken, he caught Alfred's wrist, wrenching the knife down, then twisted and struck up at the man's chin with his left fist. Alfred's open jaw slapped shut on his squeal of pain; his head pushed backwards, his teeth snapping together.

Penrod jumped onto the bench, grabbing hold of the edge of the varnished wooden luggage rack above his head, and launched a flying kick at the side of Alfred's head. He caught him above the ear, sending him sprawling across the carriage, blood and spittle fountaining from between his fat lips.

Penrod leaped after him, slamming the heel of his sturdy work boot into Alfred's right wrist. The man screamed, dropping his knife and rolling into a ball, clutching his crushed hand to his chest. Penrod side-footed him under the nose, booted his knife away and pulled his own blade from its hidden sheath.

Cecil span round, roaring with anger and charged towards Penrod. His first knife-strike was aimed at Penrod's bicep, a decisive, whip-like lash to disable and disarm. Penrod span his body sideways, so that Cecil's blade grazed his arm instead of rendering it useless, and slashed at his opponent's wrist. He knew from experience that if he struck deep enough, Cecil would never hold a knife again. Penrod judged the weight of the blow, the trajectory of it, but the knife caught and was almost yanked from his grip. Penrod rocked back. There was a pale gold slash on the arm of Cecil's jacket – his sleeve was reinforced with a band of thick leather up to the elbow.

A deafening blast filled the coach. Barney had fired his revolver. The bullet grazed Penrod's cheek and caught the edge of his blade, spiralling it out of his hand and wrenching his wrist sideways. Cecil lunged forward, his eyes wild, but Penrod dropped to the floor of the carriage, catching his weight on his wrists, and kicking out with both feet in front of him, straight into Cecil's shins. Cecil howled and threw himself on his tormentor, his weight driving Penrod flat on his back, pinning him to the floor. He felt the urgent churn of the iron wheels speeding along the track under him, his nostrils filled with the stench of coal and gunpowder. Cecil bared his rotten teeth again and lifted his knife.

Penrod shot out his hand and caught Cecil by the wrist, while Cecil used the full weight of his body and force of his bloodlust to bring the knife closer and closer to Penrod's throat. Penrod gritted his teeth and sucked air into his lungs. Cecil's face was so close that he could see every detail of the ragged stubble on his chin, the flaking skin round his thin lips, could smell his stinking, greasy hair. Then, at the very edge of his vision, he saw a glint in the shifting shadows under the bench – his knife! He had hope, but if he reached for it, Cecil would cut his throat before he could close his fingers round the handle. Penrod let a fraction of the strength out of his arm, enough to convince Cecil that he was winning. Cecil's grimace became a smile, and he lowered himself to Penrod, his eyes flitting over his face as if to savour every moment of the kill.

At that instant, Penrod threw his head forward, smashing his forehead into Cecil's nose. He heard the crunch of cartilage and Cecil reared away with a muffled yell. Penrod reached for his knife. His fingers brushed the bone handle. The train lurched. The knife slid into his grip. He caught it and drove the blade into Cecil's belly, twisting it upwards. Cecil screamed – a high-pitched, gargling yelp like a rabbit in a snare. Penrod shoved him sideways onto the floor of the carriage and pulled himself upright. The floor was slippery with blood. Cecil coughed and keened, his legs spasming, his hands clutching his stomach. His cries weakened in seconds then stopped.

'Get away! Get away or I'll shoot the girl!' said another voice behind him.

Penrod span round. Barney was holding the girl in front of him, his revolver cocked and pressed to her temple. Her bonnet had been torn from her head and her blonde hair billowed in the wind that whipped through the half-open carriage window. She had squeezed her eyes shut and was shaking uncontrollably; she would have collapsed if it wasn't for the gunman's grip. Sweat bloomed on Barney's sallow skin.

'Barney, isn't it?' Penrod said, in a soft Irish brogue, lifting his hands. 'Don't be foolish now. Let the girl go and be on your way.'

'My name is J-Jan,' the man stuttered in confusion.

'Jan?' Penrod said. 'Ah, well. Your friend there must have been confused. Why, mine is John. That makes us almost brothers, doesn't it?'

'You'll kill me if I let her go!'

'With what, fella?' Penrod said with a smile. 'You have the gun, and my knife's still stuck in your friend's belly.'

Jan sniffed and shook his head. He edged out of the space between the benches, the girl grasped in front of him, his thick arm around her neck, and began dragging her towards the door at the far end of the carriage. She struggled, her fingers scrabbling uselessly at his arm.

'Where are you going to go, Jan?' Penrod reasoned. 'Come on, my lad. Be a sensible fella.'

Penrod heard a bolt click behind him and glanced back into the carriage. Vintner had shouldered Cecil's rifle, aiming it at Jan's head. His daughter was still trying to twist free, panting and sobbing.

'Make him put down the rifle! I'll kill this little bitch! I swear I will!'

'Let her go, boy,' Vintner said, '. . . or die.'

Penrod Ballantyne tensed. The Boer was making it more likely his child would have her brains blown out in front of them.

'Damn you!' Jan shouted, forcing the muzzle against the girl's temple. She squealed. Jan was panicking, his finger already tight on the trigger. He might murder the child with every jolt of the train.

Vintner did not lower the rifle; he just stared at Jan. 'I've had enough of being told what to do by Englishmen like you. This is our land, my land, and you will not take it from us. I will not be made a fool of again.'

'What you doing, man? What are you saying?' Jan screeched, clutching the girl closer, trying to shrink his body behind her thin frame. 'I swear, I'll kill her.'

'I trust her to the Lord,' Vintner replied, his decision clear.

Penrod ran, sprinting down the carriage. Jan turned partly towards him as he came, the muzzle of his revolver shifting its black snout, catching in the girl's thin blonde hair.

Jan's finger spasmed the moment Penrod reached the girl, seizing her around the waist and dragging her out of the gunman's arms. Rifle and revolver shots exploded the air. Hester's body went slack and Barney was thrown backwards against the carriage door, bursting it open. His head and chest hung outside the carriage and the roar of the metal wheels on the tracks became deafening. Penrod stood, the child in his arms, and looked down at her.

Her thin chest rose and fell. She had a powder burn above her ear, but he could see no blood. Her eyes fluttered open, at first wide with terror, then she saw Penrod gazing at her.

'Does she live?' Vintner asked.

'She lives,' Penrod replied. The child was gasping for air, too terrified to cry. He carried her back to her father and set her down on the bench.

'God be praised,' Vintner said.

Penrod bit back a retort, and returned to the body in the doorway. He dragged it into the carriage then shut out the noise of the tracks once more. Vintner had shot Jan precisely between the eyes.

Alfred, the man who had held a knife to Penrod's throat, was still alive but unconscious. Penrod dragged the man's belt off his trousers and used it to secure his hands behind his back, then turned him on his side so he wouldn't choke on his own blood before they reached Johannesburg.

'Might I know your name, stranger?' Vintner said as Penrod sat down heavily on the bench opposite Hester. 'I am Gerrit Vintner, and this is my daughter, Hester.'

He put out his hand. Penrod lifted his own, apologetically. It was covered in blood.

'My name is John Quinn.'

'British?' Vintner asked.

'A proud Irishman, sir.'

Vintner grunted. 'I thank you for your help, Quinn.'

Penrod pulled a handkerchief from his pocket to wipe Cecil's blood from his hands.

'You are injured, Mr Quinn,' Hester said, her voice shaking. Penrod glanced at his arm where Cecil's blade had sliced through the sleeve. She was right. He was bleeding more than he had thought.

'Nothing that won't heal in a day or two, miss. Though I thank you for your concern. Are you hurt at all?'

She shook her head.

Vintner took his own handkerchief from his pocket and wiped his forehead before placing it over Cecil's face. They both stared at the body, then Penrod turned away. 'I'd better go up to the guard's carriage,' he said. 'Tell them what's occurred.' He grimaced. 'Wasn't my intention to arrive in Johannesburg in this style.'

'I owe you a debt,' Vintner said. 'I have some standing in this town. Is there something that I can do for you?'

'No need for that, now,' Penrod replied. 'You handled yourself well enough. Though if you know of someone who has a job going, I'll take that.'

'There's always work at my farm,' Vintner said. 'But I'd be happy to have you as my guest.'

Penrod smiled. 'I don't like to be under an obligation, but I'll work for you, willingly.' He stood up. 'Now, I'd best find that guard.'

He did not have to go far. The shots had been heard and the guard was on the way. Penrod told him about the attack, then led him to Vintner and his daughter. The guard asked a few questions, but there was little to be done – two men were dead and a third was trussed up and waiting to be handed over to the authorities. The fact that he had only heard one side of the story was not a concern to him – he knew the name Gerrit Vintner.

With his investigation complete, the guard showed Penrod to a bathroom, unlocking the door with a key he kept on his watch chain, so he could finish cleaning himself up.

Penrod shrugged off his jacket and ripped away his shirtsleeve so that he could get a better look at the wound in his arm. War between the British and the Boers was coming, he had no doubt of it. Vintner's outburst had confirmed it. The smouldering hostility between the Boers of the Transvaal Republic and Orange Free State, and the British authorities of the Cape Colony and Natal, was about to burst into flame once again. The enormous gold reserves discovered in the Transvaal thirteen years earlier had attracted ambitious men from across the globe to the mines of the Witwatersrand, and now they wanted voting rights, and complained about the high taxes imposed on whatever meagre profits they made. Paul Kruger, president of the Transvaal Republic, saw these demands and complaints as a threat to the freedom of his people, and suspected they were nothing but an excuse for the British to annex the Boer republics as part of a grander scheme to see the Union Jack fly from Cape Town to Cairo. And who could blame him? thought Penrod. It was the British, after all, who had forced the Boers off their farms in the Cape sixty years earlier – demanding taxes and manumitting their slaves. These were proud people, descendants of the Dutch Vryburghers, who had managed their own affairs in the Cape Colony for a century before it was annexed by the British, their blood mixed with that of the protestant Huguenots, fleeing another religious war in France after the Edict of Fontainebleau, and the children of Angela van Bengale.

The wound in his right arm needed stitching, but it was far from the worst injury that Penrod had received over his years of service. He tore his shirtsleeve into strips and used these to bind his arm.

Penrod examined himself in the mirror, washing off the final smears of blood with his handkerchief. The amiable Irishman had disappeared; the British intelligence officer stared back at him from the mirror. His blue eyes were steely and intent, and the high cheekbones and long nose gave him an aristocratic air. He soaked the flannel again and ran it over his neck. A little over nine months earlier, Penrod had been one of the first men into Omdurman, the air thick with gunsmoke from the Maxims, his face spattered with gore from the carnage of the battle that had raged outside the city walls. Twelve thousand killed – he could see them now, their broken bodies piled up, their blood leaching into the grey sand of the desert, turning it black in the late-afternoon sun. He had been looking for Rebecca Benbrook and Osman Atalan in Omdurman, looking for revenge and redemption. But that chapter of his life was closed now. He was not the man that Rebecca had taken into her bed in Khartoum, no longer that dashing young officer making his name in the 10th Hussars. He was forty-five, still strong and lithe, still as deadly with a blade as his younger self, but time had changed him. He was a father now and the old impulsiveness that had driven him had been tempered into something harder, something adamantine.

• • •

At the other end of the continent, Ryder Courtney handed the reins of his horse to the groom who was waiting for him on the broad gravel driveway of one of the elegant downtown Cairo villas that had sprung up during the reign of Isma'il Pasha, the grandfather of the current Khedive of Egypt. Designed by architects recruited from France and Greece, they

were light and airy, with high ceilings and thick walls to keep
the occupants cool in the oppressive summer heat. Ryder himself
was renting – at great expense – a similar villa not five minutes'
ride along the Nile. He jogged up the polished front steps as the
imposing front door was opened for him by one of the houseboys.

'*As-salaam alaikum*,' Ryder greeted the boy in Arabic then continued in the same language. 'Is my wife, Mrs Saffron Courtney,
here?'

'Peace be to you, sir,' the boy replied, surprised to be addressed
so fluently in his own language by a white man. 'Yes, *Effendi*, she
is with the other guests in the garden. If you would follow me,
please.'

Ryder shook his head. 'I'll find my own way.'

Ryder's heels echoed on the polished black-and-white tiles of the
lobby as he added: 'My friend, if you would have Mrs Courtney's
horse made ready? I am here to escort her home.'

He had promised to rescue Saffron from this party no later
than 4 p.m., and he was an hour late. He pulled at the tight collar around his neck and loosened his tie. His dark coat, waistcoat
and grey wool trousers were tailored to show off his broad back
and the powerful muscles of his thighs and arms, yet made to be
as comfortable as his travelling clothes. They still made him itch,
however.

He reached the terrace and studied the crowd, searching for
his wife, aware of the many eyes that had turned towards him.
He was famous and, as always, being pointed out to the new-
est arrivals in the city, excerpts of his storied history retold for
their entertainment. As the years had passed, the life of Ryder
Courtney seemed to have gained colour and detail that he himself could not recall, his exploits growing with each new posting
of civil servants and soldiers and their wives, so that now it left
those in front of him wide-eyed.

What was true was that Ryder Courtney had made his first fortune in trade, travelling thousands of miles up and down the two
rivers that met and became one under the mud-brick walls of Khartoum, the City of the Elephant's Trunk. His trading stations had
been strung out along the two great tributaries of the Nile from
Gondar in the east and Gondokoro and Equatoria in the south to

Atbara in the north. This was before he had been caught up in the siege, his river steamer commandeered by General Gordon to evacuate women and children to the north, to Egypt and safety from the Mahdi and his zealots. Stranded in Khartoum, he had become enchanted by the beautiful Benbrook sisters: Rebecca, the eldest, and the twins, Saffron and Amber. The Mahdists had captured Rebecca and Amber as the city fell, but Ryder had saved Saffron, plucking her from the churning waters of the Nile. Alight with General Gordon's death and Queen Victoria's telegram of rebuke to Gladstone, how could the British public not be captivated by the daughter of the murdered British consul in Khartoum and the man who had saved her from the Mahdi – the newspapers adored them. It wasn't long before he became her beau and they were married as soon as Saffron came of age.

After the fall of Khartoum, they had gone south to mine in the Ethiopian Highlands – Ryder swinging a pick, sweating and suffering alongside his men – emerging with a fortune in silver and the friendship of Emperor Menelik. It was not an easy life and there were many wounds to heal. David Benbrook was dead and although Amber had escaped the harem of the Mahdist warlord Osman Atalan, their sister Rebecca, heavily pregnant with Osman's son, had refused to leave.

On their return from Ethiopia, Ryder had gone back to what he knew best – trading – and had become the sole supplier of wheat for the British and Egyptian forces, who were marching south to Khartoum, to avenge the death of General Gordon. Meanwhile, Saffron began to paint. Her paintings were highly regarded, the bright colours of Africa bringing life to her work, reflecting the feeling in Europe – the new century was a fire of hope on the horizon.

Amber found herself writing novels about the romance and mystery of Africa, novels that became international bestsellers. Her experiences – war and famine, heroism and tragedy, the moment that hope fell away – experiences which had shaped their lives, were celebrated across Europe.

In that moment, as he waited for Saffron to join him, Ryder should have been a happy man, but standing on the terrace and surveying the curious crowd, something troubled him. He had become too rich to handle what he bought and sold himself. He now signed pieces of paper and shook hands with soft-palmed men in government offices or in the marbled splendour of board-rooms. At first it had been a game, it had amused him – there was always another deal, another opportunity to squeeze profit from a situation – but after three years Ryder found business stale. There was no more risk and the lack of it was beginning to itch him like his elegantly cut suit.

Ryder knew Amber would not be at the party. She had left for Cape Town some days earlier with her baby son, to be on hand whenever her husband returned from his loosely defined active service. Ryder missed her, not only because he was fond of her, but because Saffron had been in an increasingly foul mood over the last six months, and when Amber was away, it always got worse. He could no longer dismiss Saffron's dissatisfaction with their life in Cairo. Amber seemed content, but Ryder knew his wife – it was her passionate nature that drew him to her – and it was inevitable that her dissatisfaction would erupt in some way soon. What Ryder did not know, as he stepped from the terrace and crossed the lawn dotted with liveried servants carrying champagne flutes on silver platters, was that, thanks to Lady Josephine Smythe, it already had.

• • •

Lady Josephine Smythe was not a woman blessed by nature with intelligence, looks or common sense. Her position in society was due to her overbearing manner, the reputation she had gained as a generous hostess and her husband – a short, blustering man who had become a successful trader in cotton and wheat by dint of his aptitude for languages and Arabic in particu-lar. At the extravagant parties she threw at the Smythes' palatial, river-fronted residence, the champagne flowed as if from a well, her canapés were made by the French chef at Shepheard's Hotel and the flowers were arranged in the style of those seen at the Queen's royal garden party to mark her Diamond Jubilee. On this particular afternoon she was the guest of a well-to-do diplo-matic family celebrating the baptism of their first daughter, but Lady Smythe never missed an opportunity to hold court. She had retired to the shaded edge of the pink marble fountain to voice her opinions, culled carelessly from the week-old copies of *The Times* that her husband received from London, at length and volume to a coterie of older, poorer cronies and watch the younger people play croquet. However, it was not long before she returned to her favourite topic: the family of Ryder and Saffron Courtney.

'Of course, Amber Ballantyne is not only a delightful woman, she is also very well read and highly perspicacious. And her husband Penrod – he is travelling at the moment, you know – is the perfect officer, a credit to the British Empire.'

She waved her purple silk fan, to cool her perspiring face.

'But dear Amber's sister, Saffron Courtney, is a foolish girl.'

Some of her cronies shifted uncomfortably. They had noticed Saffron Courtney at the party, and though some of them had heard her tell their hostess that she had to leave early, they had not seen her depart.

'I know Saffron has spent most of her life out of society, but I would have thought that any Englishwoman would, by instinct, know better than to raise those two heathens, the spawn of a warlord, alongside her own Christian children,' Lady Smythe continued with a shudder. 'It is disgusting!'

'But, Lady Smythe, they are her niece and nephew!' one of the less hidebound members of the party said. 'And the girl is quite charming. Did you not see her dancing yesterday at Major Green's party? So terribly clever, too. I'm sure the boy will improve in time.'

Lady Smythe sneered. 'Oh, Matilda! What an innocent you are. I do not say that Saffron Courtney should leave them to *starve*, but surely they should be put away somewhere. There must be places for half-castes in the city somewhere, where they can be educated alongside other mulatto unfortunates.'

The chastened Matilda noticed a movement in the corner of her eye. Saffron Courtney, concealed by the elaborate fountain, had been only a few feet away the entire time. She must have heard everything. Now she began to make her way towards the group with a fierce glitter in her eye.

'Lady Smythe . . .' Matilda, to her credit, tried to interrupt, but Lady Smythe had fanned herself into a righteous fury and continued at increased volume.

'I know they are the children of Rebecca Benbrook, but it is intolerable to see them walking at Mrs Courtney's side and playing with white children,' she said. 'I am astonished Ryder Courtney allows his own sons and daughter to be corrupted in this way. Though he is an eccentric, too! They have Arabs coming to their house, you know, welcomed as their friends, through the *front door!*'

Unaware of Saffron's approach, Lady Smythe opened her mouth to continue only to find the object of her tirade directly in front of her.

'Oh! Mrs Courtney!' she said, her voice suddenly rising an octave.

Any sensible man or woman observing Saffron at that moment would have apologised and walked away as quickly as possible. Lady Smythe was not a sensible woman. She spoke in a high whine.

'Mrs Courtney, I'm sorry, but I must say, your display of affection to your niece and nephew sets a terrible example in our community. You treat those bastards of Osman Atalan's as if they were the equals of Christian children!'

Matilda was flummoxed at the transformation which had come over the beautiful Mrs Courtney. Her body rigid with rage, she took a step forward and lifted her arm. Several of the ladies had been riding that morning, but it was only now that they saw that Saffron still had her riding crop in her hand. Lady Smythe gave a choking gasp of terror.

'Saffron!' The sound of a man's voice came from the main body of the garden.

Ryder Courtney had called his wife's name gently, but there could be no doubt that everyone present had heard him.

For a terrible moment it seemed Saffron would actually strike Lady Smythe with the crop, but Matilda had seen a flicker in her expression when she had heard her husband calling her name.

Instead, leaning forward until her face was only inches from Lady Smythe's trembling jowls, her arm still raised, Saffron said something in Arabic. Matilda was certain that Lady Smythe spoke not a word of the language, and her own understanding was limited, but she saw one of the servants who was holding a tray of champagne rock back on his heels, his eyes widening in shock.

Saffron lowered the crop and took a half-step backwards. There could be no doubt that the message she had delivered was a stern one, even if the words were not understood.

Ryder walked forward, and with a slight bow to Lady Smythe, took Saffron's arm in his. Saffron allowed it, keeping her eyes fixed on Lady Smythe until the last moment before she turned away.

'Savages! They are all savages!' Lady Smythe hissed to her circle as soon as she had managed to get her breath back.

Saffron moved fast. Disengaging her arm from her husband's, she turned back to Lady Smythe. In a few short strides, Saffron was in front of the older woman, but this time instead of raising her riding crop, she pushed her forcefully – one swift movement. Lady Smythe stumbled back and tripped into the basin of the marble fountain, landing on her rump in the ankle-deep water with a yowl of surprise and an almighty splash.

Saffron returned to her husband and they walked away together while Lady Smythe floundered in the shallow water, the bronze statue of the Nubian girl that topped the fountain now pouring her amphora directly onto her bedraggled feather headdress. Someone laughed and tried to turn it into a cough. Matilda had to look away until she could recover her composure.

• • •

Consumed by his anger, Ryder did not spare his mount on the way back to their villa. He knew that he could not outpace Saffron, even though she was riding sidesaddle – she had an uncanny knack with horses – but he wanted to show her how angry he was.

Arriving alone, Ryder ignored the servants who opened the front door to him and marched to the spacious salon to the rear of their villa, threw open the walnut drinks cabinet, poured himself a large whisky and downed it. Seconds later, Saffron came in behind him and threw herself across one of the woven bucket chairs.

Ryder could not bring himself to look at his wife. He had for weeks been negotiating a joint venture on cotton futures with Sir Randolph Smythe, and he had no doubt that the deal would now collapse. He looked out of the window into the garden which ran down to the Nile.

The children were scattered outside, playing under the watchful eye of Amber and Saffron's old nurse, Nazeera. She had been with the Benbrook family since Saffron was a child, had stayed with Rebecca during her imprisonment in Osman Atalan's harem and had brought the orphaned children to Cairo after Rebecca's death.

'You were late,' Saffron said.

Ryder gripped his glass tightly, not trusting himself to reply.

His attention was caught by the voice of his eleven-year-old son, Leon, drifting across the lawn.

'I, Penrod Ballantyne, will now defeat you in single combat!' Leon was saying.

Ryder frowned. Leon was brandishing a short but sturdy stick at Ahmed, Rebecca and Osman Atalan's son. Ahmed was two years older than Leon and taller by a head, but, dressed as always in a simple white *galabiyya*, he seemed thin, almost sickly in comparison to his cousin.

'You are nothing but my former slave, Penrod Ballantyne, you dog,' Ahmed screamed, brandishing his own stick before launching a wild and flailing attack.

Ahmed fought with his eyes closed. Leon dodged the blows easily, a huge grin splitting his handsome face, then he stepped under Ahmed's arm and jabbed him in the ribs with his stick. This was definitely a death below – deliberate and unsparing.

Leon stepped back and looked around to make sure the other children were watching him.

Ryder narrowed his eyes. 'Why does Ahmed agree to play this game?' he asked, distracted momentarily from his rage at his wife's disgraceful show of temper. 'He knows he always dies in the end.'

Saffron swung her feet, and the delicate silver embroidery around the bottom of her long skirts glinted in the late-afternoon sun.

'I think he does it because in the first part of the game Leon has to be his prisoner, as Penrod was Osman's, and Ahmed makes Leon run up and down the garden until he falls over with exhaustion.' Ryder shot her a questioning look. 'It's good exercise for Leon,' she added crossly.

Another actor appeared on the stage now that Ahmed had stopped thrashing and was staring up into the sky with his eyes open. A girl of nine years old, with honey brown skin, ran towards the boys. She was dressed in white, just like her brother, but instead of an *abaya* she was wearing a European skirt and blouse. Blue ribbons fluttered in her dark hair.

'My husband!' she shouted. Ryder flinched. Nine-year-old Kahruba, sister of Ahmed, daughter of Osman Atalan, was playing her own mother, Saffron's sister, Rebecca.

'Take care of my children, it is the least you can do, Penrod Ballantyne!' Kahruba thrust the stick into herself, staggered and fell onto the grass. For a moment Ryder believed she was really hurt, the expression on her face was full of pain and sorrow, but in an instant Kahruba was on her feet and grinning.

Ryder could hear enthusiastic applause. It was Penelope, his own daughter, who was the same age as Kahruba and her good friend. Nazeera was applauding, too, and even Matthew, the youngest of his children at three years old, clapped along.

'How do they know what happened in the past?' Ryder asked, taking another glass from the drinks cabinet and pouring a double measure into it before attending to his own. From what Penrod had told him, it seemed a fairly accurate portrayal of his last encounter with Osman Atalan after the battle of Omdurman and Rebecca's suicide.

'They were there, remember,' Saffron said simply as Ryder handed her the glass. 'Nazeera tried to hide their eyes, but Kahruba would not look away.'

'Of course she wouldn't,' Ryder said with a sigh.

There was a tap at the door and one of the servants entered with a letter on a silver plate. Ryder thanked him and broke the seal. It was a short formal note from Sir Randolph Smythe, terminating their business arrangement. Ryder had expected it, but the speed of its arrival and terse tone irritated him. He threw the paper back onto the tray.

'No reply.'

The servant nodded and retreated.

'What was that?' Saffron asked.

He told her of the contents of the letter and she lowered her eyes but he could feel the defiance coming off her in waves.

Ryder had already made a decision about what he would do next on the short ride from the party. 'I'm leaving Cairo on

Tuesday, Saffron. Now you have successfully destroyed my arrangement with Smythe, I must look for some other venture in which to invest my capital.'

She looked up, her eyes full of hurt. 'And going where?'

'Cape Town. Ben Weil has written to me about a factory in the city that he thinks I should buy and improve. I have an idea of what to do with it.'

Saffron sprang to her feet. 'But that is perfect! Amber is already there, waiting for Penrod! Take me with you! Get me out of this city for a while, Ryder, before I ruin any more of your business deals. Please. I can't breathe here.'

He turned and held her by the shoulders. 'Perfect! Months of work wasted because of your temper, and you think that it's perfect! You wanted to settle here, Saffron. You insisted! Remember, my darling?'

She twisted away from him. 'That was *years* ago. Do you have to mention it? And these people! I can't escape them. You disappear off to America for weeks at a time, but I'm here with the children. And I have no work.'

Ryder tried to control his impatience. Hardly a week went by without Saffron taking their family on some adventure in the region, and he knew well that on his previous trip to America she had recruited their Arab friends to take her and the children trekking through the desert and sailing up the Nile, camping in splendour each and every night like a Bedouin sheikh.

'What work have you ever done, Saffron?'

She flew at him and he caught her wrists.

'Every day in Tigray,' she hissed. 'Every day I built houses, I built a church. I worked side by side with the women to feed you, to clothe you, to keep you safe. How dare you ask me that!'

He thrust her away from him. His frustration at her behaviour warred with his love for his wife.

'Do you think I should smile and agree with our friends, when Kahruba and Ahmed are spoken of in that way?'

'No, of course not! But that doesn't mean you should push the woman in a fountain!'

The image of Lady Smythe in the water with her bedraggled headdress returned to Saffron and she bit her lip.

'Saffy, do not laugh! You have cost me a fortune!'

'You think we have too much money already. Oh, Ryder, I know that I have been dark recently! I do. But I can't think and I can't paint here. Let me come.'

He raised a finger. 'Saffron, if I take you to Cape Town, will you at least try not to sabotage me?'

'Yes! I shall be an absolute angel.' She fluttered her eyelashes at him.

Ryder reached out and pulled her towards him. 'She was right, you are a little savage.'

'Isn't that why you love me?' Saffron said, lifting her chin, her eyes sparkling. 'Please, Ryder. Let us go together. It will be another adventure.'

She had done it again. He was seduced. He let his hand travel across the curve of her hip. She pushed herself against him and he smelled the heat of her skin. 'Saffy, there is a war coming. That means danger as well as opportunity.'

'I don't care,' she said, her voice thickened by desire.

'Very well, come then.'

• • •

Gerrit Vintner's farm was set in a beautiful part of the country. Only twenty miles from Johannesburg but a world away from that brash, dusty city, it sat in a low valley shaded with fruit trees and eucalyptus and watered by narrow, fast-flowing irrigation channels that Vintner had constructed himself. But it was the birds that came for the water that fascinated Penrod Ballantyne – black-faced waxbills, green woodhoopoe, Kalahari scrub robins, honeyguides and seedeaters. They made the farm look like a child's drawing of the Garden of Eden. Even the trees outside Penrod's window were filled with the nests of masked weavers, which woke him each morning with their endless chattering.

As the days passed, Penrod found himself growing more and more comfortable with his assumed identity – John Quinn, Irish patriot. In Cairo, Penrod was envied, feared and admired in equal measure; it was a pleasing change to become just a pleasant Irish fellow, not too bright, but cheerful, and always ready to tell stories of his country's immeasurable suffering at the hands of John Bull. The Boer farmers who met at Vintner's farm to discuss strategies for the coming conflict over Gerrit's wife's sumptuous lunches, were eager to hear stories of English perfidy. And in return Penrod learned a great deal about the readiness of the Boer republics. His lyrical despair that any nation could resist the armed forces of the Empire attracted strong counter-arguments from the proud farmers, making him aware of just how many men the Transvaal and Orange Free State governments could get into the field and just how swiftly. When John Quinn looked uncertain or showed doubt, caught between his hope that his homeland and theirs might one day be free and gloom at the current situation in both countries, the farmers, full of enthusiasm, reassured him with details of their stockpiles of weapons and ammunition. When John Quinn spoke bitterly about the unparalleled British artillery, the Boers boasted of the professional soldiers sent by a friendly foreign government to train them on how to counteract the effectiveness of this ordnance.

Gerrit assured Penrod not to fear. As the British did not want to be blamed as aggressors in the coming struggle, they were slow and over-cautious.

Penrod stayed on Gerrit Vintner's farm for three weeks, riding and exploring the vast, rich land with his host and eating at his table with his family. Gerrit's wife was a gentle, modest woman who spent her mornings reading the Bible with her daughter Hester, and the rest of the day providing for her household. There were many labourers on the farm, but Penrod saw only a few of them. He had picked up a working knowledge of the Bantu languages, but although he knew that the labourers might have valuable intelligence about the plans of the senior Boer commanders, he also knew Gerrit would be suspicious if Penrod was discovered trying to speak to one of them.

Early one morning late in June, riders arrived from Bloemfontein and remained in Gerrit's *kantoor* for some hours. Penrod was excluded from the meeting, Gerrit making sure that his study doors were firmly closed and stationing the son of one of his closest confidants outside to deter any eavesdroppers. Penrod did not waste his time idling; he went hunting for duiker in the kloof behind the farmhouse and then, when the sun climbed too high for his sport, he drank coffee in the kitchen with Hester and her mother, while the low voices still grumbled from the room next door.

As night fell, the guests finally departed and the house went to sleep. Penrod slipped out of his bedroom and made his way downstairs. With utmost caution, he let himself into Gerrit's *kantoor*. He spent several hours working through the documents he found there. He took no copies, made no notes, simply read to the gentle hiss of the oil lamp until the details were settled firmly in his mind. As he turned the last page, he heard the muffled creak of floorboards and realised that he must not be the only one awake in the house. He put away the papers precisely as he had found them, extinguished the lamp and silently left the room, shutting the door behind him.

'*Wie is daar*?' a voice rang out softly in the dark. It was Gerrit, from the stairs to the upper floor.

'Just myself,' Penrod replied without any hesitation in his tone. 'Fetching my tobacco, Gerrit. I cannot sleep tonight, so I thought that I'd have a smoke, go out and look up at the stars . . . see if I could read my fortune in them. Did I disturb you?'

The stairs creaked as Gerrit descended. When he reached the last step, Penrod could see that he was still fully dressed.

'Then I shall come with you.' He clapped Penrod on the back with a force which would have sent any other man stumbling.

They walked across the veranda and stared across the neat yard into the starlit night. Penrod settled in one of the wicker chairs and lit his pipe. In the flare of his match he saw that Gerrit had a cigar. He took a seat next to Penrod.

'So, can you see anything up there, man?' Gerrit asked.

'Can't say for sure, my friend,' Penrod replied in the voice of John Quinn. 'But whatever they are whispering, I think it is time for me to be gone. You and your wife and young Hester have been fine hosts, the best a man could fall in with. But I meant to see the country, and you've made me too comfortable. If I stay any longer, I may never leave at all.'

'I shall be sorry to see you go, John. But take some advice from me. Do not stay in South Africa. Take a boat to Cairo, or India, if you do not wish to return to your own land.'

'Now why would you say that, Gerrit?'

Gerrit stood up. 'My people are slow to anger, but we are angry now,' he said, thoughtfully. 'You may be a loyal Irishman, John, but you look like an Englishman to those who don't know you as I and my friends do. And for this reason you could suffer before questions are asked about your true identity.'

Penrod looked up at him. 'Bad as that, is it? I'm loath to leave this warm and bountiful country. I must have a fair look at it. What of Natal? I hear that's pretty country and, for all it's a British colony, I'll be safe enough there now, won't I?'

'In two months' time, John, there will be no place safe for an Englishman between here and the ocean.'

Two months. That had not been in the papers.

Penrod was silent for a few minutes, then said: 'I thank you kindly for that advice, Gerrit. I honestly do.' He hesitated. 'But might I ask you one thing? While we are alone and speaking companionably?'

Even in the starlight, Penrod could see Gerrit's expression become suspicious.

'You might, John.'

'How did those fellas on the train know to come after you?'

The question had irked Penrod since the attack. For all that Gerrit's friends and neighbours had been happy to chat about the war and the evils of the British, he had heard no hint of why the three men on the train had accosted Gerrit and his daughter. Penrod had not pursued the matter, his mission was to gather intelligence about the preparations the Boers were making for war, but now that job was completed in accordance with his orders, he was inclined to satisfy his curiosity.

'You admire the set-up I have here, John?'

'I surely do, Gerrit,' Penrod replied warmly. 'The smokehouse and the bakery, your livestock and your people, the wildlife and the hunting. It's a lovely spot.'

'It cost money. Seeing the right opportunities and taking them. Seizing the moment when it came. You'll find, John, that no man makes such a place in this world without making enemies too. Men without vision get jealous and their envy eats them hollow. Now, my brother-in-law is an envious man. He has capital, but no vision. I borrowed from him and while I prosper, he stagnates. I still owe him some money. I fetched the payment coming due from the bank in Bloemfontein when the talks were done, and he looked greatly disappointed when I put it in his hands.'

Penrod assumed a puzzled frown.

'Why did he want to hire fellas to steal his own money from you?'

Gerrit burst into laughter. 'I don't think he hired them! He's too cheap! No, I think he passed on the information that I would be travelling with a large sum in ready money. He wanted to make me lose face in front of the people here, by seeing me robbed of the means to pay him. Wanted an excuse to move against me for the rest of the debt.' His voice changed, became harsh. 'Instead, I left two thieves dead and another to hang and he must slink back into the shadows.'

Penrod thought back to the events on the train, but he said nothing – there was no need to confuse matters by hurting Vintner's pride.

Gerrit extinguished his cigar, wetting his fingers and pinching out the glowing end, then put the unsmoked half in the pocket of his shirt.

'I know the man. Trust me,' he went on. 'He sent word to a friend in Bloemfontein to let it be known in the lowest bars in the town that I'd be travelling with money. I'd swear it. Now, good-night, John. I have an early start to attend to pressing matters.'

'Goodnight, Gerrit,' Penrod replied. When he heard the door to the house close and Gerrit's heavy tread in the hall, he stretched his legs and finished his pipe. His mind and eyes lost their inno-cence and he became thoughtful. Gerrit had gambled with his only child's life to prove a point to his brother-in-law and his community at large. These Boers were a stubborn breed. Unless the British war office got its act together, and without delay, Penrod was inclined to think that Gerrit was right. Nowhere in South Africa would be safe for a British soul.

He would begin his journey back to Cape Town tomorrow morning, Penrod decided, shed John Quinn along the way, and become himself again.

• • •

Ryder Courtney left Cairo three days after the now-infamous party. Saffron announced to her family that they would be following him as soon as their palatial residence had been shut up and their servants accommodated elsewhere. Leon, Penelope and Kahruba were excited at the thought of the journey – they would take the steamer from Alexandria to Plymouth and then the Union Line from Southampton to Cape Town – but Ahmed refused to speak about leaving Cairo. Saffron was worried. The other children kept asking about the places they would stop on their trip – Malta, Gibraltar, Madeira, Ascension, St Helena – names like jewels strung out on a necklace, but Ahmed remained stony-faced until one afternoon about a week before their trip was to begin, when he stiffly declared to Saffron that he was unable to accompany her to Cape Town as it would interrupt his studies. Saffron was heartbroken. Ahmed had treated his mother's family with disdain since he had arrived in Cairo with his aunt. There had been days when it had seemed as if he might overcome his inclination to think of his cousins as his mortal enemies – Saffron recalled the afternoon of the party, when she and Ryder had returned home to find the children playing together in the garden – but more often than not Ahmed was sullen and withdrawn, refusing to speak English and eating only what he didn't consider *haram*. He was a sagacious boy, already able to recite the Quran and hungry to study his father's faith. And Saffron could not deny that Cairo boasted better teachers of Islamic Law than any they might find in the hustle and glamour of Cape Town. But she also knew that Ahmed's decision to remain in Cairo was the end of her hope that he might one day become a genuine part of their family.

Saffron dressed according to the custom for a lady of her standing, veiled her hair and went to the Old Quarter of the city, Nazeera at her side. She was eager to pay a visit to her friend Bacheet, but not as eager as her old nurse. Even though Bacheet had recently taken a wife, he remained besotted with Nazeera.

Bacheet was now a prosperous man in his own right. He had worked with Ryder, trading along the Nile in the years before the fall of Khartoum, then followed him into the Ethiopian highlands to dig for silver after Ryder had almost been bankrupted by the siege. But when Ryder had won the army contract to supply

Brigadier Kitchener with grain, and left for the United States, Bacheet had found himself adrift in Cairo. It hadn't taken him long to find his niche: tobacco.

Bacheet welcomed his visitors with absolute delight for he loved them both very dearly. They sat in the courtyard of his comfortable home, cooled by the flow of a fountain which spangled the shade provided by a jacaranda tree with moving light, and talked while Bacheet's servants brought them freshly brewed tea and honey cakes.

Saffron explained her predicament – brought about by Ahmad's wilfulness – at length. Bacheet listened, and exchanged glances with Nour, his first wife.

'Dear *Filfil*,' he said at last, when Saffron had finished her tirade. He used Saffron's Arabic name. It meant 'pepper', chosen for her temper and the tawny colour of her hair. 'Let him make his home with us. I don't like the boy myself. I know that he has made life difficult for you, and what you have told me makes me worry that his father's blood runs stronger in his veins than his mother's, but he is spoken of in Cairo as a promising scholar and his learning and piety will bring honour to my home.' He winked and looked at his wife. 'I am perhaps a little lacking in both.'

Saffron laughed while Nour filled Saffron's glass with tea.

'How old is he now, *Filfil*?' Nour asked.

'Thirteen.'

'He is a young man, then,' she said. 'Even if his soul is old and hardened. I shall try and soften him.'

'Thank you.'

'And I shall see him trained in British as well as Islamic Law,' Bacheet said firmly.

Saffron was surprised. 'But he wants nothing to do with the British, my wise friend.'

'I shall tell him that studying law is the only way to fight the oppression of the British! I'll tell him that to defeat you, he must tie you all up in your own red tape. Then he shall read my contracts with those Greeks, the ones they have drawn up by Foster and Perrot, to make sure he understands the way the British impose themselves on every aspect of business.'

He must be fifty by now, Saffron thought, but Bacheet's round, unwrinkled face seemed ageless, particularly when he was as pleased with himself as he was at that very moment. Saffron looked between him and his wife and sighed. She needed to make sure that her sister's orphan children were cared for and she could not make Ahmed comfortable in her home; no matter how she had tried to love him, he had always pushed her away. Kahruba, in contrast, had embraced the family with an open heart. She reminded Saffron of Rebecca every day. Saffron could see nothing of her sister's blood in the boy, though. Reluctantly, she had accepted that Ahmed might be happier in Cairo. She looked around the courtyard again and breathed in deeply, trying to memorise this pivotal moment of her life – the play of the water in the fountain, the cool air under the jacaranda, the chink of the tea glasses, the sweet and smoky scent of spices wafting from the kitchen. She would not miss British society in Cairo, but this, the hospitality of her Arab friends, she would miss immensely.

Saffron stood up. 'Thank you, Bacheet,' she said, her manner deeply respectful. 'Thank you both.'

Saffron wrote to her sister Amber and her husband as soon as she returned to her villa, letting them know what arrangements she had made with the help of Bacheet and advising when the rest of the family were to be expected in Cape Town.

• • •

Even the day before they left Cairo, the children worked at their lessons. In contrast, their governess – totally immersed in the packing of her trunk and thinking jauntily of how to spend her generous pay-off – was too busy to supervise them.

When Kahruba pointed out the mess that young master Leon Courtney was making of his calculations, he screwed up a piece of scrap paper covered with inky numbers and threw it at her. She dodged it with a laugh, and it became a game – Leon trying to hit her with his paper missiles as she jumped out of the way. Then Leon sent his pen skidding across the table, spurting ink, and managed to get it all over his shirtsleeves and face before he could pick up the pen and put the lid back on.

Kahruba laughed until the tears ran down her cheeks, so Leon chased her round and round the room, threatening her new dress with his inky fingers.

Suddenly the door swung open and Ahmed observed the room, regarding them with disgust. Leon slouched back to the table. Penelope fetched a cloth to clean up the mess. Ever since they had learned that they were leaving Cairo for Cape Town, Ahmed's presence had become like a bucket of ice-cold water over their games and amusements.

'Sister, come away from these children, at once. I wish to speak to you,' Ahmed said in Arabic.

Penelope sighed. 'Honestly, Ahmed. You know we've all lived in Cairo with Nazeera for ages now. Leon and I can understand Arabic. Why do you never speak English?'

Ahmed pushed his glasses up his nose. 'I choose not to speak the tongue of murderers and infidels.'

Leon rolled his eyes. 'Probably forgotten how, Penpen.'

Ahmed's face darkened in rage and he switched to English. 'I can speak it,' he snapped angrily at his cousin. 'I just choose not to.'

'I like speaking English.' Kahruba sighed. 'Next I will learn French because all the great dancers come from France, and the most beautiful dresses and shoes. Or perhaps I shall learn Russian . . .'

'Enough!' Ahmed said fiercely. 'I want to speak to my sister. Alone.'

Leon hunched his shoulders. Penelope put her hand on his arm – she could see the fight coming.

'Shall we go to the kitchens, Leon? I'm starving. You can explain Waterloo to me for the history essay Mama wants me to write. Whose side were the Prussians on again?'

'Ours, of course! Oh, all right, come on, then.'

Leon made a point of knocking into Ahmed's shoulder on the way out of the room, but his cousin ignored him.

Kahruba did not seem concerned at being left alone with her brother. He was four years older and towered over her, but she looked up into his pinched, angry face without fear or love. Just a weary disdain that made him want to slap her across her rounded cheeks.

He didn't, though. It took him all his strength to restrain himself, but he knew well what the outcome would be. He had tried it before and Kahruba had attacked him like a lioness, scratching his face so badly that he had to hide in his room for days afterwards, claiming to be cloistering himself for spiritual reasons.

'You cannot go to Cape Town!' he said to his sister, his fists clenched at his side. 'I insist you stay in Cairo with me. You are forgetting your faith and your place.'

'I want to go to Cape Town. It sounds fun. And you know well that I pray with Nazeera five times every day.'

'You humiliate our father's memory – you are visiting his murderer.'

'Uncle Penrod did not murder our father, Ahmed. You know that. They met as warriors and equals. They were blood enemies. It was as Allah willed it.'

'How dare you speak the name of God? Our father would throttle you with his own hands if he saw you now, his whore of a daughter. Our father . . .'

Kahruba sprang to her feet. 'Who are you to talk of *our* father? You think I am too young to remember him? Osman Atalan, slayer of Emperors, master of a thousand warriors? I remember *everything*, Ahmed. I remember that he despised you. That he saw you for the coward you are. He *loved* me! I don't know under what sick, unholy star you were born, but it is I who inherited his heart. You? No one would *ever* look at you and know you for your father's son.'

Kahruba did not wait for Ahmed to respond, but swept by him and into the corridor, slamming the door behind her so thunderously that even the windows rattled.

Ahmed was shaking with rage. He had spent much of the morning at the feet of a great Imam in the Old Quarter, and his learning had been praised. On the way back to this hated villa, Ahmed had worked out a speech, a thing of beauty, that would persuade his little sister that they would never be welcome in this family. Yes, their mother had been sister to Amber and Saffron, but she had died a devoted, obedient wife. Kahruba must stay with him, obey him as her older brother. He had imagined her listening to him with tears in her eyes, her sobs and apologies. Instead, she defied and taunted him. She betrayed their father's memory every time she smiled at Saffron and Amber or clambered onto Uncle Ryder's knee with Penelope to hear stories. They were so proud, these Courtneys and Ballantynes. Ryder with his fortune in thieving trade. Penrod with his murderous army. How Leon admired all that disgusting military show. Ahmed was still too young to take his revenge on them, however desperately he wanted to, but he had to do something, something to stop them laughing at him as they all went off happily to England and then to the Cape. He lifted his eyes, looking at the paper and ink on the table. Suddenly a thought came into his mind. Perhaps there was something he could do.

The following day, as the family was about to depart, Ahmed kissed his sister and wished her good fortune, bent low over Penelope's wrist and shook hands with Leon. He apologised to his cousin for his ill humour, and thanked his aunt for her many kindnesses. Saffron was too busy to be suspicious of his suddenly warm manners.

• • •

An observer might have taken the group of men gathered in the smoking room of a modest but respectable hotel in Cape Town for businessmen, or perhaps old school friends digesting a reunion dinner. None of them was under thirty years old and one or two were more than fifty, but they had the air of men used to vigorous activity and outdoor life. Their dress, though civilian, had a certain uniformity. Most had moustaches, all had their hair swept back from their foreheads.

When the waiter came in with cigars and brandy, conversation ceased. Penrod Ballantyne asked the man next to him how the big game hunting was around his station in India. The men began swapping stories of pig sticking, the boars growing larger, the danger greater, the behaviour of their comrades more buffoonish, until the waiter left the room and closed the heavy door on a gale of laughter.

The room became quiet as soon as he had left.

Colonel Robert Stephenson Smyth Baden-Powell, in the centre of the group, opened a folder which was lying on the polished table. The top sheet showed a well-executed watercolour of Cape Town as seen in the evening from the bay. The city was pictured cradled by water, the great cracked face of Table Mountain rearing above it, fringed by wooded slopes. Baden-Powell put it aside and unfolded the map which lay beneath. Here Cape Town was a neatly engraved name near the tip of the great land mass of southern Africa. The Cape Colony, Natal, Orange Free State and the Transvaal, the Bechuanaland Protectorate and Rhodesia, vast tracts of land marked with occasional hatched lines of the new railways, and the names of towns dotted across the empty spaces like the first scattering of stars in the evening sky.

'Here we are, gentlemen,' Baden-Powell began. 'Some of us have served together in the past, others of you have been asked to join us because of your particular skills and talents. Some of you need no introduction, but nevertheless I'll ask you to give your name, rank and regiment. For those of you who are wondering why we are wearing civilian clothes, we have been asked to remain out of uniform for the time being. Please avoid referring to each other by rank in public, and when you travel up country, you are asked to mark your luggage with an assumed name.'

Some of the men laughed in disbelief.

'Including our uniform cases?' one of the older men asked. 'I am pretty convinced the Boer will see through that ruse.'

'Nevertheless, we are so requested,' Baden-Powell replied. 'Now, introductions please, gentlemen.'

Each officer gave their name, rank and regiment as instructed. Penrod knew, from reviewing their files before the meeting, that several of those present had served in India and two of them had seen action in the Sudan – Major Lord Edward Cecil and a Captain Stuttaford. Penrod thought Stuttaford looked familiar and he knew that Cecil had been at Omdurman. Baden-Powell and Colonel Herbert Plumer had both played a major part in the Matabele Wars.

Penrod, seated on Baden-Powell's left-hand side, was the last to speak.

'Colonel Penrod Ballantyne,' he said. 'Lately in Cairo, though until a few days ago, I was in Bloemfontein and Johannesburg.'

Several of the other men in the room turned their heads slightly. They were distinguished officers but Penrod Ballantyne was a legend in the British Army, and some of the men gathered in this modest hotel had heard of his intrepidity, something which, though included in his official record, was indelibly marked on his character no matter the situation – war or peacetime.

'And yet,' Ned Cecil sighed, 'you still look so young.'

Several of the officers, Baden-Powell included, smiled at Cecil's remark, and Penrod gave Ned a respectful nod.

'Gentlemen,' Baden-Powell said, 'our orders are to raise and train two mounted regiments in the border territories – a thousand men, give or take. At the outbreak of hostilities with the Transvaal and the Orange Free State, we are to tie up as many of the Boer commandos as possible in that region with a series of rapid feints and raids. I am a great deal better informed now than I was when I left England about the capacities of the Boer forces, thanks to the selfless service of Colonel Ballantyne. It is clear that this will be busy and risky work; the Boers are far better prepared than we expected and the odds are stacked against us in a way that the British government seems reluctant to acknowledge.'

'What support can we expect from Milner and Butler?' Colonel Plumer asked, interrupting Baden-Powell. Sir Alfred Milner was the governor of the Cape Colony, and Sir William Butler was Commander-in-Chief of British forces in South Africa.

'Very little, judging by the meetings Ned, Penrod and I had yesterday with those gentlemen,' Baden-Powell said. Several of the officers tutted, others leaned back in their chairs with a groan.

'Though Sir William was kind enough to give us a very informative lecture on the political situation in this country,' Ned added.

The three officers had, in fact, been treated like pariahs by Sir William Butler. Butler thought forcing a war with the Boers was a foolhardy waste of men and resources and said so. He conceded that he might provide some artillery for the new regiments, but refused to provide any transport or shells, thus rendering the offer meaningless.

Immediately after this disastrous meeting, Baden-Powell, Penrod and Ned had gone to see Sir Alfred Milner. Sir Alfred had expressed strongly to the War Office that he believed the only way to bring the Boers to heel was with a short, decisive war, so they expected his support, but this meeting was another bitter disappointment. Sir Alfred refused to offer them any assistance and told them that on no account were they to recruit any men from the Cape. Their regiments would have to be made up of volunteers from Bechuanaland and Rhodesia. Furthermore, it was Milner who had ordered them to remain in civilian dress, and use assumed names when travelling. It was ridiculous, humiliating. These were some of the finest men the British Army had to offer.

'Sir Alfred is only going to get the support he needs for this war in England if the Boer look like the aggressors. He's afraid our regiments will complicate that story,' Baden-Powell informed his officers.

'Damn lot of good that *story* will do him if the Boer wipe our forces out in a week,' Colonel Plumer said, stuttering slightly in surprise. 'I thought Milner was supposed to be some sort of intellectual giant! This is idiotic.'

'He's a politician, so let's treat him like one,' Baden-Powell said calmly. 'We must go around him.'

The atmosphere in the smoking room darkened. No man there was a stranger to war, and they knew only too well the blood price to be paid if they were sent against a determined enemy without the substantial resources required.

'This is suicide,' Stuttaford murmured.

Baden-Powell gave Stuttaford a stern look, but said nothing.

'How are we going to supply our men?' Plumer asked, rapping his knuckles on the table. 'Supposing we manage to find any.'

Baden-Powell nodded. 'We must work out our own supply routes and send the bill to the government later. Penrod?'

Penrod blew out a stream of blue-grey smoke. 'Have any of you heard of Ryder Courtney?' he asked.

'He kept the army in bread when we retook the Sudan,' Colonel Charles Hore replied thoughtfully. 'Good man. Even Kitchener treated him with respect, which was a surprise . . . It had been said that he did not possess such a quality. The last I heard of Courtney, he was in Cairo.'

'He is in Cape Town now,' Penrod stated. 'He has been here a fortnight, looking into new business opportunities. He has influential contacts and access to their capital. I am hopeful that he will make use of both in our service. I am certain that he will if he can see clearly that there's a reasonable profit for him at the end of this endeavour.'

Hore looked mildly confused. 'Don't you like him, Penrod?'

'He's my brother-in-law.'

The married men among the officers made sympathetic noises.

'He's married to the artist, Saffron Courtney, isn't he?' Plumer said. 'I saw her show at the Cork Gallery in London two years ago. The Abyssinia series. Impressive imagination. Good work for a woman.'

Penrod only nodded.

'And their children?' Hore asked. 'And the half-breeds of the monster himself, Osman Atalan?'

Penrod did not answer, but something in the way he straightened in his chair and turned his gaze towards Hore made the rest of the party uncomfortable. They knew, as professional soldiers, the signs of a man preparing himself for action.

'Can't blame a child for their parentage, Hore. Really you can't,' Ned Cecil said in an exaggerated drawl, breaking the thickened atmosphere of the room. 'Must have said so a thousand times myself since Father became Prime Minister.'

Most of the officers laughed, and a little of the tension eased.

'Mr and Mrs Courtney are private citizens, quite at liberty to travel where they wish and with whom,' Baden-Powell said, keeping his eye on Hore. 'It sounds as if we should be very grateful that Mr Courtney has decided to come to Cape Town with his family.'

'My wife is holding a dinner to celebrate Saffron Courtney's arrival tomorrow evening, gentlemen,' Penrod said. 'The Central Hotel, eight o'clock. You are all invited. As are Sir William and Sir Alfred.'

'And Mr Cecil Rhodes?' Ned asked.

'Unfortunately unavailable,' Penrod replied. 'I am told, confidentially, that he has moved into a cottage on the coast – his health, you know.'

'So much for a low profile,' Baden-Powell muttered. 'Though I saw your wife's books were on the shelves in Government House,

Penrod. Perhaps Sir Alfred is an admirer? Get her to sweet-talk him into a couple of Maxims, would you.'

'I'm sure Amber will do whatever she can for Queen and Country,' Penrod replied.

Baden-Powell tapped the map. 'Penrod, I'm sorry to drag you out of Cape Town while your family is here, but the day after the dinner I want us to be on the way to Bulawayo. Ned will stay here to shake out what supplies he can from the authorities and see what use he can make of Mr Courtney's money and contacts. We, however, need to find what men are available beyond the borders of the Cape Colony. One regiment will operate out of Bulawayo. Plumer, that'll be your command. Hore, you'll command the Protectorate Regiment. You'll be based here, at Ramathlabama, just west of the Bechuanaland and Transvaal border.'

Hore craned his neck to see where Baden-Powell was pointing.

'What's the name of that place on the railway line? Is it a town of any size?'

'The largest for some considerable distance and the administrative capital. That's where I and Colonel Ballantyne will be based while we recruit and train men for the regiments. It boasts an hotel, a hospital and a convent,' Baden-Powell said. 'Perhaps two thousand whites and five thousand blacks of the Barolong tribe. They call it the "place of the stones", Mafeking.'

• • •

The first startled shouts came from the direction of the docks. A few people turned their heads, but, seeing no reason for alarm, ignored the noise. Though still early in the morning, the streets of central Cape Town were busy. Men in starched collars and ties strode down the pavements towards their places of business, passing handsome four- and five-storey stone buildings, nodding to acquaintances as they went, and dodging around the fluted metal pillars that held up the glass canopies which extended from the hotel and department store frontages to the kerb. Women, dressed in dark skirts and white pinafores, swept the front steps of offices and banks. Cape Malay traders in headscarves and red fezzes negotiated fiercely, their discussions suddenly breaking off into laughter. Flower sellers chatted across huge baskets of exotic, multicoloured blooms laid out along Long Street.

Tau jogged down the alley that ran along the side of the Central Hotel, then, with a quick look to make sure that he wasn't being observed, scrambled up the water drainage pipes with the confidence of long practice. He jumped nimbly between the stone balustrades that framed the balconies on the first floor until he reached the canopy above the main entrance of the hotel, crouching behind the wrought-iron decoration. Tau loved to climb the great stone buildings of Cape Town. On the street he was only a dark-skinned boy in clothes worn thin by repeated washing, was ignored, pushed aside and cursed at, but on the roofs and ledges he was a king, a prince surveying his empire of stone and slate. He had sleeping spots on top of the Central Hotel and several of the larger department stores, but he ranged widely over the top of any number of offices, banks and shops. Some of the workers and even the owners knew him, but as he never stole, they let him be.

As Tau settled into position, he saw a Hansom cab approaching from the docks – the white hood of the two-wheeled vehicle standing out amongst the other traffic. It was careering towards the junction with Long Street and as Tau watched it took a corner so quickly that one of the huge wheels lifted clear of the road and span in the air before bouncing back onto the ground with a bang like a gunshot, just ahead of a rattling tram. A Cape Malay woman with a headscarf of scarlet and gold grabbed her child out of the way of the spinning wheels and screamed.

Tau narrowed his eyes and peered through the thick, sea-damp morning air. The driver must have been thrown, the horse out of control. But no – he could just make out the top of the driver's stovepipe hat as he cowered behind the white canopy. He was still aboard, but someone else was brandishing the driver's long whip, expertly flicking it across the horse's ears, driving the surprised beast into a gallop. Tau laughed suddenly and then covered his mouth. He'd just spotted the face of the new driver. It was a boy, a white boy of about twelve years old. His expression one of complete delight at the chaos he was causing.

While the spectators shrieked and the other drivers cursed, the boy whooped and beamed at them. One of the carter's horses, spooked by the huge wheels flashing by so close, began tossing its head. It drove its cart backwards into the path of a polished chaise whose driver had been too busy staring at the speeding buggy to notice his own danger. The collision broke open the rear of the cart and a great cascade of green apples poured across the street in a sudden burst of colour and confusion.

The young driver didn't even notice. Tau watched him give the reins a slight twist and deliver another flick with the overlong whip. The horse pulled up suddenly and came to a steaming halt outside the glass and mahogany main doors of the hotel below Tau's perch, stamping and blowing.

The boy leaped off the back of the cab and stood grinning on the wide pavement, his hands on his hips. The official driver descended more carefully, his dark skin ashy, and tottered around to his horse, which seemed miraculously to still be in perfectly good health. The panels of the cab were folded back and two girls clambered down from where they perched. One, a white girl with cascades of blonde ringlets falling down her back and a straw boater perched on her head, looked a little shaken, but calm. The other girl, about the same age but her skin a dark olive jumped over to the boy and hugged him.

'Oh, Leon! That was marvellous! Did you hear everyone shouting?' she asked. 'Can we do it again?'

The boy looked pleased but before he could reply an older woman, her hair covered in a veil, wearing dark blue robes and carrying a small boy in the crook of her arm, shoved the beautiful olive-skinned girl aside and launched into an angry stream in a language that Tau didn't understand.

The boy did not look concerned. 'But Nazeera . . . But the driver said I might . . . Nazeera . . .'

The older lady had worked herself into a furious, finger-waving passion. As she made some particularly fierce point, the boy caught sight of Tau. Tau raised a hand and waved shyly from the canopy. The boy grinned back at him and winked.

Another Hansom cab drew up, stopping in a far more respectable manner than the first. A young woman with auburn hair, a snowy white blouse and a long travelling skirt jumped down. Tau noticed that the boy looked nervous for the first time. The woman slapped him forcefully across the face and it seemed for a terrible moment as if he might cry.

'Mama . . .' the boy began.

'Don't even speak to me, Leon,' she said in English. 'You could have killed your sister and your cousin.'

The Mama said something to the old woman in the language Tau couldn't understand, then she took a firm hold of the boy's ear with her free hand, dragging him into the hotel lobby and out of sight.

Tau sat on his haunches and considered. The doorman, Sello, was a friendly man who gave Tau the odd coin for running messages, and when he wasn't on duty would chat to him about the comings and goings in the hotel. Tau knew that Mrs Amber Ballantyne was already in residence, occupying one of the grand suites on the first floor, where kings and ambassadors slept, with her husband Colonel Penrod Ballantyne and their son David. Tau had seen her several times. The woman who had just arrived must be Amber Ballantyne's sister, Saffron Courtney. Her husband, Ryder, was staying at the hotel, too – he had checked in two weeks earlier. Leon was their son, and the two girls must be his sister Penelope and their cousin Kharuba, daughter of the warlord Osman Atalan. Sello had read him all the names from the register of expected arrivals. Tau could not read, but he could remember things very well.

Tau looked down the street, then smiled. Two men in civilian dress were walking side by side towards the hotel. The blond one with a thick moustache and an obvious military bearing was Colonel Penrod Ballantyne. His broad-shouldered companion was Mr Courtney. They made a commanding pair. The air seemed to still around them, and women turned away from the shop windows to stare with frank admiration. By the time they had reached the hotel, a cart with the Union Line logo had drawn up outside the entrance. It was piled high with a complicated collection of boxes and steamer trunks.

Bell boys swarmed out of the hotel and began to gather up the luggage. Ryder patted the pocket of his jacket.

'We might leave them to get settled for an hour or two, Penrod. Cigar and a walk?'

'Agreed.'

. . .

With their luggage safely in their suite, and the children already beginning to unpack, Saffron went in search of her sister.

Amber opened her door to a scowling Saffron, who immediately threw herself onto one of well-upholstered settees in the Royal Suite. It would be unusual for her to still be angry about Leon's stunt – rumours of which had already spread around the hotel. However tiring Saffron found it to continually discipline her eldest son, Amber knew that she loved his wild courage. Still, Amber was wary of discussing Leon with her sister. His love of all things military and his hero-worship of Penrod had grown almost unchecked in Cairo, and whatever Saffron thought, Amber was only too aware of Ryder's opinions about military men.

'I think you made just the right decision with Ahmed,' Amber said, wondering if this was the cause of the scowl as she poured tea in the English fashion and passed her sister the china cup. 'We cannot force him to like us . . . and Bacheet will take good care of him.'

Saffron swung her long legs off the sofa and took the proffered cup.

'I didn't have much choice,' she replied, her voice miserable. 'He's been getting worse and worse recently.'

'Saffron, darling, you know I couldn't be happier to have you and Ryder here.' Amber spoke with care. 'It's wonderful that he's heard of new opportunities at the Cape. I did ask him why he suddenly decided to come here, when I thought he was absolutely drowning in business in Cairo, but he started glowering, so I didn't press.'

'He *was* drowning in business. Making money hand over fist. Then I pushed Lady Smythe into a fountain,' Saffron said quietly.

Amber choked on her tea. 'You did *what*?'

'It was at a garden party and she was talking about what a disgrace it was that I was bringing up Kharuba and Ahmed with my own children – oh, the most foul things, Amber. And she was standing right next to the fountain . . . Oh, do stop laughing!'

'I'm trying, I promise, Saffy!' Amber hiccupped. 'What fountain?'

'That terrible one that the Fortescues had built in their garden for some reason, like a duck pond – all pink marble with statues of Nubians pouring out the waters of the Nile in the middle. You've started laughing again!'

'It's very funny!' Amber protested, wiping the tears from her eyes. 'Forget tea, Saffy! I'm ordering champagne. She is a monstrous old woman, and I'm delighted you put her in her place.'

'Oh, I shall drink your champagne, but it isn't funny really, you know. Sir Randolph severed all business ties with Ryder an hour later.'

Amber rang the bell and ordered the champagne, and they talked about the factory Ryder had bought and his plans until it was brought to them, perfectly chilled. The maître d' opened it so the bubbles sighed gently to life, poured for the two women, then withdrew.

'Ryder was planning to leave me and the children behind,' Saffron said.

'He was *that* angry with you?'

Her sister's marriage to Ryder Courtney had always been fiery, but sparks were inevitable in the union of two such headstrong, passionate people. Though Amber had never had reason to doubt the devotion which bound her sister and Ryder together.

Saffron nodded. 'He is. I have been rather horrible at home recently, I think. I even shouted at Nazeera.'

'I'm certain she shouted back.'

Saffron smiled and pushed her hand through her thick hair. 'Yes. I learned a great many new ways of saying "selfish", "spoilt" and "childish" in Arabic. I thought I'd learned all possible variations of them when we were little.'

Amber put out her hand and took her sister's in her own. 'You're here now, Saffy. Don't worry. Let the Cape be a fresh start for you. New places for you to paint and new things for me to write about. Cape Town is already filling with refugees from the Transvaal who fear the Boers.'

'Is war coming, Amber? What does Penrod say?'

'Yes, I'm afraid it is. And Penrod thinks the British are under-estimating the strength and determination of the Boers. The clouds are gathering, and Penrod will be right in the thick of it.'

'Are you frightened for him?'

'Oh, Saffy! I don't want him to know it, but I am terrified.'

• • •

'Ben Weil is the man to see,' Ryder said to Penrod as they strolled up Spin Street towards St George's Cathedral, where the city's Anglican population worshipped every Sunday. 'He and his brothers have been in an out of southern Africa for twenty years. Cecil Rhodes even gave Julius a medal for the Matabele Campaign. Nothing moves north of Cape Town without the Weil brothers knowing about it.'

The air was still cool from the morning mist that had blown in from Table Bay, but Penrod knew that the sun would burn it away in an hour or two and the city would simmer until late in the afternoon. He was learning about Cape Town's many moods.

'Will he give us a line of credit?' Penrod asked.

'He might. How much?'

'Half a million sterling.'

Ryder stopped dead and made a choking noise which turned eventually into a laugh.

'The governor not being very cooperative, I take it?' Ryder paused. 'Weil and I might come to some arrangement.'

Penrod's handsome face twisted into a sardonic smile.

'And what does Courtney Trading want in return?'

Ryder hunched his shoulders. 'I'm a patriotic Englishman, Penrod, in my very peculiar way.'

'I should warn you, Ryder, the situation here is grave and our resources on the ground are limited. The Boer could throw us out of South Africa in a month unless we are lucky. You might never see that money again.'

'Life is full of risk,' Ryder said. 'I owe the British Army a favour after the business we did in the Sudan. And once the situation with the Boer is resolved, it might be useful to have the Colonial Office in my debt.'

'So much for patriotism.'

'One can be patriotic and still have an eye on the future. If all army men thought a little harder about the future, rather than getting over-excited by their own heroism, this continent would be in a better and more advanced state.'

They were high above the cathedral now, climbing towards the Cape Malay Quarter and decided to turn back towards the hotel. Penrod began to speak in scathing terms about merchants who relied on the security guaranteed by the army, then complained about the taxes necessary to pay and supply them. Ryder replied with equal passion that trade had the power to bring nations together, while rampaging armies left scars on both sides that often took generations to heal.

'A noble sacrifice, offering up a little of your capital while men in uniform offer their lives,' Penrod said with a sneer.

'The army should think more carefully about how they sacrifice their men's blood,' Ryder retorted. 'Now, do you want the damned money or not?'

Penrod noticed a pair of Cape Malay men slowing down to watch their argument. He stepped back and lifted his hands. 'Peace, Ryder! Yes, I want the money.'

Ryder threw his half-smoked cigar into the gutter.

'Ben is coming to Amber's dinner tomorrow. I'll speak to him.'

They strolled back through the city streets, each of them busy with their own thoughts, an uneasy truce restored between them.

'How are your new ventures progressing here?' Penrod asked his brother-in-law politely as they made their way back into Spin Street, past the Groot Kerk, the seat of the Dutch Reformed Church. 'I have been meaning to ask you, but this business with the authorities here is keeping me fully occupied.'

'The factory has some excellent workers. Though I had to fire the old manager for thievery and blatant corruption – some officials in Government House have been purchasing shoddy goods for inflated prices, and I will not allow that to continue under my name.'

'Will you prosecute?'

'That is my intention.'

Penrod looked serious. 'Then I'm afraid the British Army has another favour to ask. Please do not. The political situation is very delicate at this moment. We cannot afford to draw any attention to anyone involved in our mission.'

Ryder looked at Penrod narrowly, then nodded. 'Very well. I shall add it to my bill in due course, then. Now, I think I better go and welcome my wife to Cape Town.'

And with that Ryder left Penrod alone with his thoughts

.　.　.

Amber Ballantyne ate a mouthful of the excellent butter-fish and gave a small sigh of satisfaction. Her dinner was a culinary masterpiece, framed on exquisite Bridgwood & Sons porcelain. In their time at the Central Hotel, the chef had made delicate miracle after delicate miracle with the splendid ingredients that nature at the Cape provided, and tonight was no different. Amber looked down the long table, glittering with Stuart crystal and Elkington silver plate and felt proud of what she and her sister had accomplished. The fresh flowers that they had purchased on Long Street lit up the walls, the guests were as surprising and interesting as the food and the service had been exemplary. Ryder and Saffron sat opposite one another in the centre of the table; Penrod, seated at the far end, caught Amber's eye and raised his glass to her.

Ryder had introduced Amber to Ben Weil's wife, Ethel, before they went into the dining room. She was much younger than her husband, not yet thirty, Amber guessed, but she had the ease and confidence of an older woman. She had shaken Amber's hand with a firm grip and said at once: 'I have read all of your books, of course – who hasn't? – but I just wanted to say that I think they are quite wonderful entertainment . . . Now, that is out of the way. I should imagine you are sick of talking of them. So, I shall tell you my stories instead, if you like – legends of Cape Town and our plans for a new synagogue. So many men and women of my faith are arriving from Europe these days, we have need of it and we have this marvellous new Rabbi! His name is Alfred Bender and he is handsome and sharp, too. I shall tell you how he manages us all and it will make you laugh.'

They were excellent stories and Amber did not want to separate from Ethel. However, dinner was about to be served and Amber had been charged with entertaining Sir Alfred Milner. After her time with Ethel, Amber found herself in high spirits and replied to his remarks about her novels with generous frankness. Her own observations about the importance of Baden-Powell and Penrod's mission, however, aired over the Windsor soup and sherry, were met with resignation by Sir Alfred. Happily, though, he was now blossoming under the wide-eyed attention of Lady Violet, Ned Cecil's wife, who was seated on his other side. Satisfied that her guests had enjoyed the splendid first course, Amber inclined her head to the maître d', to let him know that they were ready for the game course.

After their guests had departed in early hours of the new day, well-fed and in good spirits, Amber, Saffron, Ryder and Penrod moved into the drawing room on the ground floor of the hotel, which had been set aside for their exclusive use. The men were drinking whisky and the women, curled side by side on the sofa in a froth of lace and jewels, were enjoying a final glass of the excellent 1895 Krug that Penrod had chosen for them.

Saffron had enjoyed the evening enormously and spent much of it talking about art, fashion and Cairo life with Lady Butler, who was a painter herself. Before her marriage to Sir William, she had painted *The Roll Call*, which had been the sensation of the 1874 Royal Academy Exhibition. Such was the reaction to her debut work that the police had to be brought in to keep the crowds back from the canvas. She had told Saffron that she had all but finished a new painting – something new but also based on an event in Crimea.

'Oh, and Penrod,' Saffron said, twisting round to her brother-in-law, 'she said she'll speak to her husband about more guns and transport, but she emphasised that he'll never let you recruit openly for the regiment in the Cape. He fears it might drive the Boer here to throw their lot in with the Transvaal, so if you're going to do it, you'd better not let him find out.' Penrod raised his glass in salute to her. 'And she said that Cecil Rhodes used to have a young man named Ballantyne working for him. Is he a relation?'

'A branch of the family came out to Africa some generations ago, I believe,' Penrod said. 'You'd have to ask my brother. He holds all the family archives.'

The soft glow of the lamp light caught on the diamonds hanging from Saffron's ears and around her neck. Some women looked weighed down by their jewels, Ryder thought, but the life and energy that poured from Saffron outshone the largest stones he could buy for her. She looked radiant – her hair dressed high, but with a soft disorder about it, her eyes sparkling with keen intelligence in the half-light.

Once he'd come to an arrangement with Ben Weil, Ryder thought to himself, he'd take Saffron away somewhere special – New York, perhaps. The immeasurable fortune he had made with his Courtney Mine company in Ethiopia, added to the fortune that he had made on land deals in Egypt and the Sudan, would certainly guarantee a line of credit of half a million sterling with Weil's company. With this in place, Lord Edward Cecil would be appointed to use the funds to supply Baden-Powell's regiments, making sure that he was provided with every last thing that he needed for the outbreak of war. And after that, there was nothing to keep Ryder and Saffron in Cape Town. Why not enjoy their freedom for a while?

Penrod was watching his own wife as he sipped his drink. She had been a superb hostess, exceeding herself in every way. She has changed, Penrod thought, she is no longer the shy girl that I first met in Khartoum. Amber had always dressed more simply than Saffron – she enjoyed a more natural look, choosing clothes that emphasised her firm, strong figure – and she had never liked the limelight. But at that moment, reclined next to her sister, one hand holding her champagne flute, the other supporting her chin as she finished her story and widened her eyes as the others laughed, she was her sister's match. Then Penrod saw her expression change dramatically, as if she had been bitten by a snake.

'Amber, what is it?' Penrod asked.

She straightened and set down her glass carefully on the polished mahogany side-table.

'Do you smell that? Is it smoke?'

Ryder was already on his feet. He crossed the room, his quick steps making no sound on the thick Turkish carpet, and pushed open the door. The stench of burning suddenly grew much stronger. Penrod and the sisters followed him into the tiled lobby of the hotel.

'Service!' Penrod shouted, his hands cupped to his mouth.

A weary-looking man in hotel livery emerged from a door behind the front desk, but he snapped to attention as soon as he saw the concern on the faces of the four people in the lobby.

'Is there a fire?' Amber asked. The air was suddenly acrid, the hotel stuffy and airless.

The liveried man picked up the telephone on his desk as two waiters emerged from the kitchens.

'Samuel! David!' he shouted. 'Go and ring the servants' bells! Spread the word! Everyone out!' He covered the mouthpiece and spoke to Penrod. 'Please, sir! See to your family immediately. I'm calling the fire station.'

Ryder bounded straight up the stairs towards their state rooms on the first floor; Saffron followed, pausing only to rip her clinging dress along the seam to the knee so she could climb the stairs two at a time. Penrod dashed up behind them. Amber was about to do the same when she noticed an ornate brass dinner gong hanging from a carved stand below the stairs. That would wake the guests more quickly than the servants could alone. She looked around her and noticed a boy standing by the door to the street, peering through the glass into the lobby.

'Come here!' He looked unsure. 'Now!'

'I smelled smoke,' he said as he opened the door and approached her, 'from the roof.'

Amber grabbed the soft-headed beater from the top of the stand and gave it to the boy. 'You hit this as hard and fast as you can, do you understand me?'

He nodded, swung his arms back and struck the gong perfectly at its centre.

'Good lad,' Amber said. 'Keep going as long as you can.'

Then she ran upstairs.

The first-floor landing was filling up with guests, startled and curious. 'Get out, everyone!' she shouted as she pushed past them towards the Royal Suite. 'Quickly!'

'I see flames!' a woman wailed, pointing upwards. Her voice shuddered with disbelief.

Amber looked up. Grey smoke was billowing out over their heads on the second-floor landing. A man in a quilted and embroidered dressing gown leaned over the balustrade. He turned back towards the crowd. 'But I see smoke in the lobby,' he said. 'The dining room is on fire, too. How is that possible?'

A woman in a heavily laced sleeping cap pulled on his arm. 'Gerard, we must get dressed and fetch the luggage.'

'Do not wait! Get out at once!' Amber said, loudly enough for the whole crowd to hear.

The man in the dressing gown put his arm around his wife's waist and began to usher her down the stairs. 'Oh, no! But my clothes! My letters!' she protested.

'Forget them,' her husband snapped.

Amber found the door to their suite already open. Penrod was standing in the middle of the salon with Nazeera, who held baby David. As soon as she saw Amber, Nazeera put the baby in her arms, then turned back into one of the bedrooms. Penrod placed his hand on her shoulder.

'Penrod! The fire is on the floor above, too.'

Outside someone shrieked – a high, panicked wail. Penrod looked past Amber, into the corridor.

'Don't worry about us,' Amber said quickly. 'Saffy, Nazeera and I can manage the children. You must do what you can to help the others, my darling.'

'Go at once!' he said, then kissed her. He pulled a handkerchief from his pocket and, holding it over his nose and mouth, left the room.

'Nazeera!' Amber called. 'Nazeera!' But then the smoke hit her lungs and she began to cough. She pulled the thin gauze of his baby blanket over David's face as her old nurse reappeared at last, a bag slung over her shoulder.

'Go, my flower,' Nazeera said. 'Take the baby and go.'

'But Saffron and the other children!'

Nazeera pushed her fiercely into the corridor. 'They are next door. *I* shall help them. *You* shall go.'

Amber stumbled out of the suite, her eyes beginning to water from the smoke. She could hear Penrod and Ryder on the floor above, ushering people down the stairs. So many of them! The guests stumbled, half-blinded and choking, to join the throng on the first-floor landing, abandoning trunks and bags as they went.

A man twice Amber's size was pushed violently against her by the crowd and she tripped over a suitcase, already burst open, the loose clothes tangling round her feet, and fell against a woman with her hair in papers. She kicked herself free and held David closer to her. From the far ends of the first-floor corridor more and more people were coming, surging forward. There was no room for them. Husbands tried to keep hold of their wives, mothers pulled along frightened children. Above them a woman screamed, not just a yelp of fear, but a full-throated yowl of terror. It triggered chaos. People began to elbow and push each other out of the way in a frenzy to escape down the main staircase.

Amber reached the first stair then stumbled forward. She felt a strong hand on her shoulder and twisted round, a brief burst of hope rising in her chest that Penrod had come for her. To her surprise, it was a stranger, a young man. He didn't look at her. He was using her to lift himself above the crowd. She would have slapped him if she could, but he was already moving sideways to reach the bannister. She watched him start to swing himself over. A girl ahead of her squealed.

'Daddy, I can't breathe!'

'Get back!' The girl's father shoved the man closest to his child in the chest. His meaty forearm struck the leg of the man clambering over the bannister. He lost his footing, his arms windmilling.

Hands reached for him, but there was no time. He fell backward with a strangled scream. A wave of terror washed over the people on the stairs. Crying, prayers, threats, wails of fear. Amber was trapped between them, desperately trying to keep her head up before the press of bodies forced the last air out of her lungs.

Panic rose in her blood. No way back, and nothing in front of her but the deadly crush. How far down the stairs was she now? She kicked off her shoes and elbowed and shoved her way sideways towards the bannister. She grabbed hold of it with her left hand, holding David to her chest, and dragged herself on top of it, then over. She couldn't see how far the drop was. It didn't matter – there was no choice anyway. She and David would be crushed if they didn't jump. Amber hung for a second, then her grip on the polished marble gave way and she fell.

The shock of the fall, the shuddering strike through her ankles, knocked the air out of her lungs. She fell backwards with a gasp, winded and stunned, then as her senses returned, she scrambled to her knees and lifted the gauze from David's face. He opened his eyes and began to wail – a good sign.

Amber looked around her. The staircase was packed with a crushing mass of terrified men and women, with yet more coming down from the upper storeys. The boy was still hammering at the gong, his skin shining with sweat from the effort he had put into his work. Amber got to her feet and stumbled towards him, a fit of coughing seizing her. The boy dropped the beater and a second later she felt his hand on her shoulder.

The world swam for a moment as she gasped and recovered her breath.

'What is your name?'

'Tau, madam. Can I help you?'

Amber looked around her again. She could not see any of her family.

'Tau, have you ever held a baby?'

'Yes, madam.'

'Good.' She thrust David into his arms. 'Support his head.' The baby coughed and mewled. 'Don't mind his crying, Tau. Now, this is my son, his name is David Ballantyne. Can you remember that?'

'David Ballantyne,' the boy repeated.

'Tau, I need you to take David outside and keep him safe. When the fire is out, come and find me, and if you cannot, you must give the baby to the hotel manager, or one of the adults who works here, someone you trust, and tell them his name. Can you remember it?'

'David Ballantyne,' Tau said again.

'Thank you, now go. Keep him safe for me.'

Another scream, wild and frightened. Amber stared upwards, horrified at the sight of a woman falling from the top storey. Her shift was on fire, and she blazed as she tumbled, shrieking through the air. Amber threw her arms around Tau and the baby, pushing them further away. She heard the body hit the lobby floor and the scream cut off. The air was filled with the stench of burning flesh.

Amber grabbed Tau by the shoulders. 'Look at me,' she said urgently. 'Don't look at that. Where are the stairs for the servants?'

Tau looked sick and terrified, but pointed to a discreet door hidden in the panelling in the south-west corner.

'Thank you. Now go. Look after my child.'

Amber did not watch Tau leave. She did not think she could bear it. Instead, she ran towards the concealed door and wrenched it open. The panelling and marble floors gave way to roughly plastered walls and floorboards. The stairs were ahead of her, narrow and steep. A few people were hurrying down and heading out of the hotel through the service entrance. Amber ran up to the first floor, pushed open the door and felt her way along the corridor.

'Saffy! Nazeera!' she called into the smoke.

No answer. How far along was their suite?

'Aunt Amber!' Leon's voice, and not far away. 'Is that you?'

The heat in the air felt as if it was sealing her throat.

'Leon! This way!' she called, ignoring the pain.

'*Al-Zahra*!' Her nurse emerged from the smoke, coughing and weeping. 'The stairs are blocked by mad people! We did not know where to go!'

'Put your hand to the wall, Nazeera! The servants' stairs are clear, just twenty steps past me.'

Nazeera was dragging a weeping Kahruba by the wrist. Behind her was Leon, white as death, carrying his little brother. Matthew was wriggling and crying for his Mama, but Leon was keeping a firm hold.

'Where are Saffron and Penelope?' Amber said sharply.

'Little Penelope has locked herself in the bath chamber,' Nazeera said, coughing again. '*Filfil* is talking to her through the keyhole.'

'I'll go and help her. Nazeera, look after the children.'

She crouched down until she could look her nephew in the eyes.

'Leon, you must swear to me you will not try and come back. Swear on our lives.'

'I swear, Aunty Amber.'

'Good. Now go.'

• • •

Saffron had sent her husband upstairs to help the other guests without a second thought, just as Amber had. She was certain that she could get the children to safety without Ryder's help, but Penelope, sweet, pliable Penelope had locked herself in the bathroom the moment she had smelled smoke, before the other children were even awake, and would not come out.

Saffron had found Kahruba and Leon rattling at the doorknob and shouting at her in English, pleading in Arabic, while Matthew sat at their feet wailing.

The moment Nazeera arrived, Saffron put the children into her care with strict orders to get them out at once and crouched down next to the lock. She could see her little girl, a bundle of night clothes and blonde hair, curled under the porcelain wash basin. She was holding her rag doll and the key to the bathroom door.

'Penny, it's me. You have to open the door now.'

The bundle shook its head.

God, the floor itself seemed to be hot. How was that possible? Wasn't the fire in the corridor above them?

'Penelope Courtney! Stop being such a baby. You are nine years old! Open this door at once or we will both burn to death. And dolly.'

The bundle gave a small shriek and dolly disappeared from view. Saffron cursed herself.

She wasn't imagining it – the floor *was* getting hot. Saffron looked behind her. In the gaps between the heavy rugs the polished floorboards were beginning to smoke. She had no time to reason with her daughter. She got to her feet and holding onto the door frame with her slim, muscular arms, she kicked at the lock.

Once, twice, three times . . . She felt something break. Summoning all her strength, Saffron drove the short heel of her exquisite Parisian court shoe into the wood below the lock. The wood splintered and the door burst open. Saffron ran in and hugged Penelope into her arms. The girl did not fight her, just curled her legs around her mother's waist, arms around her neck and rested her head on Saffron's shoulder.

'All safe soon, my darling,' Saffron said, swaying her slightly.

'Saffy!' It was Amber's voice.

Saffron stepped out of the bathroom. The smoke was black now and the heat had intensified. Through the darkness Saffron could see her sister in the far doorway, her hand over her mouth.

'Saffy! Hurry up!'

Saffron took two strides forwards, then heard a terrible screeching groan. The floor suddenly heaved under her like the deck of a ship in stormy seas. She staggered until she felt the window at her back, then, with a great shuddering crash, the floor fell away from the west end of the room. Saffron saw a brief glimpse of the dining room where they had entertained that evening, their carefully curated flower arrangements consumed by flames, then the fire roared upwards through the gaping hole. The ceiling above Saffron's head crackled and caught and flames licked up the walls to the right and left.

'Saffy!' she heard her sister scream – her voice was coming from the other side of the void.

'Amber, get out!' Saffron yelled through the choking heat. She shifted Penelope higher in her arms, her muscles already aching with the effort of carrying her daughter. The table in the window where the children had been doing their lessons was still standing. The scattered papers on its surface beginning to blacken and burn.

'Saffy! No!' Amber called.

'We'll climb out of the window! Hurry and get ready to catch us!'

'I'm going!'

'Wrap your legs tighter round my waist, Penelope,' Saffron whispered to her daughter.

She grabbed the heavy brass inkstand from the table and swung it at the window behind her. It shattered into knife-like shards. Saffron swept the edge of the frame with the flat base of the stand

and then, with Penelope still clinging to her, she clambered out into the chill night, holding her daughter on her lap.

Saffron's eyes were streaming from the smoke – she could barely see. How high up was she? Twenty to thirty feet, perhaps. High enough to break both of their necks if she jumped. She tried to remember what she had seen when looking out from this point earlier in the day. She recalled that just below the window and the little stone balcony on which they now sheltered was the ornate metal canopy that extended from the front entrance of the hotel over the pavement. Could she reach it? A twist in the breeze, and a sudden blast of flame poured out into the air above her head. She had no choice – her hesitation was pushed aside.

Penny screamed, then started to sob into her shoulder.

'Don't worry, darling, we are going to be just fine,' Saffron said to her daughter. 'Now, I need you to cling onto me very tightly.'

Penelope didn't speak, but Saffron felt her knees dig into her sides and her arms tighten around her neck.

Saffron twisted round, holding onto the stone balustrade. The heat in the room was now so intense that she was sure that nothing could survive it, the stone under her hands warm to the touch. On the other side of the balustrade, her foot found a narrow ridge of stone that ran from the balcony along the wall of the hotel. Clambering over, she inched her foot along the moulding, searching for the place where the wrought-iron canopy extended from the wall. She could not let go – with Penelope's weight on her back she would surely fall – but she could not reach any further with both hands still on the balustrade.

Saffron let go with her right hand. She had to fall. The pain in her left hand made her want to scream. But then, with the side of her shoe, she touched the ornate metal edge of the canopy. At full stretch she could rest one toe on top of it. She felt along the smooth stone wall with her hand for some halfway grip and could find none.

Saffron breathed in and out once, then threw herself sideways, pushing off with her right foot. She landed heavily on her side and felt her ankle strike sharply on the iron edging. The pain made her gasp, but she had fallen five feet not twenty. She was on the canopy.

Penelope whimpered.

Saffron dragged herself along the ironwork, away from the raging flames, coughing and choking, Penelope still clutching tightly onto her waist and neck. But it wasn't far enough. She could still feel the fierce heat. Saffron gasped, looking up at the hotel. Fire poured from every window.

'On the canopy! I see her!'

Thank God! Amber had escaped from the burning hotel and was in the street. Saffron looked down into the confusion below her – a crowd, dense gusts of soot-laden smoke and Amber. Amber had seen her.

'Jump, Saffy!' Amber shouted. 'We will catch you!'

Saffron felt the ironwork shake and heard the crack of the glass panels. She pulled herself up into a crouch, pulled Penelope onto her lap and kissed the top of her daughter's head. Then, standing up, she walked to the edge of the canopy, closed her eyes and stepped into the smoke-drenched darkness.

It was sickening and sudden. A moment plummeting through the air, then the rough strength of a dozen hands breaking her fall. She heard the grunts of effort and surprise. Then she felt a sensation of gentleness as they managed to hold her and set her lightly down.

'Thank you, thank you,' she panted in relief and surprise, her arms still tight around Penelope. Amber was pulling her further away from the flames, but Saffron didn't want to go. Where was Ryder? Where were Leon and Matthew?

A shuddering crash threw her stumbling forward as the canopy came away from the hotel frontage, crumpling and exploding in the heat, sending a great shower of glass and sparks into the air.

• • •

Ryder had left Saffron to deal with the children and was sprinting up the stairs to the second floor when the dinner gong began to boom its warning below them. The rooms were more tightly packed here; frightened families emerged onto the landing in various states of undress. The smoke was already dense and black. It seemed that the fire had started in a linen room next to the staircase. He called to the crowd below: 'The fire is on the second-floor landing, top of the stairs and spreading fast!'

Then he urged the guests past the flames and down the stairs.

Penrod joined him.

'The girls?' Ryder asked.

'They are with Nazeera and the children,' Penrod answered.

The fire was running up the walls of the staircase and the heat was intense. Ryder heard a scream above him. A woman on the third floor was wailing – too scared to come past the flames, she was being jostled by the crowd on the landing.

Penrod ran upstairs and disappeared into the crowd. Ryder followed him, taking the steepening risers three at a time. At the top of the flight he grabbed the shrieking woman round the waist and carried her past the flaming walls and down to the second-floor landing. A man wearing a porter's jacket took her from him.

'The back stairs!' the man shouted to the guests. '*Hamba*!'

The guests stumbled blindly past him and into the smoke. Ryder turned to race back up the stairs again, but too many people were flooding downwards. He struggled forward, as above him the press of people shoved a woman too close to the flames licking up the walls. Her dress caught at once. Around her people pulled away, screaming. Ryder could not reach her. In her panic she tumbled over the bannister and fell screaming into the lobby below. Even over the sound of the fire and panic, Ryder clearly heard her skull crack on the marble floor.

Ryder paused, sickened. If he was to save anyone else from the same fate, he needed to get higher. Ryder ran down the corridor until he found the man in the porter's jacket. He was standing by the door to the back stairs, calling people to him. Ryder pushed past him and continued upwards. A young Cape Malay woman was in the doorway to the back stairs on the third floor, she had found a handbell from somewhere and was ringing it, covering her mouth and nose with a handkerchief, her eyes streaming. A few frightened men and women were feeling their way towards her through the smoke.

'Quickly, quickly,' she said as they went past her, touching each of them on the shoulder as they went.

Ryder saw one more flight of stairs heading up towards the attic. As he prepared to climb, he saw Penrod coming down. He was carrying a young girl in his arms, her face blank with terror.

When he saw Ryder, he nodded upwards.

'Servants' quarters, all clear now.'

'Good.'

The girl was still ringing her bell and peering into the dark corridor. Ryder stood at her shoulder and looked in the same direction. In the thick darkness, he could see sudden ribbons of fire running along the walls and across the ceiling. He closed his hand around the girl's wrist and the ringing stopped.

'No one else is coming,' he said. 'Go now.'

The girl turned and ran down the stairs. Ryder followed, catching Penrod up at the first floor.

A young woman was struggling towards them through the stragglers at the bottom of the flight.

'My children!' she screamed up at them. 'I locked them in while I fetched bread! They're on the top floor.'

'Are you sure they are still there?' Penrod shouted.

'I told them to be quiet as mice.'

Penrod swore fiercely under his breath.

'Take the girl out, and the mother, too,' Ryder said to Penrod. 'Find our family. I'll go back for the children on the top floor.'

Penrod looked as if he were about to argue, but he saw the expression on Ryder's face.

'Good luck,' he said.

'Fourth floor?' Ryder called down to the woman.

'Fourth door in the left-hand corridor. Please, sir! My little girl and boy.'

'I understand, now get out of here.'

'The key, sir!' She held it above her.

'I won't need a key,' Ryder said. Then he turned and sprinted up the stairs.

• • •

The narrow landing under the eaves was ablaze. Flames licked out where ceiling and wall met, eating the fabric of the building. Ryder heard a crash outside and the whole building shook.

Most of the doors had been left open as the occupants fled, but the fourth door was shut. Ryder lowered his shoulder and charged, throwing his weight against blistering paint, it shuddered but held. The fierce smoke choked him; tears streamed from his eyes. He charged again. This time the wood around the lock burst and the door fell open.

Ryder tumbled into a narrow room with a single bed. Above it was the faint outline of a small, high window. Ryder could see nothing else. He dropped down to all fours, searching for the last clean air the room had left. He put out a hand and touched human hair. A soft moan. The boy and girl had huddled together in the far corner.

'I've come to get you,' he said. 'Can you hang on to me?'

The girl wrapped her thin arms tightly around his neck, but the boy was already unconscious. Ryder gathered him to his chest, span round and ran out of the room and down the corridor. Letting memory and instinct guide him, he lunged through the dark for the stairs. He got down the first two flights, but it was already too late. The flames had reached into these narrow back corridors and were falling on the new fuel with a hungry roar.

Ryder turned and retreated back onto the floor where the porter had been standing guard and pushed open the door with his foot. He was met with an inferno, the flames twisting and spinning in the air, walls and floor ablaze. He let the door close again and turned back to the service stairs. He would have to dash through the fire and pray he was too fast for the flames.

'I'm going to start running,' he said to the little girl. 'You must take a deep breath and hold it. Do not let it go until we are outside, do you understand?'

She nodded. Ryder breathed deeply, filling his lungs, then he ran. The fire was eating the stairs from under him and rippling up the walls. He could feel the tongues of flame reaching for his clothes, scorching the back of his hands. He thought of nothing but the cool night air beyond. It would only take moments and he would be free.

Someone had dropped a bag between the second and first floors, it had burst, sending papers and clothes across the narrow stairs. They were already aflame. Ryder stepped around it, but then felt the half-consumed stairs give way beneath him. He threw himself forward. His right foot hit solid wood, but the weight of the children pulled him back, the step under his left foot cracked like a log exploding with sap in a fireplace. He could do nothing, he was about to fall into the fire.

A hand grabbed him at his elbow and hauled him forward. The world righted itself and the boy was lifted from his arms. Penrod had come back.

Both men half-fell down the final stairs. There was a pain in Ryder's chest like a steel bright beam of light, but he threw himself down the corridor towards the service entrance of the hotel, bursting through the doors and into the night air, Penrod just behind him. Men from the watching crowd grabbed them, taking the children from their arms. Someone pulled Ryder's blazing jacket off his shoulders. Behind him, an explosion tore the night apart. He span round in time to see part of the roof collapse, turning the service entrance into a furnace.

Someone was handing him water. Ryder drank. He heard his wife calling his name, and opened his arms to her with his eyes closed.

• • •

The fire brigade had arrived. The blinkered horses shook their heads as the pumps on the wagons rattled and shook, teams of fire fighters in blue tunics with brass buttons spraying great jets of water over the flames. The fire had destroyed the entire hotel in less than twenty minutes.

Tau saw Amber Ballantyne embrace her husband. Saffron Courtney was sitting on the pavement by Mr Courtney, his hands in a bowl of water that someone had brought him. Her children were close to her – the two little girls had their arms around each other and Leon had the small boy on his lap.

Amber was scanning the crowd. Tau's arms had grown tired carrying the baby, so he had found a basket and put the child in that. He picked it up and jogged over to Amber. She fell on her knees beside him, lifted the baby and held it. Then she pulled Tau over to her and kissed him, too.

'This is Tau,' Amber said to her husband. 'He sounded the gong and looked after David for us.'

Penrod looked at Tau and smiled. 'Thank you, my friend.'

He reached his hand into his pocket as if looking for a coin, but Tau shook his head and took a step back. He did not want to be paid. It was not like running a message.

Penrod understood. 'Very well, but will you take this?' He pulled a leather wallet from the inside pocket of his coat and plucked something out of it which he handed to Tau.

He took it. It was a photograph of Penrod and Amber Ballantyne and the baby. In it Penrod was wearing evening dress, just as he was now, though his face was not masked with soot. His wife was seated in front of him, and the baby was standing on her lap. Something was printed in gold letters along the bottom.

'Those are our names: *Colonel Penrod Ballantyne, Mrs Ballantyne and their son David.*'

'I know your names,' Tau said.

Penrod retrieved a silver pen from his pocket and took the picture again. He wrote something on the back before returning it to Tau.

'On the back it says: *This young man, Tau, is my friend. Anyone offering him aid and assistance is my friend also.* I have signed my name underneath.'

'Thank you, sir,' Tau said.

'Ballantyne!' Two tall men were pushing through the crowd towards them. Penrod turned away, and Tau stepped back into the shadows.

Tau placed the picture in the pocket on the front of his shirt. He shivered as he watched the water from the fire engine play over the flames. The crowd was getting bigger as news of the fire spread and the residents of Cape Town came to offer their help. The managers and staff of the other hotels in the area threw open their doors and woke their kitchen staff. Soon carts were arriving with blankets, flasks of coffee and sandwiches. Clerks circulated with lists of available accommodation. Even Tau had a shawl put over his shoulders and a salty meat sandwich placed in his hands. Nurses in short grey capes moved through the crowd with bags of ointment and bandages. Those who were badly hurt and could not walk were carried on stretchers to waiting wagons for medical treatment. Families were being invited into the homes of strangers, offered food and a bed for what remained of the night.

. . .

The Courtney and Ballantyne families were taken to the newly opened Mount Nelson Hotel and seen by the doctor retained by the establishment. Saffron was given a cane to take the weight off her injured leg and they were ordered to rest. The female guests, hearing excitedly about the new arrivals over breakfast the next morning, took up a collection and provided the whole family with fresh clothes by lunchtime.

It was a relief to bathe and rid themselves of the stench of the smoke. The children huddled round Nazeera in the drawing room of their palatial suite, sipping honey and lemon mixed into a weak black tea while she promised them stories and cakes. Kahruba was curled up on Nazeera's lap like a cat, stroking Penelope's hair. Only Matthew seems unaffected, playing on the floor with a set of coloured blocks.

Amber could not put David down – leaving him with Tau and going back into the hotel had panicked her in a way that she had not thought possible. As previously arranged, Penrod had left for Mafeking at dawn. He had seen them to the hotel and offered to stay, but, despite her anxiety, Amber was sincere when she told him to go – there was no point in wasting a minute of the fresh morning and he had left as the *adhan* rang out from the Dadelboom Mosque on Long Street.

'Saffy, has Ryder said anything about how the fire started?' Amber asked.

Saffron frowned. 'Only that it looked "damn strange". What did Penrod say?'

'The same. He thought it might be the act of some employee with a grudge. I worried it might be someone looking to murder him and Baden-Powell, but he reminded me that in that case they would have set the fire before our guests left.'

'Yes, he has a point. And if Ryder has made any enemies here, he hasn't mentioned them to me.' Saffron paused. 'I can't forget how frightened poor Penelope was. She is normally such a brave little soul.'

'We all have our particular terrors, Saffy.'

Saffron shook herself. 'Shall we go to the hospital?' she asked. 'We might be able to help and I can't bear just sitting about.'

'Can you manage?' Amber, wrapping baby David in a blanket, nodded at her sister's ankle.

Saffron twirled her cane. 'Of course!' she answered with a smile.

• • •

The hospital in which the injured found themselves was a clean, modern building paid for by contributions to the Prince Edward and Princess Alexandra Charitable Fund, staffed by Irish and Cape Malay nuns, under the supervision of a young English doctor and his wife.

It was the wife, a Mrs Clifford, who came to meet Saffron and Amber in the high-ceilinged entrance hall and invited them to visit the ward where the victims of the fire were being treated. She spoke with a soft West Country burr and was dressed in a modern, practical style, in a long grey skirt that fell in soft pleats from her waist and a dark blue blouse with slim sleeves.

She shook hands with the sisters.

'It's good of you to come,' she said. 'We lost two more, I'm afraid, including one of the little ones, and I don't think Mrs Porter will last until nightfall. We can't stop the burns from becoming infected and she's too old and weak to fight it. We can make her comfortable, though.'

'Do you take a hand in the nursing alongside your husband, Mrs Clifford?' Saffron asked.

'I'm an M.D. myself, as it happens,' she said, waving away Saffron's apologies. 'Yes, one of those strange "lady doctors"! One fellow from the docks told me to my face I was unnatural and

Sister Mary gave him such a telling off that he now brings fruit for the children's ward every week with his humble apologies.'

Despite her cheerful tone, Mrs Clifford looked exhausted.

'How many dead?' Saffron asked.

'Eight now, including the child,' the doctor replied.

Baby David began to fuss and Amber bounced him in her arms to soothe him.

'What a handsome child!' Mrs Clifford said warmly.

Saffron rolled her eyes. She had never understood the world's fascination with babies. She loved her own children, and would murder without hesitation anyone who hurt them, but she did think infants rather dull. Amber worshipped her baby, and the little creature had turned into a tyrant. Saffron wondered disloyally if the one had led to the other.

The ward – flooded with sunlight from the tall windows that lined both walls – provided a contrast to the quiet and calm of the corridor. Most of the injured had been staying in the cheaper rooms on the upper floors. Whole families, just arrived in Cape Town from Europe, were huddled together on the narrow hospital beds, shocked by their losses. Some had their faces or limbs bandaged, others were in casts, having broken bones during their escape.

Mrs Clifford led them from bed to bed, but Amber soon retreated with an apology as David began to squall again. Saffron told Mrs Clifford to go and rest for a minute and Mrs Clifford, seeing Saffron was at ease, did so. Saffron hopped between the beds on her one good foot, sympathising with the parents and hearing again and again about the heroism of her husband.

One young woman was curled up in her bed alongside a little girl. As Saffron approached, she saw that both were sleeping. Thinking that this was the best medicine for them, Saffron was about to move on when the young woman's eyes fluttered open and she put out a hand.

'Oh, please, don't go!'

Saffron sat on the bed next to her.

The woman's eyes were red and swollen. Not just from the smoke, but also from weeping.

'You are Mrs Courtney, aren't you?'

'I am. How is your little girl?'

The woman smiled tenderly at her sleeping child. 'She'll be well soon enough, the doctor says, and I have your husband to thank for it. He ran into the fire to fetch her. Broke down the door and carried her out as if she were his own. Will you thank him for me? Tell him that he'll be in my prayers every night I'm spared.'

Saffron knew Ryder did not believe very much in the efficacy of prayers, but felt no need to say so. She felt her heart catch as she remembered seeing him and Penrod bursting from the hotel with the children in their arms.

'Of course I shall, and he'll be glad to know the little girl is well, but don't you have a boy . . .'

Too late Saffron realised the reason for the mother's swollen eyes and remembered what Mrs Clifford had said about losing a child that morning.

'He was too far gone with the smoke, ma'am,' the woman said. 'But he lived long enough to die in my arms and I thank the Lord for that. Well, God and Mr Courtney.'

Saffron felt her throat tighten.

'I'm so sorry, Mrs . . .'

'Essie is my name, miss. Just Essie. I've been cleaning staff at the hotel for three months, now. I'm not supposed to have the children with me, but they didn't like the lady that I put them with and it was only going to be for a night or two, until I found a better place for them.'

If Leon died, Saffron thought with sudden clarity, I do not know if I'd have the strength to go on living, even for Ryder and Penelope and little Matthew.

'Can I do anything for you, Essie?'

The young woman shook her head. 'Only thank Mr Courtney for me . . .' Then she added more quietly: 'I was only going to fetch some bread.'

· · ·

Amber retreated to a corner of the ward with baby David and tried to quiet him. She turned her head and caught the smile of a rather plain girl lying in the bed closest to her. The brush of Amber's hair against the baby's face was enough to set him off again. The girl put out her arms, and Amber, over-whelmed with frustration at not being able to soothe her child, handed David over to her.

The girl sat up in bed and laid the baby on her lap, cradling his head in the crook of her right arm, then with her left hand she began to rub the baby's belly. David had been readying himself for a fresh scream, but, surprised by the girl's touch, stopped suddenly.

The girl continued to rub his stomach and crooned something to him, something like a rhyme in a language Amber did not rec-ognise. The baby examined her face, then put his pudgy fist into her long hair and smiled.

Amber sat down on the bed. 'You are a miracle worker,' she said.

The girl flushed a furious red and mumbled something Amber couldn't catch. For a minute or two she kept up the sing-song chatter with the baby, and soon David was asleep.

'I am Amber Ballantyne,' Amber said, introducing herself.

The girl blushed again. 'I know, ma'am. Will you tell your husband that I am sorry to put him to the trouble of carrying me? I wanted to go down the stairs myself, but I had fallen down in the dark and near snapped my foot off. He said not to be silly and it was much quicker his way.'

Amber smiled as she studied the girl more closely – she was a bony creature, with a square face and a thick crop of freckles across her neck and cheeks.

'Did I say the wrong thing, ma'am? I am sorry.'

'Don't be sorry. You said nothing wrong. Tell me, are you injured at all, other than your ankle?'

The girl shook her head. 'No. Not much. Only my throat hurts and the doctor said I cracked my ribs as I fell. But they aren't so bad.'

'What is your name?'

'Greta, ma'am. Greta Bauer.'

'And your country?'

'I was born near Mafeking, but my parents are German. Were. I did mending and sewing in the hotel. Lord knows what I shall do now.'

'And your age?'

'Sixteen, ma'am.'

'How did you know how to quiet the baby?'

'I had a little brother used to be this way,' the girl said. 'One of the blacks at my uncle's farm saw my ma was going half-mad with it, so she taught us this trick. Seemed like the same sort of crying, so I thought I'd try with your little one.'

'It's not just that,' Amber said, her tone friendly. 'I think he likes the sound of your voice.'

Greta lowered her eyes.

'Would you like to come and work for me, Greta?' Amber asked.

• • •

Greta came to the hotel the moment Mrs Clifford told her that she was well enough to take up her duties as a nurse-maid. Nazeera was delighted to leave David's care to the new girl. She taught Greta what she knew about the proper way to serve a member of the family, and Amber gave Greta enough money to buy a new supply of suitable clothes, toiletries and a sensible brown leather case to keep them in. Before the end of the week, Amber received a telegram giving her permission to join Penrod in Mafeking.

• • •

Amber found the journey to Mafeking thrilling, even though much of the talk on the train was the same as she had heard everywhere in Cape Town – the coming war and how it would be won. She watched the countryside transform – the train leaving the temperate oak-strewn plains near Cape Town, passing through steep-sided, scrub-covered valleys of sandstone until they reached the top of the great escarpment. After that they were in the Karoo and the landscape became unchanging – vast empty plateau after vast empty plateau. There were moments when the mountains seemed so far away that Amber thought that they would never reach them.

David was uncharacteristically calm, the rhythm of the train lulling him in and out of a long, light sleep in Greta's arms. Amber had thought that he would find the journey difficult and had prepared herself accordingly. Eventually, Greta slept, too.

After ten hours of travel, and following a brief halt at Kimberley, they reached the highveld – great oceans of swaying grass, studded with low thorn trees. It seemed too vast, too empty. How could any group of men claim ownership of such a place? Amber asked herself as the sun began to set, turning the veld into a field of flame.

Night had fallen by the time she and Greta, with David pressed to her chest, stepped down onto the platform at Mafeking's small station. Penrod, looking gaunt and sunburned, met Amber with the news he would be leaving early the following morning on another mission to recruit the men they needed – war was coming, and soon, he said – but even this did not quash Amber's spirits. She was full of the news of her journey, illuminated by the joy of travel, and happy to be back at her husband's side.

They walked around the Mafeking parade ground in the moonlight, having left Greta to settle David and unpack in the cottage that Penrod had rented. The town was a mystery to Amber and Penrod was attempting to help her make sense of the confusing assemblage of shadows. They were passing along the northern edge of the ground, in the lee of the newly built convent, home to a small group of Irish nuns, and the Victoria Hospital. These were the most substantial buildings in town, but they appeared to Amber only as low, black hulks against the night sky, pierced with the glow of gas lamps.

'They are working late at the hospital,' Amber said. The rest of the town was in almost complete darkness.

'Making bandages,' Penrod said. He felt a slight hesitation in his wife's footstep. 'Our masters have found us a warm corner to work in, Amber. You will not be able to stay here long.'

'I understand,' she said. 'I will go back to Cape Town when I must. But I can be useful here. I shall make the cottage comfortable, and I can make bandages, too.'

'Thank you.' He stopped, his hand on her slim waist. He traced the curve of her hips with his open palm, and drew her to him, feeling the swell of her breasts against his chest.

'Penrod ...' she said, her voice husky, and turned her face upwards to look at him, her lips slightly parted.

He kissed her deeply and felt her body thrill in response.

'I need you, Penrod,' she whispered, her lips against his. 'Find us somewhere we can be together.'

Stooping, Penrod lifted her into his arms. She placed her arms around his neck and pressed her face into its curve.

He carried her to a door in a wooden lean-to at the back of the hospital. The door swung open as soon as Penrod put his shoulder to it, held closed by nothing more than a loop of string over a nail. Inside was a storeroom – Amber could see rough wooden shelves full of folded bedsheets in the moonlight, the air was filled with the smell of carbolic soap.

She twisted her fingers into the hair at the back of Penrod's head as he lowered her to the floor, pulling it down, pulling his mouth down to hers. The rough stubble under his moustache scratched her, but his lips were tender. He moved his mouth to her neck, his breath hot under her ear and his hand against her throat.

Breaking away, Penrod pulled off his shirt. His body was pale and strong in the moonlight, but Amber saw the puckered flesh on his arm – another scar, another wound that would never really heal.

'Touch me, Penrod,' she said.

Turning back to her, he took a handful of the hem of her skirt and lifted it up round her waist. He was rough with haste, his need surpassing hers, but she was the one to cry out first, breaking the night with the sound of her release.

• • •

The next morning, after Penrod left for his recruitment drive, Amber set about their small cottage. She put an apron over her dress, tied a handkerchief over her hair and began cleaning the dust out of the corners of their modest home, sofly humming her favourite song as she rearranged the meagre furniture. The cottage had four rooms – a kitchen and Greta's room in the rear, a *vorkamer* and the bedroom she shared with Penrod at the front. A shaded veranda fringed with veld daisies ran across the front of the building where Greta played with the baby while Amber worked, and to the rear of the cottage was a small garden, already planted with a mixture of wild flowering plants culled from the veld and a small patch of vegetables.

Once the rooms were habitable, Amber suggested to Greta that they should walk around the town and learn about their neighbours.

The town was a simple settlement, constructed close to where the railway line crossed the Molopo River. To Amber it seemed as if it had somehow been summoned up from the earth by magic – it was so out of place in the scrubby vastness that surrounded it on all sides. The buildings were all single-storey, carefully white-washed, built with mud bricks and crowned with roofs of corrugated iron. They were neat and well-made. Pepper trees had been planted along the wide, dusty streets. Many houses boasted window boxes and gardens full of flowers. Greta proudly pointed out the police station, the Freemason's Hall, the general store owned by Amber's Cape Town acquaintance, Ben Weil, and the establishments of his rivals.

Amber and Greta spent some time admiring the handsome convent and hospital buildings – Amber's mind running over the events of the night before, her long-needed reunion with Penrod – but very soon they found themselves on the edge of town, and Amber looked out over what seemed an endless plain of yellow grass and low bushes. After the bustle and dramatic scenery of Cape Town, Mafeking seemed an impossibly isolated place, an accidental outpost in an empty wilderness created by an irritable god in his anger.

'And your family?' Amber asked. 'Where are they?'

'On the farm, Miss Amber,' Greta said, gesturing towards the horizon. 'My parents and little brother died of fever. So then I lived with my aunt and uncle on the farm, but I think I was a terrible trouble to them. I wanted to see the city, the way girls do. When I found the city not to my liking, I was too ashamed to ask them to have me back.'

Amber did not push her to say more.

'The Barolong Stadt is on the other side of town,' Greta said, changing the topic. 'The Barolong settled here before the whites arrived. They built their huts down by the river, in a little valley, so it is more shaded and green. And the market garden for the whites is in that direction.' She pointed to the south. 'It is a sort of island in the river and very well laid out, but you cannot see it from where we are now. Dixon's Hotel use it to grow all their greens.'

They strolled past Dixon's Hotel, a grand establishment with staff in waistcoats. Greta remarked to Amber that Dixon's had a proper cook and was known for its Sunday lunches. They stopped at the rail yard and watched a goods train being unloaded. Ammunition, Amber thought, judging by the shape and size of the boxes. As she watched the men work, she began to realise that the railway meant Mafeking was not as isolated as it might first appear. It was a staging post, like an island port in the vast ocean of the veld, where travellers and adventurers might stop and swap stories, and some might see the chance to dig roots into the sandy soil.

A man in khaki, a broad-shouldered fellow, older than Amber, but still shy of forty, approached them. His features were heavy and pronounced, a good-looking face if a little distorted somehow. He hunched his shoulders and touched the brim of his hat. 'Morning, ladies!' He smiled. 'Just wanting to say, Mrs Ballantyne, how I'm glad that your husband recruited me into the regiment. I was a businessman before, so I'm managing the stores now. Anything I can get for the wife of Colonel Ballantyne, just let me know.'

Amber thanked him. 'More and more seems to be arriving by the hour, Trooper . . .?'

'Cressy, ma'am. Indeed it does. Flooding in. We've had to start work on a new warehouse – to keep it all well stored. Seems someone high up has good contacts in Cape Town.'

Amber made no comment.

'Well, I shall leave you to your walk, ladies.'

The trooper went back to his duties, but Amber noticed Greta frowning after he had left. 'What is it worrying you, Greta?'

'Nothing, Mrs Ballantyne, only I could swear I've seen him before. Well, I lived in Cape Town for a year, so I think I saw just about everyone under the sun.' Her face became serious. 'War's coming soon now, isn't it?'

Amber linked her arm through Greta's. 'I think it is.'

'What does war do to a place like this, Miss Amber?'

Amber looked round her at the people coming and going, people who had embraced adventure and travelled to this place, built a home, a place in the harshness of the world, planted their flower boxes – a community finding its feet.

'Nothing good, Greta, I'm afraid,' she said. 'Nothing good.'

• • •

'I am sorry, Amber,' Penrod said, reading the paper the messenger had just handed him. 'I have been summoned to a meeting between the Barolong headmen and the magistrate.' She paused, and Penrod guessed she had thought of asking to join him, then decided against it. She only smiled, and promised to have supper waiting for him when he returned.

For some reason this brief exchange made Penrod angry with Ryder Courtney. Ryder could involve his wife in his work as much as he or she wished. The command structure of the British Army and his work as intelligence officer did not give Penrod the same opportunity. He loved his wife, and admired both her spirit and intelligence, but they lived in separate spheres. He was astute enough to realise that this saddened her, and was irritated by the vague feelings of guilt her sadness engendered.

Penrod walked briskly towards the residence of the magistrate, Charles Bell, an elegant single-storey house on Mafeking's main street. He had already formed a favourable impression of Bell. He spoke the local languages with admirable fluency, and had, Penrod suspected, the sort of dry sense of humour that Amber would appreciate lurking under his slightly stiff, business-like exterior. Still, this meeting was not a social call to which he might bring his curious wife.

To add to his irritation, Penrod found Bell, Baden-Powell and the deputation from the Barolong Stadt waiting for him. He was welcomed into the large dining room where Bell seemed to do much of his business, and introduced to the other guests. All were dressed, like the rest of the Barolong in Mafeking, in European style, and Bell moved between Setswana and English as made the introductions. He also introduced a tall, immaculately dressed Marolong man with a high forehead and wide-set, intelligent eyes as his translator, Sol Plaatje. He couldn't be much over twenty, Penrod thought, but carried himself with the ease of an older man.

'Chief Wessels Montshiwa and these gentlemen have brought us useful intelligence of the Boer and their preparations in the Lichtenburg district,' Baden-Powell said when the introductions were complete.

One of the headmen, Silas Molema, handed Penrod a buff folder.

'*Ke a leboga*,' Penrod said and Silas smiled. 'A pleasure,' he turned to the translator. 'Sol, if all the English officers learn Setswana, you will be out of a job.'

The younger man smiled. 'I shall endeavour to find a way to be useful.'

Silas pointed to the folder. 'It was my young friend Sol who gathered together these notes and endeavoured to render them intelligible, Colonel.'

Penrod opened the file. Maps neatly drawn and typewritten notes. He saw at first glance that Mr Plaatje had added notes as to how reliable or otherwise he thought the person who had supplied the information.

'This is excellent, thank you. And you may call me Ballantyne or Penrod. We have been asked not to use our ranks at this stage.'

Sol was translating for the chief, a strongly built man whose narrowed eyes glanced between the whites and his own headmen with lowering suspicion. He said something, apparently exasperated.

'Chief Wessels says he tires of these polite fictions. War is coming and our people will be caught in the middle of it.' Sol translated evenly, tilting his head to listen as he spoke. Penrod could understand one word in ten, the anger in the chief's voice obscuring the rest. 'We ask you again for arms, Mr Bell. We must defend our families and our cattle.'

'If hostilities break out,' the magistrate said, casting a look at Penrod and Baden-Powell, 'they will be between the Boer and the British forces. There is no need for your people here to be involved, Chief Wessels. You have my assurance.'

Whatever the single-word response was from the chief, Sol decided to not to translate it.

Another of the headmen, Motshegare, got up sharply from his seat at the table and stalked across the room to stand behind Bell's chair.

'Perhaps what you say is true,' he said. 'When the conflict commences, we shall shelter behind your back, like this, while you fight the Dutchmen. But what if they win? What if you fall? Are we to also surrender?'

'My good fellow, we have every expectation . . .' Bell began, twisting round, but Motshegare shook his head. He took off his coat and opened his shirt, pulling it clear of his shoulder so Bell, Baden-Powell and Penrod could see the puckered scar on his flesh.

'I had this from a Boer rifle before you British came to Mafeking. I know what bullets do.' He did up the buttons of his shirt again. 'Unless you can prove to me that your white troops are not wounded by bullets, I insist on my right to defend myself, my wife and my children. I have a rifle. I need only ammunition.'

Bell sighed. 'I understand you and I will pass on your concerns to the government in the Cape Colony. But I am certain they will say the same as I have. That this is business between the British and the Boer. None of the natives will be involved.'

'Tell your bullets and shells that,' Wessels said in Setswana. 'I do not think they are as particular about the colour of a man's skin.'

The rest of the men got to their feet, and it was clear the meeting was at an end. Silas shook hands with them, but Wessels and Motshegare were obviously too irritated to offer more than a curt nod before they left.

Sol watched them go, then turned to Bell. 'If you don't need me anymore this evening, Mr Bell, I have some paperwork to do before I go home.'

Penrod held up his hand. 'If you wouldn't mind waiting a little longer, Mr Plaatje.' Sol nodded. 'Are you of Chief Wessel's people?'

He smiled. 'I am Marolong *wa ga* Modiboa, Ballantyne. You might say the Tshidi Barolong of the Stadt are my cousins. Before taking employment with Mr Bell here last year, I was at Kimberley. But I live with Silas Molema.'

He stood with his hands clasped lightly in front of him.

'Sol speaks eight languages,' Bell said. 'And he's a bloody good typist.'

Sol laughed. 'Do you have some other question for me, Ballantyne?'

Penrod studied him carefully. 'A simple one. Will the Barolong fight with us against the Boer if it comes to it?'

Sol did not hesitate before answering. 'The Tshidi Barolong will. Our cousins – the Rapulana – are traditional allies of the Boer, however.' He paused. 'You are welcome to visit me in the Stadt and we might discuss it further there. Of the other natives present in Mafeking, I know less, though I believe the Mfengu refugees arriving in town will be happy to work for the British.'

Penrod put out his hand. 'Thank you. I shall call on you, Mr Plaatje.'

Sol hesitated only for a fraction of a second before taking his hand. 'The Barolong fighters need only ammunition, Ballantyne. You can trust them to make good use of it.'

• • •

Penrod came and went as August became September, making discreet trips into the Cape Colony to recruit men – despite Sir Alfred's dictat – and discovering what he could about the Boer forces massing in the Transvaal. Halfway through September he arrived back in Mafeking late in the evening and went straight to headquarters, despite his travel-stained appearance. Ned Cecil was sitting in the outer office, staring disconsolately at a great sheaf of paperwork on his desk. Penrod nodded to him and was just about to enter Baden-Powell's office when Ned held up his hand. Penrod waited, his eyebrow raised. A moment later he heard the sound of voices from inside the room. The door muffled the words, but Penrod could not mistake Baden-Powell's angry tone.

'Hore is in with B-P,' Ned said softly. 'And not getting a good time of it. A drink?'

'Thank you.'

Penrod pulled a chair across the room and sat down. Ned produced a bottle of brandy from one of the drawers and a glass which he examined in the lamplight. Satisfied that it was clean enough, he filled it and pushed it across to Penrod.

'Half a dozen of your new recruits arrived yesterday from Hopetown and I thank you for them.'

'Good,' Penrod said and drank. The glass might have been cloudy, but the brandy was excellent. 'Not the best riders, but they are all handy with a rifle and have some experience handling munitions. Most were working in the goldfields, but fear of the war has driven them out of the Transvaal. Another twenty are on their way to us now.'

Ned pushed his hands through his hair, staring down at the papers. 'I'm glad to hear it. Yesterday I made a list of the previous occupations and skills of the newly arrived recruits and we have more masons and cooks than anything else, but we are nearly up to strength.'

Another sharp exchange was audible behind the door.

'Exercises did not go well today, then?' Penrod asked.

'It would be funny if it were not so serious, Penrod.' Ned looked up at him. 'We want a regiment of cavalry, and half of the men can't even keep their seat. Three were thrown or fell off yesterday. Only one in ten is capable of following orders. The others hang onto the necks of their ponies and shut their eyes. We have horses who've never seen a man, and men who have never seen a horse. I understand it's much the same in Bulawayo.'

Penrod's mouth twitched.

'And then one of the idiots almost shot B-P during firing drill. No, don't laugh! He missed him by an inch. So, now poor old Hore is catching it and it'll only fuddle the man.'

Penrod reached for one of the sheets of paper lying in front of Ned and as he read it, pursed his lips and made a low whistle.

'So, some of the munitions are getting through at last?'

'Yes, we now have half a dozen Maxims, and a handful of muzzle-loading seven-pounders. I think our Mr Weil has emptied his stores in Cape Town to fill his warehouse here, too.'

'Good for him.'

Ned shrugged. 'Perhaps. We've brought in a few men from the camp at Ramathlabama to guard the munitions, but having all this ordnance here is making the townspeople nervous. They are certain that as soon as war is declared the Boers will sweep in and take the lot. The mayor and his council are asking for guarantees of defence and they have a point – if we are harassing General Cronjé on the veld, who will protect the town?' He ran his hands through his hair and sighed deeply. 'We've made plans to summon the Town Guard, but they'll have even less training than our boys. What is going to stop our Boer friends riding in and making themselves at home as soon as hostilities are declared?'

'Judging by your description of the exercises today, very little.'

They were quiet. Ned returned to his paperwork and Penrod savoured his brandy, watching the shadows gather in the dusty corners of the room. Baden-Powell was giving Hore a long oration. Penrod felt pity for the older man. Hore was a competent officer who looked after his men, but he thought slowly, and their current predicament had reduced him to a state of cowed confusion. He should never have been sent to South Africa on a mission like this. Quick wits, fresh ideas and imaginative strategies were required, and poor Hore possessed none of these. Not to mention that their situation was growing more serious with each passing day.

'Ned, how would you defend Mafeking?'

Ned didn't look up from his papers. 'It's all but impossible, I'd say.'

'The old fort on Canon Kopjé would be the key. It overlooks the whole town,' Penrod mused quietly. 'We would have to make the Barolong Stadt part of the defensive line, of course. And we could put riflemen in the brickfields . . .'

Ned put down his pen. 'One would have to dig an outer and an inner ring of trenches around the rest of the town.' He spoke lightly as if indulging Penrod in a game.

'A fair number of railway workers are living here, I believe?' Penrod said.

'Yes,' Ned said cautiously, 'but the Boer forces will rip up the tracks north and south of the town the moment war is declared. What use is a railway that can't go anywhere?'

'Think on it,' Penrod said. He turned over a bill of sale, plucked a pencil from the pot on Ned's desk, and in a few swift strokes had sketched a map of the town, including the curve of the Molopo River through the Barolong Stadt and the railway line running in a north–south direction. 'Imagine an armoured train, going back and forth along the rails within the perimeter of our defences, with one of the Maxim guns on board. That would prove a powerful addition to our defence.'

Ned was leaning over the drawing and nodding. 'Go on.'

'We might construct a length of rail going east along the edge of the European Quarter into the bush and past the brickfields. An armoured train running along that stretch would make it impossible for the enemy to launch a full-scale attack from that direction.'

'That *could* keep the Boer out of town.' Ned tapped his finger on the sketch.

'Of course it could,' Penrod replied.

'B-P has managed to get a detachment of the British South African Police added to our numbers,' Ned continued. 'They seem likely lads. They might hold Canon Kopjé if it could be reinforced. But all this is more than the Town Guard could manage.' He leaned away again. 'We would need the whole regiment in the perimeter trenches and our orders are to mount raids on the Boer. We are to be mobile. Keep them busy.'

Before Penrod could reply, the inner office door opened and Colonel Hore, his face scarlet, hurried past them and out into the night.

'Should've given him my brandy,' Ned muttered.

Baden-Powell appeared at the door to his office and saw Penrod waiting for him. 'Ballantyne. Good to have you back. Come in.'

Penrod followed him into his spartan office and waited until Baden-Powell waved him into a chair before sitting down. Penrod saw a bunk bed had been set up in the corner of the room, but aside from this recent addition the room was still bare of comfort or ornament.

Baden-Powell listened to Penrod's report on the growing numbers of Boers collecting on the other side of the border with grim attention. When Penrod had finished, Baden-Powell was silent for a full minute before he spoke again.

'No doubt you have heard about the showing the regiment made on exercises today. What chances would you give our men in the field against General Cronjé's forces?'

'None, sir.'

Baden-Powell's face was dark. 'That's my opinion, too.'

'But I have a plan, sir,' Penrod said sharply. 'It involves a loose interpretation of the orders we have been given, but it will work.'

Baden-Powell looked at him coolly. 'Colonel Ballantyne, as long as you remember you are under my command, I am ready to listen.'

'I understand, sir.' Penrod leaned forward, his elbows on his knees, the light from the table lamp exposing his thin, unshaven face. He looked like the itinerant engineer he had once claimed to be. 'I had a thought about a defence of Mafeking.'

'That was the map you and Ned were scribbling?' Baden-Powell replied. 'What do you propose?'

'An extra track for an armoured train heading east out of the railway yard on the far side of the convent.'

'An unnecessary use of limited resources,' Baden-Powell said dismissively. 'We must get out and do what we can against the Boer in the field.'

Penrod suppressed his irritation and spoke calmly. 'I know our orders, sir, but to obey them to the letter would be committing suicide. Surely it is better to obey their spirit! We need to buy time for reinforcements to arrive in southern Africa or the British Empire will lose the Cape Colony. That is the whole reason for our mission, is it not?' Baden-Powell nodded. 'Now, you and I both know, sir, that our men would be beaten in a day on the veld, but what if we draw Cronjé into a siege here in Mafeking? That could tie up his men for weeks and their superiority on horseback would become irrelevant.'

Baden-Powell raised his eyebrows, appeared serious for a moment, then waved his hand. 'But why would they stop, even for the stores Ned has managed to build up? They don't need the munitions – they are well-supplied,' he said, his voice prickling with exhaustion. 'And you yourself have told me often enough that the Boer commandos don't need rations – they can supply themselves from the countryside.'

Penrod spoke quietly. 'Yes, sir. If we had only infantry here, they might bypass us entirely, but they do not know how bad our men are in the saddle and Cronjé is said to be a cautious man. He will want to knock out our regiment at once, so he does not need to worry about raids on his flanks. Add to that the temptation of the stores and Cronjé might well think it is worth the effort to encircle the town and demand a surrender.'

Baden-Powell had picked up a pencil from the table and now he began rolling it between his fingers. 'By your own account Cronjé has six times as many men as we do. Our lines would be so thinly manned, a concerted attack at any point would overwhelm us instantly.'

'Sir, I only know that our men have no chance in the field and this plan gives us a chance of tying up the Boer advance until reinforcements arrive from England and India. And I am certain that a slim chance is better than no chance at all.'

Penrod waited. He did not think many officers in the British Army would have given his plan so much as a second's thought. Even the best of them had a tendency to hang on to their traditional methods of waging war and followed procedure no matter what the conditions on the ground or the larger consequences.

'It would mean arming the Barolong in the Stadt,' Baden-Powell said at last.

'They have the right to defend their homes, same as the whites,' Penrod replied.

Baden-Powell nodded. 'We will talk it through. I am happy to bet my reputation on a chance of survival, rather than accept martyrdom, but we must make a better case for this plan to work and we must present it well if we are to convince the other officers.'

'Surely they will obey your orders?'

'Damn right they will,' Baden-Powell said fiercely, 'but if the plan is to draw the enemy into a siege and put the civilians of this town as well as the fighting men in danger, I want them to obey gladly and with conviction. I have no doubt you have the ability to lead men, Ballantyne, but here you must learn to work alongside your fellow officers, not around them.'

Penrod held his temper, biting back the retort that had risen to his lips. He was aware of how often his own pride has cost him in the past.

Baden-Powell stood up and crossed the room with swift, sharp strides before pushing the door open. 'Ned,' he called, 'leave the book-keeping for now and come in here. Bring that sketch of Ballantyne's with you.'

Within minutes the three men were using chess pieces from Baden-Powell's travelling set to represent the Cape Boys, the squadrons of the Protectorate Regiment and the Town Guard. Penrod's irritation dissipated as he discussed tactics with the two highly intelligent officers. The Black Queen was given the role of the armoured train, and the knights stood either side of the river in the Barolong Stadt.

Ned traced the line of trenches that would form the outer perimeter, then threw down his pencil in disgust. 'But the Boer have spies all over town! Every day some concerned citizen of Mafeking comes to inform me that he has heard his neighbour speaking Dutch.'

Baden-Powell picked up the pencil and flourished it like a weapon.

'That might work to our advantage, Ned,' he said with a twinkle in his eye. 'A little misdirection.'

Penrod watched as Baden-Powell traced his hand across the open, exposed bank of ground between Canon Kopjé and the brickfields.

'The minefields will go here.'

Ned looked confused. 'But we don't have any mines.'

'The Boer don't know that,' Baden-Powell said. 'A hundred of those small wine cases that Weil uses to ship in his excellent brandy. Painted black and filled with sand. Do you think we might fool them?'

Penrod nodded. 'We might announce a test. Drop some dynamite down a couple of anthills. It will need to be staged well.'

'Theatrics are my speciality,' Baden-Powell said, 'leave that to me. Penrod, I'm making you Base Commander, effective immediately. Ned, get this plan written up, then I want you and Penrod to start work on the defences as soon as it's light. Take Major Panzera with you.'

'Yes, sir,' Ned said. 'Those Fengu refugees who came in from the Witwatersrand look like they know how to dig a trench.'

'Excellent. Hire them all. And tomorrow I want every officer in Mafikeng here first thing in the morning for a briefing. Every Dutch spy we have in the town is going to hear how the only thing we fear is a siege! Given the excellent horsemen and the amount of ammunition we have at our disposal we are not defeatable in the field.' He looked at his watch. 'I shall go and see the civil authorities this evening. We need to get as many women and children out of their homes as possible. Mafeking is about to become a military town.'

Penrod smiled. It was clear that once Baden-Powell had the bit between his teeth he could act with authority. 'And the Barolong, sir?' he asked.

Baden-Powell nodded sharply. 'Yes, of course. I shall visit Chief Wessels tomorrow. This is, and should remain, a white man's war, but I shall make it clear to the chief that if the Boer attack his people or try to rustle his stock, he has the right to defend himself.' He sighed. 'And perhaps you should go and speak to that young man who works for Bell, and tell him what's actually going on. I think he might prove to be extremely useful to us.'

• • •

Penrod left Baden-Powell and walked towards the outskirts of the European Quarter, crossing the railway line and walking the path which curved past the stables and ran along the river to the Barolong Stadt. The moonlight limned the world in front of him with an unearthly silver, making the occasional heaps of volcanic stone, studded with low thorn bushes, look like ancient burial mounds.

The Stadt was made up of large round houses with thickly thatched roofs, each standing in a compound surrounded by a stone wall. At the eastern edge of the town stood the Lutheran church, and near it a number of houses built in the European style where the chiefs and headmen lived. He must have been spotted, because Sol Plaatje came out to meet him, and led him up to his veranda.

'Emang,' he said to a young girl leaning against the open door to the house. 'Tea for our guest, please.'

Then he invited Penrod to sit on one of the wicker chairs which looked out over the dusty garden. 'I am teaching her English. If she brings brandy or cigars, I shall think myself a failure.'

Penrod sat down with a smile, but when the girl returned she did so with a teapot and cups, which she set down carefully on the low table between them.

While Sol poured the tea, they spoke of the weather, the longing everyone in Mafeking felt for the rains to come. A pause in the conversation which seemed to indicate a turn in subject settled between them.

'Baden-Powel will be speaking to Bell and Chief Wessels officially in the morning,' Penrod said, 'but I am here to tell you we mean to provoke a siege, and discuss what that means for the people here.'

Sol's teacup hovered in the air only momentarily. 'I see,' Sol said eventually. 'Do go on.'

Penrod outlined the plan he had so recently discussed with Ned and Baden-Powell. Sol pointed out the importance of the Stadt immediately.

'You will be supplied with ammunition, of course.'

'You are asking us more than that,' Sol said, studying the silhouettes of the thorn trees under the moonlight.

'Are we?'

'Of course,' he replied. 'How do you intend to get news in and out of Mafeking? Will it all be done under a white flag?'

Penrod put down his teacup. 'No, we cannot hear only what the Boer see fit to tell us. The encirclement will not be perfect and Bell has messengers who know the country.'

Sol frowned. 'I have heard enough stories about the Boer to doubt their safety. Any white man crossing the lines is likely to be killed. I think, Penrod, you will have to rely on Barolong runners to carry your messages. They know the paths the whites do not, and there are many Tshidi Barolong scattered through the countryside outside Mafeking. That means our runners can lie about where they are going and why. A white man cannot do that.'

Penrod nodded and for the first time the reality of what he was proposing became suddenly real. They were asking the Boers to put a noose around their necks, inviting all the dangers of siege with little but hope on their side. He clenched his fist. It had to be done, whatever the risk.

'Are you a married man, Mr Plaatje?'

Sol's eyes grew soft. 'Yes, my wife is Elizabeth. She and my little boy are staying with my family in Pneil. Given what you have said, for the first time in weeks I am glad they are not here.'

'I have a wife and child in Mafeking,' Penrod said quietly.

'I know. I have read your wife's novels. I hope for your sake that they leave soon.'

• • •

While Penrod came and went, Amber spent much of her time at the hospital, taking lessons from the nurses and spending hours cutting and rolling bandages. That was until little David suddenly developed a fever. His agonising cries broke Amber's heart and this time not even Greta could quiet him. Amber did not dare travel back to Cape Town with him until he was better.

'I want you to leave as soon as possible, Amber,' Penrod told her firmly the day after his first discussions with Ned and Baden-Powell about the defence of the town. 'Very soon this place will become a charnel house.'

Amber felt a wave of frustration, she was resilient and strong-minded, but being sent from one place to another with her baby and hardly seeing Penrod was beginning to weaken her resolve. 'I shall decide what is best for David, Penrod!' she snapped at him. 'A day or two more and then you will no longer be inconvenienced by your sick child.'

He frowned at her. 'Amber, I do not understand you. You hire a nursemaid, but as soon as David sneezes you only let the girl have charge of him when you are too exhausted to stand. You claim you do not want to leave my side, but every time I open or shut a door in this house you say I am disturbing the infant.'

Amber held her son close to her, and he clearly felt her distress because his thin, high wail started up again. Some part of her thought that there might be some justice in what Penrod had said, but she was fatigued and frightened of what lay ahead of them. 'Is it unnatural that I want to be with both of you, is it wrong of me to want us to be a family? Tell me, my husband,' she said.

'No, but at the moment it is impractical,' he replied angrily.

David began to wail more loudly.

'You are making him worse.' Amber began rocking the baby again.

Penrod stalked out of the house without replying.

• • •

By mid-September Ryder Courtney's ride from the Mount Nelson to Salt River, the manufacturing district on the edge of Cape Town, had become a familiar pleasure. Even in the early morning, the air was already thick with the smells and sounds of industry. Ryder breathed in deeply, savouring the taste of the bitter coal dust and the sharp ammonia tang from the tanneries. He heard the clank of iron striking iron from the railyards, and from every direction came the sound of hammering, flywheels spinning and the hiss of steam. The wagon drivers and their boys threw inventive curses at each other in four different languages as they steered their loads up and down the wide busy streets. The men leaning in the doorways of dark workshops, wearing thickly grimed overalls, wiped the sweat from their foreheads and exchanged greetings with clerks hurrying towards their offices, with order books under their arms. Ryder was happy – he enjoyed being a part of this community of men creating whatever the swelling population of the Cape demanded. Where others might have only seen dirt and noise, Ryder saw enterprise in action. Men from all walks of life met here to combine their skills and ingenuity with capital, to create something new. Trade and manufacture had made England rich and powerful, not soldiers sent out to parade in ranks and die of disease and festering wounds on the fringes of Empire. His boy, Leon, refused to see what Ryder admired about this world, his son sneered at men like these. Leon's desire to dedicate himself to a life of military glory enraged Ryder. His contempt for his father's work had been more overt of late, and Saffron had become more and more impatient with them both.

Ryder had no doubt a war was coming, and he knew the character of the men the British would be fighting. They were like him. The Boers were a proud breed, used to unholy hardships and struggling against steep odds, and more than that, their belief in their own independence ran through their cores. So, while the elite society of Cape Town had convinced itself that the conflict between the British and the alliance of the Transvaal and Orange Free State would be over in a month, Ryder thought differently. He believed that even if the initial military victory was swift and decisive, the British would have to keep a force in the field for some considerable time to prevent the Boers rising against them again. That force would need to be supplied with equipment suitable for southern Africa and its particular challenges.

Ryder had formulated a plan based on this belief as soon as he had arrived in Cape Town and put it into action. First, he took boxes of cigars and bottles of whisky to all the junior officers stationed at the Castle of Good Hope, the military headquarters in Cape Town, and discussed with them the field kit provided for the infantry and how it might be improved. Next, Ryder had bought the small, floundering factory in the Salt River area of the city, the one that Ben Weil had told him to visit, and dismissed the incumbent manager – a vicious and lazy individual. He had done as Penrod had asked and declined to prosecute when the time had come, but there was no doubt that the man belonged in gaol.

With the Cape Malay foreman, Mr Yusuf Baderoon, his senior workers and a former sergeant of the 80th Regiment of Foot, the Staffordshire Volunteers, who had fought in the Zulu Wars, Ryder designed a camp kettle for the infantry to use in the field. It was lighter and stronger than the models imported from England and it would soon be ready to take back to the Castle, to be tested by the officers. Ryder was confident that they would want ten thousand. All he needed now was for war to be declared.

• • •

Rumours reached the residents of Mafeking that the Boer were forming commandos. The younger men put on uniforms, and family men who could afford it sent their wives and children south into the Cape Colony. Penrod had made sure that the Boer had heard that Mafeking was a prize they could not afford to miss. His satisfaction that his plan to delay them might work was tempered only by his concern that the town might have to pay a high price for his success.

As the time went by, Amber kept finding reasons to delay her departure and Penrod was too distracted with preparing the defence of the town – often napping at odd hours at headquarters rather than returning to the cottage – to demand her immediate departure to the safety of the Cape. Sir William Butler had been recalled to England, and with his departure some of the desperately needed artillery that he had denied Baden-Powell arrived into Mafeking. The railway yard seethed with activity as the workers used metal sleepers to turn goods wagons into armoured trucks, and laid rail heading east out of the town. Baden-Powell received official sanction to move the Protectorate Regiment into the town itself. Then, on 10 October 1899, President Kruger issued an ultimatum – unless the British government withdrew all its forces from the borders of the Transvaal and Orange Free State in the next two days, he would declare war.

On the evening the ultimatum was delivered, the officers in Mafeking received word that men had been spotted forming *laagers* around the edge of the town. Penrod and Baden-Powell rode out to see for themselves. They left their horses a mile and a half from the most southerly of the Boer camps and walked through the tall grass towards the orange glow of the campfires. Guided by the starlight, they found a small rise from where they could observe the men waiting to attack Mafeking.

Wagons had been positioned defensively, in a wide circle, and the two officers could hear the bellows and bleats of cattle and sheep in the darkness – the mobile larder the commandos had brought with them to feed their men. Cooking pots steamed over the campfires, and in the light provided by these fires Penrod and Baden-Powell observed the men who had been sent to take Mafeking. Penrod studied individual faces through his field glasses. Some were young, still smooth-cheeked, and appeared dwarfed by the rifles they held across their laps and the canvas bandoliers strung across their chests. Other men he saw in the flickering light were clearly over fifty, their thick beards shot through with grey. Penrod let his vision rest on one after another, then suddenly he felt a shock of recognition.

'What is it, Ballantyne?' Baden-Powell was also observing the camp through field glasses and did not lower them as Penrod answered.

'Do you remember the name Gerrit Vintner, sir?' Penrod asked.

'Yes, the farmer you stayed with. You learned a great deal under his roof, as I recall.'

'Third fire from the western edge of the camp, the man with his head up and looking in our direction. That is Gerrit Vintner.'

'By God, it's as if he can smell us out here in the dark.' Baden-Powell lowered his glasses and rubbed a hand across his eyes. 'I hope your conscience isn't troubling you, Penrod.'

'For abusing his hospitality to gather information? No, sir, not in the least. Though I think if he saw me and recognised me, he would crawl across any minefield, real or otherwise, to call me a blackguard and shoot me himself. I only hope that Cronjé does not have many men like him under his command.'

'As do I,' Baden-Powell said. He looked through the glasses again. 'I would estimate there are more than five hundred men in this camp alone, all well armed by the look of it.' He paused. 'Penrod, you know you must get Mrs Ballantyne out of Mafeking at once, don't you?'

'I do,' Penrod replied. 'Shall we fetch the horses and take a look at the northern camps?'

'Excellent notion,' Baden-Powell said dryly. 'I think that friend of yours can see in the dark – he is beginning to make me nervous.'

When they returned to headquarters, Ned handed Penrod a note. It was from Amber. *I know I must go*, it said, *please come and have supper with me.*

He could not refuse her that and started to get ready to go home.

Penrod was about to leave Headquarters when a runner arrived. He took the message and read it, knowing instinctively that it could only be bad news. As he read, Penrod felt as if the air was being forced out of his lungs – it was the worst possible news.

The rails had been taken up to the north and to the south of the town. Amber and the other remaining women and children in town could no longer be evacuated by train.

• • •

The front door of the Ballantyne cottage opened into the small living room. Amber was waiting for her husband and stood as he entered. Penrod stared at her as if he was seeing her for the first time. Occasionally he forgot how beautiful his wife was. The dress she wore was cut low and fitted tightly round her hips. Her hair was washed and loose, lying across her shoulders and tumbling down her back in thick golden curls.

'Amber?'

She crossed the room and reached up to kiss him tenderly on the mouth. He let his hands slowly circle her narrow waist, savouring the warmth of her mouth, the familiar shape of her back under the thin material of her dress.

'Are you apologising to me, Amber?'

She undid the top button of his jacket. 'Absolutely not. You are a pig. But David is better again, so Greta has taken him to spend the night with the nuns. I have heard about the railway and hired a cart and a pair of mules. We leave at dawn, but if we must go tomorrow, I want to take a good memory with me, something that will last.'

She looked up at him and bit her lip even as her long fingers undid the next buttons on his jacket.

'You have it all planned out, my dear.'

'I do. I spoke to Mr Plaatje and he has found a man to go with us. We will go to Setlagole first. It is in British territory, they will have no right or reason to trouble me there.'

She slid her hand under his jacket, and he felt the cool of her fingers through the thin fabric of his shirt. He lowered his head to gently brush her neck and shoulders with his lips, his grip around her waist tightening, pulling her closer to him.

'That might not be far enough,' he whispered against her skin and she shivered deliciously and shifted slightly, pressing her hip against him. Her hand under his jacket plucked the cloth free of his waistband and her fingers reached the skin of his back, her nails lightly tracing their way up his spine. Her other hand gripped his bicep. She licked her lips.

'I can improvise, Penrod,' she whispered. 'Now, about that memory . . .'

'I'll see what I can do, Mrs Ballantyne,' he said, then swept her up and carried her to the bedroom.

• • •

'How dangerous is it, Penrod?' Amber asked some time later, when they had taken their fill of each other. 'And do, please, tell me the truth.'

She was lying across his naked chest, looking up at him. He smoothed her honey-blonde hair, turned silver by the moonlight shining softly in through the shutters. He owed her the truth.

'We have staked everything on the hope that we can tie up the Boer commandos in a siege and now some seven thousand fighters are camped in the immediate vicinity. If Cronjé realises how thin our defences are, he will attack and we shall have to fight our way out. It will be very bloody, my darling.'

'If we didn't have David I would pick up a rifle and fight beside you.'

He laughed softly. 'I know you would, and you'd be worth a dozen of our new recruits. But you must go, Amber. If I am to fight as I must, I cannot spend every hour worried about your safety.'

She shifted slightly, but said nothing.

'Amber, I need to be certain that when you do leave here, you will speak only about the strengths of our defences. Even to those who you take for allies and friends.'

'You know that I will do my part, my love,' she said.

Outside the cottage the wind was beginning to pick up and it rattled the shutters. Penrod had longed for these moments of intimacy with his wife since their child was born, but when he thought of the battle to come, he wished with all his heart she was a thousand miles away.

'If all goes well, the war will be over in just a few weeks,' Amber said. 'But what are the chances of us getting news of each other in the meantime?'

He let his hand drift across her shapely body. No artist could ever draw a line more beautiful. 'Sol and the headmen of the Stadt have a number of men they trust to be runners. But it will be difficult, and dangerous. You must have faith, and I shall do the same.' He ran his hand through her hair. 'You think I am a monster, sending you away with our son.'

'No, Penrod. I know you are convinced we are safer out of Mafeking. But I dread not knowing how you are each day when you are in such danger. Sometimes I think David is such a fretful baby because he senses my fear for you.'

It sounded like nonsense, but at the same time Penrod felt a truth in what his wife had said. She reached up to him in the darkness and stroked his cheek with her hand.

'What time is it now?'

He glanced at his watch, where it lay in a splash of moonlight – it had been a present from Amber many years earlier.

'Nearly one.'

She pulled away from him.

'Then we had better have a quick late dinner and then I will finish my packing.'

Amber climbed out of bed, slipped on a silk dressing gown and went to their small kitchen. She had made a beef stew, to be served with mashed potato – Penrod's favourite dish. While her husband ate, she began to pad around the other room. Penrod heard Amber opening and shutting drawers while the wind sighed against the cottage walls and rattled the wooden door – a storm was brewing out on the veld. Penrod thought about the men he had seen around their campfires, readying themselves for war. Some of them would be awake now, feeling the change in the wind, also wondering what this new dawn would bring. Suddenly Amber came running back into the kitchen and threw herself into Penrod's arms, clinging to him fiercely.

'Don't die, Penrod. I'd never forgive you.'

He stroked her face gently.

'I'll try not to, my darling. Take care of our son.'

•   •   •

The following afternoon, after Amber had left, Penrod found himself in headquarters, with Ned and Baden-Powell, as the deadline given in Kruger's ultimatum approached. Penrod noticed Baden-Powell glance at the clock, then he fetched brandy and glasses and poured them all a drink. The wind outside the building moaned, rattling grit against the windows. How soon, Penrod thought, would the sounds be the moan of shell fire and the spatter of rifle rounds?

They waited, staring at the clock ticking away on the wall, until a minute past the top of the hour.

Baden-Powell lifted his glass. 'The war has begun,' he said. Penrod noticed there was no triumph, excitement or fear in his voice. It was a simple statement of fact. 'God save the Queen and good luck to us all.'

'And let us pray that this plan works,' Ned said and knocked back the contents of his glass.

'I'll drink to that,' Penrod said.

• • •

Penrod slept lightly that night and was up at dawn. With no wish to go to headquarters or stay in his silent cottage, he walked towards the railway depot through the empty streets. As he walked, he imagined his fear for his wife and his son like a block of cold matter in his heart, heavy and dragging, poisoning his blood. The memory of her sighs during their last night together seemed to swarm and itch under his skin like his old cravings for opium.

He lit a cheroot and crossed to the depot and greeted the guards. They looked nervous, peering up and down the street as if they expected a Boer to pounce on them from the shadows at any moment.

'Will they be coming today, then, sir?' one asked – a skinny boy with a strong Northern Irish accent and the faint, brave beginnings of a moustache on his upper lip.

'They might, Corporal Parland,' Penrod replied. 'If they do not, then I think we should probably go and get them, don't you think? Seems a little dull to wait.'

The boy grinned and looked encouraged. Penrod turned to walk away again, but the lad called after him: 'Sir, may I ask you another question?'

Penrod tapped the ash from his cheroot and nodded.

'The matter of it is, sir, all the dynamite in the store, sir. I know it's useful stuff, but if the Boer shell us, and Walshe standing here says they have bloody great guns with them – pardon me speaking so free – there's enough to blow the whole town sky high. So I was just wondering to myself, sir, why are we hanging onto it? I mean, quite much anyway. Sure now, keep a fair bit handy, box or two in a few places about the town, but why so much in a great big pile? I mean . . .'

Penrod walked towards them, unhurried but attentive. 'All the surplus dynamite was sent up to Bulawayo before our Boer friends tore up the rails. I signed the order myself.'

Parland scratched behind his ear and shifted awkwardly from foot to foot. 'I wouldn't know about that, sir. See now, I was working there that day, and one lot of dynamite went out on the Bulawayo train, just as another lot came in from the Cape. It's happened a fair amount, double shipments, one coming a few days after the other.'

That much was true, Penrod thought. First, the private stocks of Mr Weil had arrived to add to his considerable reserves, gathered in Mafeking to avoid a threatened tax on goods in Rhodesia. Then, a great rush of vital materials had come – ammunition, rifles and rations – purchased on account thanks to Ryder Courtney's guarantees. Finally, Milner and the new Commander of the British Forces at the Cape had apparently discovered Baden-Powell's requisition slips, and another glut of goods had been shunted up the railway. They hadn't managed to send any more artillery, but Ned had still been forced to build another storehouse for the government's bounty. Orders had been replicated a number of times, and if more dynamite had arrived on the same day as a surplus had been shipped off to the relative safety of Bulawayo, it would have been an easy mistake to miss the duplication. Easy, but potentially fatal. Penrod felt his frustration building inside him. These things should have been checked. Now civilian lives were in danger, as was the whole enterprise of the siege, because some fool with a clipboard hadn't bothered to do one final check.

'Show me,' Penrod said.

Parland gave a messy but enthusiastic salute and led him into the dark of the storehouse.

The interior was crammed with crates and boxes. Some attempt had been made to keep the military and civilian supplies apart, but in places they seemed to have bled into each other. Sacks of flour and crates of tinned salmon perched incongruously on the metal crates containing the munitions for the Howitzers.

'They keep moving everything about, sir,' Parland complained in the gloom. He pointed. 'Here we are, sir, on the right.'

Parland was quite right. He was looking at a wall of wooden cases, each containing sixty pounds of dynamite, neatly stacked although partially obscured by boxes of tinned peaches. Penrod made a closer examination and a swift calculation. Five hundred cases. If a shell caught them, the whole European Quarter of Mafeking would be a crater.

'I did right to mention it, sir?' Parland said nervously.

'You did indeed, Corporal. Now, wake one of the engine crews and the rest of your squadron and bring them here. Immediately.'

Parland caught the tone of his voice, and moved fast. While he fetched the men, Penrod wrote a note to Baden-Powell reporting the discovery and his plan of action, and gave it to one of the boys who always seemed to be hanging around near the engine sheds. The boy came back at a run with a folded slip. Penrod flicked it open. One word. *Proceed.*

Within fifteen minutes 'D' Squadron of the Protectorate Regiment found themselves trundling wheelbarrows back and forth, ferrying the cases to two goods trucks, quickly shunted into position to receive them. The engine driver was watching proceedings at Penrod's side, his freckled skin pale and sweaty even in the morning chill. 'But we don't know how close to town they've pulled up the rails, Colonel,' he was saying to Penrod. 'I'll have to go slow, or we'll be off the end of them before we can bring the engine to a stop. Do you know how close the Boer are? What if they come before we can uncouple and blast away at us? We'll be blown to nothing, scattered over the veld for the hyenas.'

'We'll go as slow as you need to,' Penrod said. 'As to where the rails run out, we are about to discover that for ourselves. The Boer's laager is north-north-east of here. Depending on their patrols, we should have time to reach a safe distance from the town before they spot us. Is your fireman ready?'

'He's ready.' The driver took off his cap and rubbed the top of his head fiercely.

'Do you need anyone else to assist you with uncoupling the trucks?'

The man hesitated. 'No, we'll be quicker on our own, or *as* quick, at any rate. No point risking anyone else.'

One of the men passing cases onto the truck lost his grip and went down on one knee, grimacing. For a moment everyone held their breath, waiting for the explosion. It did not come. The man got back to his feet and the loading continued.

Penrod saw an officer approaching, pulling on his uniform as he crossed the yard towards them. Captain Charles FitzClarence. Commander of 'D' Squadron. He was a veteran of the Royal Fusiliers but had never seen action, being restricted by ill health to administrative rolls. It was said by some that his father – Captain George FitzClarence – had pulled strings to keep him in the army, a rumour that enraged FitzClarence and had caused him to volunteer on numerous occasions for front-line duty – requests that had been turned down until war had threatened in South Africa. Penrod knew that his twin brother, Edward, had been killed at Abu Hamed – his commanding officer in Egypt, Herbert Kitchener, had spoken warmly of the man. But Penrod had struggled to match Kitchener's words to the individual who now strode towards him.

'Ballantyne!' FitzClarence bellowed, his handsome, aristocratic face crumpled with sleep and annoyance. 'It is customary to ask a fellow if you are going to make free and easy use of his squadron.'

Penrod looked at him coolly. 'My apologies, Captain. I thought the matter too urgent for such niceties.'

FitzClarence glanced at what his men were carrying to the trucks and blanched. 'Dear God! This had been left in the store?' He took a step back and saluted. 'Carry on!'

'Ready soon as you like, Colonel,' the driver said, pulling his cap onto his head and striding off to the gently hissing engine.

• • •

They crawled out onto the veld, the engine nudging the wagons away from the town with nerve-shredding slowness. Penrod hung out of the cab, looking past the trucks and their deadly cargo, studying the ground ahead through his field glasses. The driver exchanged occasional remarks with the stoker who shovelled coal into the hell-mouth of the firebox, adjusting the levers and valves, and when he had no other task, polishing off an imaginary speck of soot from the gleaming brass of one or the other with the orange rag that he kept tucked into the pocket of his overalls.

The vegetation around Mafeking was scrub and thorn bush – sweet thorn, umbrella thorn, camel thorn and candlepod thorn. The dry red earth beneath the sparse grass was desperate for the summer rains and the only interruption to the horizon were low rises of weathered rock. Penrod scanned the horizon with regular unhurried sweeps. The smoke billowing from the engine would be visible for miles. The Boers must have sent out a scouting party by now, to see what the residents of Mafeking were up to. Penrod was counting on it.

'How far are we from the town?' he asked.

'Six, seven miles, I'd say,' the driver said. 'That has to be enough now, doesn't it? Shall we uncouple and head home? I've got a bit of bacon back at the yard. I'll cook you your breakfast on the shovel as the fire cools.'

'Let's go just a little further,' Penrod said firmly.

Soon afterwards they spotted the place where the tracks had been torn up, and Penrod gave the command to brake. The ground below had been dug away. The wind was picking up, thickening the air with dust and making the thorn bushes shiver and rattle. Penrod felt the sting of it on his face, then he saw a thicker plume of dust low to the ground. A party of men on horseback was emerging from behind a low ridge of rock and scrub to the east.

The engine hissed to a final halt. The driver caught sight of the riders in the distance then stared at Penrod. 'You want them to fire on the trucks!' he said as Penrod's plan suddenly became clear to him. 'You're tempting them! You want them to blow it up! That's why we are out so far!'

'We are not going to make them a gift of this dynamite,' Penrod said. 'And it seems a waste of explosives to blow it up ourselves.'

'You're insane,' the stoker hissed.

'You may uncouple now,' Penrod replied.

At once both driver and the stoker were out of the cab. Penrod heard the clank of metal as they worked.

He counted the horsemen as they rode towards them – twenty men, at an easy trot.

'Come on,' Penrod said quietly. 'Take a close look.'

The driver and stoker scrambled back into the cab and began working the levers.

'Wait,' Penrod said sharply. 'We're not moving yet.'

'For God's sake, man!' the driver whined.

The engine hissed and Penrod could hear the driver's panicked breathing over the steady moan of the wind, but the man did as he was ordered.

The horsemen were speeding up as they approached, forcing their horses through the dust kicked up by the howling winds. Seven hundred yards. Penrod could almost feel their suspicion, their eagerness for a fight, for the first blood of the war. He leaned out of the cab, unholstered his revolver and fired four rounds in quick succession. He had no chance of hitting any of the riders at this range, but that wasn't the point. He needed them to fire on the truck. It wasn't armoured. A few rounds from the Boers Mausers should be enough to blow the dynamite sky high.

The Boers returned fire at once.

'Now,' Penrod said.

The driver threw himself on the levers and brakes and opened her up. The engine pulled away with a groan of iron, and the firebox roared as the stoker furiously shovelled on more coal.

The Boers were firing on the trucks as they cantered towards them – Penrod could see the dust kicking up by the tracks.

The wheels thundered along the rails, putting precious yards away between them and the deadly load on the trucks. In the wind and dust the Boers had not realised that they were no longer being fired on. Through his field glasses, Penrod saw a thick splinter of wood fly from the side of the truck containing the explosives. Were they far enough away?

At last one of the bullets struck home, and the dynamite exploded in a rippling, thunderous blast, throwing the trucks into the air and smashing them into a storm of flying shrapnel. The shock wave drove the breath from Penrod's lungs and threw him sideways, half out of the cab, leaving him clinging from a single handhold over the charging pistons. And then the light of the morning was blotted out as the earth thrown up by the exploding trucks came raining down upon them. Thick clods bounced off the top of the cab like mortar fire. Penrod wrenched himself up – away from the spinning iron – and fought to find a footing on the edge of the cab, the muscles in his arms burning with the effort of holding him in place. He managed to lift himself another inch, found purchase, and then threw himself sideways into the cab.

The driver was swearing in a florid mix of English and German, but seeing Penrod appear in the cab and finding that he was still on the rails and powering towards Mafeking, he let out a great hurrah. Earth pattered around them like heavy rain.

Pulling himself to his feet, still fighting to regain his breath, Penrod went back to the edge of the cab and looked out again, wiping the dirt from his field glasses. A great plume of smoke and debris still filled the air behind them. Penrod could see no sign of the twenty men who had attacked them, only the emptiness of the veld around the twisted remains of the trucks, and a horse, riderless and panicked, racing away through the burning grass.

· · ·

Baden-Powell was waiting for them when they came to a halt at the railyard. Penrod jumped down from the footplate and brushed the earth from his uniform, straightening and saluting as his commanding officer approached. The driver and stoker were being feted by the rest of the railway workers and were carried away on their workmates' shoulders, no doubt to the best breakfast available.

'That blast of yours rattled the windows,' Baden-Powell said as he returned Penrod's salute. 'At ease, Colonel. And well done.'

'We encountered a patrol of twenty horsemen, sir. Came from the north-east.'

They began to walk together towards HQ, Penrod stooping slightly so he could hear Baden-Powell – his ears were still ringing after the thunder of the explosion and his commanding officer had a habit of talking quietly whenever they were in the open.

'We are cut off,' he said simply. 'The telegraph lines are down and Cronjé is sending out patrols from the south and north to survey our defences. Shots were exchanged near the brickfields, but nothing more than a skirmish.' He paused. 'A party of twenty tried to come in along the riverbed, through the Stadt.'

'And?'

'The Barolong saw them off. Mr Plaatje delivered the chief's report. He believes they killed or injured six before the Boer retreated. No injuries in the Stadt, other than one young man who got a nasty graze from a ricochet.'

Penrod smiled briefly, imagining Sol delivering the message, then became serious again. The Boers were moving fast. 'I am surprised they are making serious attempts so soon, sir.'

'Indeed. Perhaps your little escapade this morning will put the wind up them, but I shan't sit here quietly, waiting for them to come at us. Damned if they should be allowed to take their time to find our weak spots. If there is no further action today, we'll send out Bentinck with "A" Squadron tomorrow morning and see if he can run down a patrol or two and send them packing.'

Lord Charles Cavendish-Bentinck was one of the men recruited for Baden-Powell's irregulars in India, a lieutenant in the 9th Lancers. He and Major Alexander Godley could often be found together – two tall 'Irishmen', as they styled themselves, united by their love of polo, horses and hunting.

'If Bentnick fails, and it causes a gap in our lines, all Cronjé will have to do is walk through it,' Penrod replied.

'We are all aware of that, Colonel,' Baden-Powell snapped. 'You may not believe it, but there are one or two other men here who know their work well enough.'

'Though not well enough to check whether or not enough dynamite to turn this whole town back into veld had been sent to Bulawayo or simply tucked away in the back of the stores,' Penrod snapped.

Baden-Powell came to a halt and Penrod caught a flash of anger in his eyes. 'Ballantyne, you are a brilliant man, but I was warned that you are also unyielding and proud. Do not let the less generous side of your nature get the better of you. I see you treat the lower ranks in a far more friendly and open way. You have their loyalty as a result. You will need the loyalty of your fellow officers, too, before this is done. Perhaps you can extend the blessing of your friendship beyond Ned Cecil and avoid giving the impression of always sitting in judgement of the rest of them.'

Penrod was tempted to reply that he expected nothing from the other officers that he did not expect from himself, but managed to hold his tongue.

Baden-Powell began walking again. 'If Cronjé breaks through our lines, we will fall back to headquarters as planned and fight our way out to the south. You left us enough dynamite to blow up the stores if necessary, I hope?'

'I did.'

'Good.'

• • •

The explosion had rattled more than the windows. The women and children had been ordered into a laager to the west of the railway lines some days previously. They had moved reluctantly, and made only a show of setting up home in the bell tents provided. Now the streets were busy with dogcarts and wheelbarrows as the wives of Mafeking gathered up their pots and pans, their travelling stoves and little locked caddies of sugar and spices, and wheeled them to the laager through the swirling dust. The women's faces were anxious, and the children, slapped or scolded out of their initial excitement, watched their mothers with suspicion.

Penrod walked the mile from Dixon's Hotel to the lookout tower on Canon Kopjé in a thoughtful mood. The British South African Police forces manning the post seemed calm enough, given their exposed position. Penrod had placed Captain Stuttaford in command. He was an awkward man, but had proved to be a decent officer thus far. He had been using his time to build up the defences and had several of his men digging a trench behind the hillock in spite of the wind and dust. It was agonisingly slow going – the ground was like iron.

'I've seen movement out there,' Stuttaford said to Penrod, lowering his field glasses and pointing. 'Though it's hard to tell with this dust. Perhaps they are being cautious. Either that or they are gathering themselves for a full assault.'

He looked around to check he was not overheard and leaned towards Penrod.

'It's a hell of a risk, isn't it? All these false mine fields, fake wire, defences half-dug or not dug at all. Our men have courage and the Cape Police boys are well trained, but we have no artillery to speak of. Wouldn't we be better to ride out west before they encircle us? Blow up the stores and live to fight another day?'

Penrod shook his head. 'If Cronjé's men find nothing and no one to delay them in Mafeking, they will sweep down through the Cape and knock out what forces we have in the country before sufficient troops arrive from India. Every day we can keep their best general and seven thousand of their men at Mafeking is crucial for our victory.'

'I feel like a sacrificial chicken left out for the fox.'

'It's a game of nerves, Stuttaford,' Penrod said and Stuttaford coloured. 'Cronjé doesn't know we are undermanned, undergunned and only half dug in.'

Penrod lifted his own field glasses – the wind had finally dropped and the dust was settling. He could see the great dry expanses of the veld reaching for miles into the distance. Two horsemen were riding at an easy rolling pace among the grass and scrub. The lead rider was Gerrit Vintner. Penrod wondered if the fortunes of war would bring them face to face before hostilities were over, and if Gerrit would recognise him before one was forced to kill the other.

'Sir?' Stuttaford said, seeing Penrod lost in thought.

'Carry on, Stuttaford,' Penrod said, looking away from the horizon.

Stuttaford watched him leave, his long strides taking him along the track towards town, then he pulled his handkerchief from his pocket and dabbed at the gritty sweat on his forehead. He had spent most of his undistinguished career in Africa, but his body still refused to adapt. In the deserts of the Sudan he had spent his days parched and gasping, here his body either shook with the chill or was scalded in the sun. Penrod Ballantyne always looked as if he'd just stepped in from a country rose garden.

Stuttaford's sergeant came to the lookout for orders. The man followed Stuttaford's gaze and noticed Penrod's retreating figure.

'He looks as if he's settling to enjoy himself, doesn't he, sir?'

'Colonel Ballantyne is blessed by the gods, you know, Timpson,' Stafford said bitterly. 'He can throw fortune's gifts into the ocean if he likes, and they'll come back in on the next tide to be dropped at his feet, while another man might make one remark, say one foolish thing and fortune leaves him forever in the dust like a rag.'

He managed to stop himself. Timpson was looking at him sideways.

'We are lucky to have Colonel Ballantyne with us, of course,' Stuttaford added. 'Now, let's see what we can do to make this anthill more defensible, shall we.'

• • •

Penrod couldn't sleep that night. The wind that had died down earlier that afternoon – giving the residents of Mafeking a break from the swirling dust – had returned. Without Amber, the cottage felt empty and strange, as if the rooms were the wrong size for the furniture.

Penrod sat out on the veranda and smoked his pipe, looking deep into the veld and thought about the men he had known, those who had shaped his life and those he had killed. His life had turned – he was now closer to death than he was to the boy who had grown up dreaming of being a soldier. The images of the battle at Omdurman came back to him and he looked down to see that his hands were shaking. If he was to die here in Mafeking, what would become of his son, and Amber? Amber was wealthy in her own right, and even if she hadn't been, Ryder would have taken care of them financially, of course, but David would grow up without a father and Amber . . . Would she take another man into her bed? Would another man become father to his son?

And these men, the men he commanded now – what of them? And the townspeople? They hadn't asked for this siege, to be starved and shelled and shot at by snipers. Penrod had been in Khartoum and he knew what a siege could do to men. This had been his idea. Penrod Ballantyne – hero of Abu Klea and Omdurman.

• • •

The next morning, Penrod was at headquarters to watch 'A' Squadron head out into the veld. Their mission – to show the Boer fighters that Mafeking was well defended – was pivotal. Penrod itched to go with them. It was a clear, crisp morning with hardly a cloud in the sky.

A telephone system had been installed at headquarters so that they could speak to the outposts and forts that dotted the perimeter. The officers tried to focus their work, ignored the clock and tried not to jump as the telephone rang.

Ned picked it up and listened for a moment, then spoke to Baden-Powell.

'Corporal Saunders of second patrol requesting that the armoured train be sent up in support of "A" Squadron, sir. Seems they've run up against a party of five hundred. Lord Charles has been cut off from the main body of his men.'

'So ordered,' Baden-Powell replied with equal calm.

Ned spoke into the phone, cut the connection and once again the staff returned to their work. Five hundred Boers. 'A' Squadron was a quarter of that size, and now split! The battle for Mafeking might be over already, Penrod fumed, while he and the other officers were sharpening their pencils in this glorified telephone exchange.

Within half an hour they heard the pop of the Hotchkiss one-pounder firing from the armoured train to the north like a distant hand clap, and the far-off rattle of the Maxims. They strained to listen. The sounds of firing continued for some time and then ceased abruptly. Had the armoured train been taken? Penrod had his side arm and a good supply of ammunition on his person. If the town was overrun from the north, he would man the final fallback position in the centre of Mafeking with the Town Guard while the rest of the Protectorate Regiment fought their way out to the south-east. Penrod would fight alone if he had to. He suspected that few of the townsfolk would choose to fight alongside him if their defences were overrun so quickly.

Baden-Powell was leaning over a large plan of the town. Penrod began to push back his chair, ready to tear the map out of the man's hands and demand action. Before he could move, Baden-Powell spoke: 'Ned, perhaps you could call Hore. Have him send FitzClarence and "D" Squadron out in support of the armoured train, please.'

Ned picked up the phone at once, fumbling briefly with the receiver before confirming the order. 'D' Squadron was their reserve force. They were committing everything to this action now.

Penrod did not speak. No one in the room needed the situation explained to them. Either FitzClarence would succeed and drive off the Boer attack, or most of the men in the room would be dead before lunch. More than once Penrod realised that his hand was drifting to the handle of his revolver.

The telephone rang again. Ned seized it. He listened for a few seconds then spoke: 'FitzClarence is pressing back the enemy,' he said, the tension he felt evident on his face.

One of the other men in the room stifled a curse and Penrod clenched his fist. The meaning of the report was clear – FitzClarence had managed to relieve the armoured train, but instead of returning to Mafeking, he was pursuing the Boers into the veld.

FitzClarence had too little experience and too much confidence in his own dash. If he had managed to save the armoured train and 'A' Squadron, it was vital he disengage and get the men back into the town. To pursue the enemy into their own territory was suicidal, exactly the sort of action the siege had been planned to avoid.

Baden-Powell frowned. 'Send a messenger out to FitzClarence at once,' he said. 'He is to retire immediately. All possible despatch.'

Ned gave the order and broke the connection. The tension in the air was oppressive. Penrod could bear it no longer. 'Sir, I might ride out myself, with your permission.'

'If you must, Colonel,' Baden-Powell said and continued to stare at the map.

• • •

Penrod had left orders that his horse should be kept ready for him outside headquarters. He swung himself into the saddle and patted the sturdy pony's neck, then clicked his tongue, kicked his heels and rode at a steady trot to the edge of town. There was no need to alarm the townspeople any further, but as soon as he was a decent distance past the last house – and sure that he was out of sight – Penrod let fly, following the line of the railway tracks into the wilderness until he reached the armoured train. It was still on the tracks and showed minimal signs of damage, yet the Hotchkiss was quiet.

He galloped towards it, low in the saddle, pulling up sharply as he came level. The sergeant in command hailed him. Penrod's sweating horse shook her head and snorted at the smell of cordite and oil.

'Report.'

'Came up in support of "A" Squadron, sir. They were split up and badly outnumbered. It was pretty fierce, but we bagged a few and only two of Lord Charles's lads were wounded. Then "D" Squadron came up the line causing a ruckus and engaged the enemy – got between us and the Boer, so we couldn't be of any help to them.'

'Where are they now?'

'FitzClarence coming up all cheers and sabres put the Boer off a bit, sir, so the captain went off in pursuit. Boer started to wheel off to the right and I daren't try for them now with the Hotchkiss. "D" Squadron's somewhere in the middle. Can't tell where.'

'FitzClarence has been outflanked?'

'Hope not, sir. He was still heading after them happily enough thirty minutes ago, over that rise.'

Penrod swore under his breath. FitzClarence had been drawn into a trap, tempted away from the armoured train by the Boers. If Gerrit Vintner was involved, then Penrod was sure it had all been done with forethought. It would be impossible to defend Mafeking for a week if they lost a whole squadron.

'Send a man to the nearest telephone point and have them call headquarters,' Penrod said. 'My compliments to Baden-Powell and a recommendation that he sends up one of the seven-pounders at once, to cover "D" Squadron's retreat.'

He turned his horse's head and drove her into a fierce gallop across the gently undulating ground. Within five minutes he had reached the top of a shallow rise and saw the field of battle laid out below him. Ahead he could see a kraal – three or four round thatched huts built close together. They looked abandoned – the vegetable plots which surrounded them overgrown, and the rough fencing which encircled them broken down. Penrod could see some twenty of the Protectorate Regiment's horses in the lee of the buildings with two 'D' Squadron troopers in attendance, trying to calm them as they jerked and pulled at the tumbledown fence to which they had been tethered. Beyond the kraal was a great expanse of shifting grasses some three feet high, which ran to a ridge of stone topped with scrub and thorn trees.

As Penrod began to ride towards the kraal the air was split by the screaming whistle of an artillery shell. It struck one of the thatched huts which exploded in a shower of earth. The horses bellowed. One mare escaped her tether and began to canter back towards the town. Penrod cursed as his own horse shied away, terrified, but it yielded to his heel on its flanks and his firm words of command and he forced it into a gallop, racing towards the wreckage.

The two troopers were sprawled on the ground, alongside two of the horses, the other animals fighting desperately to free themselves. One of the horses was already dead – its guts torn open by shrapnel. The other was writhing and trying to stand. As Penrod approached, the nearest trooper staggered to his feet, walked over to the injured animal, raised his rifle and shot it between its wild and frightened eyes. The second trooper was clutching his face and moaning.

Penrod swung himself from the saddle, tied his own mount next to the others, and turned just as the army surgeon, Major Anderson, staggered out of one of the remaining huts. He leaned up against the wall for a moment, then dropped to his knees to attend to the trooper injured in the blast.

Penrod crouched beside him.

'Four wounded so far, Colonel,' Anderson said. The man he was treating groaned and spat blood, his eyes were open but blank with pain and confusion. The side of his face was ripped and bloodied, the work of splinters from the exploded kraal.

'Steady there, trooper,' Anderson said. 'You'll live. Let's get you inside and clean you up.'

'Where is FitzClarence?' Penrod demanded.

'Three hundred yards to the north,' Anderson said gruffly. 'If you are going to join him, move quick and low. We had them nicely on the run, then they got to that bloody ridge. Looks like nothing until you are almost on it, but there are trees and rocks enough to give them good cover, and it's an elevated position, or what passes for one in this country.' He looked at the ruin behind him. 'And they have artillery.'

'What cover has FitzClarence?' Penrod asked. He resisted the temptation to tell the Major that the Boers knew every rock and bush in this country and the manoeuvre had obviously been planned.

'None. He's pinned down, in the grass.'

Anderson got the injured man to his feet and steered him into the remaining hut. Penrod went to the trooper who had shot the horse.

'May I borrow your rifle?'

'Welcome to it, sir,' the man said and handed the weapon over, unbuckling his ammunition belt and passing that to Penrod too. 'Bag a Dutchman for me. I hate to see the horses hurt.'

Penrod checked the bolt, filled the magazine and slung the rifle over his shoulder. Then he ran out of the kraal and through the long grasses in the direction Anderson had given him. Rifle rounds sung through the air and kicked up the dust at Penrod's

feet as he sprinted, crouching through the low grass. He cut sideways as another bullet whined past his ear.

'Here, sir!'

Penrod dropped to the ground and crawled forward towards
the voice. One of 'D' Squadron, almost invisible in his khaki
among the pale stalks, was lying on his belly, his rifle raised. Next
to him lay a body, its face destroyed, a mass of flesh and bone
already providing a feast for the flies.

'Damn,' Penrod said. 'Who is that poor devil?'

'Corporal Walshe,' the trooper said through his teeth. 'I swear
he barely twitched, just reaching to reload and some devil on the
ridge spotted him. They can see like bloody eagles, these bastards.' Penrod looked right and left. The whole squadron was
caught in the grass. 'Captain FitzClarence is north-north-west
of us, sir. The buggers are trying to move wide on the west and
cut off our retreat. He's making it hot for them in that corner,
so they're taking their time over it, but we need some luck. I can
shoot a rook off its nest at this distance, but I can't get a target,
and now they've got that bloody field gun in action.'

Penrod heard a movement to his left and turned in time to see
Corporal Parland, the Irishman who had noticed the dynamite
in the stores, get to his knees. He lifted his rifle and fired with
the steady determination of a man who had seen his mark and
knew he could hit it. One of the Boers had shown himself shifting
his position. Penrod saw the Irishman's bullet hit. The Boer was
spun round by the force of it, his hands reaching up to his neck
to stop the sudden fountain of blood, then he fell backwards, his
limbs already loose in death.

'Drop, Parland!' Penrod barked. 'Get down!'

Too late. Parland had waited on his knees to see the result of
his shot. A bullet hit him square in the middle of his forehead
and exploded the back of his skull onto the grass. He collapsed
instantly, dead before he hit the ground.

'Bastards, bastards, bastards . . .' the man next to Penrod
muttered.

'How good a shot are you, soldier?' Penrod asked.

'Trooper Wormald. Best in the Squadron, sir. If only I had
something to shoot at.'

The Boer field gun roared again. Soon they would score another hit on the kraal, and then, having taken out the horses, they would concentrate their fire on the men in the grass and finish off what the snipers had started. They had minutes.

Penrod lay on his elbows and lifted his field glasses. A flash of white caught his eye, a scrap of paper fluttering down from a high point.

'Fourth tree right from the rock shaped like a lion's head,' he said. 'Ten feet up in the cover.'

Wormald breathed out steadily then squeezed the trigger. His Lee–Metford rifle cracked and echoed and Penrod saw the branches of the tree shake, and the body of the Boer sniper drop backwards, then tumble down the rocky slope.

Wormald pulled back the bolt on his rifle and the cartridge sprang free into the grass.

'Good stuff, sir. Give me another one.'

Penrod stared intensely at the pattern of low trees and scrub in front of them, looking for any movement in the branches and foliage not caused by the wind.

'Two stumps left of the head, in the thorns.'

Wormald was still and steady, his world narrowed to the small universe in his sights.

'Show yourself, you bugger,' he said. In the same moment the man moved again, twitching the thin cover of the thorn bush, the dark cloth of his coat just visible. Wormald fired, the dark cloth was gone.

Penrod caught the sound of voices from the ridge.

'That's put the wind up them,' Wormald said.

The Boers had lost faith in their positions. Several figures were instantly on the move, looking for better cover but exposing themselves to fire as they did. Wormald shot again. Penrod left him to find his next targets, pulling the borrowed rifle from his shoulder and finding his own. From the grass around them other rifles snapped and echoed.

The air rippled with a new note of thunder, the croak and breathy roar of a field gun firing from behind their own lines. The round sent up a narrow plume of dry earth just in front of the ridge. Baden-Powell had sent up one of their precious seven-pounders.

Thank God! Penrod kept up a steady rate of fire, picking his targets when he could, but even when he saw nothing but rock and scrub he fired. The Boers had to believe the field gun was the harbinger of considerable reinforcements coming to the aid of 'D' Squadron. It was now or never. Either the Boers withdrew, or the fiction of Mafeking's defences would be exposed as a conjuring trick.

Everything hung on this moment. If the Boers held their position and directed their artillery at the men of 'D' Squadron who lay scattered in the grass, they would be flesh and dust in minutes and the way into Mafeking would be wide open. The town would be overrun and Cronjé and his commandos would sweep through the Cape. The pink of the British Empire would be drained from every corner of the country. A major port would be lost, British dominance in India threatened, and the rebellious forces in that country encouraged; the whole future of the British Empire depended on this moment.

Penrod picked another target, just visible in the midst of a stand of trees. He saw the edge of a slouch hat, a thick beard. His target was shouting at a group of other men, and waving his arm towards the dust and grass where 'D' Squadron was pinned down. He was telling them to hold their positions – Penrod knew a professional soldier when he saw one.

He drew back the bolt and then pushed it home, breathed out softly and fired. The bullet hit the man through his cheek and punched him sideways. The two men he had been haranguing staggered backwards from his body. They, too, were waving their arms now, but pointing north-east towards their laager, away from the fight.

'That's right,' Penrod muttered to himself, 'get out of here.'

Behind him he heard the seven-pounder cough again. The shell fell higher up the ridge, sending up another spurt of rock and earth into the air.

'Keep firing, Wormald,' Penrod said through gritted teeth. 'Pepper them.'

Wormald started to firing more quickly and Penrod watched as the panic began to show itself on the ridge – the trees shifting and shaking as men scrambled down from their positions. He kept firing as another shell tore up the scrub and turned the volcanic stones at the top of the ridge into shrapnel. The dust settled and the ridge was still and silent. The Boers had withdrawn. The skirmish was over.

'Cease fire!' came the order from up the line and the men pinned down in the long grass gave a ragged cheer. Penrod lowered his head slightly, took his hand from the trigger of the rifle and stretched it to ease the ache in the small muscles of his fingers and palms. The little patch of rust-coloured earth and scrub grass below his eyes seemed an entire universe. Looking down on it, he was reminded of the dream-like clarity he had experienced on occasion when smoking opium. On this patch of ground, he thought, under my hand, we saved the British Empire – for now, at least.

FitzClarence got to his feet, and seeing that he was not shot, the rest of the squadron followed his example. He gave the order to fall back towards the kraal to collect the wounded and the horses, then he noticed Penrod.

'You here, Colonel Ballantyne? That was a lively one, wasn't it?'

Penrod examined FitzClarence's face for any sign that he realised what he had just done, that he had risked the whole of the Cape Colony by pursuing the Boers into a trap. He looked as pleased as if he'd just led his school team to some unlikely victory on the cricket pitch.

'Men held up well, I think,' FitzClarence continued with pride.

Penrod thought of the Irishmen, Parland and Walshe, and the wounded men back at the kraal and scattered over the field. Two, three hours exposed under that fire and not one of them had turned and run.

'Yes,' Penrod said, brushing the dust off his jacket. 'Yes, they did. But you, FitzClarence, are a bloody fool.' Then he walked back to the kraal to return the rifle and retrieve his horse without giving FitzClarence a chance to reply.

• • •

That evening, Penrod made a careful inspection of the lookout posts around the town, exchanging news and greetings with the Cape Boys, irregulars and South African Police Force who occupied the trenches. Then he visited the Stadt, and gave Sol the dispatches he hoped could be carried over the lines. Sol received them solemnly. Two runners would go out the following night, he said, the papers sewn into the linings of their bags.

The moon was full and seemed to hover over the town, stained red by the dust that rose from the veld. All around him, it seemed, the Boer camps glowed in the darkness – a noose of fire on the horizon threatening to choke the life out of the town.

At the hospital, Major Anderson was grey with exhaustion and bloody to his elbows. Two of the men wounded in the day's action were unlikely to survive, he said. For the rest, their chances were good if infection did not set in. The nuns who were working alongside him were, he reported, excellent nurses.

Penrod returned to HQ just after midnight. Baden-Powell was still at his desk, working in the halo of a paraffin lamp.

'Colonel?'

Penrod gave his report on the wounded and Baden-Powell leaned back in his chair.

'Good. Well, we have survived the day, Penrod. Sit down. Pour yourself a brandy.'

Penrod did so. He could tell Baden-Powell was watching him, but he knew his hand was steady. He offered to refill Baden-Powell's glass, but he shook his head. 'No, too much of the stuff, and I can't sleep. So what is your assessment? Has the plan worked?'

Penrod let the brandy warm his throat and his belly before replying.

'I think it may have done. The Stadt repelling that first attack was crucial, and as for today – it was a close-run thing, but in the end it was the Boer who blinked. We were lucky they lost one of their veld coronets at a crucial moment.'

'Yes, I've heard your shot was well-aimed and well-timed.' Penrod's eyebrow flicked up in surprise. 'Honestly, Ballantyne,' Baden-Powell shook his head, 'yours aren't the only reports I receive, you know. I know you think FitzClarence is an idiot. So do I. But he was scrupulous about giving you your due.'

Penrod said nothing.

'I do believe this might have been enough to keep Cronje at our gate, and to stop him storming his way through it,' Baden-Powell continued. 'Pray God we are right.'

'We can expect the shelling to begin tomorrow, sir.'

Baden-Powell nodded, and pulled a leather folder of papers towards him.

'Indeed. Go and get some rest, Penrod. And if you pray, pray the townspeople can hold their nerve when it does.'

Part II

S hortly before the first shots of the war were fired, Ryder returned to the Castle with his prototype of the new camp kettle and encouraged the soldiers to try it out while he discussed the price and the speed with which he could make his deliveries with the senior officers. The men were enthusiastic, the officers impressed by Ryder's promises, but the final say lay in the hands of the quartermaster general, a man who reported directly to Sir William Butler.

A few days later a letter arrived from Sir William himself, containing an order for ten thousand Courtney camp kettles.

Saffron was delighted when he announced the size of the contract. Penelope and Kahruba both wanted to see the designs and the kettle itself. Ryder was surprised by how much the girls enjoyed seeing how the two matched up and Penelope continued asking precise questions about materials and the process of manufacture, even after Kahruba had slipped off to dance around the hallways of the hotel. She had heard that there was a famous ballerina staying at the Mount Nelson and was trying to catch her eye and talk her into dance lessons. Saffron took the kettle, filled it with wildflowers and painted a still life of it. The result pleased Ryder so much he hung it in the Salt River offices. Only Leon had nothing pleasant to say about all the excitement.

When Ryder told them how much the picture had pleased his workers over breakfast, Leon tutted.

'Do you have something to say, Leon?' Ryder asked curtly.

'I can't believe you are celebrating the fact men are going off to war so you can make money out of it,' he said.

'That's not what your father is doing, Leon!' Saffron said.

Penelope looked confused. 'Don't you want the soldiers to have a better camp kettle, Leon? Father is making a better one for a better price.'

'Why doesn't he just give them the kettles, then?' Leon said. 'He's happy because we are at war and he can profit from it.'

Kahruba pirouetted across the carpet. 'You were very happy to hear the soldiers were coming, too, Leon.'

He flushed.

'Go to your room, Leon,' Ryder said. 'Until you stop talking like a fool, I see no reason to waste time explaining my business to you.'

'Ryder . . .' Saffron said.

'Your room, Leon!' Ryder continued.

Leon stormed out and slammed the door. Nazeera was playing with Matthew and his blocks on the carpet. She murmured something.

'What?' Ryder turned towards her.

She cast him a look of great dignity and said more clearly in Arabic: 'Only, *effendi*, that lion cubs can be entertaining when they are small, but are difficult to contain as they grow.'

He bowed to her stiffly, then left for the office.

• • •

By the time news of the first hostilities reached Cape Town, Ryder had made Yusuf, the foreman, his manager at the factory and given him the freedom and capital to hire the best workers he could find. Now Ryder rode to the factory not more than two or three mornings each week, handed the reins of his horse to an eager office boy and spent a few hours planning, designing and going through his correspondence.

Yusuf was proving to be an excellent appointment, combining an attention to detail, vital in manufacturing, with an ability to delegate, hire the best people and trust them. Yusuf still could not quite believe his luck at his promotion and new position, however, and seemed embarrassed by his office and desk whenever Ryder came in, shooting to his feet and offering Ryder his own chair.

Ryder told him gruffly to stay where he was and when coffee had been brought they worked through the business of the day.

'I have given a position to a young mother named Essie Taylor,' Yusuf said in his precise, clipped English. 'I have been meaning to introduce you to her. She was a maid at the Central Hotel, but she can write in a neat hand and it seems she has a talent for figures. She is also . . .' He narrowed his eyes as he chose the right words. 'She is also very observant and seems to be able to spot a problem quickly. She sees where we need a little grease or a knock with a hammer to make us run better.'

'The name is familiar,' Ryder said as he ran his eyes over the figures in front of him.

Yusuf got up from his desk and opened the door into the clerks' room. 'Essie, will you come in here a moment?'

A neatly dressed young woman appeared at the door and bobbed a curtsy. Ryder recognised the young mother he had met on the smoke-filled stairs of the Central Hotel, desperate to reach her children. Seeing her, he could almost feel the weight of her son and daughter in his arms and the scorching heat of the flames. He remembered, too, that her son had not survived and was torn between pleasure at seeing her again and regret for her loss.

Ryder stood up and shook Essie's hand. She was tongue-tied with gratitude but managed to promise to reward the trust placed in her with diligent work, and Ryder tried to encourage her and ward off her thanks. As Yusuf was showing the young woman back into the outer office a call came in from the Mount Nelson. Leon had left the premises and told no one where he was going.

• • •

Many of the citizens of Cape Town had made their way to the docks that morning to witness General Buller and his troops disembark. Tau had decided to join them and earned a few pennies fetching flags for the loyal subjects of Queen Victoria to wave at the soldiers, so when he spotted Leon Courtney among the throng he decided he would follow him a while. Tau had not seen anything of Leon or his family since the fire, and he wanted to ask after Colonel Penrod Ballantyne, Mrs Ballantyne and the baby he had looked after. Tau was surprised to see that Leon was on his own. Tau, being poor and without family, was used to looking after himself, but white boys with good shoes and smart clothes went everywhere with parents, maids or other servants in the bustle of the city streets. He checked his new jacket was clean and, satisfied that it was, he began to make his way through the densely packed crowd towards Leon.

The new jacket was one of the surprising gifts Tau had received after the fire. Mr Grace, the manager of the Central Hotel, had kindly taken some time to track Tau down. And when he had been told that the boy was living under the water tank above a nearby department store, he had climbed its narrowing stairs to thank him for his bravery and help. When the new hotel was built, Tau might have a job in the kitchens, Mr Grace had told him, and in the meantime he bought Tau a new shirt and trousers, a second-hand jacket, which was a bit big for him, and gave him money for food. Tau liked the new clothes, especially the jacket, but he was not sure he liked the idea of the job. He was used to his freedom, earning his coins running messages and small errands. He thought it would be impolite to say that to Mr Grace, though, so he thanked him gravely and promised to think about it.

Leon was staring at the spectacle in front of him. The arrival of General Sir Redvers Buller, hero of the Zulu War, and the British Army on South African shores was certainly worth watching, especially when General Buller's horse was lowered from the deck in a special harness. The soldiers sang, and the whole town was garlanded with bunting which snapped and fluttered in the wind.

Tau slipped his way through the cheering throng and touched Leon on his arm.

Leon beamed at him. 'Oh, it's you! Tau, isn't it? Gosh, this is a jolly sight!'

Tau thought it would have been better if the men were wearing red coats, rather than khaki, but he nodded. Leon seemed excited. 'How is your family?' he asked.

'Oh, fine, just fine,' Leon said, craning his neck to see the soldiers marching down the gangplank. Tau pulled out the photograph of the Ballantyne family and was rewarded with Leon's full attention. 'That is Uncle Penrod and Aunt Amber! Uncle Penrod is an absolute hero, you know. He's in Mafeking at the moment and I think Colonel Baden-Powell relies on him *absolutely*. I wish he were my father. Did you hear, the garrison managed to repel the Boer, even though they are most horribly outnumbered and then, after the enemy had bombarded the town with shells for hours and hours, the Boer demanded they surrender "to prevent further bloodshed", and Baden-Powell sent back a message saying: "What bloodshed? Four hours bombardment – one dog killed." They are remarkable men.'

'What about Mrs Ballantyne and the baby?'

'They are waiting for Uncle Penrod nearby, I think. Mama had a letter from Aunt Amber, saying that she would stay near Mafeking as long as possible so she might hear any news. When we lived in Abyssinia, Aunt Amber had a pet lion. She found it as a cub and raised it herself. That was before she married Uncle Penrod.'

Tau found this information both interesting and surprising, even if it was not very much to the point. He asked Leon to read the sentence Penrod had written on the back of the card. Tau could remember the way the message made him feel, but he wanted to make sure the precise words were fixed in his memory. Leon turned the card over and obliged: '*This young man, Tau, is my friend. Anyone offering him aid and assistance is my friend also.*' Then he looked deflated.

'You are lucky, Tau, to have a message like this from Uncle Penrod. I'd give my right arm for it. I didn't have the chance to do anything brave in the fire at the hotel, apart from carry my brother and he's not very heavy.' Leon suddenly seemed miserable. 'Aunt Amber made me swear not to come back and help.'

Tau frowned. 'But Colonel Penrod Ballantyne is your friend already.'

'Only because I'm his nephew, not because I've done something impressive, something courageous, like you. My name is Leon, by the way.' He stuck out his hand.

Tau looked at it in surprise for a second – he wasn't used to white boys offering him their hands – then he shook it.

'I know your name.'

Leon was watching the soldiers again, though with less enthusiasm than before. 'My parents never let me do anything brave. You're lucky. Why can't you read?'

'I do not go to school,' Tau said. 'I would like to read.'

'It's easy, really. I'll teach you, if you like.' Leon looked him up and down. 'You speak English very nicely, though. Where did you learn?'

'In my father's house,' Tau said quickly. 'Do you mean it, Leon Courtney? That you will teach me to read?'

The offer seemed generous to Tau, though Leon shrugged as if it were nothing.

'Of course! We're staying at the Mount Nelson. Come and see me and I'll teach you.'

Tau knew he could not simply arrive at the reception of the Mount Nelson and ask for Master Leon Courtney. He might, however, be allowed to wait outside. He smiled to himself, thinking of how the words he saw on the sides of the rattling trams or above shop windows would soon release their meanings. He put the Ballantyne postcard back into his pocket and turned his attention to the soldiers. Leon was soon pointing out the different insignias on the men's uniforms, telling him which ones were the officers and providing full regimental histories. Tau asked every question he could think of, and by the time they had bought samosas from a man passing through the crowd, he was convinced he had become an expert on the British Army.

They were still sucking the grease from their fingers and Leon was halfway through a description of the Charge of the Light Brigade, when he stopped speaking and gazed, horror-struck into the crowd on the other side of the line of soldiers. Tau saw the unmistakable figure of Ryder Courtney, Leon's father. Ryder had also seen Leon and pointed at him then held up the flat of his hand, obviously indicating he should stay where he was. He looked, Tau thought, extremely angry.

'What is *he* doing here?' Leon said, his brows drawn together in a fierce frown.

'You did not have your father's permission to come and see the troops?' Tau asked.

'I didn't ask,' Leon said. 'I knew he would never let me come. He hates the army and I hate him. He's just a shopkeeper. I wish my father was a man like Uncle Penrod. He'd bring me down to see the troops. I'd be in Mafeking with him. I could help him.

Father just wants me to learn maths so I can add up his money and tell him every morning how rich he is.'

Ryder had reached their side of the street and was bearing down upon them, his dark face flushed with rage. Tau knew that Ryder Courtney had no reason to be angry with *him*, but the urge to run away was almost impossible to resist. Tau glanced sideways at his friend. Leon looked pale, but did not turn and flee. Tau thought this was heroism indeed.

'Your father saved many people when the hotel burned, Leon,' Tau said, watching Ryder shoulder his way towards them.

Leon snorted. 'He was probably worried that their jewels might get burned, or thought they'd give him a reward,' he said and turned away to stare at the troops again.

'The little girl your father saved, I saw her once or twice,' Tau said. 'When I waved at her through the window she smiled and waved back. Her mother was only a maid and poor, so I do not think she had any jewels and still Mr Courtney risked his life to rescue her. Do you remember when he came out? His hands were burned and his hair and clothes all smoking.'

Ryder had reached them. He grabbed hold of Leon's arm, and if he recognised or even noticed Tau, standing beside his son, he gave no sign of it.

'Leon! How dare you sneak away without leaving word?'

Leon span round and stared up at him. 'I did not *sneak*! I just came. I wanted to see the troops and I knew you wouldn't let me.'

He tried to pull free of his father's grip.

'Why should I let a lazy, spoiled child like you do what he wants?'

'They are great men!' Leon said, pointing at the troops. 'And I would give anything to be one of them. I wish you were not my father. You don't care.' He was scowling with anger and frustration, but Tau saw something else which he recognised and understood. Leon was trying not to cry.

'You're only angry because you had to come and look for me rather than drinking coffee and talking money with all your shop-keeper friends. Any one of these soldiers is worth more than all of you put together! You have no honour!'

Tau saw a flash of pain and hurt cross Ryder's face, replaced almost at once with renewed anger, then, without another word, he picked up his son and carried him through the crowd. Leon struggled, desperate and enraged, but his father was too strong for him.

Tau slipped through the crowd after them. He did not mean to follow, only the entertainment of seeing the troops arrive seemed suddenly a little stale and if he could he wanted to find a chance to wave at Leon, or smile at him, something to let him know he was not alone and that Tau thought he was brave, but father and son had already disappeared in the sea of people and waving flags.

• • •

Saffron was sitting with Penelope and Kahruba, helping them with the history essays that their new tutor had set them as homework, but neither Penelope's careful diligence, nor Kahruba's brilliant flights of fancy could distract her. She had rung Ryder from the hotel in a fit of anger – annoyed with her oldest son for heading off without a word. She was certain that she knew where he had gone and after she had left the telephone booth in the lobby she had begun to wonder if she shouldn't have gone looking for the boy herself.

The door crashed open and Ryder flung Leon into the sun-soaked luxury of the suite's main salon and grabbed his riding crop from the stand by the door. Nazeera dropped her sewing, then at once gathered up little Matthew and began to usher the girls towards the bedroom.

'No, Nazeera!' Ryder said, his voice thick with anger. 'Keep them here.'

Saffron stood, her hand on the back of the chair. She had feared Ryder would be angry, but this rage frightened her.

'I just went to see the troops come ashore!' Leon shouted. 'What's wrong with that?'

'You know you should have asked permission,' Saffron said, shocked at his defiance. She had expected Leon to be sulky and sorry, not angry with them.

'*He* would not have given it to me,' Leon said, turning and spitting the words at his father.

'You will be beaten for it,' Ryder said. 'And for your words when I found you.'

'What in God's name did you say, Leon?' Saffron asked.

'I . . .'

'Tell her!'

Her son seemed suddenly trapped and desperate. He looked at the comfortable couches, the carved mantelpiece, the polished mahogany furniture and sparkling glass of the mirrors and chandeliers. He reminded Saffron of a wild animal backed into a dead-end gully by a skilled hunter.

'I said Papa was only angry because he had to come and find me, not drink coffee and count money with his shopkeeper friends. And that none of them have any honour, not like Uncle Penrod, and I meant it!'

'How dare you?' Saffron said. 'You should be proud, Leon, proud of your name and your family and what we have achieved, but all you do is sneer and complain. Have you forgotten all the work your father and I are doing for the refugees coming into Cape Town from the Transvaal? Kahruba and Penelope are always willing to help. But you sulk and complain when we force you to come.'

'Charity is women's work!' Leon spat. 'And Papa gives you the money so he can boast about it.'

Saffron felt her blood go cold. 'Leon, I am so very disappointed in you,' she said.

That word 'disappointed' caught him unawares and for a moment she thought he was going to apologise. Then Leon looked at his father and all his resentment seemed to return in a black tide.

'He cares for nothing but money . . . It is true, Mama!'

Ryder pushed the boy over the arm of the couch, lifted the crop and struck the first blow. Saffron felt it as if it had landed on her own back. Leon gasped but did not cry out and the short leather whip hit him again, squarely on the seat of his serge trousers.

His mother sprang to her feet. 'Ryder! No!'

Ryder cast a stern look in her direction and struck again.

Penelope had started crying and Kahruba took her hand and squeezed it. Matthew began to wail and struggle, reaching out towards his brother, but Nazeera kept a tight hold on him. Again,

Ryder brought down the crop and this time Leon gave a short gulping cry.

Ryder lifted his arm again, feeling his rage increase, but before he could deliver another blow, his hand was stayed. Saffron had crossed the room and grabbed hold of his wrist. 'Nazeera,' she said. 'Get the children out.'

Her old nurse bustled the others away, leaving Saffron and Ryder facing each other over their sobbing son.

'Saffron . . .' Ryder said, his face like thunder.

She stared back at him. 'Enough, Ryder!' she said. 'You have punished him enough. If you wish to strike him again, you will have to strike me first.'

Ryder curled his lip. His forehead was filmed with sweat. He stared for a moment at his wife then dropped the crop and stalked out of the room without a word.

Saffron watched the door close behind him, her heart thudding in her chest. She had never seen a look like that on her husband's face before, he was like a raging animal, and it frightened her more than she could say.

She knelt down by her oldest child, smoothed his hair from his sweat- and tear-stained face.

'Leon, can you walk? I shall help you into your room.'

He made a snuffling sound, allowing her to support his slight, limping frame, biting his lip to make sure he didn't cry out.

In his small chamber she made Leon as comfortable as she could. He did not try and justify his behaviour in running away, or complain about his beating. She did not try and explain his father to him, or his fear for young men who joined the army with their eyes clouded by dreams of glory.

Saffron noticed a parcel of books that Mrs Weil had sent for the children. Mrs Weil had chosen well and one in particular, *The Adventures of Huckleberry Finn*, looked like it would appeal to Leon. It didn't have a soldier in a red coat on the cover, so Ryder would not sneer at it when he saw it either. She placed it next to her son, kissed his forehead and left him to recover in the privacy of his room.

• • •

The shelling of Mafeking was cruel in its random, unpredictable nature. Hours could pass without a shell being fired, but then again, one could come at any moment. The people of the town lived under an unceasing strain of expectation and fear. The Boer gunners sometimes waited for a target – herdsmen and their cattle gathered near the Stadt, or groups of soldiers or civilians in the town – at other times they simply took out a building, seemingly for sport. The Fengu refugees dug bomb shelters in the town and trenches around it, and a warning system of bells and bugles was set up, designed to indicate what part of town was being targeted, but day after day one unfortunate or another was injured or killed by a shell. The stories of near misses and maimings became commonplace. Snipers took their chances from posts around the town. Sometimes the distance meant that the bullets only tore clothing, or bounced off a gatepost or some other piece of metal to sparkle in the dust at the feet of the astonished target. At other times they got lucky, and a man would collapse in the streets, and only the pooling blood would show he had not fainted.

The mood was grim, fatalistic. Still, the plan had worked. General Cronjé's six thousand men were camped around the town rather than driving the British forces out of the Cape Colony.

Occasional skirmishes took place around the perimeter as the Boer tested their strength, or when the British forced a confrontation to distract their enemy from the movement of the runners.

Cronjé sent protests about the arming of the black population under a white flag; Baden-Powell replied by return that the Barolong had the right to defend themselves. The fiction they were not actively fighting alongside the British was maintained.

Some fortnight after hostilities had begun, Baden-Powell was sitting at his desk in HQ, reading through his daily stack of reports and requisition requests, appeals from the town council and notes from Chief Wessels demanding more ammunition, when Penrod visited him with the suggestion of some more decisive action.

'Agreed. What is your suggestion?' Baden-Powell asked, looking up.

'A night raid,' Penrod said, turning to face his commander. 'I want to take "D" Squadron across the brickfields to the trenches under Louw's command. Bayonets only. Two parties of the Cape Boys to providing flanking rifle fire in support.'

'Why?' Baden-Powell asked, leaning back in his chair. 'I can't see what tactical advantage such a raid would bring.'

Penrod shook his head. 'It's a matter of morale, sir. Theirs and ours. We cannot intimidate Cronjé's men with our numbers, but perhaps we can keep them sleepless with the fear of stealth attacks. And it would be good for the townsfolk, I think, to see that we are not simply waiting for the Boer to pick us off one by one.'

'How many men has Commandant Louw in his camp?' Baden-Powell asked.

'According to the herdsmen in the area, approximately six hundred, sir.'

Baden-Powell set aside his papers. 'Fifty men against six hundred? Even with supporting fire from the Cape Boys, that is a very risky proposition.'

Penrod did not reply; Baden-Powell tapped his pencil on the pile of papers in front of him.

'This said, I cannot deny the effects of cold steel on enemy morale. However, "D" Squadron are FitzClarence's men and he is not fit.'

FitzClarence had taken a rifle bullet through his left thigh during an action the previous week. He was recovering well, but was still using a crutch.

'I have fought alongside "D" Squadron,' Penrod said. 'They will follow me, and most importantly they have the nerve for this raid.'

'When do you want to go?'

'Tonight.'

'Very well, Ballantyne. So ordered.'

• • •

The men of 'D' Squadron moved silently into position at the edge of the veld at a few minutes after eleven in the evening. The air was warm and still and the only sounds were the frogs croaking in the pools formed by the first summer rains.

Penrod glanced right and left at the shadows of his fifty men. They might be a rag-tag assembly of civilians, impatient with the endless drilling and military regulation, but he had seen them withstand Boer fire.

'Silence is essential,' Penrod said. 'If the Boer sentries get wind of our approach, "D" Squadron will be cut down in the open veld by rifle fire.' The troopers exchanged glances. 'I am not asking you to do this for me, or for the British Empire,' Penrod went on, his voice low and fierce. 'Do this for the town. Do it for the men we lost out on the veld. Teach them that they cannot kill our friends, then expect to sleep easily in their beds.'

He turned to the Cape Boys. 'We're relying on you to get us back out of there, gentlemen.'

The Cape Boys nodded and moved silently into the cover of the brickfields, then Penrod gave the word and 'D' Squadron began to move, half-crouching towards the deeper darkness of the Boer trenches, a smear of khaki in the dark blue haze of the night.

• • •

With Penrod at their centre, the men moved forward through the tall grass. The air was full of the sweet scent from the blooming whitethorns – the trees had begun to flower with the first rains. Everywhere around him, it seemed to Penrod, new life was beginning, and into the middle of it he brought death.

On Penrod's left, Trooper Moxley caught his foot in the tangled weeds and fell forward into the grass, but he bit back his curse and the silence of the night continued unbroken, there was only a rustle as he stood again. No call of alarm from the Boer trench. The advance continued. The tension in the air was like the charge of an electric storm. Penrod could feel it lifting the hairs on the back of his neck.

One hundred yards from the Boer earthworks, Penrod quietly gave the order to fix bayonets and drew his sword. The metallic ripple of the long double-edged blades locking into place on the rifle barrels echoed down the line. As the starlight caught on the sharpened steel, a lookout gave the first shout of alarm.

'Guard!' Penrod shouted, and the men brought their rifles to their sides, points upwards, their faces shadowed with determined rage.

'Charge!' Penrod swept down his sword. They sprinted forward. The Boer fighters scrambled for their rifles as the first troopers of 'D' Squadron leaped to the top of the low earthworks, then fell on them in the trenches like a plague of devils.

Penrod swung right and the blade of his sword, almost invisible in the moonlight, sliced through the carotid artery of a sentry raising his gun. To his left he saw a trooper thrusting down into the belly of another man, caught as he rolled out from under his blanket. Penrod could hear the man repeating his bayonet drill under his breath. 'First, two-three, second, two-three,' as he pulled the blade free and struck it into the man's stomach again. The Boer's scream of alarm and pain became a blood-soaked gurgle.

'Forwards!' Penrod shouted, and raced across the fifty yards between the earthworks to the second trench. Now they faced fighters who had been blessed with a few vital moments to wake, realise the danger and arm themselves. Penrod's men must close at once before that slight advantage coalesced into coordinated rifle fire. He had ten seconds, maybe less.

Penrod sprinted like a cheetah, his sword held low, the chill of the African night cool on his cheek, the scent of the turned earth in his nostrils. The darkness exploded with muzzle flashes, and cries of panic. Penrod covered the last yard in a split-second, then struck upwards, pushing aside the rifle of a thin-faced man in a ragged waistcoat with the hilt of his sword. He brought his knee up sharply into the man's groin then twisted his wrist to slice through the man's shoulder as he stumbled. The man tumbled sideways screaming and Penrod plunged over the earth and sandbag parapet into the second trench. Moxley leaped down next to him and caught a half-dressed Boer in the chest with his bayonet, roaring as the blood spattered across the front of his uniform. Some of the Boers were running back towards their laager now, and the flashes of muzzles in the deeper dark showed that they were being caught by the defensive fire of their own men.

Trooper Moxley span left, looking for another target, and Penrod saw him hesitate. His bayonet was ready for the thrust, but he seemed to stumble back. For a moment Penrod thought the man had been shot, but then he saw that the Boer in front of Moxley was a boy of no more than fourteen, white with terror and fumbling for his rifle.

Penrod shoved Moxley aside and struck the boy on the jaw with his closed fist. The boy fell to the ground insensible.

'Low guard,' he shouted, and Moxley swung his bayonet down and pushed upwards, catching a bare-headed Boer as the man leaped forward, his knife in his hand.

They fell back against the trench wall together, Moxley pinned under the man he had bayonetted. Another Boer appeared on the ridge in front of them, drew his revolver and fired downwards. The single shot, delivered with unhurried accuracy destroyed Moxley's face. Penrod felt the bodies of the two men crumple against him, pinning him to the back of the trench like grain sacks.

The fighter swung his revolver towards Penrod, jumped down into the trench and thumbed back the hammer. Penrod strained every muscle in his body against the dirt, pushing Moxley's corpse aside and throwing himself forward towards the muzzle of the gun, his sword forward, held against his own flank. The warrior had no room to fire, and stumbled backwards out of range of Penrod's sword point, squeezing the trigger. Penrod twisted sideways, feeling the bullet slice the air barely an inch from his side, then swung forward. In his haste to back away, the man had tripped on something in the trench and was now lying on his back, his head and shoulder and his revolver raised. Penrod kicked out with the full momentum of his turn and caught the man's wrist hard enough to hear the bone crunch. The revolver spiralled away into the darkness and Penrod plunged the point of his sword into the man's belly. The man screamed, and curled into a ball as Penrod withdrew.

Cries and curses and the thud of rifle bullets burying themselves in the ground filled the air. The sharp bite of cordite stung Penrod's nostrils and he could smell the coppery heaviness of blood. The muzzle flashes were too quick to show anything, but the Boers were screaming at each other, cursing and crying for help and unable to hear the instructions that their commanders were giving them. The raid was complete. Penrod lifted his silver whistle to his lips and gave three short regular blasts. 'D' Squadron broke off to retreat and the Cape Boys opened fire on the reeling Boers from the flanks.

• • •

The morning after his beating Leon was, with a good deal of wincing, able to sit up, but was told to stay in his room. Saffron came in to see him throughout the day, bringing him his lunch and then his supper. Leon could tell she was waiting for him to apologise and the guilt of being the cause of her unhappiness was sour in his belly. He loved his mother, but he could not talk to her about his father. Her tawny eyes were full of reproach and he looked away. She sighed and put her arms around him, holding his head against her shoulder, her cheek against his hair, then kissed him smartly on the forehead and left the room.

Part of Leon *did* want to say he was sorry and for a moment he wondered if that might, in the end, be the best thing to do. When he remembered what he had said to his father, his cheeks burned with a sudden instinctive shame, but then he felt his spirit rebel. He clambered awkwardly out of bed and went to his travel chest, opened the lid, and recovered from under the stock of his personal treasures a thin bundle of letters. He took them back to bed and read them until the urge to apologise disappeared and was replaced by a righteous fury.

In these few pages he found comfort, strength and resolve. They had been written by a fellow sufferer of his father's tyranny, his cousin Ahmed, now free and studying in Cairo. Leon had always disliked and distrusted Ahmed when they had lived under the same roof, but now they had a bond, a secret correspondence. Penelope would listen to Leon when he complained about their father, but her answers were always so reasonable and mild that he had become convinced that she would never understand, and Kahruba could never stay still long enough to listen to anyone. Ahmed understood, though.

It was Ahmed who had written first, soon after Leon had arrived in Cape Town, and in a friendly way, telling Leon the news from

Cairo and hinting that he was sorry Leon was still trapped – when he had escaped. Leon had found himself pouring out his frustration and unhappiness in his reply. He was mocked for his love of military history, tortured with mathematics, forbidden from mentioning his ambitions to be a soldier. Ahmed's next letter was balm to his soul. Ahmed wrote with warm fluency, sharing Leon's outrage at Ryder's behaviour and his disdain for soldiers and warriors. Ahmed was careful to emphasise the fact he did not blame Saffron. Saffron was a paragon of wifely virtues, charitable and beautiful, just as her sister Rebecca, Ahmed's mother, had been. At last, Leon felt someone understood. Leon wrote again, and now he had two further letters from Ahmed. As Leon read the pages he felt his outrage burn brightly again and his resolve stiffen. His father's actions the previous day had proved it – he must act.

The door opened suddenly and Kahruba swept into the room. Leon stuffed the letters under his pillow and picked up his book.

'I brought you chocolates,' Kahruba said, shutting the door behind her. 'They are from Penelope, too, but we've been told that we are not allowed to speak to you today, so she is keeping Nazeera out of the way. We have to go out in a little while for another walk, but it's not a proper walk because Nazeera goes so *slowly*.' She sniffed. 'And I think it shall rain again. No wonder there are so many flowers here.'

She placed a folded handkerchief on the coverlet next to him, then unfolded it carefully so he could see the rich cocoa dusted truffle balls within.

'Thank you,' he said and, with a grimace, pulled himself upright.

'Does it hurt an awful lot?' Kahruba asked. She was more curious than sympathetic, which Leon liked.

'Just stings a bit,' he said.

'We thought you were very brave, you know. Penny and I,' Kahruba said.

She lolled on her back on the tumble of sheets and pillows at the end of bed and stretched out her legs and arms into the air. The kitchen in Cairo was patrolled by an old sleek cat, who was made much of by the servants. When it woke it would stretch in this way; Kahruba would copy it to make Penelope and Leon laugh. He grinned now, glad that the girls thought he was brave, and comforted by the chocolates and Kahruba's games. She sprang back to the floor and began performing her ballet steps, using the end of the bed for balance. She wasn't trying to entertain Leon now, though, it was simply that she could never stop moving.

'You didn't yell or anything for ages,' she remarked mid-pirouette. 'I think you would make a good soldier.'

'Kahruba . . .' he said, then stopped. The temptation to tell her what he intended to do was almost overwhelming, but he could not risk it.

'What?'

'Nothing, only look after Penny, won't you?'

'I think she looks after everyone else, actually. But if you like. Why?'

'You should go, and thanks for the chocolates.'

She leaned forward and kissed him noisily on the forehead. 'Don't make yourself sick, General Courtney,' she said, then scampered out of the room.

When she had left, Leon folded up the handkerchief and put the chocolates to one side. He would need them later.

• • •

Tau had learned to be patient, but as evening came he began to think Leon might not emerge from the hotel at all. He had arrived early in the morning and gone to the rear of the hotel where he had made the acquaintance of a pair of Cape Malay matrons who worked as washerwomen. They had confirmed that Leon and his family were in the hotel and, pleased with Tau's formal courtesy, they had smuggled out a pocket full of bread and two slices of beef from the kitchen for him. Tau had found himself a dry perch in the tree branches above the hotel driveway and waited.

A storm had broken over Cape Town in the middle of the afternoon, an explosion of water from the sky that turned the streams that ran off Table Mountain into little rivers. Tau remained warm and dry under the thick foliage of his chosen tree, watching the carriages fighting through the sudden torrents. He expected Leon and the girls to emerge after the weather changed. The older lady did come out with the children when the rain stopped, but Leon was not with them. Kahruba raced across the damp grass like a springbok, bounding in wild circles with her arms flung wide. Penelope walked alongside her nurse, looking about her with wide, serious eyes, and examining the unfurling flowers. The little boy careered from one flowerbed to another, falling into most of them.

Late in the afternoon, two Englishmen, fresh off the boat, stood under Tau's tree smoking cigars and talking about how they might get to the frontline in Natal. They had come up with some elaborate scheme and were sure it would get them to Lady-smith ahead of the other reporters who would travel with the troop ships. It sounded like the sort of thing that Leon would be interested in, so Tau listened carefully, enjoying the smell of the men's cigars and the fierce excitement with which they spoke, and repeating the names of the places they mentioned to himself to fix them in his mind. He liked to think how surprised the men would have been to know that he was perched in the tree above them, listening to every single word they said.

As the day passed into evening and darkness fell, another carriage arrived at the front of the hotel, and Tau had a brief glimpse of Ryder and Saffron Courtney stepping into it. The carriage rattled away, taking the road into town – Tau could hear the horses' shoes on the new setts that had been laid on Orange Street in the months leading up to the opening of the Mount Nelson.

A few minutes later there was movement in the first storey of the hotel. Tau saw a window being opened, and a small head emerged, followed by a body. Even in the twilight, he could tell it was Leon. He had a knapsack on his back. Tau watched as Leon clambered awkwardly out onto the sloping slates of the roof of the veranda and scrambled along it until he reached the far corner of the building. Swinging himself down, he gripped onto one of the columns that supported the roof and slithered to the ground. He looked around him and chose a line through the patch of trees where Tau was watching.

When Leon was three or four yards away, Tau coughed. Leon looked up into the branches, Tau waved then scrambled from his perch to meet him.

Leon looked wary. 'What are you doing here?' he whispered.

'I was waiting for you.'

'Shhhh!'

Tau dropped his voice to a whisper. 'You said that you would teach me to read,' he said. 'But now it is too dark to see the words. Where are you going?'

Tau saw a look of bitter determination pass across Leon's face. 'Mafeking,' he said. 'I cannot live with my father any longer. I shall go to my uncle and put myself under his protection until I am old enough to be a soldier. I want nothing from Papa ever again.'

Tau considered. 'Did he beat you?'

'That's not why I'm leaving!' Leon's voice was high and wild. He looked around quickly and then spoke carefully, making sure that his voice was under control. 'I can take a beating. But I cannot live with a man who would beat his son just for cheering the troops. He is a man without character.'

Tau was considering this when Leon shrugged suddenly. 'I cannot stay here talking to you. I must go before anyone sees us or notices I am gone.'

He strode off and Tau went with him. They left the grounds of the hotel in silence, the warm air was thick with moisture and the scent of the garden flowers after the rain.

'Where is Mafeking?' Tau asked.

'I have a map, from the newspaper,' Leon said.

'How are you going to get there?'

'I have money.' Leon stopped and turned to him. 'Do you want to come too? Uncle Penrod likes you – he gave you that photograph, after all. You could be our servant.'

'I do not wish to be a servant.'

'Just as you like,' Leon said, but Tau could see his shoulders slump.

'But I will come with you, Leon. You can teach me to read and I will help you.'

Leon beamed at him again. 'Do *you* know how to get there?'

'No. Let us go and eat meat pasties and we shall consider it,' Tau said.

The boys walked down Government Avenue. Tau considered the practicalities. He had not left Cape Town since he was an infant, though he knew that when most people did, they took the train.

They found a pasty seller and Tau negotiated with skill to make sure that the price they paid was fair. They walked on, chewing happily.

'Shall we go on a train?' Tau asked when he had finished the last delicious morsel. The streets were quiet, only the last office workers hurried by without looking at them.

Leon's footsteps slowed for a moment. 'Yes, I think so, but the railway lines have been ripped up south of Mafeking, so I don't know if that will work.'

'What was your plan, after leaving the hotel?'

'I thought I would find some of the soldiers and ask them,' Leon responded.

Tau halted under the light of a streetlamp and looked at Leon. His new friend was brave, and Tau had decided he was also kind and generous – he had paid for the meat pies – but he was not showing himself to be a great strategic planner.

'I do not think that is a good idea, Leon. Your parents will find you easily if you do that.'

Leon looked uncertain, then sat down on the stoop of a shuttered shop and took a map from his pocket. Tau dropped into a crouch at his side and stared at the piece of paper he was holding.

'Mafeking is here,' Leon said, pointing his finger at a word.

Tau had seen maps in the house where he had grown up, the house where his mother had worked as a servant, but they had been coloured in, so that you could tell what was land and what was sea.

'How far?'

'Nine hundred miles,' Leon said.

'That is a long walk,' Tau said after a pause.

Leon sighed. 'Yes, and it's desert or sort of desert for most of the way.' His eyes widened. 'Tau, do you know how to hunt in the desert?'

'No. I live in Cape Town. We do not hunt here.'

Tau was beginning to understand the lines on the map. He traced his finger along a hatched line that ran between Cape Town and Mafeking.

'This is the railway, yes?' Leon nodded. 'And this is the sea. And boats and trains are better than walking?'

'That's right, but there are no *boats* to Mafeking.' Leon looked at Tau suspiciously. 'Are you *sure* you don't know how to hunt? Perhaps you could if you tried?'

'I am sure.'

Tau touched the map again, drawing his finger along another hatched line which headed east and north, then south, then let his finger follow the edge of the coast, then up again along another hatched line towards another word, which seemed on this map to be near to Mafeking.

'We must go round,' Tau said. 'It is like climbing in the city. Sometimes the straight way is too dangerous, it has no place to hold on. So then I go sideways and then up.'

Leon looked dubious. He scowled at the map.

'I heard some men talking today,' Tau continued. 'They worked for newspapers.'

'Well, they should know what they are talking about, but that is a very long way around,' Leon said doubtfully. 'I know that the direct way doesn't work, but still . . .'

'But it is trains and boats,' Tau said firmly. 'Not walking through a desert where there are no meat pasties to buy.'

Leon pouted and screwed up his eyes, staring at the map. 'Tell me again, Tau.'

As Tau described the route the men would take – the mail train through De Aar to a port called East London, then a boat to Durban and another train north – Leon's frown of concentration intensified.

'I think it might work! At least, one way or the other, I'll be away from my father and closer to the action.' He reached into his pocket and produced a silver pocket watch. 'But we must hurry if we are to get the train they were talking about. Do you need to fetch anything?'

Tau considered his meagre stock of possessions on the roof of the department store. They were of little use to him. His pocket knife and the photograph of the Ballantynes were his most valued possessions and he always carried them with him, so he shook his head and said: 'No.'

Leon smiled, folded his map and slipped it into his knapsack.

'I am afraid, Leon, that I have no money.'

'I do!' Leon was cheerful. 'I got it for my birthday.' He fussed over the buckles and straps of his knapsack. 'I got this for my birthday, too. Uncle Penrod and Aunt Amber had it sent to me. It is made from the same material as the real army ones.'

Tau waited for him to be done.

'I think we must sneak onto the train, Tau. The man in the ticket office might ask questions.'

'Then this time we shall sneak,' Tau said.

.   .   .

They reached the rail yard a little after eight o'clock. The mail train was already at the platform and while a small number of passengers clambered on at the front, the heavy wagons at the back of the train were being filled with mail sacks, trunks and crates.

The two boys waited in the darkness next to the warehouses until they saw their chance to dive through the shadows and into a goods wagon.

Leon tumbled into the darkness inside, knocking his shin against the sharp angle of a crate, his quiet laugh of triumph turning into an exclamation of pain. He felt Tau grab him and drag him into a corner where something dusty was thrown over his head. He was about to complain when he heard a voice outside and froze.

'In this one?' a man's voice asked.

He sounded bored and impatient at the same time, and the darkness lightened momentarily as someone swung a lantern into the wagon.

'You're mistaken, mate.'

Another voice, too low for Leon to hear, but the words were insistent.

'No, I'm telling you, no one's in there, and if you think my lads are unloading that lot because your eyes are playing tricks on you, you'd better think again. The train has to move in ten minutes or the boss will have my guts, and we've still got all those bloody crates to shift into the last wagon.'

Leon heard a groan and bang as the great doors of the wagon slid into place, and then the rattle of a chain being fastened. The sudden reality of escaping from the cage that his father had built to contain him, to restrain him, to make him into someone he did not want to be, made his heart beat fast, so fast that it felt as if it was going to burst out of his chest. He had won. For the first time in his life he had broken free of his family, and was on his own in the world – no mother, no nurse, no teacher, no sister or brother to fuss over him. He felt as if he had thrown himself off the top of Table Mountain and was flying on the currents above and beyond the foaming clouds.

The cover that Tau had thrown over him was some sort of tarpaulin, heavy and stiff. It was sour-smelling and airless underneath it. Leon tried to get comfortable, but Tau put a warning hand on his shoulder, so he did not dare to move. He knew Tau was right, those men were still nearby, and might not give up so easily a second time if they heard something moving about inside the wagon.

Leon heard the hiss of steam and the train lurched forwards, the couplings taking the strain, the carriages groaning as the wheels began to turn. He pulled off the tarpaulin as Tau pushed past him, dragging something heavy.

'We are almost ready now,' Tau said.

Leon blinked. He could not see clearly, but it looked as though Tau had started to build some sort of den under the edge of a stiff canvas sheet – a couple of sacks with a blanket thrown over them.

Tau scrambled on top of the sacks, patted the space beside him, then rolled onto his back, put his hands under his head and shut his eyes. Leon found his way to the gap between Tau and the rough slatted walls of the wagon and settled down.

'I can feel the wind between the slats,' Leon said. 'That means we'll be able to see when the sun comes up, and I have a book with me, so I can teach you to read as I promised.'

'That is good,' Tau said and yawned, exhausted after the excitement of the previous few hours.

Leon wriggled. Lying on his side was more comfortable than lying on his back. The deep, bruising marks from his father's riding crop would take a while longer to heal, he knew that, but the humiliation of his beating had been lanced somehow. Leon had been sleeping between aired and ironed sheets on a soft mattress for a long time, but now, instead of their hot, clean scent, softened with lavender, he smelled grease and hot metal, raw wood and paint. The blanket was rough and his sack mattress was soft in some places and hard in others, but he grinned in the darkness. He was free, and able to live his own adventures at last. He closed his eyes and dreamed about reaching a small town in the middle of the veld, a scene of heroism which was attracting the admiration of the whole Empire – Mafeking.

• • •

As the trading post at Setlagole came into view, Sergeant Blake touched his heel to the flank of his horse and the animal obediently picked up its pace. Mrs Amber Ballantyne came out into the road to meet him as she always did. Since Amber, her nursemaid and her baby had taken up residence with Mr and Mrs Fraser at the trading post, Sergeant Blake had seen her several times. She listened to the scraps of news he was able to gather from Mafeking with grave attention, and asked questions which showed both a keen intelligence and a thorough understanding of the dangers that Baden-Powell, her husband and their men were facing.

The day when he told her that the Boer forces had brought up a ninety-four-pound gun, with which to bombard the town, her face had lost its usual animation and she had become quiet.

'But the garrison holds on,' she said. It was what she wished to hear – a statement not a question.

'They do, ma'am,' Blake had replied, noting the determined set of her fine jaw.

Today, as soon as he came alongside Amber, he dismounted and walked with her, leading his horse into the yard. He did not wait for her question.

'I have heard news that your husband led a bayonet charge against the Boer trenches two night ago, ma'am. A surprise attack and by night! Killed dozens and scared the hell out of the rest of them.'

'And Penrod?'

'Only injury he got was from the townsfolk slapping him on the back.' Blake winked at her. 'How is the baby?'

'Thank you.' She flashed him a tight smile. 'David has another fever. Not a bad one and I am trying not to worry.'

'I saw Mr and Mrs Bauer, your nursemaid's relatives from up by Mosita, yesterday and I carry a letter to her from them. They told me that Greta wrote to them of you and Colonel Ballantyne with great warmth.'

'I wouldn't know what to do without her, Sergeant. David is a fretful baby. I would never sleep if it were not for her help.'

'I am glad,' he said.

'Any letters from the Cape?' she asked.

He reached into his pocket and retrieved an envelope which he handed to her with the letter to Greta from her aunt and uncle.

Jabu came across the yard and took the reins of Blake's horse. The animal whinnied in greeting.

'Faithless beast,' Blake said, as Jabu led the horse away. 'I think she prefers your servant to me.'

'Jabu is a good man. He would much rather be fighting the Boer than looking after me, but Chief Wessels persuaded him that it was both honourable and necessary to accompany us.'

Blake had other news. He would speak to Mr Fraser first. Let Mrs Ballantyne enjoy the letter from her sister before she learned the rest.

Mr Fraser and his boys arrived back from their day's work as Amber reached the veranda and gave Greta her letter. Mr Fraser went to wash his hands at the pump in the yard and Sergeant Blake went to join him. Sitting, Amber took the baby onto her knee and broke the seal of her own letter with one thumb. Saffron was not a great letter writer, but she sent her love and that of the children and boasted about Ryder's new factory. Kahruba had persuaded a ballerina to give her dancing lessons, and Penelope was excelling in mathematics. Then Amber frowned. Leon and his father were more and more at odds, and even in Cape Town, Saffron was bored, confined with the children while Ryder built up yet another fortune, frustrated by the behaviour of some of the other women who were caring for the refugees.

Greta's letter was longer. The young woman's face glowed with pleasure as she read, and she kept wiping tears away with the back of her hand. Over her shoulder, Amber noticed Sergeant Blake and Mr Fraser were still talking. She watched them, noticing the serious expressions of both men and the glances they kept casting in her direction. She began to feel anxious. She handed David to Greta and walked across the yard. The men fell silent as they watched her approach.

'Good evening, gentlemen,' she said. 'Sergeant Blake, I think you had better tell me the truth, don't you?'

Mr Fraser, an older man, with a heavily wrinkled face, but clear, friendly blue eyes, nodded to her. 'Told you that we wouldn't be able to keep her in the dark for long, Blake.'

'I did not wish to frighten you, ma'am,' the sergeant said. 'But I do have some other news, bad news. Not from Mafeking, but bad news all the same. I wished to get Mr Fraser's opinion before giving it to you.'

'Tell me now,' Amber demanded.

Mr Fraser replied for the sergeant. 'Of course, my dear. We have been speaking of the Boer commandos in the area. They are small raiding parties under the nominal control of General Cronjé, but acting independently. They are stirring up trouble, trying to get any men of Dutch or German descent to join them, stealing livestock. And they are reaching further and further across the border. My boys and I will be driving our cattle well out west as soon as it's light tomorrow.'

'Jabu told me about them already, Mr Fraser,' Amber said calmly. 'They are not likely to slaughter us in our beds, are they, for the sake of the supplies at the trading post?'

The Scotsman scratched his chin. 'No, shouldn't think they'll do that, but that's not the end of it, I'm afraid. Tell her, Blake.'

Amber turned her attention to Sergeant Blake.

'Mrs Ballantyne, some of those boys have heard talk that an English spy dressed as a woman rode out of Mafeking just before they slung a noose around it. And the commandos might not be interested in Mr Fraser's store, but an English spy is another thing entirely. Some of them say you are Dr Jameson himself.'

Amber laughed. She had seen a picture of Dr Jameson, the man who had caused scandal and embarrassment by leading an unsuccessful raid into the Transvaal four years earlier. She spread her hands wide. 'I think, sergeant, that anyone who saw me would know that I am not Dr Jameson wearing a dress.'

'That's as may be,' Blake said, frowning. 'But they shot two native boys this morning, five miles north of here. They accused them of spying for the Mafeking garrison and killed them on the spot.'

'Jabu is in danger, then,' she said, shocked, her mouth suddenly dry.

'Just so, Mrs Ballantyne,' the sergeant said. 'But that's not the end of it. Another rumour has it that the spy is Queen Victoria's granddaughter and if she's captured then the British will hand over the Cape and Natal to get her back. No war, no argument. They might not take you for a man, but they might well take you for royalty.'

For a moment Amber thought this was a joke, but something in Mr Fraser's face told her that it was no laughing matter.

'Can anyone believe such nonsense?' she asked.

'I'm afraid so,' Blake said. 'Maybe not many, and maybe not much of it, but some of these Dutch fellows, raised out here with nothing to read but the Bible, might think there's something in it. They don't want war – they want the British to get out of the way and let them live how they wish – and now, well, you're like a winning lottery ticket. They scoop you up and Queen Victoria will give them the land forever for your safe return. No war. And here you are, right by the main road to Vryburg, for everyone to see. They are searching for you. If they think Jabu is your man, they'll kill him, and if Mr and Mrs Fraser hide you, they'll pay a very high price for it.'

'And we won't give you up, my dear,' Mr Fraser said.

'We must leave,' Amber said in a hollow voice.

'And go where?' Mr Fraser asked. He looked at the sergeant. 'Blake, no one has seen Mrs Ballantyne here other than us and our boys, and none of them would say or do anything to help the Boer. They can stay tonight, can't they? While we think on it.'

Blake considered carefully. 'I wouldn't advise more than one more night. Won't be long till someone thinks to look down here – they know the country.'

Mr Fraser invited Sergeant Blake to share their evening meal, but he declined. Then he stretched out his arm to Amber.

'The best of luck to you, Mrs Ballantyne,' he said.

She shook his hand and watched him walk away to his horse and the road.

• • •

Amber and Mr Fraser returned to the house to find that David was still no better, even after so many hours. When Amber touched his forehead she could feel that he was burning with fever. Greta went into the garden, and returned with a handful of willow bark. She brewed a weak tea with it while Amber walked the baby up and down the central corridor of the house. Once the tea was cool they helped him to drink it with a teaspoon, and he seemed to grow calmer before settling into a disturbed sleep. Amber told Greta about what the sergeant had said.

'They are shooting people?' Greta blinked back tears of surprise. 'Might they hurt you and David, Miss Amber?'

She laid a hand over the little boy's tiny fingers as she spoke, though she showed no concern for her own predicament.

'I don't know,' Amber said.

'We must go to my aunt and uncle,' Greta said without hesitation. 'The farm is a good forty miles west of here, and away from the road. It will be difficult to get any news from Mafeking, but you will be safer there.'

Amber considered. It would be agonising to be even further away from Penrod than she already was, but she had to keep David safe. If Greta's aunt and uncle could hide them on the farm, they might live there comfortably enough for a few weeks, and the child would be safe. Surely the siege could not last much longer than that?

'That would be good of them, dear Greta,' Amber said. 'Yes, let's do that. We shall leave in the morning.'

Greta's face flushed pink with pleasure. Amber handed David to her, praying he might sleep a little longer than he had the night before. Then, kissing his forehead gently once again, she left the house and crossed the back paddock to the kraal where the Frasers' workers lived with their families and Jabu had found lodgings.

Jabu saw her coming, and after they had exchanged greetings he led her into one of the round huts and offered her a low stool. She thanked him and sat down. Nearby, a young woman was working a loom, and outside a chubby toddler chased chickens between the houses. The floor was cleanly swept and piles of coloured blankets were stacked neatly against the walls. The air smelled of woodsmoke and the evening meal that was bubbling on the fire.

When Amber told him the news, Jabu showed no sign of fear for his own safety, dismissing her concern with a wave of his hand. 'We shall leave at first light. And do not worry about me, madam. The Boer have been trying to kill me half my life, yet I live.'

'You had better not call me "madam" either, Jabu,' she said. Then told him about the rumours that she was either Dr Jameson or the granddaughter of Queen Victoria. He laughed until the young woman abandoned her work at the loom and another turned her head round the doorway of the hut to see what was so amusing.

Jabu translated the story for them and the infectious laughter rippled out through the kraal, Amber joining in.

When Amber shook Jabu's hand and wished him goodnight, she noticed him looking at her wrist.

'Is this a new fashion, Mrs Ballantyne?' he asked.

She glanced down and laughed. It was a piece of blue ribbon which had come loose from David's jacket. She had bound it around her wrist for safekeeping just before she noticed Sergeant Blake arriving.

'No. I had forgotten it.' She shook her head.

'It is pretty. You should leave it, I think, for good luck,' Jabu replied, then accompanied her back to the farmhouse.

• • •

A strange creeping watchfulness fell over them as darkness covered the veld that night. The moon was just bright enough to shed a pale light over the farm. It tricked the eyes and more than once Amber found herself looking out through the windows, not sure if the flickering shadows were real riders approaching the trading post or just her imagination. She remembered a story she had read once of a man who was lost in some dark northern forest, a place of steep mountains and ravines and bone-freezing cold. He knew that packs of wolves were moving somewhere in the darkness, that they had the scent of him. When she had read the scene, even in the heat of Cairo, the details had made Amber feel that chilling cold, the threat of something hostile lurking out of reach of the firelight. She felt a similar sense of dread now as she watched through the windows for any sign of movement on the road. Finally, she fell into an exhausted sleep.

Amber woke suddenly, from a dream of forests, wolves and firelight into the heart of the African night. She lay still, trying to recall what had woken her, then she heard it again – hushed voices on the veranda outside her room. Mr Fraser was speaking to someone in his low, lilting voice, and she could hear horses shifting their hooves in the dust and gravel. She slipped out of bed, feeling the rug under her bare feet, then slowly crossed the room to David's cradle. He was sleeping soundly, his face angelic in the thin moonlight, his breath rasping.

'What is it?' Greta asked from her bed, her voice low from the other side of the room. She was already on her guard.

'I don't know,' Amber whispered, reaching for her skirt and stepping into it.

Someone scratched the door, then pushed it open. 'Don't make a light, girls.' Mrs Fraser was standing in the doorway, a shawl over her nightgown. 'Boer riders. They came quicker than we thought. Tom might be able to get rid of them. Don't make a noise.'

She shut the door again.

Shrugging on her blouse and grabbing her boots and stockings, Amber moved closer to the window and concentrated on the conversation outside.

'No stranger's been past that I saw,' she heard Fraser say, but the reply was muffled and indistinct.

'Could have turned off on the north road after Treat's place. How should I know where they might be going? I've told you already, I've seen nothing and heard no rumours of travellers from Mafeking coming down this way since the siege began.'

Peering through a gap in the shutters, Amber could just make out the shapes of three, perhaps four men on horseback, the light of Mr Fraser's lantern glinting off the long barrels of their rifles. She grabbed her stockings, pulled them on and slipped her feet into her neat ankle boots.

'If you want to wait, I guess I can't stop you,' she heard Mr Fraser say.

As she laced her boots, Amber could hear the sounds of men dismounting, their feet hitting the earth as they jumped from their saddles. She watched David in his crib, knowing that the moment he cried they would be discovered.

Greta was half-sitting up in her bed and Amber crossed the room to crouch next to her. 'We must go now. Get dressed and gather what you can, then follow me out to the back of the house. I'm going to find Jabu and get David away before he wakes.'

She heard a heavy step on the veranda, the creak of a chair as a man lowered himself into it. The riders were not coming into the house yet, but they could at any time. Amber went to the window and looked out again, then withdrew suddenly. The man was sitting inches away from the glass and in the light of Mr Fraser's lantern she could see one side of his face clearly. He was a young man, younger than thirty, with high cheekbones and dark stubble across his square jaw. He turned as if he could sense her watching and Amber saw he wore a patch over his left eye, the skin around it puckered with pink scars.

Amber waited for her heart to slow, then she crossed to the cradle and scooped David up, praying that he would not cry out. He opened his eyes and seeing his mother in the half-light, recognising her scent, closed them again and went back to sleep. Amber walked to the door to the passageway, which opened without a sound, and stepped into the pitch-black centre of the house. David shifted in her arms and yawned. Amber turned right towards the kitchen and the back door of the house, hardly daring to breathe, moving as smoothly and quietly as she could in the thick darkness.

After fifteen feet the toe of her boot touched a threshold and she could smell the last breath of Mrs Fraser's evening baking – she had reached the back kitchen.

The door to the backyard was to the left of the window above the sink. This window was also shuttered – the frame only just visible in the moonlight – but Amber knew the room well and walked towards the door unerringly, calmly drawing the bolt and gently pushing it open with the flat of her hand. It creaked softly and she froze instantly, expecting the men outside to storm into the cottage. After a few minutes, when everything remained silent, she opened it fully and felt the sudden cool breath of the night air on her face. Looking up, she saw that the sky was bright with millions of stars, not the stars she had been born under but still the stars of an African sky.

Amber paused in the doorway, suddenly terrified that the Boer riders might have brought their horses round the back of the house for water and pasture. David was beginning to wake in her arms. She was desperate to reach the kraal where the farmworkers lived. If David began to cry when they were on the other side of the fence, then the Frasers could tell the Boers it was one of the Barolong children. She ran into the darkness, searching for the low silhouette of the native huts against the sky. David gave a brief squalling yell. She covered his tiny mouth with her hand.

'Shush, my darling!' she said and began to hum into his ear, rubbing the palm of her hand over the crown of his head.

Amber quickened her steps, but the toe of her boot caught on the uneven ground. She stumbled, landing on her knees, throwing out one arm to break her fall while clutching David tightly to her chest with the other. Footsteps came towards her in the darkness, light and swift. Amber saw a sudden flicker of light as a shaded lantern was briefly held up and she shielded her eyes with her grazed and bleeding hand.

'Jabu!'

'Come, Mrs Ballantyne!' He pulled her to her feet and kept his hand on her arm as he led her into the shadow of the kraal. David yelled, and Jabu ushered her hastily into one of the huts.

'We are borrowing two riding mules for you and Miss Greta,' Jabu said as soon as they were inside. 'We will leave as soon as we are able.'

By now David had started to scream, so Amber put him over her shoulder and rubbed his back, rocking him gently, trying to soothe him. 'How long until dawn?'

'Three, perhaps four hours. We cannot reach the farm in that time, but perhaps we have time to escape these riders. We will not be able to hide our trail, Mrs Ballantyne, we can only hope that they will not find it.'

'We should have left last night,' Amber said, continuing to rock David from side to side. 'Why am I always so slow?' David hiccupped and became calmer. She touched his forehead and found it was still warm from the fever. The door swung open and Greta rushed in, her face ashen with panic, carrying a travelling bag in each hand.

'Greta! Do you have some of the tea from last night?'

David began to wail again from the top of his lungs, sensing the tension around him.

'He is hungry,' Amber said.

One of Jabu's relatives came in carrying a horn beaker in her hands which she handed to Amber. 'For the baby,' she said softly. 'Milk porridge.'

'*Ke a leboga, mma,*' Amber said as woman bowed and left.

'The mules will be ready soon,' Jabu told her.

'We will leave the moment they are equipped,' Amber replied, starting to feed the porridge into David's mouth. 'Greta, did you see anything more of those men?'

'No, but I spoke to Mrs Fraser. She says that there are five of them and they think we were staying on a farm north of here. Its owners are Dutch and left to stay with relatives in the Transvaal when war was declared.' Greta paused. 'Miss Amber, if someone here is able to sell me a cloth then we can make a sling to carry young David. Shall I go and ask?'

'Yes, Greta, but hurry, please,' Amber answered, rocking her child, her body tense with fear. She had never been afraid before he was born, not like this. He squirmed and she tried to relax, afraid she was holding him too tight. 'Sorry, my darling,' she said, bowing over his small body, speaking softly. 'I'm so sorry, my angel.'

Finally, she felt him going back to sleep.

• • •

I t was still dark when they finally crept out of the kraal and started out to where the mules had been tethered in a dry riverbed almost half a mile from the trading post, but even as they walked

Amber could feel the quality of the cool air changing against her skin – dawn was coming and soon a ribbon of gold would appear on the horizon, a foretelling of the heat of the day to come. The mules were fractious and jumpy and they huffed and bumped each other in the dark as Jabu helped Amber and Greta mount them.

They travelled south and east from the road, keeping the kopje between them and the trading post. The plan was to walk for an hour or so before looping back and recrossing the road as they headed west towards Mosita and the Bauer farm. If the men looking for Amber did find their trail from the Frasers' place, perhaps they would follow it south-east and miss the place where they changed course towards the farm.

• • •

They were within ten miles of the farm when they saw the riders behind them. Greta had begun to point out landmarks that were familiar to her and Amber had felt hope flicker, bright and dangerous, in her heart – they needed an hour more to reach safety.

Amber looked back to where Jabu pointed. The specks on the horizon seemed to barely move. Surely, they couldn't overtake them now. But Jabu assured her that they could. And if they did? What lay before them? A prison camp? Ransom? Would Jabu even escape with his life? Amber's hope collapsed into ash and smoke.

But at the moment she lost all hope, Amber found something else – a calm certainty she had not known since she became a mother. Her thoughts suddenly became clear.

She passed David to Greta and arranged the sling around her nursemaid, then dismounted, her skirts swishing through the dew-dampened weeds.

Five horsemen, travelling fast across the veld, were heading towards them.

'Have they seen us, Jabu?'

'Yes, Mrs Ballantyne.'

'And we cannot outpace them, or hide here.'

She pulled off her wedding ring, then took hold of Greta's left hand and pushed the ring onto her finger.

'Miss Amber, what are you doing?' Greta squealed.

'They are going to take me prisoner, but you are just a farmer's daughter with her servant and child. You bought a riding mule from a neighbour, stayed the night there and now you're taking it home. Your husband has joined the Bechuanaland Police, so you've come to stay with your aunt and uncle until the war is over. David is your child and Jabu is your man.'

Greta could not hide her terror at what Amber was proposing. Amber seized her wrist and jerked it towards her. Greta looked down at her from her perch on the mule, her bottom lip trembling.

'They must believe it, Greta, or they will shoot Jabu. I can face whatever comes, torture or hardship, but I can only do that if I know David is safe. This is up to you now. My story is that I stopped you on the road and offered you money for somewhere to stay tonight. I have no luggage. That is all you know about me.'

Tears welled up in Greta's eyes.

'Do you understand me, Greta?'

'Yes, yes, Miss Amber.'

'You must take David to safety. You must say he is your child. Make them believe it. What would your aunt say if men like these challenged her when she was going about her lawful business? You have to, Greta, if you care for us at all.'

Amber's heart was in turmoil, but her head told her that the only way to keep her child safe was to let him go.

'Perhaps they will not take you prisoner!' Greta whispered.

'You know they will. Be brave, Greta. You have survived worse,' Amber urged her.

Greta wiped away her tears and straightened her back. 'I will take care of David. I swear it on my life, Miss Amber.'

Amber took out her pocketbook and pulled out all the money she had and thrust it into Greta's pocket. By this time the horsemen were moments away.

'The money is for you and your aunt and uncle. I will give them anything they ask. And if you can get word to me, Greta, please tell any runner I will pay handsomely for news of my child.'

Jabu's hands were tightening around the rifle. Amber spoke to him, low and urgently: 'Please, Jabu. Remember, I am just some strange traveller. Your mistress picked me up on the road.'

'I promised to protect you, Mrs Ballantyne.'

'You *cannot*. I am begging you, Jabu, do not put my child at risk and your own life, too. I have no idea what will happen if they take me as a spy. Make sure Greta and David get to the farm – that is the greatest service you can do for me and my husband.'

Jabu hissed with displeasure but did not protest further.

Amber could see the lead rider clearly now – their pursuers had slowed to a trot. It was the man with the eyepatch and the scarred face. Amber prepared to play her part. If she said goodbye to David, if she went to kiss him, or rub his small hand against her cheek, if she took one last breath of the scent of him, his sweet-sour smell, the man with the eyepatch would see through their pretence. She could not look at her child. She stared at the ground until the men surrounded them, then looked up at their leader. The man with the eyepatch met her gaze for a long moment, then swung down and took off his hat.

'*Wie is jy?*' Greta asked, her voice firm and annoyed. '*Ons het gesien hoe jy ons volg.* Are you lost?'

The man with the eyepatch laughed. 'No, we aren't lost. *Ons is lôjale Transvalers en ons jag Britse spioene. Hoekom is jy so vrug hier en wie is deel van jou group?*'

Greta began to repeat the story Amber had prepared for her, adding the detail that they'd met Amber as she climbed out of a dogcart on the road from Vryburg, not far south of the trading post. She was doing well, keeping up the tone of an irritated housewife, but Amber could see that the men were suspicious.

Two were watching Jabu – the rifle over his shoulder and his glowering expression were not helping the situation. Amber could confess to being a spy straight away, but that might make it worse. No, a desperate spy fleeing through this wild and empty country would not hand themselves over.

If the men searched the mules and went through the travel bags they'd find a dozen letters and her own fine clothes, not the sort of thing a country wife such as Greta was pretending to be would carry. The silver rattle Saffron had given David would betray him as the baby of someone wealthy. A search would expose them all – their pursuers would kill Jabu and throw Greta into a cell alongside Amber and her child. What could she do? She could pretend to beg Jabu and Greta for their protection, and hope they'd realise it was part of the ruse and react with disdain. Too risky. They might think she had changed her mind. What would a spy, a lone and desperate woman, who had just bargained her way into lodgings with strangers do?

Amber knew what to do. She ran!

Greta shrieked in alarm and for a few precious seconds the riders were confused. Amber sprinted as if the hounds of hell were after her, stumbling over the loose rocks and stones, the stiff veld grass pulling at her skirts. She heard the scarred man shout and the thunder of hooves behind her.

I must get further away, she thought, pushing on, praying they would want to capture her alive, knowing her back was an easy target, waiting to feel the hot sting of a bullet between her shoulder blades.

No bullet, only the shout of the riders as they drove their horses after her. In no time they were beside her, hooves and horseflesh throwing up a cloud of choking dust. A narrow-faced rider swiped at her back with his whip and she fell onto her knees, feeling the strike tear the thin fabric of her blouse and cut through the delicate flesh on her back.

'*Staan terug!*' a voice commanded.

At the command, the men retreated. She heard a man's boots thud to the earth as he dismounted, the chink of his spurs as he walked towards her. She stayed still, feeling the blood beginning to run down her back – the pain was excruciating but she would not give these men the satisfaction of hearing her cry out.

The man grunted and bent over her, pulling her wrists together behind her back and tying them, tightly, with what felt like a leather strap. He fitted his hands under her armpits, lifted her up, and set her on her feet, then twisted her round to face him. He looked her over carefully. Amber didn't resist or meet his gaze, staring into the air over the top of his head. He sniffed, then turned to where Jabu and Greta were waiting.

'*Ons sal julle nie vêrder steur nie,*' he shouted. 'On your way.'

Amber watched them move off, happiness and despair tearing at her heart, then she looked into the face of her captor for the first time. 'Take me to General Cronjé,' she said confidently.

• • •

The Mount Nelson Hotel in Cape Town was built to flood its elegant rooms with light in the mornings. Saffron woke and stared at the ceiling. Ryder's place in the bed next to her was already empty and cooling. The thought of her husband and the frigid politeness with which they had treated each other since he had beaten Leon made her miserable. She had to do something to heal her family – somehow reconcile with Ryder and bring him and her son together. But what? Leon's snubs over the last few weeks had eroded Ryder's patience. Still, he should not have lost control of his temper. She knew, deep in her heart, that Ryder knew that he was in the wrong and was angry with himself. He was just too proud to admit it.

Leon's behaviour was more of a mystery to her. Her son had always worshipped anything connected to the military, that was true. She remembered how he had hung on stories of battle even as a small child in the mining camp. Cairo, with all those men in braid, the parades, the pomp and swagger of Empire, had made it worse, but something had changed in him, though she could not place exactly what it was. His love of the military had been untainted by contempt for his father's work before they came to Cape Town. Perhaps he was simply reaching the age when children needed to demonstrate their independence from their parents? Saffron and Ryder, having lost their parents young, had never had to face such a struggle. Maybe that was what made it so difficult for them to understand their son. She would have to spend time with her son, just the two of them, and see if she could get to the core of what was causing Leon's behaviour.

Now she had the beginnings of a plan, Saffron began to hum one of her favourite songs as she brushed her hair. In the main salon, she found Penelope at the breakfast table, buttering toast while she read the newspaper. She ruffled her daughter's hair and stole the piece of toast she had just buttered, taking a bite and swallowing greedily.

'I am going to take Leon out today, the two of us, but is there something you would like to do?'

Penelope rolled her eyes, then began buttering her next piece of toast so the entire surface was covered in a thin layer right up to the corners.

'Mrs Weil told me that she had riding lessons when she was my age,' she said. 'Do you think Kahruba and I might take riding lessons? Proper ones? I asked the hotel manager and he said that he would send up a list of reliable teachers in the area.'

Saffron poured herself a cup of coffee from the silver pot on the counter and drank it, her eyes bright with amusement, proud of her daughter's resourcefulness. Penelope was always, quietly, two steps ahead of the rest of them.

'You wish to learn to ride? But, of course, my darling,' Saffron said. 'Just make sure that you get references for those teachers before you start. I am sure that you have already told the manager to add all the charges to our bill.'

'Thank you, Mama.' Penelope stood and went to hug and kiss her mother. 'I promise you, Mama, Kahruba and I will become *exceptional* horsewomen. You will be so proud of us.'

Saffron set down her cup. 'I am certain of it. Now, where are the others? Why is it so quiet this morning?'

'Kahruba is still asleep, and Nazeera has taken Matthew down to the hotel kitchen. The chef lets him make animals with the leftover pastry after the early breakfast rush.'

'And your eldest brother?'

Penelope just shrugged her shoulders.

Saffron stood up, kissed her daughter's forehead and then went to Leon's room. These days she knocked before opening his door – you never knew what kind of mood he might be in and Saffron had learned the hard way that it was best to test the water first.

There was no reply, so Saffron opened the door and let herself in to Leon's room. The first thing that she noticed was that his bed was unmade, and she would have reprimanded him, except that there was no sign of Leon. She hurried out, heading for the room which Penelope and Kahruba shared, slamming open the door with unexpected force.

'Have you seen Leon?' Saffron asked Kahruba.

'No,' Kahruba said, slowly sitting up in bed and yawning.

Saffron looked swiftly around the room and left without saying anything more.

Kahruba blinked into the morning light and realised that she was ravenous. Springing out of bed, she padded to the bathroom, then dressed, adding a scarlet shawl she had borrowed from Saffron a week or two earlier to her outfit, before going in search of sustenance. Penny looked like an illustration out of a magazine, Kahruba thought, when she saw her sitting and reading the newspaper. One of those stories about young noblewomen doing good works among the poor, only Penny's feet didn't reach the floor. As Kahruba hauled herself into the chair next to her cousin, she wondered what sort of story she'd be in herself one day when she grew up. She hoped it was the sort of story she wasn't allowed to read yet. She reached for the toast and jam and the tassels of her shawl trailed across Penny's plate.

'Kahruba!' Penny whined, exasperated.

'Sorry! What's happened to Leon?' Kahruba asked, gesturing to Leon's empty chair.

'I hope he's in the kitchen with Nazeera and Matthew. Mama went downstairs to look for him. Papa will be furious if he's gone to watch the soldiers again.'

Kahruba ate her toast and stared out of the window, thinking about her future. 'Penny, when we are old, like Amber and Saffron, what shall we do?'

'I shall run Papa's company, and you shall be a dancer with loads of famous friends from all around the world and we shall live together in a big house in London,' Penny replied with absolute certainty.

Kahruba had seen pictures of London in magazines and it seemed to have plenty of theatres and shops. She loved her cousin's plan and accepted it happily.

'What about Leon and Matthew?'

'Leon will be a soldier, no matter what Papa thinks, and Matthew . . .' Penny pondered. Her younger brother was too small to be of much interest to her, but he always tried to throw himself into the shrubbery whenever they went on walks with Nazeera. 'He will be a great, intrepid explorer like my grandpa. He will send us exciting presents from faraway places – gold, diamonds and emeralds from India . . . Spices and pearls from Ceylon. Silk from China . . .'

'Or maybe just some monkeys from Africa.' Kahruba laughed, but her laugh was cut off by Saffron's return.

Ignoring the two girls, she ran straight to Leon's room. When she emerged a few seconds later, she looked heartbroken. 'Girls, my girls, Leon has taken his knapsack. Oh, God! I think he has run away.'

She came to the table and sat down, putting her head in her hands. Penelope slid from her chair and tucked herself under her mother's arm. Saffron kissed her daughter on her forehead and held her tight to her chest. 'I am worried about him, my loves. If either of you knows anything, please tell me . . . I don't know what might happen to him. He has never had to take care of himself. I know secrets are important, but I also know that you wouldn't want him to get into trouble.'

Saffron's voice was shaking with fear. Kahruba felt a strange and uncomfortable stab behind her ribs, a feeling such as she had never felt before. Maybe it was because she had never seen Aunt Saffron in such a state. Her aunt was always one thing or another: alive and bright and full of adventures or deadly serious, angry with them – though only ever for a very short time – or delighted with their noise and nonsense. But she was never scared, never afraid, and Kahruba did not like it. She got down from her chair and silently padded to Leon's room.

When Kahruba had given Leon the chocolates the previous day, she had seen him hiding letters under his pillow and recognised the thin, sunset-yellow paper Ahmed used to write to her. His letters had arrived regularly since they left Cairo. They were delivered to her by Nazeera, who always received fat bundles of correspondence from the city. Ahmed's letters to his sister were exactly two full sides of homilies and bitterness in excellent Arabic. She read them, then threw them away without giving them another thought.

Kahruba did not know *why* those letters from her brother to Leon might have something to do with his disappearance, but she had noticed how Leon had become angrier with his father lately, and she knew, too, that Ahmed hated Uncle Ryder. Something bitter and poisonous had trickled into the blood of her happy family, and Ahmed's letters to her were so full of bile, Kahruba wondered if they might be the source.

Kahruba went straight to the pillows and found the pages, which Leon had hidden there. She picked them up, returned to the breakfast table and dropped them on the table in front of her aunt.

Saffron looked puzzled, then began to read. Ahmed had chosen to write to his cousin in English. The voice in his letters was warm and understanding, indignant on Leon's behalf, designed to enflame the boy's resentment and sense of injustice. Saffron felt a chill creeping through her veins as she read.

I cannot write the name of Penrod Ballantyne without pain. I know you will understand and forgive me for that, cousin. He killed my beloved father and took away from me the warm sunlight of his love, but even so, I think you are right to seek his protection, whatever dangers you must face and whatever obstacles your father places in your way. Penrod is, at least, a warrior as my father was, a man so skilled in the arts of battle he could defeat even Osman Atalan. I can never forgive him, but I must respect him. How could any young man, with the vision of such a noble warrior in front of him, live in a shadow of those dirty hagglers, their hands greasy with coin from the souks and bazaars, or the banks and offices? Still, it will take great bravery and resolve to separate yourself from the tendrils of Courtney's money, and instead live a free and honourable life under the protection of a true soldier. I do not know if you have that courage, though I think perhaps you do. It might be safer, wiser even, to wait until the conflict with the Boers is over before you escape the counting house and find a new guide through the noble endeavour of your life, but those tendrils might have wrapped themselves around your throat by then, or your father might succeed in destroying your noble dreams and leave you fit for nothing but a stool in a clerk's office, adding up columns of scratched out numbers until you are half-blind . . .

There were pages and pages of it. Saffron stood up, backing away from the letters as if a living cobra had fallen onto the tabletop.

'Did he write to you, too, Kahruba?' she said, with a shiver of revulsion.

'Yes, Aunt Saffron, but I never listen to Ahmed.'

Saffron looked at her now, her honey eyes ablaze. 'But Leon *did*?'

Kahruba felt uncomfortable. 'I don't know,' she said.

Saffron turned away from them. She was used to an enemy she could see but she did not know how to fight this malice which had found its way into her home like damp in a grain barn, and rotted out the heart of it.

'I am going downstairs to telephone Ryder. When Nazeera and Matthew come back, you may tell her what has happened.'

Saffron left the suite and went into the busy lobby of the hotel to place her call. She had to fight her way through a throng of newspaper correspondents and army officers newly arrived in the country on the *Dunottar Castle*, a pushing, shouting, noisy crowd of men unable to contain their excitement at the prospect of war, all laughing too loudly. She loathed all of them.

• • •

Essie arrived at the Courtney Manufacturing Offices early every morning. She liked to greet the workers on her way through the yard, then settle herself at her desk in the outer office she shared with the other clerks while it was still quiet. Already she had developed a ritual. After greeting Mr Yusuf – who was always already in his office when she arrived – she would make sure her desk was neat and the inkwell full, blotting paper, scrap paper and order sheets laid out in front of her, then she would close her eyes and put her hands together and offer up her prayers. She prayed for her son, and asked him to watch over her from heaven. She prayed that her daughter would work hard at the mission school, and then she prayed for the Courtney family. Lastly, she would ask for the wisdom to do her job well.

This morning the roads had been clogged with troops and army carts, so Essie almost didn't stop at the yard to say good morning, but then she remembered that they had shipped out the latest consignment of camp kettles to the front by train late the previous evening, and she was anxious to know that they had been sent off safely and to hear if the railway porters had been helpful and efficient.

'They are good boys in the yard for the most part,' the foreman reported. 'Helps Mr Yusuf sent me with a little grease,' he rubbed his fingers together, 'and a crate of beer for them to enjoy after their work. I promise you, goods from the Courtney Works will be carefully handled up the line.'

Essie was pleased. The crate of beer had been her idea. She had worked at the hotel long enough to see that the guests who tipped generously could rely on their luggage being treated with care. She was about to go on her way, when the foreman added some muttered remark.

'What did you say, Mr Abercrombie?'

The man shrugged and scratched his chin.

'Only that the guard was a sour old fusspot. Nothing we can do about him, but I'd swear I saw a pair of boys scrambling into a freight car between us finishing the loading and them securing the doors. A native lad, and a wee blond fellow with a knapsack. Guard wanted to make sure that the train left on time, and I suppose that's fair enough, but he did no more than glance into the carriage when I told him what I had seen. Then I thought: well, it was only two lads grabbing a free ride, not grown fellows thieving, so I didn't push him.'

Essie always felt any mention of boys like a hot blade pressed to her skin. She wondered how long she would feel so raw.

'I'm sure you did the right thing, Mr Abercrombie.'

The foreman looked comforted and Essie was glad. Her life had been a hard scrabble which had started with a poor education, an early marriage and widowhood. As a result most of her days had been a blind panic of trying to earn enough to keep her children fed. Now she had a good wage, a clean room for her and her little girl to sleep in and could even take the time to make Mr Abercrombie feel better.

Essie let herself into the office and hung up her bonnet, greeted Mr Yusuf, and set her table straight. She had enough time for her prayers after all, and set to her day's work. Mr Courtney arrived and greeted her by name, touching his hand to his forehead as if tipping his hat. He was such a civil man, and handsome, and for a while she worked to the sound of the low rumble of masculine voices next door. The telephone in Mr Yusuf's office rang, which made her jump, and it was only luck which prevented her from smudging her work, and right at the bottom of the page, too.

The voices next door grew louder, and she heard the rattle of the phone being slammed down. The door opened and Mr Courtney stormed through the outer office. He went straight to the yard door, thrusting it open so hard that it banged against the outer wall and the whole wooden frame of the building shook. Essie could hear him shouting for his horse before the door swung closed again with another crash. She stared at it, her mouth slightly open, as Mr Yusuf emerged from the inner office. Glancing at him over her shoulder, Essie saw that he was looking serious, but not guilty or ashamed. She was relieved – at least the cause of Mr Courtney's anger was nothing they had done.

'His oldest boy has disappeared,' Mr Yusuf said.

'Again?' Essie said.

Mr Yusuf smiled and Essie felt herself blush and laughed a little to hide her embarrassment.

'I fear it is more serious this time, Mrs Taylor. Mrs Courtney just called from the hotel. The boy took his knapsack and some clothes. I do not think it is a case of slipping away for a morning to watch the soldiers on this occasion.' He shook his head. 'It is a problem to be the father of sons.'

At once he realised what he had said and stood up, his face a picture of dismay. 'Mrs Taylor, that was most thoughtless. I offer you my apologies.'

'Please, do not give it a thought, Mr Yusuf.' She turned back to her work and the familiar figures, but then went still, her face frowning and thoughtful. A drop of ink fell from the tip of her fountain pen onto the page, and bloomed shining on the paper, but she did not notice.

'Mr Courtney's son had a knapsack, you say? He is a blond boy, is he not?'

'That's correct. Of course, he has not visited the factory since you joined us.'

'Do you have a picture of him?'

Something in the urgency of her tone made Mr Yusuf blink. He disappeared into the inner office and returned with a framed photograph which he handed to her. They had taken it when the sign bearing the Courtney name had been hung over the workshop. Under it stood Mr Yusuf, Mr and Mrs Courtney and their children. The boy was not smiling. He looked bored and distracted.

Essie stood up. 'Excuse me one moment, please.'

She headed to the works shed at a run, still holding the photograph. The noise of hammering and hissing, rolling machines and metal stamps washed over her. She spotted Abercrombie in the western corner of the huge shed. He was with two other men, filling the finished kettles with water and checking them for leaks before emptying them and setting them on the racks to dry.

She scurried across to him, the long hem of her grey cotton skirts snapping round her ankles. The workers glanced up and smiled – it was as if a rare bird had come into the shed and was fluttering between them.

'Mr Abercrombie?' she called, holding out the photograph. 'Was this one of the boys you saw getting into the train last night?'

Abercrombie was surprised by Essie's presence and her question, but recovered quickly, taking the photograph from her. He examined the image carefully. Then he nodded. 'That's the lad.'

Essie thanked him and ran back to the office through the sparks and hammering.

• • •

Ryder arrived at the Mount Nelson while Saffron was on the telephone to the factory. The lobby was a fug of tobacco smoke and loud male voices but he caught sight of her in the telephone booth. Her image was splintered by the engraved glass, but he would know that turn of a shoulder, the colour of her hair anywhere. He shoved his way through the crowd towards her, his vision flickering with the buttons and stripes of military insignia.

Saffron had seen him. She pushed the door open and stepped out while a man in civilian clothes, his face red and sweating, bustled in behind her and snatched up the telephone. Ryder caught her by the shoulders.

'That was Essie Taylor on the telephone,' she said.

'From the works?'

'Yes, and thank God for her,' Saffron said. 'One of the men saw Leon and a native boy jumping the train out to East London at nine o'clock last night.'

Ryder thought for a moment. 'A native boy? I am a fool. It was that lad from the fire. They were together at the docks when the troops were arriving. Tau.'

'Good,' Saffron said, then seeing Ryder's expression of surprise, she added hastily: 'I would hate to think of Leon alone and without friends, Ryder.'

She looked up at him, his strong features and dark eyes. 'Ryder, we must go after him.'

'We shall.' He spoke without doubt or hesitation.

A middle-aged man, clean shaven and wearing a shabby tweed jacket, cleared his throat. He was standing close beside them, waiting his turn at the precious telephone.

'Couldn't help overhearing, sir, madam,' he said, with a nod to them both. 'Did you say the nine o'clock train for East London?'

'That's right,' Ryder said.

The man elbowed the fellow next to him who was making strange, scribbled notes on a pad of paper, seemingly indifferent to the crush around him.

'Oi, wake up, Stammers! Weren't Philip and John on the last train to East London last night?'

'What?' The man with the pad was young, but his greased-back hair was already thinning. 'Yes, clever bastards scooped all the rest of us on that.'

Saffron looked between the two men. 'I don't understand.'

'Our esteemed colleagues, war correspondents from *The Times* and the *Daily Post*, ma'am,' the older man said. 'They worked out a way to get to Natal ahead of us – taking the train to East London, then the mail boat up the coast to Durban. From there it's not far to the frontline at Ladysmith. By the time the rest of us had figured out what was going on, they'd already headed off, hence my friend's salty language.' The younger man shrugged. 'Turns out it was the last train going that way. So you can't follow, I'm afraid. Not by that route, anyway. Is the lad trying to get to Ladysmith?'

'He is trying to reach Mafeking,' Saffron said firmly and Ryder looked at her in disbelief.

The younger man scratched his nose. 'Long way round! War will be over before he gets there,' he said nonchalantly.

'Rubbish, boy's got his head screwed on,' the older man replied in a sudden roar. 'If he can jump the trains in the Transvaal, then he'll be in Mafeking long before the army can send a relief column to lift the siege. He'll be in plenty of time to see the fun.'

The two men began to argue about the alternatives, waving their arms to trace Leon's imagined route in the air.

Saffron clenched her fists. 'I'll ride. I'll sail. I'll walk every foot of the way if I have to, but I'm going after my son.'

Saffron took her husband's arm and he led her upstairs. Before they opened the door to the suite, Saffron told Ryder about Ahmed's letters.

'I thought if we let him stay in Cairo and study, he'd stop resenting us so much,' she said, 'but it seems he is willing to go to great trouble to keep on hurting us.'

'How did Leon get the letters?' Ryder asked.

'Nazeera.' Saffron saw his face darken. 'Ryder! We did not tell her that she should not pass any letters on. She is a close friend of Bacheet's. None of them knew what the letters contained. How could they?'

He took his hand from the door and leaned against the wall. 'We've made quite a household for ourselves, Saffy.'

'It wasn't all our doing,' she replied.

'No, that is true. What shall we do with the girls and Matthew while we are gone?'

'Leave that to me.'

'Gladly,' he said. 'I am going to telegraph the railway and have the train searched at De Aar.'

Saffron turned to him, her eyes bright. 'That is a *good* idea! Then we might even know they are safe and waiting for us before we leave Cape Town.' She stretched to kiss his lightly stubbled cheek. 'They will be safe, won't they, Ryder? I feel sick to my stomach not knowing anything and thinking of them out there.'

Ryder cupped Saffron's face in his hand and wondered if he could ever forgive his son for worrying her in this way, or forgive himself for letting his child make him lose his self-control. 'We will bring them back home, Saffy. I swear it to you.'

• • •

When Leon awoke the morning after his escape from Cape Town, the first thing he saw were the words stencilled on the side of the wooden crates between which he and Tau had slept: COURTNEY MANUFACTURING. Leon huffed, then lifted himself up on his elbow so he could look between the slatted planks of the carriage at the passing scenery. He caught glimpses of a huge expanse of rust-coloured earth and scrub reaching out to the horizon, low rocky mounds dusted with yellow and gold grasses. In the distance he could see the purple of rising hills. His mouth was dry and his stomach rumbled. For the first time he began to consider the necessities of his journey. He had a full water bottle in his knapsack, the chocolates and some sweet biscuits he had stolen from the tin on the sideboard in their hotel room.

Leon got out the water bottle and took a swig, then shook Tau awake and gave him some too. Then they ate the biscuits and began to explore the wagon, sliding past the closely packed stacks of boxes, or clambering over them, until they had discovered all of their new home's secrets. Leon found a dozen packing cases stamped with the legend FORTNUM & MASON and used his penknife to ease out the nails of the lid of the top one. Inside was a stack of large square parcels, each labelled with the name of an officer. Leon licked his lips. Sometimes Amber's English publishers, or the London gallery where Saffron showed her paintings, sent packages which looked like this to their house in Cairo. They were a cause of great celebration. Once the thick brown paper was removed, Leon knew that he would find a wicker basket filled with savoury biscuits and jams, anchovy paste, cheese and Dundee cake in tins. His stomach growled.

Tau scrambled into the gap next to him and peered over his shoulder, then looked at him quizzically. 'What is it?'

Leon explained what was in the parcels, then ran his hand through his hair. 'But it would be such a rotten thing to steal one, Tau. These men are fighting for the Empire, and how would it be if they got this present from home and then opened it up and there wasn't anything in it?'

'You have money?'

'Yes, but still. Who wants a shilling when you were looking forward to Dundee cake in a tin?'

Tau didn't know what Dundee cake was, but he understood the principle. 'Take only one thing from each basket,' he said. 'Each man will have a little less, but only a little less, and a shilling. And if you take cake from a man who wants it very much, his friends will share.' Tau frowned. 'And if he has not got friends who are happy to share, then he is probably not a good man and so does not deserve cake, don't you agree?'

Leon agreed.

For the next hour the boys occupied themselves with opening packages, selecting their purchases, albeit at prices they invented themselves, then rebuckling the hampers and reknotting the string. They retired to their hiding place behind the crates to feed themselves on a mixture of potted beef and water biscuits.

• • •

Leon and Tau digested their feast as the train sped them across the great open spaces of the Karoo, then Leon spent a couple of hours trying to teach Tau to read. He discovered it might take longer than he had thought, but puzzling over the problem for a while, a memory of his own first lessons in the mining camp in Abyssinia bubbled up from the depths of his memory. On the blank pages at the back of his copy of *Huckleberry Finn*, he drew an illustrated alphabet, beginning with A for apple, accompanied by a small drawing of the fruit, and B with a rather good bat, and so on all the way to Z. Leon's work was not, he had to admit, anywhere near as good as his mother's. Her pictures had been little stories in themselves, but after Leon explained which creature was a horse and which a zebra, and replaced the camel – an animal Tau did not know or recognise – with a smoking cigar, it seemed it might work.

Leon left Tau to study and went on another tour of their domain. They had found a tin bucket in one of the crates to act as a chamber pot, but the day was hot, and even with the motion of the train whipping eddies of air through the wagon, the smell was getting unpleasant. Leon had decided that there must be some sort of trapdoor in the roof of the wagon, so while Tau studied his alphabet, Leon set himself the task of finding it.

It took him the best part of an hour to discover the hatch and manoeuvre enough crates into position so he could reach it. Only then could he start on working the rusted bolt free and pushing it open. The blast of light, air and flying dust as he put his head outside was exhilarating. The wind stung his skin. The sound of the wheels on the track and the regular beat of the engine's pistons pounded against his ears and the air was full of smoke and soot.

Getting up to the hatch a second time, encumbered with the bucket, was less enjoyable. Tau watched carefully from below as Leon's upper body and then the bucket disappeared outside the carriage. He heard a clank, and then a thumping sound. After a pause Leon made his way back down the stack of crates. Tau sniffed cautiously.

'It didn't hit me,' Leon said, a defensive tone in his voice. 'But we'll need another bucket.'

Tau shifted over so that they could sit together and continue to examine the mysteries of the printed word.

• • •

Darkness fell and the train pulled smoothly along the tracks. Both Leon and Tau were dozing when the hiss of the brakes jolted them awake.

'De Aar!' a deep voice called out on the platform. 'De Aar! It is a half-hour halt, ladies and gentlemen!'

It was too dark in the wagon to look at the map, so Leon decided to climb up to the open hatch and see if he might be able to read it by moonlight. He hauled himself up, set the map on the roof and stared at it. It was not a very good map, designed for newspaper readers in London to gain a rough idea of the theatres of war, rather than for someone on the road like himself. He stared at it, willing himself into some sort of comprehension.

While he was lost in concentration, two men in railway uniforms walked past on the platform.

'We don't have time to search for runaways,' one complained in a thick German accent.

Leon felt his blood run cold.

'At least we aren't searching the passenger cars,' said the other. 'Having to wake people up, or asking the passengers in the waiting room if they saw anything unusual. I'll take the goods wagons any day.'

Leon heard the barn-like doors of one of the wagons nearer the engine being unchained and dragged open, then a grunt as one of the men clambered in. Leon ducked back down through the hatch.

'Tau!' he whispered, and beckoned upwards.

Tau was already packing Leon's knapsack with the remains of their feast, the book and a rough, greasy blanket that he had found and commandeered. He slung the bag over his shoulder and sprang up the packing case tower.

Leon shoved the map into his pocket, pulled himself out through the hatch and rolled onto the roof. Tau appeared through the hatch behind him, seeming to spring through the hole like a jack-in-the-box. Leon could just about see his face in the gloom, tight with concentration. Tau reached for the cover, aiming to flip it closed but Leon shot out a hand, grabbing his slim wrist. Tau turned towards him with a frown, and Leon shook his head, putting his finger to his lips. Tau nodded.

The men had finished with the first wagon, jumping down onto the gravel between the tracks with a crunch. The boys waited, hardly daring to breathe, as the footsteps came closer. Leon tried to slow his hammering heart as the chain on their wagon was unhitched and the doors slid back heavily.

They heard a grunt as the German man helped his colleague climb in. After a few moments the Englishman called out: 'Yes, they've been here, all right! Little devils have shifted things around and made a home for themselves. Come on and have a look.'

They heard more grunts as the German man made his way into the wagon, and a series of thumps and curses as the railway workers moved between the crates. Leon closed his eyes, willing them to go away.

'I see no sign of them now,' the German man said. 'How have they got out? The chain and padlock had not been tempered with.'

'Check the roof hatch,' the Englishman replied.

Tau and Leon looked at each other. If one of them put their head out of the hatch, they would be seen at once.

Tau pointed down the side of the wagon and Leon shook his head but Tau pointed again more emphatically. Leon inched his way towards the edge of the curved roof, moving sideways like a crab, and looked down. The wooden boards which formed the sides of the carriage were bolted to an external steel frame – verticals every eight feet or so, diagonals crossing between them. Below, Leon saw darkness and the glint of metal tracks. The rivets were painted and smooth. The diagonal bands stood out a little from the side of the wagon, but even if he could rest a toe on them, he couldn't see what to hold on to.

'Do what I do,' Tau whispered.

Leon watched, his stomach churning. He could hear the men's voices inside the wagon.

'Made themselves a little ladder, the monkeys!'

Tau sat on the edge of the roof and twisted sideways, grabbing onto it with both hands, then he lowered himself down until his feet touched one of the diagonals. His bare toes seemed to grip onto the narrow space. Then he let go of the edge of the roof with one hand and braced himself against the nearest steel vertical. He released his other hand and hooked his fingers into a gap between the wooden planks, then looked back up at Leon.

'You can do it,' he encouraged Leon.

Leon's mouth was dry. He had to act. He closed his eyes, forcing himself to imagine being caught by the collar and sent home in disgrace, and decided he'd rather break his leg than give up without a struggle. He slid to the edge of the roof and swung himself over as Tau had done.

'Right foot down! Down!' Tau whispered.

Leon's foot found the solid support of the diagonal.

'Left foot down, Leon.'

Leon stretched out with his left foot. He was breathing heavily, his right foot was cramping and his left could not find a place to land. The edge of the roof was pressing against his chest and his hands were slippery. At last his left foot hit the diagonal.

'Good! Now hands.'

Leon stared at his fingers and willed himself to let go of the edge of the roof. He heard a curse from under the hatch and managed to unclench his right hand. For a nauseous second he thought he was going to fall backwards into the darkness, but his desperately searching fingers found a sharp-edged hole on the underlip of the roof's narrow overhang and he clung to it. *One more hand now, please,* he begged himself, staring at his white fingers. *Please.* A head was emerging from the hatch. Leon released his left hand and reached blindly for a hold, dropping his head below the edge of the wagon at the same time. He found it, a crack in the planks just big enough for two fingers, but the grip with his left foot was weak and slipping. The muscles of his thighs felt hot and torn, the jagged metal cut into his fingers and he closed his mouth on a yelp.

'Got out this way, most certainly.'

The man's voice was close. Leon stopped breathing and bit his lip until it bled, struggling to ignore the pain and stay silent.

'Any sign of them?' the voice inside the carriage asked.

The man did not reply immediately. Leon prayed he would not climb out onto the roof after them. He was certain he would fall any second, sprawling and twisted on the gravel below – he could not cope with the pain for a moment longer.

'No. They're long gone.'

The hatch slammed shut, but it gave Leon no relief. He could not move and he could not hold on. His left hand lost its grip and slipped, and he flailed out desperately. At that moment his left foot went from under him, but even as it did, a hand grabbed his own and he heard Tau's fierce whisper from above: 'I have you, Leon!'

Leon managed to find his foothold again and the panic slowly left him.

'Give me your other hand!' Tau ordered.

Now all he could feel was pain – his legs had begun to shake with the effort of keeping him on the side of the carriage and his fingers were cut and bloody. Leon managed to reach up his other hand and felt Tau grab him, hauling him up and onto the roof. He lay on his back and closed his eyes, waiting for his heart to stop thumping in his chest.

A whistle blew and a long hiss of steam escaped from the engine. Leon opened his eyes and turned towards Tau. Tau had been lying across the roof. Now he rolled on his side and rubbed his forearms and wrists.

'Thank you.'

Tau shrugged. 'You emptied the bucket.'

A sudden jerk and the train began to ease forward. Leon shuffled to the hatch and tried to prise it open. It rattled and held.

'Bolted,' he said. He had a sudden image of being ripped off the top of the train and thrown onto the tracks. 'We must get inside the train! We can't hang on all night.'

Panic gripped his chest once again.

'We can hang on,' Tau said. 'Many times have I seen men travelling into the station at Cape Town sitting on the roof.'

Leon took a long deep breath and slowly the fear drained away, leaving only an ache in his muscles and the stinging of his fingers. 'We are having a real adventure now,' he said, a triumphant tone in his voice.

For some reason this made Tau laugh. Tau's laugh was high and musical and that made Leon laugh, too. Soon, tears were rolling down their cheeks, and whenever one managed to stop the other started off again.

• • •

The novelty of riding on top of the train wore off a few hours later. Leon knew that they would fry in the sun if there was no cloud cover and the train was bound to go through more stations on its way to the coast, where they might be seen by railway officials or passengers. They must find somewhere else to hide. He turned onto his belly to tell Tau his thoughts. Tau was sitting cross-legged on the roof, his head nodding sleepily. Leon put out a hand and shook his knee to wake him. Tau's eyes opened and he looked at Leon in surprise.

'I had a dream,' he said.

'What about?' Leon asked with a yawn.

'My brother,' Tau replied. 'And my mother, and the place she came from, I think, but she left there before I was born.'

Leon was struck by the thought that he knew nothing much of Tau, other than the fact he liked him and he was good at climbing.

'Are they alive, your parents?' He pulled himself up until he could sit cross-legged, too. The train moved evenly along the rails. 'Why don't you live with them?'

'My father and my brother are alive. My father is a white man. And my brother has pale skin; he is called Jacob. They used to live in Cape Town. Then they left. I saw them sometimes on the street. Jacob goes to school. He wished to be a priest like my father.' Tau glanced at Leon and saw the confusion on his face. 'You have your mother's face. I have my mother's colour. She was Barolong, from Kimberley, and my father took her to Cape Town with him. When Jacob was born, he said he was a miracle from God and told the people in the city that he was a widower and Jacob was his son. My mother died giving birth to me, and he saw my colour and told his cook to raise me. He married a white lady, Jacob called her Mama, and they left Cape Town without me.'

Leon was staring at Tau. The idea that Tau was the son of a white man, and had a white brother, was confusing.

'What is your other name, then?' Leon asked. 'I am Leon Courtney, so you are Tau . . .'

'I am just Tau.'

'But what was your father's name?'

'Shepherd,' Tau replied at last. 'But I do not want his name.'

Leon yawned. 'Shame, it suits you.'

'Modisa,' Tau said slowly. 'That is "shepherd" in Setswana, the language of my mother and the cook. I shall be Tau Modisa.'

'What languages do people speak in Mafeking, do you think?' Leon asked.

'I only know what we spoke in the kitchen,' Tau said. 'But I think perhaps Setswana.'

Leon looked up at him. 'Is that why you agreed to come with me? Because you might find your people there?'

'I came because I want to learn to read.' Tau stood up and stretched, easy and balanced, as if he was standing on a pavement rather than a moving train. It made Leon feel uneasy. 'Shall we go inside, do you think?'

· · ·

Leon spent the next few minutes dividing his energies between not looking scared and avoiding a sudden and messy death under the clanking wheels of the train. Tau led the way, running along the roof of the goods wagon and leaping onto the next with the confidence of a circus acrobat who has grown bored of the applause. Leon watched and then copied him – his sprinting run along the gently curved roof, then his leap like a deer across the rumbling, crushing space between the wagons. Leon was so surprised to find himself clearing the gap that he lost his concentration and landed with a stumble and sprawl rather than Tau's elegant crouch, but any chagrin he felt about the landing was dispelled by the delight that he had managed the jump at all. He would have gone back and had another go, but Tau was already at the far end of the wagon, his hands on his hips, examining the track in front of them and the next wagon. Leon put his hands in his pockets and attempted to saunter along the roof.

'What is it?' he said as casually as he could when he reached Tau's shoulder.

Tau pointed ahead along the tracks. The sun had risen, bathing the world in the fresh light of morning. The landscape around them was furred with green, new growth from the first rains of summer, and was not as flat as it had been the previous day. The horizon was still vast, but low green hills had begun to appear, like ruffled waves on the surface of a pool. Leon narrowed his eyes to see what Tau was pointing at and saw a sort of unnatural bulge on the edge of his vision. Buildings, he thought, a town of some sort. They must find a new place to hide soon, before they were seen.

Leon went down on his hands and knees. Looking down over the end of the wagon, he could see that it was coupled to a passenger carriage. There was a door leading into the carriage, but it would certainly be locked. He sat down and rubbed his chin.

'We can't stay on the roof, someone will see us as we arrive in town. Do you think we could find somewhere to hold on down there before we get into the station? Perhaps some passengers will get on, and we can pretend to be with them.'

'I shall see,' Tau said and swung from the roof.

Leon leaned over the edge to watch him. When he looked back up, the town seemed to be much closer. A hot cinder flew into his eye and as he blinked and recoiled the carriage jolted and his hand slipped. For one second he thought that he was going to fall, blind and thrashing under the charging wheels. He seized onto the edge of the roof and tried to control the sick lurch in his stomach.

'Hurry, Tau!' he called.

'Come! I have a place.'

Leon approached the overhang again and twisted, slithering heavily down the rough boards of the wagon. He felt Tau's hand on his foot, guiding him to a foothold, and, after a few breathless and unsteady seconds, found himself rattled but secure, standing on the coupling bar. The sound of the wheels was deafening and the air smelled of hot oil and coal, but he was confident he would not fall and the dizzy speed and noise made his blood fizz in his arteries. Too soon the train began to slow and hiss and as it dropped into a sedate crawl, the boys could hear the sounds of people on the approaching station platform.

Tau and Leon jumped down from their spot and sprinted to the front of the train, keeping close to its shadow as it entered the station. Joining the crowd on the platform, they stepped into a carriage unchallenged in the confusion of harassed mothers, crying children and luggage. Tau touched Leon's arm, then nodded towards two young men dressed in tweed travelling clothes in a corner of the carriage.

'The newspaper men,' Tau said.

'They are the ones taking the boat to Durban?' Leon asked.

Tau nodded.

'Tau, we must follow them. And stay close without them noticing us. Do you think we can manage it?'

Tau grinned.

• • •

The ride to the outskirts of Mafeking was painful and humiliating. Amber shared the horse, a sturdy Basotho pony, with the lightest man of the scarred man's band. After much deliberation, the Boers had tied her hands in front of her and then roped her to the rider while he sat complaining in his saddle. Her back was against his and her skirts trailed down the back of the pony, making it kick out every now and then at the fabric tickling its heels. The rope bit into her chest and tore at her hips and she was sure it was no more comfortable for the man she rode with – shoved forward into the pommel of his Spanish-style saddle to accommodate her bustle.

After a couple of miles the ponies began to settle into a steady trot. Amber had nothing to make her life easier as a prisoner of war, nothing but the clothes she was wearing. She still had her pocketbook, true, but she'd emptied out the money and given it to Greta. All it contained now was a picture of her, David and Penrod – it was the twin of the one Penrod had given the boy Tau after the hotel fire. At least the riders would feed her. The idea struck a light in her mind like stone hitting flint. A prisoner of war was an expensive creature. You needed men to guard them, feed them, a place to hold them. Once Cronjé saw she was not Dr Jameson in disguise or the granddaughter of the old queen, surely he would want to get rid of her. He could not just let her go, and the Boers were too careful of international opinion to shoot her, but perhaps he would let her return to Mafeking. She closed her eyes and prayed, silently, in every language that she knew as the miles bled away, bringing her ever closer to the besieged city.

• • •

Cronjé heard riders were coming, and bringing an English woman with them. When Amber and her captives trotted slowly into the yard of the old schoolhouse, in which

Cronjé had set up his headquarters, he was waiting outside. A short man, stocky and black-bearded, wearing the usual dark waistcoast, jacket and corduroy trousers of the Boer fighters, he glowered at the incoming party. Amber counted a dozen other men with him, scattered round the yard and dressed much the same. The Boers wore no insignia of rank, just the occasional cockade on their caps in the colours of the Transvaal flag. Cronjé returned the greeting of the scarred man with a nod, his thick arms crossed over his chest.

The scarred man dismounted, untied Amber and lifted her from the pony on which she had been transported and set her in front of the commander. They began to speak in Cape Dutch.

Amber could not understand more than the odd word, but she could see that the scarred man, initially boastful, began to look more doubtful and then sullen under Cronjé's questioning. Amber rolled her shoulders to release the ache in her back from the ride and looked around her discreetly.

A scattering of bell tents surrounded the school and then, at a hundred yards distance, the main body of Cronjé's men were encamped. Hundreds of wagons spread towards the horizon, and beyond them one could clearly see a lowing, rippling mass of cattle and sheep. The Boers larder walked itself to the battlefield.

'Who are you? I know, even if this fool does not, that you are no princess.'

Amber realised that Cronjé was addressing her. She had planned to lie, but she could think of no lie which could not be easily disproven, and now she had set her sights on entering Mafeking she decided that the truth might be her trump card.

'I am Mrs Amber Ballantyne,' she said clearly. 'And I ask permission to return to my husband, Colonel Penrod Ballantyne, in Mafeking.'

A groan of rage went up around her. One of the men who had been sitting on the veranda sprang to his feet and pulled out his revolver, aiming it at her head. She had expected some sort of reaction, but not this.

Cronjé held up his hand. '*Gaan sit*, Ricus!' he said sharply. The man with the revolver holstered his weapon and sat down again, slowly, but Amber could still feel his eyes on her.

'He came in darkness!' Cronjé shouted the words at her, his breath hot on her face. 'He came crawling among us like a snake!'

The bayonet attack Sergeant Blake had told her about.

'The strongest lions hunt at night,' she said quietly.

Cronjé stepped away from her, disgusted. 'You are a spy, sent out by your husband to bribe the blacks for information and send it back to Mafeking. Ricus wants to shoot you and I stayed his hand. But perhaps we should shoot you? It's no more than the wife of Colonel Penrod Ballantyne deserves.'

The others seemed suddenly uncertain of how to react to Cronjé's fury, now that their initial shock at hearing her name had passed.

'I am no spy!' Amber shouted back, her voice ringing in the still air. 'Am I carrying messages? Did you find me drawing plans of your positions or counting up your men? No! I was taken while trying to seek a night's shelter away from the front with a family of honest farmers, like yourselves.'

Cronjé looked back at her over his shoulder.

'And how will all those European nations who are lending you their support react if you shoot a woman, sir? A kidnapped, innocent woman, shot without trial or process, while her hands were tied and with the flesh of her back cut open by a Boer whip?'

All eyes turned towards the riders who had brought her in. The narrow-faced man who had struck Amber with the whip said something in Dutch to the rest of the men, his voice high and angry.

Cronjé screwed up his face like a child forced to drink a spoonful of bitter medicine.

'Your actions will make me a martyr,' Amber said loudly, proud and confident. It was clear many of these men knew enough English to understand her. 'My name is well known in England, France and in Germany. Try to imagine my picture on the front page of every newspaper in Europe, under the headline "Murdered by Boer Savages without trial, without reason". See how readily their governments will sell you arms after that.'

One of the men behind Cronjé slouched towards Ricus on the veranda and whispered something to him, then shoved him inside the schoolhouse.

'We shall send you to Pretoria,' Cronjé announced after a few minutes of silence. 'They will decide what to do with you and the blood will be on their hands not mine.'

Amber had not expected such an outcome. She did not want to go to Pretoria. Far away from her husband and child, to become a bargaining chip, an embarrassment to her own government.

'I want to go into Mafeking, nowhere else,' she demanded. 'If you try and send me to Pretoria, I shall do my best to escape. The city must be two hundred miles away. Think of all the chances I shall have to run away. Send me to Mafeking.'

'You think we are so careless of your life, woman?' Cronjé roared at her. She felt the formidable force of him, the power of the man. '*Savages* though we are! We are pouring hell into Mafeking every day, Mrs Ballantyne, and we are not done yet. If I send you into Mafeking, it would be murder itself! Too much blood has already been shed by my men to offer mercy.'

'I do not care. I wish to be with my husband. Would a Boer's wife desert him while he is fighting for his life?'

The men were looking at Cronjé now, not her. He stared at her, then lifted his hands. '*Sluit hom in die agterste kamer toe*,' he said to one of his soldiers. 'The fate of Mafeking will be decided in a few days. Till then keep her safe and out of my sight.'

• • •

Two of Cronjé's men escorted Amber into the schoolhouse and to a room at the back of the building. They took her pocketbook and untied her hands, then shut the door on her. She heard the metallic rasp as the key turned in the lock. Amber leaned against the door and counted her blessings. She was alive and not on her way to Pretoria. David was safe. Jabu was alive. But then a bubble of anxious questions rose in her heart. How would David cope without her motherly love and protection? Would he know her when she saw him again? What if she was held for years? What if Greta ran out of money and they all starved?

'Stop it,' she said out loud to herself. 'Greta would give her life for David and he's better off with her right now than with you, Amber Ballantyne.'

Having calmed herself, Amber looked around her prison cell. The place had been used as a store and workshop. A rough sort of couch had been shoved under the one dirty, barred window, though what stuffing it still had was sprouting through its upholstery, and chairs with broken backs, three-legged tables and tea chests were stacked in the corner, with rag bundles piled on top of them. Everything in the cramped room was waiting to be reused, remade or burned as scrap. She sat on the couch, thinking about David and Jabu and Greta. They would be at the farm by now and Greta would be fussing over David. And, of course, her uncle and aunt would love the baby as soon as they saw him.

Amber worked through the tables until she found one which had four study legs and a pair of chairs which could be sat upon without risking life and limb, then she plucked a cloth from the top of a pile of rags and began to clean. She couldn't clean properly without water, but the work kept her unwelcome thoughts at bay. She worked until she felt the sweat prickling her skin, and then she kept going.

• • •

As the light faded outside a girl brought Amber a bowl of stew, a jug of water with an enamel cup tied to it with a length of grubby string and a hurricane lamp. She shook her head when Amber tried to speak to her, and scuttled out of the room as quickly as possible. The stew was tasty, rich with onions and barley. Suddenly Amber realised that she was ravenous. A memory of the butterfish that she had eaten at their dinner in Cape Town, before the fire at the hotel, returned to her as she scraped her spoon in the bowl. She almost laughed at the contrast between herself then – in a gay mood, diamonds around her neck, her husband beside her and the whole world promising her a bright and happy future – and now, eating her stew in a storeroom that had been turned into a makeshift prison cell, covered in sweat and dust and her own blood. Amber wondered where Saffron was at that moment. She wished she could talk to her sister, hold her hand. If only she could get some word to her. In her mind's eye, Amber could clearly see her twin in the palatial rooms of the Mount Nelson, sitting in one of the wide, comfortable armchairs upholstered in fabric imported from France, a leather-bound book in one hand, a glass of champagne in the other.

The door opened again, but not with a clatter this time. Amber put down her spoon and sat up rigidly in her chair. It was a man, alone. He was in his fifties, perhaps. He reminded her of Cronjé, except he was much taller. He held her pocketbook in his large, tanned hands and what looked like a novel. He stared at her with ferocious intensity. She felt her skin prickle, an instinctive sense of danger waking in her chest – she was a woman alone and he should not be in this room, at this time of night.

The man closed the door behind him, but he did not lock it. Perhaps, if he attacked her, tried to rape her, she could use the lamp, swing it at his head, Amber thought, and even if she did not knock him down, it might give her enough time to get out of the room.

He took a stride forward, pulled the photograph from her pocketbook, and laid it on the table in the pool of yellow light made by the lamp. The man jabbed his finger at Penrod's face. 'Who,' he said in a heavy accent, through gritted teeth, 'is this?'

Amber made him wait for her reply – one breath, two. 'That is my husband. Colonel Penrod Ballantyne. You all seem to have heard of him.'

His hand formed into a fist and he slammed it down on the photograph. '*No*, that is John Quinn. My *friend* who was a *guest* in my home.'

He opened the novel, *Waverley* by Sir Walter Scott, at the title page. *To Gerrit Vintner, my good friend, from John Quinn.* She recognised Penrod's handwriting and understood. This man was one of Penrod's sources.

'That, too, then,' she said.

He moved too fast for her, striking her across the face with the flat of his hand and sending her toppling sideways off her chair onto the floor. 'You do not even deny it?' he yelled. 'That this man, this *skelm*, this spider crawled into my home and abused my trust? For weeks? He is beneath contempt.'

Amber could taste blood in her mouth. The man's rage was murderous. Her mind was in overdrive. If Cronjé had decided not to shoot her, he could not want her beaten to death now. The girl would be back to collect the bowl soon. She just needed to stay alive until then. She scrambled to her feet and righted the chair, keeping it between her and Vintner.

'Did he steal from you? Did he seduce your wife? No, I know he would not do that. He used you to learn as much as he could of your men and your fighting strength because that is his duty and his profession as an intelligence officer.'

'Profession?' Vintner lurched towards her, grabbing the chair out of her hands and throwing it aside, driven on by his rage.

'Have you told Cronjé this?' she asked quickly, moving round behind the table. 'Have you confessed you had a spy under your roof for weeks and never noticed?'

He leaned forward, the lamp light chasing shadows across his face, making him appear monstrous. 'I thought he was my friend,' he said.

'I'm sure he would be, were it not for this war.'

Vintner lunged towards her, hands raised. Amber feinted in one direction, then went in the other. Running away again, when there was nowhere to run; it had been the story of her life. He grabbed hold of her wrist, slammed her against the wall and put his hands around her neck, choking her. Black spots appeared in the corner of her eyes. The last time she had come this close to death, she had accepted it. But she was a mother now. Forming her hand into a claw, Amber went for Vintner's eyes, and he staggered back. At that moment the door opened.

It was the silent girl. She looked between them, curious and confused.

Amber spoke fast, her voice husky. 'Mr Vintner brought me a book to read but he is leaving now.'

Surely the girl could not believe such nonsense. She stayed frozen where she was.

Vintner hesitated. That's right, Amber thought. There's a witness now. You'll have to murder the both of us.

Finally, he turned on his heel and left the room, slamming the door behind him.

Amber collapsed against the table. There was still water in the jug and she poured a cup and drank it greedily, her hands shaking.

'Please tell me your name,' she said at last.

'Rachel Malherbe,' the girl replied.

'I am Amber.'

Rachel picked up the bowl and spoon. Amber's wrist and neck were painfully sore. She tried to clear her throat, wondering if Rachel could see the red marks where Vintner's fingers had gripped her.

'Miss Malherbe, when you close and lock the door behind you, please could you take the key with you?' She hoped her voice didn't crack as she said it.

The girl didn't answer. She looked down silently at the bowl and spoon in her hands, then turned to leave.

Amber waited. The key turned. If the girl left the key, Vintner could come back and murder her at his convenience. She'd wake up and find a knife at her throat, then darkness. She heard a tiny rasp of metal on metal.

'Oh, thank God!' She ran to the door and dropped to her knees, examining the keyhole. The key was gone. She turned her back to the door, relief flooding her body and making her shiver as if she had a fever, then she wrapped her arms around her knees and waited.

• • •

Neither Cronjé nor Vintner came near Amber for the next two days. She paced her room, ate her meals and read her book. Once she heard someone try the door handle, late in the evening, but she could not tell if it was Vintner considering another attack, or a curious passer-by. The only time she left her cell was on her twice daily visit to the necessary house, accompanied by Rachel Malherbe who walked quickly and would not speak to her.

Each time they left the schoolhouse, Amber cast slow, sweeping glances across the camp. On the first day her impression was simply of a wall of men and canvas, but slowly she began to develop a picture of how Cronjé's camp was laid out. She could see no opportunity for escape, though. The old schoolhouse was surrounded by soldiers, their tents closely packed. Even if she could get out of her room without alerting anyone, she had no chance of escaping through such a multitude. She did not understand why they would not send her into Mafeking. Cronjé had saved her from being shot only to then say he was considering having her executed as a spy, before refusing to send her into Mafeking, claiming to be concerned for her safety. The complex codes of men baffled her sometimes. To kill her as a spy was acceptable, but once she had protested her innocence she had to be protected, even if women and children in Mafeking had already been killed by Boer shells. While she remained in the camp, her only protection from Vintner was a locked door. What if Penrod did something else to further enrage him? Or the men Vintner led discovered he had entertained a spy in his house? Amber did not think a locked door and a witness would stop him then.

Fear and frustration and her circling thoughts were driving her insane.

But on the third day of her captivity, as she was escorted to the necessary house, sweeping her eyes right and left, searching for Vintner or Cronjé or anything on which to focus her whirling mind, she saw a face which startled her so much she stumbled.

'Mrs Ballantyne?' Rachel said with genuine concern in her voice, turning round.

Amber smiled at her, trying to control the flush in her cheeks. 'Nothing, Rachel. I'm just clumsy.'

The girl eyed her suspiciously, but kept walking.

Jabu! He was butchering a sheep close to the schoolhouse. He gave no sign of having noticed her, but Amber was certain that he had. The rest of the day was a torture of hope and impatience. She saw no sign of Jabu on her evening march to the necessary house, but then, in the middle of the night, with the moon hidden behind thick cloud, Amber heard a careful tapping at the window and found him on the other side of the dingy glass.

'Mrs Ballantyne? I am come to speak to you.'

She pressed her face to the wall by the window. The window itself had been nailed shut, but Jabu was so close that she could hear him breathing.

'Jabu! I am so glad to see you. But you shouldn't be here! They'll shoot you if they find you!'

Jabu chuckled softly. 'What will they find, Mrs Ballantyne? I am just another kaffir to them, doing their chores.'

'Jabu, is David safe?' She couldn't hold the question back any longer.

'He is, and Miss Greta, too.'

Amber sighed with tremendous joy and closed her eyes.

'The baby's fever is gone and it is a nice farm, Mrs Ballantyne, that the Bauers have. Trees, fat sheep and good water.'

'Please, tell me more,' she begged.

'The aunt was so happy to see Miss Greta that she cried, and her uncle kept coughing and looking sideways, like a man trying to hide his heart's gladness.'

He made a little coughing noise, mimicking the old man, and Amber smiled.

'Oh, thank you. Thank you for coming to tell me.'

'It is nothing.'

Amber felt deep gratitude at having a friend so close.

'What is happening in the camp, Jabu?' she asked.

'Much, I think,' he replied. 'The men talk bravely and loud about their victory which is coming soon. They promise to buy each other whisky in Dixon's Hotel. They talk about the stores of champagne and jam owned by Mr Weil and how they will send parcels of it home to their wives and sweethearts. I unloaded three carts of fresh ammunition today, and they have moved their gun to this side of town.'

'Another assault, then?'

'I think so, Mrs Ballantyne. A great assault.'

'When?'

'Not tomorrow, but the day after. Tonight they are sleeping, tomorrow night they will be polishing their rifles.'

A thought struck Amber. 'That's why they are keeping me here. They mean to take many prisoners in the assault, and send us all to Pretoria together.'

'It may be. Good luck to you, Mrs Ballantyne.'

Then Jabu melted away into the night before she had a chance to say another word.

• • •

A little more than twenty-four hours after Amber had spoken to Jabu, the big guns boomed into life just before dawn, startling Amber awake from violent, bloody dreams. Rachel Malherbe came to take her to the necessary house and as she walked through the camp, Amber could feel the anticipation in the air – the younger fighters calling out to each other, laughing loudly, while the older men checked and rechecked their rifles.

Her guard was beginning to outpace her. She could not spend another long, solitary day locked in the schoolhouse, ignorant of everything that was happening. If she did nothing she would go mad.

A group of senior men was standing some yards away from the schoolhouse as she and Rachel returned to it and she recognised one grizzled face among them. 'General Cronjé!' she called out. 'I must speak to you!'

He turned his back on her.

'I am a nurse!' Amber shouted desperately.

The girl tried to pull her towards the schoolhouse, but Amber shook herself free.

'Let me help!' she insisted.

Cronjé said something to the men with whom he was talking, then approached across the heavily trodden grass.

'What do you want, Mrs Ballantyne?' He paused a few feet in front of her, as if she had some disease and he feared to put himself at risk of infection.

'You are attacking the town this morning. Let me work in your field hospital. I have training. I would rather make use of it than sit locked up in that room.'

'You will use any liberty you are given to try and escape.'

'I give you my word that I will not, not while the assault is under way,' Amber said.

'Your word is of no use to me.'

Amber spoke quickly before he turned away. 'I will not try and escape today, General, because if I managed to get close to Mafeking, soldiers who should be defending the town from your attack would feel honour-bound to try and protect me. Including my husband. I would be an unnecessary distraction and could cost them the day. However, once your attack has *failed*, I shall make every effort to escape, I promise you.'

Cronjé's expression remained fierce and determined. 'Now, that I can believe, Mrs Ballantyne. The attack will not fail, I promise you. But why should you offer help to your husband's enemies?'

He was a blunt man, and she suspected he liked plain dealing. She decided to tell him the truth. 'Simple. I will know how the battle is going if I am working in the hospital. If you shut me in that room, no one will tell me anything.'

Cronjé examined her narrowly. 'How do I know you will not do further harm to the fighters in your care?'

The thought had never occurred to Amber. 'That would be . . . despicable!' she said, her face flushing with indignation.

In the near distance the guns coughed and boomed while Cronjé considered. Someone called his name and he lifted his hand in acknowledgement.

'Very well,' he said, before adding some instruction to Rachel in Dutch and walking away.

Amber felt a sudden concern that her excellent plan was not so excellent after all. 'Rachel, do you know where Gerrit Vintner is today?'

'Not in camp today,' she said.

Amber breathed out heavily in relief.

'Now, come with me, Mrs Ballantyne.'

• • •

The doctor in charge of the Boer field hospital was a small, spare man in a dark blue coat with a neatly trimmed beard. Amber found him sitting outside the tented operating theatre. Inside, she could see a kitchen table and the air smelled strongly of bichloride of mercury. Field panniers around the edge of the tent had been recommissioned as tables for his instruments and large pitchers of water. The doctor himself was sitting on a school chair, his legs elegantly crossed, reading a small volume entitled *Wounds in War*. He looked as if he would be at home in London or Cairo, advising rich men on their gout and aristocratic women on their nerves, but he was incongruous out here on the great sea of the highveld, in charge of a circle of bell-tents clustered about a central fire, with a wagonload of straw outspanned nearby and a group of children sitting on the grass and winding bandages.

He looked Amber up and down, with a wry twist to his thin mouth, and when he spoke it was with a strong Irish accent.

'The fair captive, is it? You're a nurse? How experienced are you?'

'I'm not,' Amber said. 'Though I did help out at the hospital in Mafeking.'

He waved his hands, shooing her away like an errant chicken. 'I don't need some fine lady who's going to faint at the sight of blood here. Get away with you now.'

The children winding the bandages stared in fascination.

'I saw plenty of blood in Khartoum and in Abyssinia, and I haven't fainted yet,' Amber said. 'I was there when Khartoum fell to the Mahdists and worked among the wounded after the Battle of Adowa. I held down a man while his arm was cut off with a hot blade. I've seen gangrene and cholera and I can work better than any *boeremeisie*.'

The doctor spat into the grass. 'Now, that's a proud boast. And I doubt it. But I'm partial to a wager, so I'll give you the chance to prove me wrong. My name is Riding.'

'Amber Ballantyne.'

'I know who you are. A writer.' His lip curled. 'Well, you'll have more yarns to spin by the end of today. Perhaps you can explain to the British that they can't go round the world ordering free men about without getting their lily white fingers snapped off.'

'The British bringing wealth and expertise to the Transvaal have rights, too,' Amber retorted.

'I am not going to debate politics with you, woman, so stand down.' He closed his book. 'I'll let you work but I can't speak to your safety. That bayonet charge against us a few nights ago, which your husband led, skewered some good men. They hate him like they hate the devil and all his works. Even I do not want to speak your name. I think I shall call you Queen Victoria, since you speak for her.'

Riding's voice was bitter, and she did not reply. Setting his book aside, he stood and handed Amber a coarse and badly scrubbed apron. Then he nodded to a covered cart behind one of the tents.

'There's straw there. Get it down on the floor of the main tent. I've four in there who took wounds during your husband's attack and I don't see them getting better. Make sure they have water before today's wounded start arriving.'

'You are the only doctor here?'

'Only one for twenty miles. But don't worry yourself. Half the men won't come to me, not even if they're so full of bullets they'd rattle if shaken. Only cases we'll get are the ones carried here by their mates.'

• • •

Amber did as she was told, and after the straw was down she began filling the men's bottles with fresh water, the canvas sides of the tent glowing pale gold in the morning sunlight.

As she replaced the bottle of the last patient, he reached out with his left hand and grabbed Amber's wrist, pulling her towards him. He was in his early forties – sweating with fever. His other arm was splinted, black with bruising from hand to elbow, and his stomach was thickly bandaged, the skin showing above it discoloured and dark purple.

'I know who you are, woman,' he said in English, his eyes focusing on her face. His sweat had a rotten sweetness to it. Amber recognised the signs of a putrid fever. He would not survive.

'Your husband broke my wrist and filleted me in the dark. I am dying by his hand.'

'Can I fetch you anything?' Amber asked, trying to keep her voice level and compassionate.

'Anything you want to tell your man? I'll be seeing him in Hell soon enough.' He gave a sudden bark of laughter then muttered something more, as if talking to someone Amber couldn't see.

She tried to pull away but he had a strong grip, as if being so near death had given him some peculiar power.

'You'll have to wait for him there awhile,' she said.

'No, I'll see him *today*!' The man laughed again, pulling her closer, drawing her down until he could whisper in her ear. 'Even if the bombardment hasn't flattened the fort at Canon Kopjé, Eloff's men will take the flank, and Jacobs will drive through the Barolong Stadt. *Pow pow pow* with our pretty Mausers. The British won't even know it's coming.'

Again, Amber tried to pull away and again she found herself unable to break his grip.

'Trust me.' He was speaking slowly, his words coming out in one smooth sigh. 'I'll be shaking your man's hand and introducing him to the devil before nightfall.'

Amber finally shook herself free and backed away from the man. She looked up and down the tent, but no one had observed their exchange.

Perhaps it was all lies, some nonsense he had made up to frighten her, she thought, but if it was true that the main attack was going to be supported with two surprise waves, then she had to try and get word into Mafeking. The defenders would be stretched so thin that to have even a few minutes warning might make all the difference.

Amber left the tent. There was no way that she could escape and make it to the lines, let alone get through them. Jabu might be able to, though. He knew every possible route in and out of Mafeking from his time herding cattle. But she didn't know if he was still in Cronjé's camp, and if he was, how would she find him among the mass of men around the schoolhouse and beyond without jeopardising her own safety?

Her fingers brushed the scrap of blue ribbon from David's jacket that was still tied around her wrist and she remembered Jabu telling her that she should wear it for luck the evening before they had left the trading post. He might recognise it and come to see what she needed – if she could find a way of making sure that he saw it. Amber ducked round to the back of the tent, which faced towards the main camp, and tied the ribbon around the guy rope. It looked small, so easy to miss.

'Victoria?' The doctor was shouting for her. She span round, praying he hadn't noticed her tying the ribbon to the rope. 'I've heard rumours of clean bedsheets in the schoolhouse. Fetch them and give them to those wee ones to tear into bandages.'

• • •

When Amber returned from the schoolhouse, the scrap of ribbon had gone. Had Jabu seen it? She had her answer almost at once – he was walking towards the tent with a load of firewood on his shoulder. She gave the sheets to the children and went calmly to meet him, taking the fuel, and in a rapid hissing whisper told him what the dying man had said, watching his face grow serious, then angry.

'I will relay the word across the lines,' he said.

It was all the conversation they had time for.

'Thank you,' she said in Setswana.

'They are coming for my people, too, Mrs Ballantyne,' he said sharply. He pushed the scrap of blue ribbon into her hand.

'Jabu!' she said and he paused. 'Take it, for luck.'

He nodded and tied it around his wrist.

• • •

By the time Amber had carried the wood to the fire pit, stacked it and washed her hands – trying to stop them from trembling – there was movement on the road.

'Where's the doctor?'

Amber looked up to see three men approaching on foot. All three of them were wounded – to judge from the blood on their clothes – but the one in the middle was being half-carried by the other two, his head down and his feet trailing in the dust.

The doctor emerged from his tent and looked them over. 'Get your mate in there,' he told them. 'Then have Queen Victoria wash out and bandage your wounds.'

They took their friend inside, but when they came out, the taller one shook his head at Amber, said something in Dutch and headed back down the track.

'He says it's only a scratch,' the other man said in English. 'But I'll take your help.'

He pulled his shirt off his shoulder, hissing with pain as the fabric came away from the wound. The round had gone straight through the soft flesh of his upper arm.

Amber cleaned the neat, oozing hole with alcohol and boiled water. The fighter gritted his teeth, but didn't flinch.

'You've been lucky,' she said.

'Naa, I wouldn't have come in, but my mate caught one in the belly, and with me not able to hold a rifle right, thanks to this flea bite, I thought I'd drag his ugly old hide back here. But I'd give my best pony to be in the fight that's coming now.'

Amber started to bind his wound, and if he felt any pain, he did not show it.

'Shame so many of your boys are going to cop it,' he said. 'Should've let us come and take the place.'

'Mafeking is in the British Bechuanaland Protectorate,' Amber said and tied the bandage with a stronger tug than she had meant to.

He flinched. 'All right, lady!' Then he twisted his neck to examine her work. 'Not bad.' He gave a heavy sniff. 'I'm done shooting for the day, but I can lend a hand here. What do you need?'

'How about persuading your friends to stop shooting at my husband?'

His smile disappeared. 'How about you leaving my people to live as they see fit?'

Amber bit her lip. This was not the right time for a confrontation.

'We have water and fuel enough for now,' she said. 'Can you help get other wounded men to us?'

'That I shall, though I doubt you'll have many more customers from our side.'

He ambled off and Amber took the chance to breathe. She realised something had changed, and for a moment she couldn't work out what it was – then it came to her. The Boer artillery had ceased firing. That could only mean one thing: the Boer fighters were about to storm Canon Kopjé. Amber thought of the men crouched behind the thin cover provided by those old low walls. The Boer guns had been firing all morning, so the chances that anyone in the fort had survived the bombardment were minimal. Would Penrod lead the rest of the garrison out of town to meet the Boers? She pictured him, revolver in hand, urging his men forward and her heart felt squeezed in her chest. He was too brave and too stubborn, and they had so few trained men in Mafeking. Even if Jabu managed to cross the lines and warn the garrison their chances were slim. No wonder Cronjé's men seemed confident. Amber felt a wave of nausea shudder through her, seeing herself wandering a battlefield, searching for Penrod among the corpses.

'Victoria?' the doctor shouted. 'Get yerself in here!'

Amber returned to her duties.

• • •

Baden-Powell and Penrod watched the end of the bombard-ment from the lookout on top of Dixon's Hotel. The old fort on Canon Kopjé had been reduced to rubble, leaving a low sandbag parapet to shelter the few visible defenders. Stuttaford was keeping as many of his men under cover as possible while the shelling continued. The Boer riflemen had begun to advance ten minutes earlier and were now within five hundred yards of the fort but the rain of shells still hadn't ceased. Penrod only realised how tightly he was holding his field glasses when his hands began to cramp.

'How much longer?' Penrod said between gritted teeth.

'Give Stuttaford a chance, Penrod,' Baden-Powell replied.

As the words were leaving his mouth, the shell fire came to a halt. Stuttaford turned from the parapet and shouted a com-mand. Sheets of corrugated iron, half-buried in dust and rubble, were shoved aside and from below them, from the narrow trench scraped into the rock by Stuttaford's men, crawled the rest of the small force of British South African Police tasked with defending the fort. Two Maxim guns were being passed up and assembled, then moved behind the remains of the rampart on top of the low hill. The movements were urgent, but controlled.

Penrod swept his glasses over the approaching Boer troops. He estimated the force at more than five hundred men; they were arrayed in a broad arc and approaching the fort at walking place. Stuttaford's men were still manhandling the two Maxims into position.

'How many men has Stuttaford?' Baden-Powell asked.

'Forty-five this morning. Forty-two now if those bodies behind the sandbags are his only losses.'

One of the Maxim crew members stumbled and dropped an oak box of spare parts. Penrod flinched. He could feel it as if he were with them, their muscles aching and cramping after crawling out from the narrow trench, their heads sore and ears pounding from the continual bombardment that had kept them buried alive. Their hands would be clumsy and slow, their minds dazed and exhausted, and they could probably hear no more than a fog of dulled voices, an echoing ring and the thud of their own blood.

The Boers were walking steadily forward and beginning to bunch closer together as they approached the hill. In three minutes at most, the forty-two men would be overrun. With Canon Kopjé gone, Mafeking would be impossible to defend. Cronjé's men would take the town and then advance towards Cape Town and Britain's subjects at home would give up hope, humiliated and defeated while her enemies crowed.

Penrod watched the barrels of the Maxims being locked into position, the boxes of ammunition thrown open and the canvas belts cranked into the feed block. The gunners found their positions. Penrod could almost feel his own fingers curling round the spade handles, his thumb raising the safety catch and then . . . pressing down on the brass firing button.

The Maxims spluttered into terrible life and the arc of traversing fire from the easterly gun cut down the enemy in a long sweep like the swing of a scythe. Those not hit by the bullets dived immediately to the ground. Stuttaford had given the order to fire at the perfect moment. The Boer artillery could not begin shelling the fort again with the attackers so close, and the Maxims were keeping them pinned in position.

'Good,' Baden-Powell said quietly.

Suddenly, the westerly gunner fell backwards from his seat, a burst of blood exploding out of the back of his head. Penrod cursed the expert marksmanship of the Boer fighters.

The gunner's comrades rolled him away and the man who had been loading the ammunition took his place while another man set down his rifle behind the parapet and moved to hunch over the ammunition box. The front rank of the Boers was beginning to dig in, scratching some kind of cover in the loose soil.

A movement in the corner of his eye attracted Penrod's attention. Two native men were crossing the empty ground in front of Dixon's Hotel, one was obviously wounded and leaning heavily on his companion. The other looked up, spotted the officers and hailed them.

'See what's happening,' Baden-Powell said.

Penrod scrambled down the ladder and jogged across to the two men. As he got closer he saw that it was a man and a youth. The man was by far the larger of the two and the youth trying to support him – one of the boys who herded cattle round the town, avoiding sniper nests and occasional shells – was staggering under his weight. Penrod increased his pace and put his arm under the wounded man's free shoulder. The man winced in pain and looked at him.

'Jabu?' Penrod said. His white shirt was red with blood. 'Where is Amber?'

Jabu tried to say something, but his breathing was ragged.

'No, wait till we get you under cover.'

Penrod and the boy carried Jabu around the back of the hotel and Penrod barked an order for water and stretcher bearers.

'Fetch the surgeon,' Penrod told the boy. 'Fetch Anderson . . .'

Penrod examined the wound as the boy ran off towards the hospital and saw at once that a bullet had gone through Jabu's back and out through his shoulder, smashing through his collarbone. He had been shot from below, by a man crouching in a trench as he crossed it, was Penrod's guess. What would occasion such a foolhardy attempt to cross the lines? Penrod gathered the fabric of Jabu's shirt in his hands and pressed hard over the wound, trying to staunch the bleeding, then lifted his canteen to the injured man's mouth and let him drink.

He glanced up the street – a pair of orderlies were running towards them with the boy.

Jabu feebly pushed away the canteen. 'Eloff's men are coming from the south-west, this side of the railway, and more along the river into the Stadt.'

Penrod felt his blood run cold. The Stadt was well defended, but the line on the south-west was thin. 'How many?' he asked urgently.

'Many, many,' Jabu said. 'Eloff's men hidden in the grass like snakes.'

'You saw this yourself?'

'I saw . . .' He took a slow, painful breath.

Penrod hailed the cattle boy.

'Go tell Chief Wessels an attack on the Stadt along the river is imminent.'

The boy was off at a low crouching run before the words were out of Penrod's mouth.

Jabu touched Penrod's hand. 'Mrs Ballantyne . . . very brave . . .' he said, then his eyes fluttered shut – he had lost too much blood.

It cost Penrod every ounce of his own resolve not to try and shake him back to consciousness. One of the stretcher bearers had a satchel over his arm; he crouched by Jabu in the dust and began to pack his wounds with bandages.

'This man risked his life bringing vital information across the lines,' Penrod said. 'Treat him like he is Baden-Powell himself or answer to me. Do you understand?'

The men nodded as Jabu was laid on the stretcher.

Penrod watched them go. For one moment he allowed the fear for his wife, his son, the possible interpretations of those few words Jabu had spoken, to blossom in his mind. Then he closed his fist over them, jogged along the street and climbed swiftly up the ladder to the lookout.

'A considerable force approaching through the grassland to the south-west,' Penrod reported.

Baden-Powell swept his field glasses in the direction Penrod had indicated. 'Damn! I can't see them, but that doesn't mean they aren't there. Do you trust this native?'

'Yes,' Penrod said. An image of Amber with David in her arms flashed across his mind.

'I need the reserves to support Stuttaford,' Baden-Powell said. 'The police lads are doing well, but they are losing men fast, and the Boer keep on coming.'

The Boer attackers who had managed to find any scrap of cover in front of the fort were picking at the defenders with accurate fire. Any sight of a uniform showing above the parapet or between the ravaged defences was a target.

'The seven-pounders, sir,' Penrod said. 'And it must be now.'

He knew that if the attack from the south-west was going to come, it would be soon. The Boer commanders must have understood that they were being held at the kopje by now and would order it at once. If the defenders were lucky, however, and

Jabu was right about the position of Eloff's men, then the small seven-pounders might be able to hold them back.

'Go, Colonel!' Baden-Powell said and Penrod left him.

• • •

Lieutenant Murchesion had been drilling the gun-crews daily. It was time to see if he had managed to teach them anything. Penrod watched as the men unlimbered the guns and took their positions.

'Shrapnel, Murchesion. Probably twelve hundred yards. Between the railway and the fort.'

The lieutenant stared out at the gently waving grasses, then back at Penrod. 'Why?' he asked. 'I can't see a damn thing.'

'Do it.'

'Colonel Ballantyne, may I offer you the command?' Murchesion's voice was dripping with sarcasm. Penrod chose to ignore it.

'Very well.'

In truth Penrod was glad to take control. The shots the seven-pounders were about to fire had to be accurate to within a few feet.

'All guns! Load shrapnel!' Penrod barked. 'Ten degrees elevation. Trail right three fifty!'

The shells were checked and loaded and the guns positioned, then they waited. He had to have a target. Three or four minutes ticked by as they watched, listening to the rapid beat of the Maxims from Canon Kopjé and the crack of rifle fire.

'I think your information is inaccurate,' Murchesion said angrily. 'We should reposition the guns to support the men on Canon Kopjé. I've been expecting *that* order for the last fifteen minutes.'

No doubt B-P was desperate to give it too.

'No. The information is good, Lieutenant,' Penrod insisted.

Another minute passed. Penrod felt each second of it pulse in his blood. Then he saw them: 'There!'

The dry grass stirred – figures small and distant emerging and moving towards the town in number. They were more like thirteen hundred yards away. The target was tiny, at the very limit of where Penrod had been expecting it.

'They are there! But you can't possibly hit them, man,' Murchesion hissed. 'It's like hitting a postage stamp with a revolver across the recreation ground. Wait for them to get closer!'

'No,' Penrod replied. 'Our only hope is to panic them into retreat while they are still grouped together.' If he could land the first shells in their midst, the shock and confusion might be enough to stop the attack before it began. If he missed them, the attackers would scatter and continue their advance.

'It's impossible!'

Penrod allowed himself two seconds, then let instinct and experience speak for him. 'Number one gun, two degrees trail right forty-five!' he shouted. 'Number two gun four degrees! Number one gun, fire! Number two gun, fire!'

The lead gunners repeated the fire order, tugged sharply at the lanyards and almost in unison the guns coughed and rocked back on their carriages. Without waiting to see where the shells landed, the crews began to swab out the barrels and reload. Murchesion had managed to teach them something, after all.

One second, two, three ticked by with agonising slowness, then the shells burst and threw a cloud of red dust into the air. Penrod altered the elevation of number two gun by three degrees and gave the order to fire again.

'By God! You are a devil, Ballantyne.' Murchesion whistled through his teeth. 'I think you got the poor bastards.'

Some of the Boers were still moving forwards, but the horror of those sudden blossoms of deadly ordnance among them was completely paralysing.

The second volley was more accurate than the first. The distant figures collapsed and scattered. Penrod watched through his field glasses as men dragged their wounded comrades back towards whatever cover they could find.

'Fire!'

To the west Penrod heard the sound of rifle fire coming from the Barolong Stadt. The Boers would have no hope of getting through that warren of houses without support or the element of surprise. Penrod listened for a moment to the cries of triumph of the Barolong, and then turned towards Murchesion.

'Your gun crews are good, Lieutenant,' Penrod said. 'I'm returning command to you. See if you can reach the reserves on the approach to the Canon Kopjé, and drive them back.'

'Delighted you enjoyed making use of my men,' Murchesion said and began barking out orders to the sweating gunners.

• • •

P enrod returned to Baden-Powell in his lookout. The bodies of the Boer attackers scattered in front of Canon Kopjé were like worshippers prostrated in front of an ancient idol.

'The attack has been repelled,' Baden-Powell said. 'And Murchesion is driving off the reserves.'

Penrod picked up his field glasses and began to count the bodies on the Mafeking side, sprawled and unmoving. Already stretcher parties were jogging along the road towards the fort.

'Go and see that they have all they need at the hospital, Colonel,' Baden-Powell said. 'And I hope your informant survives. He saved our hides today.'

• • •

W hen Penrod arrived at the hospital, Jabu was still uncon- scious. He asked Anderson what his chances were, but they were already receiving the first of the wounded from the fort and the doctor only had time to shake his head doubtfully.

Penrod stood by Jabu's bed for a moment. 'Where is my wife, Jabu?' he said quietly. 'Where is my child?'

Jabu's eyelids flickered, but he did not wake to answer him.

• • •

W hen the first of the casualties were brought in from the abortive attack on the south-west flank, Amber had to hold onto the side of the operating table to steady herself.

One man, his shattered right leg hanging only by a tendon, died screaming as they tried to cut away his clothes. Another, gutted by shrapnel, was strangely calm and smiled at her as she placed a clean sheet over his exposed intestines. He was dead before the doctor even saw him.

'I need you, Your Majesty,' Riding shouted, and Amber hurried to his side. A man had been laid on the table, screaming and writhing, while the fighter with the shoulder injury tried to hold him down. The lower part of the screaming man's trousers had been blasted away and his leg was broken, the shocking white of the bone stuck out through the flesh in a jagged spear.

'I am here, Doctor,' she said.

The man's hair had been burned away on one side of his face and the smell of singed flesh filled her nostrils.

'Hold the thigh steady,' Riding said, taking hold of the man's foot. Amber placed both hands around the man's leg just above the knee, breathing slowly.

He glanced at her to see if she was ready and she nodded, then he pulled down hard on the man's ankle, bracing himself against the table. Amber's hands were wet with blood, but she held on as the man screamed and the bone slipped back into the flesh with a slick sucking sound. Amber felt his body go slack.

'He's passed out, lucky bastard,' Riding said, and turned to their new orderly. 'Get one of the women to wash the wound and splint the leg.'

'I can . . .' Amber said, but Riding interrupted her: 'No, I need you with me. Let one of the others do it.'

His orders and instructions came quickly and Amber moved in a trance among the torn flesh and gore. The morphine ran out after the second amputation and the straw under the table was soon matted together with blood.

She sluiced the chest of a young man with water while the doctor dug shrapnel from between his ribs. She put a hand on the man's shoulder and felt his blood warm on her hands.

'Doctor?' She showed him.

'Help me turn him,' Riding said, and when they shifted him onto his side they saw a shell fragment sticking out of his back below his right shoulder blade.

'Get over the other side and hold him steady.'

Amber ran round the table and put one hand under the young man's head, the other on his flank. Riding pulled at the fragment, Amber heard the foul sound as it came free and she realised with a jolt the patient had his eyes open and was looking at her. He coughed once and black blood ran out of his mouth and over her palm, then his eyes went glassy and still. Riding swore fluently while the body was carried away and Amber washed her hands, her mind numb.

Then, as quickly as it had started, the flow of wounded slowed down to a trickle.

'Fetch me coffee, Victoria,' Riding said. He spoke gruffly, but Amber knew he wanted to give her a moment away from the charnel house now that the worst was done.

Amber felt like a traveller watching a dry riverbed that, in its sudden spate, then decline, told simply and vividly the story of a storm further up the valley. As she stepped outside, she was astonished to see that the sun had not yet reached its zenith. She fetched the coffee and took the tin cup back into the tent. The doctor was sewing up a thigh wound. When he had finished, he dismissed the injured man with a wave of his hand, took the coffee from her with a grunt of thanks, and sat down heavily on the schoolroom chair in the middle of the tent.

It was clear that the attack had failed and that Mafeking was still in British hands. She began to gather soiled bandages and shredded clothing into piles and used the last of the water in the basin to rinse some of the blood from the operating table. She found herself wondering if the grass would grow thicker and more luxuriant in this spot having been fed with the blood of these men, and if the local people would know why. The image distracted her, so she did not notice at first the Boer commanders entering the tent.

It was General Cronjé himself and Gerrit Vintner was with him. Amber took a step backwards and kept her eyes lowered, but she could feel Vintner studying her. If he knew that she had tried to warn the men in Mafeking of the surprise attacks, she was certain he would shoot her where she stood.

'What happened?' the doctor asked in English.

Cronjé took off his wide-brimmed hat and wiped his high forehead with his sleeve. 'I am not here to discuss tactics with a surgeon,' he spat. 'How many men have been wounded?'

'I can't tell you that,' the doctor replied. 'I have treated thirty men, two of them lost an arm, one a leg, but at least four died before I could help them, and others may have died since, and God alone knows how many of your people are treating themselves with folk remedies and *dop*.'

'"Your people", *rooinek*?' Vintner said.

The doctor waved his hand in the air. '"Our people", then. To guess by other actions, if it rains at all I'll have four dozen more men turning up with pus-filled wounds in the next day or two. Half of that if it continues dry. But what happened?'

'The British had two seven-pounders in position to repulse our flank attack,' Vintner said, 'and a bloody magician firing them. They managed to dig in on Canon Kopjé, too. It shouldn't have been possible, but they did it. When our fighters approached they were ready with Maxims.'

Amber glanced up and found Vintner staring at her.

'And they armed the blacks!' Cronjé said with sudden heat. 'This is a white man's war, but your Baden-Powell is no gentleman, I tell you that, woman! He uses mines and arms his blacks. It is disgusting, not civilised, and they say we are backward. I will write to him to protest.'

Amber wanted to scream at him. They had sent armed men through the Barolong Stadt. Why shouldn't the Barolong defend their homes and their land?

'Shall I can carry your letter, General?' she said instead.

He stared at her with a mixture of disgust and surprise but did not reply at once. Instead, he turned to the doctor. 'So, Doctor Riding, has your nurse been of use?'

'What?' The doctor looked at Amber. 'Oh, Queen Victoria? Yes, she's done well enough.'

'A prisoner exchange,' Amber said quickly. 'There are Boer men in the town gaol. Why bother with the expense and inconvenience of housing me here, when you can send me into Mafeking with your letter and exchange me for one of your own men?'

The doctor swallowed his coffee. 'Viljoen is in their gaol. And a useful man.'

'You are so ready to give up your nurse, Doctor?'

He shook his head. 'She's still a Brit. And she just cost me money on a wager.'

Cronjé swung his attention back to Amber. 'You have courage, Mrs Ballantyne,' he said. 'But think about what you are asking. The assault today failed, that is true, but the siege continues. If we must be patient and starve and shell that hole into submission, we shall. How old are you, Mrs Ballantyne?'

'I'm twenty-nine,' she said, 'and I wish to be with my husband.'

'And does he want you with him?'

'Of course,' she said blinking with surprise.

The expression on Cronjé's face was strange, and she thought that he looked at her in that moment with a fatherly eye. For a terrible moment, it seemed he pitied her.

'I will think on what you have said.' He glanced back at the doctor. 'Viljoen, you say?'

The doctor nodded.

• • •

Once the tent had been cleared, Amber took her turn going among the wounded men with water and bowls of stew for those who could eat. Eventually, her silent guard came to fetch her and took her back to the old schoolhouse. As she passed the field hospital, the doctor was reading his book on war wounds by the fire and the children were rolling more bandages, ready for another day.

From the dirty window of her prison room, Amber watched two carts coming from the direction of Mafeking. Each had a long pole lashed upright on its side from which flew a flag of truce. She realised that these were the wagons bringing back the Boer dead. A grave had been dug in the shade of a stand of black bean trees along the road, and she watched as the bodies were lifted from the wagons and carried out of her view. She counted fifty-seven of them. No one brought her food that night, but she had neither the energy to demand anything, nor appetite to eat it.

She lay back on the lumpy couch and closed her eyes. As soon as she did images of the man with his abdomen split open by shrapnel flashed on her inner eye. For the first time she allowed herself to understand that what Cronjé had said about the failed flanking attack could mean only one thing – Jabu *had* got through the lines with her message. And so, to some degree, she was responsible for the terrible wounds that she had helped Riding treat.

'I did the right thing,' she said aloud to the darkness. She thought of David, the sweet-milk smell of him and the infinite softness of his skin. 'I am doing the right thing,' she whispered, swallowing to dislodge the lump in her throat.

• • •

Penrod had left word with the hospital that he should be sent news of Jabu's condition every hour. In the meantime, he went about his duties in town. He was arranging the burials of those killed at Canon Kopjé when Sol Plaatje found him at the gates of the town's small cemetery.

Penrod watched the young man count the graves, and raised his eyebrows.

'You are burying the Cape Boys alongside the whites, Ballantyne?' Sol asked.

'We are,' Penrod said firmly. 'What were your losses in the Stadt?'

A shadow passed over Sol's face. 'None. Montshiwa picked the place well. When we have warning of the Boer's coming and rifles, they cannot come close to us in daylight. Is it true that Captain Marsham is among the dead?'

'It is.'

'He was my friend, I am grieved to hear it.' Sol studied the ground under their feet.

Penrod nodded. Marsham had been popular in the town. 'A sniper caught him while he was assisting the wounded.'

'I have news for you Penrod. Baden-Powell just sent a message to the magistrate. We have been asked to release a horse thief called Viljoen from the town gaol. He is to be exchanged for your wife in the morning.'

Penrod's heart seemed to spasm in his chest, and his pulse increased for the first time that day. 'The Boer have Amber as a prisoner?'

'So they say,' Sol replied. 'Of your son, I am afraid, there is no word.'

• • •

T he next morning Rachel took her to the necessary house and returned her to the schoolroom with coffee and a roll. Amber ate and drank slowly, trying to eke out the pleasure of it and prepare herself for a day of frustration. She had read through *Waverley* twice during her captivity and was not sure she could face it for a third time.

She still had coffee in her cup when Rachel came in again. She handed Amber a sealed letter addressed to Baden-Powell.

'They will let me deliver it, then?' Amber said, delighted.

Rachel nodded. 'Yes. You are to be exchanged for one of our men. We go now,' she said.

Amber scooped up her pocketbook and the novel, put on her dark straw hat and tied the ribbons under her chin, her hands shaking. Cronjé's letter she put into the pocket of her short, dun-coloured jacket.

'Am I to say farewell to the general?'

'No, Mrs Ballantyne. Dr Riding will walk you out of the camp and to the front line. Then you must cross, and they will send our man back the other way.'

Amber felt a sudden fear as she imagined her slow walk from the Boer lines to Mafeking, imagined Vintner with a rifle in his hand, watching her. He had almost choked the life out of her with his bare hands. Would he be able to resist the temptation to shoot her in the back? 'Where is Vintner?'

Rachel looked at her coolly before speaking. 'The general gave me the letter an hour ago. I waited until Mr Vintner was sent to the north laager to fetch you.'

Amber relaxed. 'Thank you.'

Rachel led Amber out of the schoolhouse and handed her over to Dr Riding at the field hospital. Amber wanted to thank her properly, to acknowledge her help in some way, but the girl was gone before she could find the words.

Dr Riding and Amber walked together in silence a half mile or so northwards, towards the front line. None of the men going to or fro paid them any attention, but Amber noticed that the number of them carrying their rifles across their chests rather than slung over their shoulders gradually increased.

Riding stopped and drew a large white handkerchief from his jacket pocket. 'I'll have to blindfold you, Your Majesty,' he said. 'You're a clever woman. We shall send you into Mafeking, as that is what you want, but we shan't let you take a map of our trenches with you.'

Amber hesitated, then nodded and allowed him to tie the linen square over her eyes. It smelled of wild thyme and she had a sudden idea of a wife or daughter laying sprigs of the herb among clean laundry as she felt him take her arm.

'Now stay close to me. We'll go slowly and I won't let you stumble.'

It was a long walk over the stony ground. Robbed of her sight, Amber's hearing seemed to sharpen and she could hear the sound of horses and mules cropping the grasses, the shifting steps of men and the occasional thud of kit being lifted into a cart. Riding began to lead her in a zigzag, but she did not know if this was because they were moving through the trench lines or to confound her sense of direction. Amber breathed slowly and steadily.

'Tell Mrs Perkins her people are well!' a male voice called out and Amber jumped slightly, then nodded in the direction of the voice.

'And tell Charles Smith that his sister had a boy, ten days ago. Both well,' another voice called out on the other side of her.

'And inform Mr Weil,' said another, 'that Kurt Vulpine has paid for his Christmas pudding and will take delivery as arranged.'

That made some of the other men laugh.

'Enough chatter, boys,' Riding said, his voice was friendly, but it ended the shouts and the quiet became oppressive. At last they came to a halt.

'You know the story of Lot's wife?' Riding said.

'I do,' Amber said and swallowed. 'She was ordered not to look back, but she did, and was turned into a pillar of salt.'

'She was. Now, I'm going to unbind your eyes and you are going to walk, slowly, and straight ahead. You're heading for Canon Kopjé. You will see our man, Viljoen, coming the other way. I'm going to give you that handkerchief so you can hold it over your head. The General's orders to our men are clear. If you turn back to look at our position and trenches, they are to fire without further warning. If you run, they are to fire. If our man is shot, they are to fire. Do we understand each other?'

Amber wet her lips. 'Yes, Dr Riding, we do.'

'Remember, move slowly. The boys in that fort took a beating yesterday, and they might be a bit quick on the trigger. They know you're coming, but they also don't trust us. Keep waving that handkerchief, and don't look back.'

Amber felt his hands on the side of her head as he reached out to untie the handkerchief, but she placed her own hand over his.

'Thank you, Dr Riding.'

He grunted.

The sudden light made Amber blink. She felt the doctor press his handkerchief into her right hand. By the time her vision had cleared he had moved behind her.

'Remember, my girl, go slow, and do not look back.'

• • •

Amber could see the rise of Canon Kopjé in front of her, with the ruined fort above it. A mile beyond it smoke curled up from the chimneys of the European Quarter and also, to the west, from between the thatched roofs of the Barolong Stadt. She wished she was wearing something more brightly coloured – the rich blues and greens Saffron favoured would have been a good choice. Her long skirt was a chocolate brown and her jacket a dull straw, the same hues that the Boer fighters wore. How would the men on Canon Kopjé know it was her for sure?

Amber began to walk forward on the rough ground, then she stopped and pushed her straw hat off her head so it hung down her back and let free her long blonde hair. Surely that would make her look less like a Boer fighter. She started to walk again, waving her handkerchief in the air, her eyes fixed on the kopje in front of her.

A tall, red-headed man was walking away from the town, on a path parallel to hers. That must be Viljoen. He kept glancing over his shoulder, as if expecting to see a muzzle flash and feel a bullet between his shoulder blades. Then he stumbled.

'No!' Amber gasped. If the Boers thought that he had been shot, then she was dead. The blood seemed to freeze in her veins, making it impossible to put one foot in front of the other. This is what Lot's wife felt, she thought.

Viljoen did not fall, just staggered a pace or two then recovered himself and walked forward again. Amber was released, but it was impossible to forget the rifles aimed at her back.

'Tell Mrs Perkins her people are well, and Charles Smith's sister had a baby ten days ago,' she whispered to herself.

Somewhere on the ruins of the hill that stood in front of her, a sentry, exhausted by the action of the previous day, was about to catch sight of her, a single figure moving across the open ground. Would he panic, shoulder his rifle and fire before he saw the handkerchief and her blonde hair? They knew she was coming. The prisoner exchange had been agreed. But that didn't mean that an accident couldn't happen.

And Vintner? Where was Vintner? Amber wondered. Rachel had said that he was with the north laager, but what if he had returned? She thought of him settling into position on the heights to the south-east, or Fig Tree Hill. It was as if she could feel his hot breath on the back of her neck, hear the click of his rifle bolt – the impulse to run was almost unbearable.

'Kurt Vulpine wants his Christmas pudding as arranged,' Amber said, gritting her teeth. They must see her soon, and either shoot or signal. Her skirts whispered through the grass and the early morning breeze pulled at her loose hair.

Viljoen was nearly abreast of her now. They glanced at each other and he nodded to her. He looked very young, and his face was deathly pale. She nodded back. Their lives were in each other's hands, two strangers moving across the dead space between the lines, rifles trained on them both. What if he ran now that they had passed each other, now that he could see the Boer lines?

'Tell Mrs Perkins her people are well, Charles Smith's sister had a baby boy, Kurt Vulpine wants his Christmas pudding as arranged.'

Two hundred and fifty yards from the fort Amber glimpsed movement among the ruins on the hill. There was a flash on the ramparts. She paused, sure that the shot which would kill her had already been fired and this was her last moment in the African sun.

Nothing. No plume of dust kicked up at her feet, no crack of the rifle.

It had to have been the sun catching on a pair of field glasses, but Amber's instincts still screamed at her to run, to throw herself to the ground, to find cover, a hole to bury herself in.

Instead, she waved the handkerchief in broad arcs. And waited. Either she would be shot, or they would see the fluttering cloth.

Nothing.

She forced herself to walk forward. 'Perkins, Smith, Vulpine,' she said. 'Well, baby, pudding.'

She began to walk more quickly, then unable to help herself broke into a run. In the distance she saw a man, a tall, straight-backed figure coming from the town.

He caught sight of her and began to run too. Her heart leaped and plunged, a wave of hope and relief made her stumble. It was Penrod, her own Penrod. Let them try and shoot her now. She no longer cared. She dashed forwards and they met fifty yards east of the fort. She was in his arms. His mouth fastened on hers, and she drank him in, the dark scent of him, cologne and cigar smoke, the prickle of his moustache.

'Amber, my God! How did you come to be Cronjé's prisoner?'

'Didn't Jabu tell you?' she said breathlessly.

He held her at arm's length. 'He was shot crossing the lines, he only just managed tell us about the flanking attack before he lost consciousness.'

'Oh, God!' Amber exclaimed. 'Will he live?'

He took her in his arms again. 'It is too soon to know, but Amber, where is our son?'

She saw the anguish in his expression and in that second realised what he must have suffered in these past hours.

'David is with Greta. He's safe. I will explain everything, my darling, but please, Penrod, don't make me stay out here a moment longer.'

He had his arm tight around her shoulders and began to walk her quickly back towards town.

'We were caught by a group of Boer riders between the trading post at Setlagole and Mosita. Greta's uncle and aunt have a farm there. I had to make a choice, and I thought David would be safer with them rather than with us in Mafeking.'

Penrod's body seemed to stiffen and Amber understood with a shock that Penrod was angry with her. After the fear and frustration of the last days, she had expected joy, praise for her bravery and fortitude. She wanted to justify herself, tell him about the wounded man in the hospital, the letter from Cronjé, but he was walking so quickly she barely had breath to keep up, so she stopped.

'Penrod!'

He turned on her, grabbing her by the shoulders. 'Why did you stay at Setlagole, you little fool? God, I thought you'd be in Cape Town by now, and then Jabu came through the lines . . .'

She felt her own temper rise. 'How dare you speak to me in that tone? I didn't *know* you wanted me to run and keep on running! I thought that we were safe at Setlagole and we left as soon as we heard we might be in danger. I have information for Colonel Baden-Powell and a letter from Cronjé as well as news of your old friend Gerrit Vintner, and I have other messages to deliver in town. I would like to go to headquarters now.'

Penrod nodded angrily and began walking towards the town again. Amber followed, but refused to scurry to keep up, and unconsciously or not, he adapted his pace to hers.

• • •

Leon must have been dozing, even though it was his turn on watch. The clank of a coupling chain startled him awake, and he rubbed his eyes then peered through the heavy rain across the railyard. What he saw reinvigorated his cramped muscles, and he turned to shake Tau awake.

The sneaking had gone well. They had hidden with the mail and bribed a deck hand with the last of their ready money to get onto a steam packet named *Umzimvubu*, to Durban. Tau had been seasick on the boat.

From Durban, Leon and Tau had charmed and bluffed their way to Estcourt, the nearest British base in Natal to Ladysmith. But in that town they had come to a standstill. However they pleaded, the officers in camp and the civilians working on the railroad were adamant that they could not go any further. Leon had recognised Walter Kitchener, younger brother of Penrod's old commanding officer, on their second day in town and went to him to demand advice. He only narrowly avoided being carted off and locked in a storage cupboard until his parents could fetch him.

While Leon was trying this direct approach, Tau learned from some of the railway workers that armoured trains were regularly being sent on dawn runs as far north as Colenso. When Leon returned breathless and indignant, Tau suggested they stow away on one of these patrols. Once clear of the army, they could continue on foot deep into enemy territory where they could find another train to take them to Pretoria. It was a better plan than any Leon had managed to come up with, so they began haunting the railyards, waiting for the next sortie that might be arranged. They took turns watching at night, sheltering from the cold and regular rainstorms in empty carriages, and spent their afternoons scavenging for food around the camp.

And now their persistence had been rewarded. Leon pointed across the yard to a siding where an engine was being coupled to four armoured cars, two in front of the engine and tender, and two behind. The armoured cars were open goods wagons with four steel walls bolted to their frames to a height of six feet, with loopholes to fire through. The soldiers, the Dublin Fusiliers and the Durban Light Infantry, looked awkward and ungainly as they struggled up and over the smooth sides with their blankets strapped to their backpacks. The rain was falling heavily through the last cold shreds of night, and it was difficult to see in the dripping darkness, but Leon felt his hope turn sour and his excitement slacken. It would be impossible to hide anywhere on an armoured wagon – it was too tightly packed with men. Then he noticed another wagon being hitched to the rear of the train, three cars back from the engine. It was low and had no steel plating.

'What is that?' Tau asked.

Even as he spoke they saw a team of railway workers loading this final wagon with tool bags, short lengths of metal rail and huge wooden sleepers. With their work complete, they began to arrange a swathe of oiled tarpaulin over the wagon and two of the workers scrambled nimbly into the last armoured car. The patrol was carrying everything it needed to make repairs to the line, and now the boys had a place where they could hide.

In the commotion caused by the hauling of a field gun into the front car, no one noticed the two boys swinging themselves into the wagon and ducking under the tarpaulin. They waited, scarcely daring to breathe, listening to the rat-a-tat of the rain, until finally the engine hissed, the wagon jolted into movement and they were on their way. Leon shifted a wooden sleeper to the edge of the wagon so that he could use it as a bench and pushed the covering up between its ties so he could watch the gently undulating land pass them slowly by. They crawled forward, halting for long periods in small, abandoned towns before the train pulled on again. At last, they came to rest at a halt with a proper platform, and a station sign.

'Col . . . en . . . so!' Tau said, proudly deciphering the name on the battered board. 'This is as far as the train goes now, isn't it?'

Leon fitted his knapsack over his shoulders, pushing up the tarpaulin and causing cold water to run along his spine.

'Yes, Tau. The question is, do we wait, or jump now?'

'Now is always better,' Tau said.

Leon undid the rope loop holding the tarpaulin to the wagon and eased it up. Putting his head out, he glanced right and left, then slithered out, with Tau jumping onto the tracks behind him.

As Leon straightened and lifted his head he found his view blocked by a solid wall of khaki. He raised his gaze further and saw the uniform was that of the Durban Light Infantry, and between the damp uniform and the dripping helmet was the bright red face of an angry sergeant.

Leon made to run, but the sergeant took a firm hold of his upper arm. 'Oh, no you don't, lad!' the sergeant said, his fierce grip forcing a gasp of protest from Leon. Tau could have run, but he would never desert Leon, so he waited with sulky resignation until his arm was seized, too, and they were hauled to the front of the train, onto the platform, into the station office and the presence of the British officer in charge of the train that morning. The sergeant greeted him as Captain Haldane.

Haldane was tense and angry already, and when he caught sight of the boys and heard they were stowaways, he lost his temper. During the following four minutes the captain delivered to Leon one of the most thorough and humiliating dressing downs of his life. He was an irresponsible, stupid child, who had no business on a battlefield. He was endangering Haldane's men and their mission – they had the Boers to worry about, swarming invisibly in the hills around them, and no time to play nursemaid to a truant.

'We don't want a nursemaid! We are going to Pretoria and then Mafeking!'

'And why the hell would they want you there?' Haldane said, his face flushed with fury.

Leon opened his mouth to reply, but could not find any words. He had always assumed everyone in Mafeking, particularly Amber and Penrod, would be delighted to see him. The idea they might not welcome him was new and shocking.

The telegraph operator interrupted with a folded piece of paper. Haldane read it; his lips grew thin. He said something quietly to the operator, who saluted and returned to the front of the train.

'Forget this ridiculous idea of going further into Natal,' Haldane snapped at Leon. 'You are coming back to Estcourt and you'll remain in custody in the town until we can evacuate you. Mafeking! I've never heard such nonsense. As if they'd have any more use for you than I have.'

Tau noticed Leon's jaw tighten and his eyes narrow, so he nudged him sharply and made his eyes wide in appeal. An explosion of Courtney temper was unlikely to help at that moment. Leon relented and said nothing, though he still glowered.

'You'll have to go in the last armoured car, where the sergeant can keep a close eye on you two. How you will fit in, I have no idea.

Perhaps one of the corporals can use you as a footstool,' Haldane said. 'Sergeant, take these urchins back to your armoured car, and don't let them out of your sight.'

From ecstasy to misery in ten minutes. Pretoria and Mafeking had seemed so close, and now Tau and Leon were squeezed into one of the armoured cars with a dozen infantry men. All but the sergeant seemed reasonably friendly, and one private slipped them a half-bar of chocolate. Leon thanked him and handed Tau his share but the sweetness melting in his mouth could not compensate for his heartbreak. They were moving in the wrong direction. And once they were back in Estcourt, Leon knew it wouldn't be long before he would find himself back in Cape Town. Fate seemed to Leon at that moment unspeakably cruel, to let them get so far, then, at the last moment, drive them back towards the rage of his father. Rain-drenched and cramped against the cold steel armour of the car, he rocked to and fro, deep in his misery, his nostrils full of the smell of the soldiers, damp khaki and sweat.

The first shots hit the side of the car with a high-pitched clang, like pebbles thrown at an empty tin can. At first Leon didn't recognise the sound, and wondered why the soldiers were drawing back the bolts on their rifles and adjusting their positions. Only when the automatic cannons, the pom-poms that pumped out sixty one-pound shells a minute, started to thump in the near distance did he realise the train was under attack.

Leon felt his heart leap with excitement. The rattle of bullets hitting the steel became a continual storm, and the sergeant had to shout to make himself heard. Shells burst above them, puffs of white smoke and booming claps like tropical thunder. Leon stared up at them, amazed, until one of the soldiers shoved him out of the way against the front of the wagon.

'There must be hundreds of Boer out there!' Leon said excitedly, listening to the sting and rattle against the steel.

'Plenty enough,' the private who had given them the chocolate muttered, 'and I can't get a shot on any of the buggers. Keep your heads down, lads.'

The rapid crumps of the automatic cannon were getting closer and Leon watched with an otherworldly fascination as a shell tore through one metal side of the car and out the other before exploding outside. He felt the heat of it as it passed, a flash of deadly metal. The wagon rocked and the private whistled between his teeth.

'God, they are crawling all along the slope.'

The train picked up speed until it was rattling forward in a charging flight. Leon was thrown forwards onto the rough planking of the floor. He realised he could see the track through the gaps between the boards and for a moment the sound of the shells was replaced by the storming clatter of the iron wheels. Everything around him was sharp and vivid, the texture of the wood under his fingers – the smell of oil and coal dust, the sound of his own breath – then a deafening wrenching grind tore the air, the metal screamed and the carriage was thrown upwards.

Leon was in flight, untethered, his senses twisted and confused, like a speck of glass in Penelope's kaleidoscope being rattled and thrown into new patterns. He slammed against the steel side of the wagon and fell in a sprawling heap onto cold metal. The double impact drove the breath from his lungs, paralysing him for a moment, then the air returned in a gulping rush that tasted of earth and iron. He shook his head, trying to understand how the world had suddenly turned upside down.

A bullet slammed into the steel wall above Leon's head, striking a white-hot spark. Scrambling blindly into the nearest corner, trying to wipe grit and dirt from his eyes, Leon found Tau curled into a ball.

He shook his friend's shoulder. 'We've been derailed! Tau, are you hurt?'

Tau looked up, but Leon saw a blankness in his eyes as if he didn't recognise him.

Leon looked around – the wagon was on its side, and the men had been flung from it like toy soldiers from an upturned box.

The private who had given them chocolate was already on one knee, firing up the slope. 'Run, boys!' he said, working the bolt on his rifle to fire again. 'Run, now, and don't look back!'

Another soldier was sprawled against the floor of the wagon, his neck was at a strange angle and his eyes were closed.

Leon grabbed hold of Tau's shoulders and screamed into his face: 'Tau! We're going!'

Some sense returned to his friend's eyes and he nodded, unfolding his limbs.

'Now!' Leon screamed.

He shoved Tau to what had been the front of the armoured car and pushed him into a sliver of cover. The low wagon in which they had travelled up to Colenso had been thrown off the rails and turned over. Leon blinked, the telegraph operator was lying half under it, one arm thrown out sideways, and his eyes staring sightless into the grey sky. The line where his body disappeared under the wagon was a wet mess of red and purple flesh.

Their armoured car was on its side and twisted at an angle, half on and half off the rails, its great metal wheels spinning slowly.

The bullets thudded into the ground around them, throwing up fountains of wet earth and gravel.

'Stay here, Tau!' Leon said, then ducked round to the far side of the fallen car in search of more cover, but the bullets were flying into the earth here, too. Leon saw figures above them on both sides of the tracks, calmly firing down at the struggling men. A bullet hit the soldier beside him. Leon heard the smack of it tearing through the flesh of the man's arm. He was thrown against the wagon by the force of the bullet and groaned.

Leon moved to help him, but the soldier pushed him away.

'For God's sake,' he said through gritted teeth. 'Get out of here. It's a blood bath. Just go!'

But go where? Ahead of them, on the track leading towards Estcourt, he saw the cause of the derailment, a great pile of rocks placed where the track bent round steeply at the bottom of the slope.

It was a trap and the train had dashed headlong into it. Leon looked in the other direction. The engine was still firmly on the tracks, but it could not escape south while the toppled armoured car blocked the way. Haldane was barking orders, gathering a party to uncouple the fallen car and shove it clear of the tracks. Leon watched him talking to the engine driver, clapping the man on the back as the bullets rattled around him. The driver nodded cautiously, and returned to his position – steam hissed and iron groaned.

The sergeant who had found them was lying with his back against the car to Leon's left. 'Oi, lad!' he said hoarsely to Leon.

'Can you get my rifle? My leg's broken, but if you pass it to me, I can still get some shots off.'

Leon looked where he was pointing. The Lee–Enfield lay out of the man's reach. Leon pounced, sprawling across the cold, wet tracks, closing his hand on the butt of the rifle and then hauling it towards him and under his slim body. The bullets zipped and flew around him. Turning over, he crawled back to the sergeant on his elbows, the rifle slung over his shoulder.

'Good lad!'

The sergeant took the gun, loading it and preparing to fire, looking north and south along the track. They were pinned down. Until the track was cleared, they were cornered in a killing field.

'Son, you and your friend have got to get out of here, and be quick about it. Run up the hill and hope that the Boer decide not to waste a bullet on you.'

'I want to help!' Leon said.

'You got me my rifle, didn't you? Now, go! And that ain't just a friendly suggestion.'

Leon twisted around. Tau was where he had left him, his arms wrapped around his thin legs.

'Tau! Come on!'

The sound of his name seemed to rouse him, and Tau looked gratefully at Leon and twisted his limbs into a crouch, ready to run.

A sudden burst of white and slate blue obliterated the sky above them and pushed them to the ground again, but Leon was back on his feet at once. The smoke of the blast would hide them from the Boers for a moment and in the seconds of slackened rifle fire, Leon saw their chance.

'Now!' he shouted. He dragged Tau up the slope away from the tracks. As the shell smoke cleared, he aimed for a gap in the Boer lines on the hilltop, pulling and shoving Tau with him, his legs and arms burning with the effort. Leon and Tau scrambled and struggled through the shallow mud to the top of the rise. As soon as they were out of the field of fire, they fell to the ground. Tau turned on his back, staring up into the rain but Leon twisted onto his stomach and looked down at where they had been.

The sergeant had been killed by the shell blast, his right arm reduced to a mess of flesh. Leon blinked, shocked at the sight of the dead sergeant, and turned away. The sound of the guns roared around them and each shell sent up a fountain of smoke and debris, but Leon could still make out Haldane in the midst of the chaos, moving among his men, giving orders and encouragement. The armoured cars behind the engine were being decoupled.

'Why are they doing that?' Tau asked.

'If they can get the armoured car off the tracks, the engine will still have to push past that pile of rocks. It needs all its power for that.'

Two privates picked up the sergeant's body and carried it to the side of the tracks, while one of soldiers provided covering fire. A dozen men then began the work of shoving the armoured car clear of the tracks, straining at the wounded beast of the wagon with their shoulders. Seeing the bravery of the men, right in front of him, thrilled Leon to his core. They were heroes. The wagon rocked, swaying back and forth. Leon willed them to succeed. It lurched, then, and as the men yelled and pushed, it turned over. With a grind of gravel it slipped back towards the tracks. Leon could not see if it was properly clear. If it was not, the engine would remain trapped and none of the surviving men would make it through the Boer fire and back to the safety of Estcourt.

The engine huffed and heaved against the overturned car, and with agonising slowness, began to push past it. The sound of gunfire was drowned out by the screech of metal on metal. Finally, there came an ear-shattering squeal and the engine lurched forward and began to edge through the pile of rocks.

The tender was loaded down with wounded men, and more were being lifted up to join them. A shell struck the fat belly of the engine firebox and a great plume of fire and smoke exploded into the air, hiding men and train from view. Leon gasped; everything was lost, surely, but somehow when the smoke cleared the engine was limping forward, dragging the tender full of wounded with it back towards Estcourt. They had done it. The men left behind cheered.

'Surrender,' Leon whispered. 'Surrender before every one of your men is dead.'

Haldane was firing at the Boer attackers above him with his service revolver, pausing only to reload, even when a shell exploded no more than two yards from the tip of his polished boots. Leon flinched as more of the soldiers fell, but Haldane continued to issue his brisk commands and his men calmly kept up their fire. Haldane meant to keep the Boers busy until the engine and wounded were out of range. Another man dropped his gun and fell sideways onto the gravel.

'It's enough now,' Leon whispered desperately. 'They can't be followed now! They are clear! Surrender, please!'

As if he had heard Leon's appeal, Haldane holstered his revolver and barked something to his remaining men. They ceased firing and the fierce fusillade of the Boers sputtered to a halt.

The sudden silence was disorientating. Leon could suddenly hear the groans of injured men, and somewhere in the distance a bird began to chirrup in the damp air. Leon felt devastated, not from fear, but with sorrow at the British loss. They had fought so bravely, it did not seem fair to Leon that they be forced to surrender and be carted away like stray cattle. Some grit must have got into his eyes, and he rubbed them with the heels of his hands as the soldiers laid down their arms and Haldane offered his revolver to the Boer commander.

'How did you do that?' Tau asked quietly.

'What?' Leon said, twisting round to where Tau lay in the mud.

'The noise, and the bullets. The telegraph man cut in half. I could not move and all I could think was that it should have been us in that last car. We would have been cut in half. The blood and shouting, but you could move. You could speak and talk to that sergeant.'

Leon rubbed the side of his nose with his finger. 'I just did, that's all.'

The excitement that he had felt during the battle was draining away, leaving him cold and weary.

'I could not.'

'You didn't cry or scream or anything,' Leon said, consolingly, and noticed for the first time that Tau was shivering.

Already the Boers were packing up, shouldering the field guns back into ox carts, while the prisoners were ushered along the track in the direction of Colenso. Within half an hour, only the British dead and the abandoned armoured carriages were left to tell of what had happened.

'Stay here.' Leon patted Tau on the shoulder. 'I'll get our stuff and be back.'

Leon ran back down to the overturned wagon and found their knapsack, then scouted around amongst the wreckage for anything useful, avoiding the eyes of the dead. Some of the soldiers' packs had been abandoned on the trackside. He chose one with a blanket strapped to it, and making sure that it contained rations and clean socks, he emptied out all the heavy ammunition. The body of the sergeant lay close by. He paused, crossed over and looked down at what was left of the man, then crouched and closed his eyes.

'Go with God,' he whispered, then turned and ran back up the hill to Tau.

• • •

Leon and Tau followed the tracks back towards Colenso. Leon thought through the action as they walked and concluded that it was sending the armoured train in the first place which had condemned the men to death or surrender. The Boers could move, and they could hide. The landscape around the train tracks might look bare and flat, but those gentle undulations hid a thousand gullies and low hills which gave cover, and the Boer knew the landscape so well, they could move as if they were invisible. The British, in their armoured train, were a gift; caught on the rails, they could be assaulted wherever the Boer wished to attack. The British might as well have delivered their men to the enemy tied with a bow.

• • •

Leon and Tau wandered into the deserted town of Colenso as evening came on and Leon decided that they would make camp. The shop fronts had been broken down, the doors kicked in and the signs that men had made camp here before them were everywhere. Leon lit a fire in the fireplace of the general trader, and while Tau laid their possessions out to dry, Leon made a tour through the building. He found a small stack of notebooks and took one for Tau to practise his writing in, and a pencil, then he found a tin of soup which had rolled under a sideboard in the back kitchen. When he returned in triumph he found Tau examining *Huckleberry Finn*. The leather cover was bent, and the damp had made the pages swell. As Leon approached, Tau held it up with a look of amazement – a vicious-looking shard of metal had been forced through the leather lining and stuck deep in the pages of the book.

'Shrapnel!' Leon said, handing Tau the tin and taking the book.

'It went right through the bag,' Tau said. 'I shall sew up the tear.'

After they had eaten, Leon stared into the flames while Tau worked on the knapsack.

'When we meet the Boer,' Tau asked, 'what shall you tell them? You cannot say you want to fight against them in Mafeking. They will take you away like the men from the train.'

Leon scratched the back of his neck. 'I think I have a plan.'

• • •

They woke as dawn began to lighten the darkness outside and packed their belongings into the knapsack and soldier's pack. Tau had gone on from repairing the knapsack to adapting the pack to his needs, shortening and padding the straps so it would sit comfortably over his narrow shoulders. Now that he had a pack of his own, Leon made him a gift of the scarred copy of *Huckleberry Finn*, and Tau received it with proper seriousness, packing it with the reverence due to a holy text. The notebook and pencil he placed in his jacket pocket because he had seen the journalists on the train carry theirs in that way.

As they stepped into the street, Leon heard the click of metal on metal and turned sharply towards it. A young man, thin and long-limbed, with a heavy chestnut beard and a wide slouch hat shadowing his face, was leaning against one of the posts on the veranda, his rifle pointing squarely at Leon's chest.

'Morning, sleepyhead,' he said in English. 'And what are you boys doing creeping round Colenso?'

'Nothing,' Leon said. 'We were just leaving.'

The man shifted his weight, but kept the rifle pointing towards them. 'Not sure about that, son.'

Another man, older and with only a day or two's beard growth, appeared round the corner of the building, his spurs clicking and jangling. He said something to the younger man in Dutch. The story that Leon and Tau had decided on last night seemed weak in the morning light, but Leon launched into it with all the confidence he could muster.

'We're going to Pretoria,' Leon said, 'to stay with my aunt. My father was killed at Ladysmith, and he said if anything happened to him, I should go and find her there. Are you the *veld-kornet*?'

Leon was proud of his knowledge of the organisation of the Boer forces. The men of fighting age from each ward elected a *veld-kornet* to lead them, then they banded together to form a regional Commando.

'I am, and you are English, little man,' the older man said.

'My father was English by race, a Natal man by birth, and a Boer by choice,' Leon said quickly. He thought the sentence had a fine ring to it.

The two fighters looked at each other – they didn't seem convinced, but Leon was counting on the fact that the Boers would not want to be encumbered with a couple of children as they ranged across the country harassing the British troops, and so would be willing to accept any plausible explanation he could come up with.

'Your aunt lives in Pretoria?' the older man said, his English had a German tang to it. 'I lived in that city many years, perhaps I know her. What is her name?'

'Smith,' Leon said promptly, and the younger man snorted with laughter. 'Her name is Smith and her husband Piet works on the railways.'

The man frowned and jerked his rifle towards Tau. 'Who is the boy?'

'My friend,' Leon replied and their looks of suspicion deepened.

'Do you have family in Pretoria still, sir?' Tau said to the older man. 'We might take a letter to them, if you like.'

The Boers exchanged glances, and the younger of the two slowly lowered his weapon.

'I can't write, lad,' the *veld-kornet* said, leaning against the post on the veranda. Leon thought he was looking a bit friendlier now, his eyes had a weary amusement in them.

'I can write,' Leon replied, 'and I'm sure you wouldn't bother the military messengers with a personal letter, but I'd be happy to take a message from you. Perhaps some of the other men with you would like to send letters home, too? We could take them all.'

'My ma lives in Waterkloof,' the younger fighter said, looking at his commander hopefully. 'She'd like to hear a word or two from me and my brother.'

'I have paper,' Tau said, producing the notebook from his pocket with a flourish. 'What words would you like to send her?'

The *veld-kornet* shook his head. '*Ach*, I suppose it would cheer the boys to send a letter home. Come then, we're camped outside town, and we'll give you a meal for your trouble.'

•   •   •

They left Colenso two hours later with half a dozen carefully written letters folded in their knapsacks. They carried blunt declarations of affection, husbands reminding their wives of tasks on the farm, sons saying they were well and complaining about the food, a request for a waistcoat or a new scarf. Tau and Leon impressed the men with the care they took, reading each message back to its sender and checking the street names or directions to the outlying farms. The *veld-kornet* went so far as to sign with his X a page of writing saying that he had recruited the boys as temporary messengers, and asking that they be allowed to pass to Pretoria without hindrance. Leon was not sure how to spell hindrance, but it sounded impressive, so he wrote out his best guess.

It was that page that got them past the lookouts on the other side of the Tugela Valley. They picked up the trail of the British prisoners from the train the following day, caught up with them camping on open ground, and showed the guards their pass and the stack of letters they had already collected. Before the men and prisoners settled to sleep that night, Leon and Tau had added another dozen earnest notes to their parcel, and been given permission to ride on the train taking the British prisoners to Pretoria. The Boer guarding the British officers was so impressed with Leon's penmanship, he even allowed him to speak briefly to Haldane. The Captain looked miserable, but his relief at seeing Leon unharmed and free was palpable.

'You still insist on this foolish plan to reach Mafeking?' he asked. 'I suppose I can do no more than wish you luck now.'

Leon felt his conscience stir uneasily. 'Sir, if you do have the chance to send a message back to the British, might you just say that Tau and I are well?'

'I shall. Thinking of your poor mother picking through the corpses at the armoured train giving you pause, is it?'

Leon had not imagined such a concrete image, and it struck him deep in his heart.

'Don't worry, lad,' Haldane said, passing a hand over his unshaven chin. 'My lieutenant was injured and safe on that engine when I left him. Private Green saw you and your friend taking cover on top of the hill and told us you were safe. They'll have got the message back.'

Leon was surprised at the power of the relief which swept through him.

'Thank you, sir. Anything we can do for you?'

'Since you won't go home, then no.' He looked at Leon, then grinned. It made him seem much younger all of a sudden. 'You're pretty good under fire though, and took care of your friend. How about when you get your first commission, you drop me a line?'

Leon beamed and managed a credible salute. The Boer guard growled and Leon left to find Tau before his goodwill was exhausted.

• • •

Two days after the failed assault on Mafeking, Amber wrote to Mrs Weil in Cape Town, giving her an account of her time as a prisoner in the Boer camp and the action that had taken place while she was working alongside Riding in the field hospital. Mrs Weil obviously thought Amber's letter too important and entertaining to keep to herself and shared it with a newspaper editor of her acquaintance.

Two weeks later, a runner managed to cross the Boer lines in darkness with, among other things, a message from the editor of *The Daily Chronicle* – an edited version of Amber's letter had resulted in a doubling of their usual circulation, and he was eager to publish any other news of the siege or impression of the people of Mafeking that she could get to them. This new focus helped Amber's spirits. She knew that little David was safe and loved, but the continual physical ache created by his absence was unbearable. Amber had volunteered at the hospital, throwing herself into her duties to help her distract herself from her feelings, and even though she had been encouraged to hear two of the Irish nuns whispering in their rolling Irish brogues that Mrs Ballantyne was shaping up to be a good nurse, she knew that writing for *The Daily Chronicle* offered her a way of truly making a difference.

Jabu recovered slowly and was amazed to hear he was the hero of the town. On the day after he woke, he took Amber's hand and pressed the blue ribbon from David's jacket into her fingers. She burst into tears when she saw it, as Jabu reminded her how nice the farm was where David and Greta were sheltering, and how safe. She hugged him and tied the ribbon around her wrist again.

The nurses who were not nuns were a lively bunch, and once they had learned that they didn't need to treat Amber as a grand lady, they quickly grew fond of her. They formed the habit of meeting for tea or a glass of beer at Dixon's Hotel after their duties were done for the day, and, as the newspaper men were often in attendance, they made a merry party. The men told their stories, the young women laughed along, and Amber played the indulgent chaperone.

In the days since the battle of Canon Kopjé, Amber had noticed that Captain Stuttaford seemed to be spending more and more of his time at Dixon's. He didn't join their crowd, but would remain at the bar, occasionally talking to one man or another from the town, drinking steadily from the bottle of whisky that was always at his elbow. Sometimes Amber thought he was watching her, but whenever she turned towards him, he was staring into his glass again.

•   •   •

t was the end of November when Penrod told Amber, as they sat together over their modest supper, that General Cronjé had left Mafeking and taken most of his men with him.

Amber looked hopeful. 'Will you attack the men that are left, then?'

Penrod shook his head and pushed away his empty plate. 'No. They still have two thousand men and all their artillery. We cannot defeat them in the field. And we cannot break out. To do so would be to sacrifice the town to them.'

'So we are stuck here. But the British reinforcements have all arrived in South Africa now, haven't they? The war and the siege cannot last much longer.'

'I hope not,' Penrod said. 'But until the relief forces reach us, we must put up with the shelling and the snipers.'

'And the rain, and the heat. Though it is wonderful to see the land green.' Amber paused. 'We should do something for morale,' she added. 'Something to take people's minds off their situation. Is Cronjé's replacement going to keep the Sunday truce?'

'That is what we are told,' he replied, watching the soft lines of her face, his eye catching on the scrap of blue ribbon round her wrist. It was a strange quirk of the siege that the Boers believed strongly that no non-religious activity should take place on a Sunday and it was therefore a great sin to shell or shoot the inhabitants on this day.

'Good. I shall see what can be arranged.' She plucked at a loose thread on the tablecloth. 'And Penrod, so you know Captain Stuttaford?'

'I do.'

'Can you get him off the frontline? I'm not sure he's well.'

'Stuttaford must do his duty like the rest of us.'

'But it is not wise to drive men beyond their limits, surely.'

'How else are we to know what a man's limits are?' He spoke lightly, but Amber could hear a warning note in his voice.

He had continued to keep her at a distance since her reappearance in Mafeking, treating her, in the day at least, with a careful formality. She responded by treating him in the same way. She looked at him now with longing, but dared say no more about Stuttaford.

• • •

Amber began planning a Sunday entertainment, and recruited Trooper Cressy to help her. He was eager to do so and proved useful. She arranged a talent show with the nurses while Cressy organised cricket and soccer matches, pitching the Town against the Regiment. The editor of *The Mafeking Mail*, a news-sheet for the town now published daily, shelling allowing, refereed the sporting events. He did so with rough good humour, and the parade ground echoed with the cheers and groans of the populace.

The Masonic Lodge was chosen as a venue for the evening's entertainment, and as it filled with cigar smoke and laughter, Susan and Barbara, two of the civilian nurses, performed half a dozen music-hall numbers to ecstatic applause. Amber persuaded each squadron of the Protectorate Regiment to put on skits or musical numbers of their own, and as the men fumbled and blushed and played up to the enthusiastic crowd, she awarded prizes based on the volume of the cheers.

The evening was chaotic, ridiculous and a great success. It was also perfectly timed – the news from the frontline was bad, and the mood of the town had taken a downward turn in the previous week. As Amber looked around the hall she noticed Baden-Powell leaning against the back wall with Penrod at his side.

When Amber finally escaped the stage to laughter and applause and ushered on Susan and Barbara for the evening's finale, she circled towards the back of the room and joined the men. Baden-Powell nodded to her with a warm smile, then after a final word to Penrod, he left them.

Penrod slipped his arm around her waist and pulled her towards him with the affection of loving husband. 'Baden-Powell told me that he thinks you are worth a squadron to this town,' he whispered into her ear. His moustache tickled her skin, making her squirm deliciously against his side. 'And you are requested to put on something along these lines every week. I think he is almost as glad as I am that you made it back.' Out of sight of the cheering crowd he ran his hand over the curve of her hip. 'Almost.'

'Are you really glad I am here, Penrod?' she asked.

'Amber . . .?' He said it with a stern frown, moving his hands away from her waist and stepping back. 'Everyone is glad you are here. News about David and Greta in Mosita is received with as much pleasure as news from the front.'

Her triumph turned to bitter bile in her mouth.

Ned Cecil struck up the National Anthem on the battered piano in front of the stage. Civilians and soldiers jumped to their feet and sang the familiar words with such force and fervour that the walls of the hall seemed to shake and the corrugated iron roof lift into the evening sky.

Amber tried to smile and join in. When she turned around, Penrod had gone.

• • •

Penrod slipped out of the hall and made his way towards the Barolong Stadt. The people who lived there remained crucial to the defence of Mafeking and Penrod had taken the role of an informal liaison between Chief Wessels and Baden-Powell, though he spent most of his time with Sol and Silas, or with Jabu's family. These social visits were part of that role – they did not always have formal business to conduct, but Penrod traded hunting stories on the veranda of the chief's home or discussed literature with Sol several times each week, and he could almost always be found with one or other of them in the Stadt on a Sunday evening.

The moon was full and high. Taking advantage of the relative peace, Penrod decided to walk along the Molopo River before returning home. It was a mercurial stretch of water. Further out of the town it poured through wide, shallow pools, but as it neared the Stadt it cut itself a deeper, narrower channel and switched in sharp turns north and south. Mud and shingle collected in the lee of low riverbanks, thick with thorn bushes and tangled greenery.

Penrod exchanged a few words with the men at the pickets which overlooked this section of the defensive perimeter, then continued along the edge of the river. He moved easily through the moon-shade, sure-footed over the rocky shore, enjoying being unseen and alone in the cool of the night, listening to the movement of the water and breathing in the scent of the dew-damp earth.

Penrod had never suffered the full strain of a siege before. While Saffron and Amber were trapped in Khartoum, he had continually slipped through the lines, trekking over the desert and carrying news between the besieged and the relief column or his masters in Cairo. He had not understood how being confined in this way was like a slow pressure, a strangulation. No wonder the nerves of some of the men were strained.

In that moment, he heard the sudden click of the hammer of a revolver being drawn back.

'I do not think I believed it until now,' a voice said. 'Even after talking with your wife.'

Penrod turned, hands raised, his boots shifting the pebbles under his feet in a soft series of clicks, as the shape of a man emerged from the low trees which lined the banks. For a moment the only sound was the running water and the rippling sigh of the foliage in the faint breeze.

'Gerrit Vintner. How did you find me?'

Vintner kept his distance, but held his revolver steady, aiming it at Penrod's belly. 'When you were my guest, you enjoyed walking by the river on my property. I have watched you coming and going from the Stadt many times. This time, I decided to risk crossing the lines to meet you.'

Penrod lowered his hands. Vintner was clear of the shadows now, disgust transfiguring his face. Amber had told Penrod of Vintner's rage at discovering how he had been deceived and it would seem that his feelings hadn't mellowed in the intervening weeks.

'I did my job,' Penrod said calmly. 'It is not the first time such things have happened, it will not be the last and I feel no need to apologise or explain myself to you.'

'My friend John Quinn is a liar. Worse, he is a lie.' Vintner stared at him. 'You have no right to live. None of you. I told Cronjé you were liars, that we could take Mafeking with one assault.'

'We beat you back,' Penrod replied.

'Luck! Sheer chance! Cronjé is too careful with his men. If we had launched an attack from the north, you would have crumbled in on yourselves! But he sees a dozen men killed by your seven-pounders and his faith fails. He had six *thousand* fighters!'

Penrod said nothing. Vintner was right, but Penrod saw no reason to tell him that. Vintner appeared to want to talk rather than try to kill him at once. Penrod took a cheroot from the pocket of his tunic and lit it.

'And now,' Vintner said, his voice shaking, 'your treachery has murdered my family.'

'Nonsense,' Penrod replied, flicking his match into the twisting waters of the river.

Vintner took a step forward, lifting his revolver. He was still too far away for Penrod to reach him, but only just.

'Truth! Mrs Ballantyne's account of her capture and the assault on Mafeking was published in London and illustrated with your wedding photograph.'

Penrod raised an eyebrow. 'Indeed. I understand it was a popular story. The British love a heroine, and when that heroine is as beautiful as my wife, naturally they print her portrait. But she wrote of the Boer fighters with grace and restraint.'

Another step forward. Vintner's rage was his weakness. That dark, all-embracing anger had once been Penrod's Achilles heel. He recognised it well.

'You think my friends in Pretoria did not recognise you?'

The thought had not crossed Penrod's mind. 'An embarrassment for you, I am sure.'

'My wife was a proud woman,' Vintner said in a bitter, choked voice. 'She did not write to me herself but the day after news of this story reached Pretoria she took to her bed with a fever and died three days later.'

'Coincidence,' Penrod said shortly. 'People only ever die of shame in novels. Your wife was ill. My condolences for your loss, but the idea that I am in some way responsible is ridiculous.'

Vintner inched forward. 'They have taken my farms,' he said. 'I told you I owed my brother-in-law money, but when I had standing among my people, he could not touch me. The day my enemies saw *your* photograph that protection disappeared. I received word last night from some lemon-sucking lawyer in Pretoria: my brother-in-law has thrown my daughter out of the house, to live with my oldest sister, fired my workers and now he is sleeping under the sheets my wife sewed in her final days of health.'

His voice trembled and broke and at the same moment the muzzle of his revolver wavered. Springing forward, Penrod drove his shoulder into Vintner's chest, forcing him to fire blindly. Penrod felt the bullet explode the air as the force of his attack brought Vintner down heavily on the rocky ground. Seizing Vintner's wrist, he smashed the hand that held the gun – once, twice, three times – into the rocks, while the larger man was still dazed. Vintner yelled, the bones of his fingers snapping, and the gun fell from his grip.

Vintner struck back with his left hand, a closed fist with the power of madness behind it, knocking Penrod sideways and onto his back. Vintner rolled on top of him and his left hand closed around Penrod's throat.

The force of his hold was so powerful, so immediate, that black spots formed in front of Penrod's eyes. He gasped and writhed, the rocks pressing into his back, his fingers searching for anything he could use to break Vintner's grip. He touched the end of his smouldering cheroot, knocked from his fingers in the first moments of the fight. Clutching it, he drove it into Vintner's cheek and heard the hiss of the Boer's flesh burning. Vintner screamed and bucked away, but he kept his grip on Penrod's throat.

Penrod struck up with his knee into Vintner's groin, pushing all the air out of the man's lungs, reaching for the knife he knew that Vintner always carried on his belt. As his fingers seized the leather-wrapped handle, he struck his elbow up and into the man's jaw, prising away his weakening grip on his throat and throwing his weight sideways. They rolled over. Now Penrod was on top of him, but Vintner blocked his knife hand with his forearm. The blade hovered above Vintner's throat.

'Yield, Vintner! For your daughter's sake!' Penrod hissed between his teeth.

'Never! I will kill you or haunt you, *John Quinn*.' He scrabbled with the fingers of his damaged right hand, closed them round a rock and slammed it into the side of Penrod's head.

Penrod felt a starburst of pain and was thrown sideways by the force of the blow. He could not breathe, could not see Vintner, but he knew that he would be trying to stand, so he could raise the rock again and beat out Penrod's brains. And if he couldn't stand, he would try and pin him where he lay and do the same. Penrod tensed every muscle in his body and rolled himself over onto his back, bringing his arm up across his chest, jabbing upwards with the last of his strength with Vintner's own blade. The Boer's knife did the rest, slipping between Vintner's ribs and into his heart as he lunged forward, his weight crashing down on Penrod's spine.

Penrod saw Vintner's face change. Rage, realisation, then, as the blood began to flow from his mouth, his expression became blank, and he collapsed finally on Penrod's body like an exhausted lover.

The blood from Gerrit Vintner's wound flowed between the stones on the shore and joined the waters of the Molopo, making its way on into the heart of Africa.

Eventually, Penrod rolled Vintner's corpse away and got unsteadily to his feet, leaving the body where it lay. He made his way back along the river towards HQ. High clouds were stretched across the moon and Penrod was grateful for the shadow that they provided – he did not want any of his fellow officers to see him, battered and bruised, his uniform soaked in blood.

Back at HQ, Penrod greeted the night watch perfunctorily – saluting and pushing past the man before he could ask any questions. He went inside and found his way to the bathroom. He was still bleeding from where Vintner had hit him with the stone, the blood had clotted thick and black in his hair.

After washing as best he could, Penrod changed his uniform and left for home.

• • •

Amber was on her way to Dixon's when Penrod arrived back at their cottage. She was wondering if two of the British South African Police in her care would survive their wounds. Most of the men shot with the high velocity Mauser bullets recovered with remarkable speed if no vital organ was damaged, but these two boys had been hit by ricochets and sepsis had set in. The doctor had confessed that he was not hopeful that they would make it through the night.

The food at the hospital was nourishing – the vegetables came from the market garden on the island in the river and the meat from the Barolong herds – but Amber thought those recuperating would do better with milk fresh from the cow. She would speak to Ned about buying a milk cow or two from the Barolong and a boy to look after them. The boy would be able to take a few pennies home to his mother, and the men recovering would have the benefits of the milk straight from the animal. Occupied with her plan, Amber strayed into the light coming from one of the hotel's windows and at once she heard a rip in the air and the dull crack of a Mauser bullet splintering the planking of the wall next to her. She recoiled into the darkness, her heart racing, cursing her carelessness, then moved slowly round the back of the building and into the long bar which stretched across the front of the hotel.

Barbara and Susan, were waiting for her and Barbara immediately saw the terrified look in her eyes.

'Lively out there this evening, isn't it, Amber, dearie?' she said, pouring tea as she spoke.

'They are trying to catch runners crossing the lines,' Susan said. 'But if they can't find any they start taking potshots at the townsfolk.'

Amber sat down and took a sip of tea. She was ashamed to see her cup rattle in the saucer as she put it down. 'The worst thing is,' she said, 'that if that bullet had hit me, my last thought on earth would have been about a milk cow.'

For some reason her statement struck them all as very funny, and when Angus Hamilton, correspondent of *The Times*, arrived in the bar, he found them wiping tears of laughter from their eyes. They told him the story and he found it amusing, too. In fact, he insisted that they share a bottle of champagne to celebrate Amber's avoidance of such an ignominious end. He summoned Mrs Peters, the manager of the bar, and when she'd also had a laugh at the story, he sent her to the cellars to fetch the best vintage Dixon's had to offer. Stuttaford watched them from his stool, but shook his head in refusal when Hamilton invited him to join them.

After a few minutes Mrs Peters returned and was carrying the celebratory bottle across the front of the bar when suddenly it shattered and the room filled with the yeasty, toasted smell of champagne. Mrs Peters stared, amazed, at the broken neck in her hand while the vintage fizzed in a pool at her feet.

'Mrs Peters, move away from the door!' Amber shouted, but it was already too late.

Mrs Peters was still looking at her, uncomprehending, when the sniper's second bullet struck her in the neck just below the jaw and she crumpled to the floor among the broken glass. Hamilton reached her first, catching her under the arms and dragging her back towards their table. Amber snatched up linen napkins and as Hamilton half-fell into his chair, tried desperately to staunch the bleeding. Barbara ran to fetch the doctor while Susan held Mrs Peters steady.

Mrs Peters had lived in Mafeking for her entire life and had worked at Dixon's for ten years. She knew every customer by name and had welcomed the arrival of Colonel Baden-Powell and his men. For her, it was as if the town had finally been put on the map. She was proud of Dixon's and what it offered these well-travelled men from around the Empire, men who had grown up in Calcutta and Perth and Christchurch. She had taken the siege itself in her stride. As long as she was busy, she was happy. And there was always work to do at Dixon's. Amber knew that her husband worked on the railways and that she had a son apprenticed in Cape Town. She was a good woman from an honest, hard-working family.

Amber looked down at Mrs Peters. She was staring up at Amber without blinking. It took her three minutes to die, the expression of bewilderment never leaving her pale, bloodless face. She choked and spasmed, and Amber saw with disbelief the moment life left her body. Her sparkling eyes turning dull like frosted glass as she became nothing more than flesh.

Silence fell across the bar. The sounds of the few minutes earlier came back to Amber: the sound of shattering glass and damp hiss of the sparkling wine, then Mrs Peters' soft collapse to the floor muffled by her thick skirts, the scrape of her heels dragging across the boards, Susan's gentle crying, and the horrible rattling gasps as Mrs Peters tried to breathe and her lungs filled with blood. Then Stuttaford, still perched on his stool by the bar, began to laugh.

'Shut up, man!' Hamilton said, through gritted teeth. 'Shut up!'

'You have to admit, that was very funny,' Stuttaford said in a drawl. 'I wonder what *she* was thinking before they shot her? How much to overcharge you for that bottle of fizz, I suppose.'

He leaned along the polished bar and picked up the little brass bell customers used to call for service. It gave a horrible jangling chime which set Amber's teeth on edge.

'Make sure they don't add that bottle to your bill, Hamilton. They hadn't begun serving you yet.'

He started laughing again and did not stop until Hamilton strode across the space that divided them and knocked him out cold with a single punch that sent him sprawling off his stool and onto the floor.

• • •

Penrod was sitting at their small dining table when Amber came home later that evening. He was looking at a map of Mafeking and a number of other documents, spread out across the scrubbed boards, but as soon as he saw her blood-drenched skirts and her pale face he got to his feet at once.

'It is not my blood,' Amber said. 'But please, Penrod, do not make me explain.'

She swayed a little and put her hand against the wall to keep from falling, and Penrod felt something change within him. In that moment, looking at her in the yellow glow of the lamp, some veil that had hidden her from him in these last days was ripped away. He saw his wife again.

He crossed the space between them and caught her in his arms. She began to weep, and a slightly garbled account of the death of Mrs Peters emerged between her sobs. He murmured words of reassurance and love, rocking her slightly from side to side, as if comforting a child.

'I have seen death many times,' Amber managed to say at last. 'Why does this feel so particularly cruel?'

She lifted her face – her skin had been gently browned by the sun, and her hair in the glow of the lamp on the table seemed every shade of gold and bronze.

She nodded and leaned forward, her forehead against his chest. 'Penrod, I told you that I had seen Gerrit Vintner at the camp. I didn't tell you that he came to the room where I was being held and tried to strangle me.'

'Good God, Amber! Why did you not tell me?'

He held her to him.

'You were already so angry with me for not managing to reach safety. I couldn't. When I was crossing the lines, I was certain he was out there, waiting for his chance to shoot me. He was so angry when he found out that you had been gathering information in his house. Enraged and humiliated. Now, sometimes I wonder if he will try again.'

'Amber, Vintner is dead,' Penrod said.

She looked at him, dazed.

'He found me by the riverbank, this evening, when I was on my way home. We fought and I killed him.'

Amber sighed, her head pressed against his chest. 'I know that I should have left Mafeking for the Cape with Mrs Weil. I know I should have done, but I was not thinking straight, and I didn't want to . . .' Her words came out in a rush, fierce and urgent. 'I am so sorry, Penrod. I am so sorry. If I had left when you told me to, then Vintner never would have found me and discovered the truth. And Jabu wouldn't be in the hospital. And David would be safe, close to me and safe. I miss him so much, every moment. All I have of him is this ribbon from his jacket, this thing on my wrist is all that connects us and I know it's foolish but I can't take it off, I just can't.'

'I have hardly dared speak to you since you came back, my darling,' Penrod said. 'I am afraid for you, and I don't want you to see me afraid. That is my weakness. When I look at you, I fear losing you.'

She sighed. 'That is why you have been so angry with me.'

He bent down and kissed her, a long, slow kiss, and felt her hand on the back of his neck. Then he pulled away a little. 'I'm not angry with you, my beautiful girl, I'm angry with myself. I could have made you leave. I didn't. I let you make your excuses because, in truth, I wanted you and our son here with me.'

She laid her head back against his chest. 'You cannot be afraid for me, please. And I cannot be afraid for David. It will make us all insanely unhappy.'

He held her more gently, one hand around her waist and his other stroking her cheek, rocking her against him.

'I will not be afraid for you,' he said, his voice husky with emotion.

'I will not be afraid for our boy,' she replied and took hold of his hand.

• • •

Captain Stuttaford was summoned to Penrod Ballantyne's office the next day. He arrived angry and sullen. The corner of the room had been caught in a shell blast the previous week, and repairs made with more speed than precision – the morning light poured through slats of wood where the brick and plaster had been torn away.

'One moment please, Stuttaford,' Penrod said, and while Stuttaford took his seat Penrod lifted the telephone and had a brief discussion with Major Godley at Fort Ayr on the north-west perimeter. Stuttaford stewed as they exchanged reports on the positions of the Boer artillery. Penrod returned the telephone to its cradle and made a series of notes in his logbook.

'You know why you are here, Stuttaford?' he said at last, setting down his pen and leaning back in his chair. Stuttaford was reminded of being called into the deputy headmaster's office at his prep school and his bitterness swelled again.

'I should imagine your wife has been complaining about my ungentlemanly behaviour last night.'

Penrod raised his eyebrows.

'No, Stuttaford. What my wife told me last week was that she thought the strain of the siege was affecting your nerves. I told her that you would remember your duty and dismissed her concerns. This morning, however, I received a visit from Mr Hamilton and a young nurse and they would both like to have you shot on the recreation ground if they could. Two members of the town council have heard something of what happened last night, and have felt compelled to write to me. They note your heroic actions at Canon Kopjé but feel it is their duty to inform me, as Base Commander, that they do not want the defences of this town or the lives of the men and women who inhabit it in the hands of a . . .' he picked up a letter from the desk beside him and glanced at it '. . . an officer who is clearly a crazed drunk!'

Stuttaford flushed, but remained silent. What had happened the previous night was not something he could explain. He was sorry for Mrs Peters, but he could not have prevented her death. His laughter had not been directed provoked by her, but at the horror of the siege. Everyone here must see how absurd their situation was, trapped in this hell-hole, blasted by the sun one moment then doused in the sudden afternoon rains the next. The shells landed at random in the confines of the European Quarter and snipers were constantly discovering some new position to take potshots at anyone who wandered into the open.

Three days ago, Stuttaford had been walking towards Weil's general store when a shell screeched over his head. It exploded in front of a Barolong man leaving the building, his arms full of parcels for delivery. The force had killed him instantly, tearing his body into hunks of flesh, and Stuttaford had been one of the men who gathered up the bloody fragments before the town dogs could get to them. He had wiped flesh off a neat brown paper package of salt and sugar destined for a Mrs Smith in the women's camp, and returned it to the store for redelivery.

He was desperate to escape, but their orders were clear. Mafeking must not fall into the hands of the enemy. Amidst the news from Natal of Boer successes and British humiliation, their resistance was being promoted as a shining example of British pluck. It was pitiful, senseless and insane, and they called him crazed. Stuttaford supposed that they would have to hold on until all the townspeople had been picked off by the snipers and the shells. He felt his leg beginning to bounce and fought to control it, clenching his fists.

Ballantyne was still looking at him, his face emotionless, like a mask. Damn Ballantyne. Damn him to hell. Stuttaford had heard the rumours that circulated about this man. He'd been told Penrod had at one stage disappeared into a fog of opium for months on end and resigned his commission, only to be welcomed back some time later after he had managed to wean himself off the drug. He was a favoured son, a golden child. But Stuttaford, in spite of his years of service in the worst disease-ridden and comfortless corners of the globe, was being hauled up like a schoolboy because he had laughed at the absurdity of one woman's death. Why should he not?

'Stuttaford, you are not well,' Penrod said.

Stuttaford blinked in surprise.

'I am taking you off active duty and putting you in charge of the food supply. You'll have half a dozen men under you, and your duties will keep you in the centre of town. Dixon's is out of bounds. Your second-in-command, Sergeant Cressy, has been given the responsibility of finding you a room near the warehouses. If I ever see you drunk, I shall have you thrown in the town gaol. Do you understand?'

A private room. An escape. Stuttaford had a brief, joyfully bright vision of himself in a cool empty space, free of the sound of fellow officers snoring, the smell of their sweat. A chair and a book, then he twisted in his chair.

'I am a soldier, sir, not a clerk. I refuse your offer.' The words were said with such arrogance that Penrod was flabbergasted.

Penrod met Stuttaford's gaze. 'At the moment you may be a soldier, but you damn well aren't an officer,' he said, sternly. 'You are, however, capable of clear thinking, forward planning, and weighing multiple demands on limited resources . . . when you are not drunk.' Penrod closed the leather folder in front of him. 'I shall need you to make use of all those talents. This is your last chance to redeem yourself. Do you hear me, Stuttaford?'

Stuttaford glanced at him, confused and suspicious. So Ballantyne could parcel out redemption from behind his desk now. The man thought he was Jesus Christ himself.

'A runner managed to get through the lines last night,' Penrod said. 'The news is bad. It seems we will have to manage on our own here for some time yet. You need to make an accurate assessment of the food on hand, and talk to Sol Plaatje and Chief Wessels' headmen about the situation in the Stadt, find out what the Barolong can provide. You'll need to plan a rationing system for the town, one that can be adapted and extended if the siege continues into the new year.'

'The new year!' Stuttaford jumped out of his seat, his voice horrified. 'The war is supposed to be over by Christmas.'

'It will not be over by Christmas,' Penrod said. 'I'm afraid it is only just beginning.'

Stuttaford opened his mouth to speak, to denounce the army, their tactics and leaders, but he found himself caught by the intensity of Penrod's gaze.

'Yes, sir,' he said, returning to his chair.

'You will also need to work out how to guard what we have with limited men in a relatively unsecured location, and any action you take to ensure the stores are secure must be done in secret. If the townspeople see barbed wire going up now, the population will panic and start to hoard.'

Stuttaford considered the different aspects of the task facing him and a clear plan of action formed in his mind. He thought about how each step would be implemented and in what order.

'Are you fit for this role?' Penrod asked. 'It is clear that the British victory in South Africa will come at a very high price, and we will all have to be better soldiers and better men than we ever imagined we could be. I must ask you again, are you fit for this role? Can I trust you?'

Stuttaford's mind felt calm and clear for the first time since he had told his men to stand down after the engagement at Canon Kopjé.

'Yes, sir.'

Part III

The camp around Estcourt was a quagmire. Even with the prodigious fortune at his command and his contacts in the higher echelons of the British military, Ryder Courtney had struggled to find passage to Natal. They had found space, eventually, on a battered steamer that was running the coast from Cape Town to Durban. It had been decommissioned years earlier, but with the trains requisitioned by the army, an enterprising group of businessmen had brought the *Dunkeld* out of retirement. It had been a dreadful journey – the boat was flat-bottomed and rolled heavily in the dirty weather off the Cape. Eventually they had been forced to put in at East London and find another vessel to take them to Durban. Not until well into the third week of November did they reach the town which had become a staging point for the British troops.

Saffron was desperate for any news of Leon. Up to their ankles in mud, swilling through the streets in the summer rains, Ryder caught hold of her wrist. 'Saffron, for God's sake, look at us! I shall get us a room. You haven't slept properly for days. In the morning, we shall make Kitchener see us, and if he cannot give us information, then no one can.'

'Go if you want, Ryder!' Saffron said, forcefully shaking his hand from her arm. 'I need word about my son now.'

He took a step back, seeing the anger building in her face. 'You look like an insane woman, Saffron. Do you have your revolver?'

'I am an insane woman. Yes. And yes, of course I have my revolver, and it's fully loaded.'

He stared at her intently. 'Then go. I am not going with you. You know where to find me.'

For a second he thought she was going to relent and join him at the hotel, but she did not. Instead, she turned away from him and set off up the street without glancing back.

Ryder made his way to the only hotel in the town, the mud sucking on his boots with every step, and paid the manager a month's wages to give up his own room and provide a tin hip bath, a platter of cold roast beef and potatoes, whisky, cigars and a dressing gown.

Once he had washed and eaten, he ordered the bath refilled again with hotter water and waited. Saffron came to the room an hour later. She was alone and desolate. Ryder's breath caught in his chest, seeing her pain, the distress on her face.

He sprang to his feet and went to her.

'You found something out? God, Saffy, what did you learn?'

She began to sob. 'Oh, Ryder, we missed him by a whole *week*. I should have let you shoot that clerk in East London, the one who wouldn't let us on the boat!'

He held her close, and for the first time since they had left Cape Town, she relaxed into his arms. He could feel her anxiety, her exhaustion, as if it was his own.

'There's more.' She sniffed. 'He was on the armoured train that was attacked near Colenso. The soldiers who escaped sent word to Cape Town, and Penelope wrote to us here . . .'

'I am glad that I have at least one sensible child.'

She pulled away. 'Ryder, stop! Why must you take every chance to . . .'

He held up his hand. 'Saffy, I see how he makes you suffer and I cannot forgive him for it.'

'Then stop adding to my suffering!' she exclaimed.

Ryder turned away slightly, so she could not see his face. 'Did you learn any more?'

She sighed. 'I went to the hospital and found a private who was on the train with him. He said he saw Leon and Tau after the engagement, both alive . . .' Her voice caught in her throat. 'Both alive and unharmed. They survived. And another patient had spoken to one of the Boers taken as a prisoner. He said Leon and Tau had offered to act as postmen, taking the Boer's messages to Pretoria.'

Ryder tried to let the tight bonds of his anger loosen a little.

'He's clever, Saffy. I'll give him that. If he is carrying letters, the Boer will let him travel through their territory.'

He moved to her and put his arms around her waist. He felt her rigid body relax a little.

'Listen, wife of mine,' he continued. 'That means he's safe.'

He felt her relax against his chest. 'Do you think so, Ryder?'

'I do. At least until he reaches Mafeking.'

'Then what do we do?'

'We will follow him, of course. But no more boats and trains. Tomorrow we shall gather our kit and get decent horses, provisions for our journey, and the next day we will leave this place. If he and Tau are delivering letters in Pretoria, we should be able to catch them between Johannesburg and Mafeking.'

'Yes, Ryder! Oh, we shall find him. We have money and even if he has a head start, we've travelled for years. I am sure we'll beat him.' She put her hand over her mouth. 'Imagine his face when he reaches Mafeking and finds us blocking his way!' She paused. 'He'll be so angry.'

Ryder turned away again with a frown. 'I don't care if he's angry,' he snapped, striding to the mantelpiece and taking down the bottle of Dewar's that the manager had produced from some dusty hidey-hole.

As he poured a double measure into his whisky glass, his back turned to her, Ryder heard his wife sigh and sit down on the narrow bed to take off her boots. Then, as he stared unseeingly into the fire, his mind occupied by thoughts of how he would revenge himself on his son, he heard the sounds of her undoing the ties on her dress.

'Ryder,' she called him.

He turned instantly. She was standing by the tin bath, naked, shaking down her hair. He could see every detail of her firm body in the firelight.

Under his gaze, she stepped into the bath. He watched as she ducked under the water, then emerged, gasping, pushing back her hair, and began to soap down her skin.

'Don't hate our son. He came from you and me.'

Finishing his whisky, Ryder set down his glass and knelt beside the bath, gently pulling her face into his hands and kissing her, running his hand down her flank under the warm water. 'Perhaps,' he said softly, 'you could make me think of something else.'

She smiled and put the sponge into his hand, then turned over in the water and looked at him over her shoulder.

'Could you soap my back for me, perhaps?'

He let the water, turned golden by the firelight, drip onto the pale skin of her back, then down across the generous curve of her backside. She wriggled slightly, and he ran the sponge down the back of her thighs, then pushed them slightly apart. With his other hand he reached into the warm water and cupped the swell of her breast. She gasped, arching her back. He let the sponge go and explored the soft secrets of her with his fingers.

When he felt her body begin to tremble, Ryder lifted Saffron out of the water, wrapped her in a bath towel and carried her to the bed.

• • •

Leon and Tau found delivering the letters in the quiet and sombre city of Pretoria proved profitable. Grateful mothers and wives fed the messengers and shook coins out of their housekeeping tins in gratitude. The women were surprisingly indulgent of the boys' ambition to reach Mafeking, and happy to give detailed and conflicting advice about which route to take. The last letter that they had to deliver took them south of the city, towards Johannesburg. They had been told that the road east from that brash new city, built on the gold of the Witwatersrand, was the best route to their final destination, so they hitched a ride with a native man driving his master's wagon, full of meal and coffee, out of Pretoria to his trading station on the edge of the mining district.

The grateful mother who received their final letter offered Leon and Tau a bed in the barn for the night. Leon was tempted, but the sun was still high, and, having been fed and watered by the matrons of Pretoria, he was keen to get closer to his goal. The housewife accepted his refusal and packed their rucksacks with *droëwors* and bags of rusks. The road east led them through the Witwatersrand itself. Leon climbed a mountain of earth and rock to stare across a landscape of machinery, mud tracks, and great wooden and iron towers. The lengthening shadows of the afternoon gave the tall pumping towers straddling the broken earth the look of thin-limbed monsters, but everything was still, none of the wheels turned, and silence thickened air. Piles of earth reared up around deep craters in the ground, signs of the works of man, but the men themselves were gone.

Tau joined him and looked around.

'I do not like this place,' he said. 'The world is not supposed to be this way.'

'The men are all at war or evacuated, I suppose,' Leon said. 'What a sight it must be when they are all at work!'

He was imagining the wheels in motion, the clatter of hammers and stamping mills, and the steady stream of gold emerging from the dirt and mayhem.

'It is a dead place,' Tau said. 'I do not want to stay here.'

Something about the shadows and strangeness frightened Leon, too, but Tau's obvious distaste for it annoyed him.

'Don't be stupid. I bet they left all sorts of interesting things lying around.'

'You are looking for gold?' Tau's voice was full of disapproval.

'All the gold on the surface has gone now,' Leon said. 'That's why they've had to build these shafts to go deeper into the earth. I mean, I bet some of these sheds have stores in them, and maybe tools or things that might be useful. We have no more letters to deliver, so if we can get extra food now, we should.'

'What need do we have for shovels?' Tau said. Somewhere in the distance a dog barked. 'I think they left the guard dogs here,' Tau continued. 'They will probably be very angry and fierce.'

Leon launched himself down the rocky slope. He wanted to explore for the pleasure of it, and if he listened any more, Tau would dissuade him. He scrambled down to the bottom of the spoil heap and looked about for a promising place to start. Tau called, a silhouette on the top of the artificial hill.

'What about the dogs?'

'I can't see any dogs,' Leon said and settled the backpack over his shoulders.

A two-storey stone building formed one side of the large dirt square on which he found himself, and opposite it were a number of single-storey wooden buildings, the sort of place mine workers might keep useful things like lanterns and kettles and stoves and tins of biscuits and tea. He set off towards them without looking back, hearing the rattle of stones and earth as Tau slid down the slope behind him.

The first shed was bolted, but the second had a window set in its side and seemed larger. Leon hurled a stone against the glass and felt a thrill as it shattered. Tau ambled across to him.

'Give me a boost,' Leon said, dropping his knapsack on the ground, and Tau formed his hands into a step. Leon knocked out the glass in the bottom of the frame and tumbled through the dark mouth of the window.

Tau heard a thump and a curse.

'Leon?'

His blond head popped up over the edge of the window frame.

'I've found *stuff* in here!'

His head disappeared and Tau waited. The mining machines seemed to grow more threatening with every moment and he wondered if they'd find enough loose wood to make a fire tonight. In the distance he heard something which might have been another bark. Then Leon reappeared in the window.

'Here!' he called, and he began to throw tins out of the shed. Catching them before they hit the ground became a game and Tau managed to get six out of seven, even though Leon threw them quite far. The boys were laughing and sweaty, the dogs forgotten.

'There's a lamp here, too. Shall I bring it?'

'Yes. For trading,' Tau answered. 'Can you open the door? Perhaps we can sleep inside tonight.'

Leon was already clambering out, but he hesitated.

'Do you want a pick-axe?'

'I do not.'

Leon dropped to the ground outside.

'I don't want to sleep in there. The door is chained and padlocked, so that means we'd only have the window to get in or out. If a guard comes we'll be trapped like rats.'

Tau shrugged. It was a good point, but the surrounding land was grim and bare, and he knew that the escarpment would be pitch dark as soon the sun fell below the horizon.

The two boys walked towards the main building, gathering up what scraps of wood they could find on the way. One building must have been a carpenter's workshop at some stage. In the shadows behind it they discovered an array of off-cuts, ends of planking which might catch a spark, and bags of shavings which would make tinder. Tau noticed that one old plank that he carried was stamped with a word, and as was now his habit, he tried to read it.

'Vint-N-E-R . . .'

A side door of the building had been forced open. The offices which opened off the long central corridor had been ransacked, furniture was broken, desks overturned and papers scattered everywhere. They found a pair of heavy leather coats in one office. They were too large for the boys to take with them, but at least they would keep them warm that night.

They made a fire in the fireplace of one of the larger offices and Tau read haltingly to Leon by its light. He was still slow, but once he had got a sentence straight in his head, he would read it again in a dramatic voice which made Leon laugh. The tins were full of some sort of meat which had an oddly gritty taste, but when it was burned in the fire on the end of a toasting fork it was quite tasty, and so they went to sleep warm, with full bellies.

Leon woke in the night with a sudden sense of dread. The fire had almost burned itself out and the air was cold. He could not understand why he was afraid – everything was quiet and the heavy leather coat was keeping him warm. His brain told him to roll over and drift back to sleep, but something in his gut was sending a powerful warning. He listened; he could hear the shifting of the embers and Tau's breathing as he slept, and something else, a click and tap on the wooden floorboards, a more ragged breathing, and a then a low growl.

'Tau?' Leon hissed. 'Tau, wake up!'

Pulling himself up, he shuffled out of the coat and grabbed a shattered piece of wood, thrusting it into the embers. They flared up and he turned to face the dark room as Tau woke with a gasp. In the sudden glow Leon found himself staring into the eyes of an enormous hound. It snarled, baring long yellow teeth along its thin jaws. Leon could see its ribs as its grey barrel chest rose and fell, then it gave a single snapping bark. Flanking it were two more dogs, compact and snub-faced with wide shoulders rippling with muscle. Leon heard a rattle as one of their discarded meat tins rolled along the floor and saw another of the same sort chase the tin across the floorboards, then hold it with his forepaw and lick out the remnants with a whine and a smacking of its long tongue.

Leon grabbed his makeshift brand out of the fire and waved its smouldering end at the three dogs in front of him, sparks spraying into the darkness.

'Get back!' he shouted with authority, while Tau scrambled to his feet and thrust their possessions into the knapsacks. The largest dog growled and reared away. Leon felt himself being examined, studied for any sign of fear or weakness.

'Back, I say!' he commanded again.

The dog took a step back but continued to growl low in its throat, moving its tail stiffly from side to side, then it barked twice and began to creep forward again. Leon took his knapsack from Tau and slung it over his shoulder.

'Do we run or fight?' Tau said.

The dog lowered its head, its eyes never leaving Leon's face.

'Run. Throw the open meat tins in the corner and sprint for the door we came in. We can shut them in behind us!'

Tau scooped up the remaining empty tins.

'Quickly, Tau.'

Leon's torch was almost out, and the hound took another step towards them. Its coat was a mottled grey.

'Now!'

Tau threw the tins in an arc over the heads of the dogs into the far corner of the office and they clattered and banged against the wooden boards of the floor. The lead dog turned its head, while the others bounded towards the tins with excited barks.

'Run!' Leon shouted, and they sprinted forward, dodging round the fallen chairs and tables. Tau reached the door first and, when Leon had tumbled out after him, tried to slam it shut. One of the overturned desks was blocking it. Leon tried to kick it away, but his foot struck the polished mahogany with no effect.

They heard a storm of angry barking and the skittering of claws on the polished floor inside the office. Tau pulled at his arm.

'Come on, Leon!'

The corridor was only illuminated by the odd thread of moonlight that found its way through the semi-shuttered offices.

'Which way?' Leon shouted.

'Forward! I don't know!' Tau said in a rush and they dashed on.

The corridor turned suddenly right, and Leon felt a cold pressure in his chest. This was not the way they had come. The passage ended in darkness, but Leon was certain a door somewhere must lead out into the yard. He sprinted, then slammed into an open office door. A sudden bolt of pain shot through his shoulder and arm, but as he stumbled sideways he saw a thickened sliver of moonlight down the passage to the left.

'Tau! A door! This way!' he shouted and the boys darted forward.

Tau reached it first and he twisted the round brass handle, his hands slippery with fear, and pushed at it with his shoulder. It opened six inches and no further.

'Blocked!' he gasped.

The dogs were upon them now. The lead hound bounded at Leon in a snarling leap, showing its long canines.

Leon cried out and lifted his arm to protect his face as the hound barrelled into him, knocking him to the floor, and fastened on his forearm. Leon yelled and thrashed as the teeth pierced his skin and wrenched at his flesh. The dog's breath was rank in his nostrils, sweet and rotten, and a wave of pain and shock washed through his body. He kicked and scrabbled, striking the dog's flank with his free hand, another of the dogs yelping as his heavy boot found its snout, but the hound only shifted its grip and hung on more tightly.

Leon heard Tau let out a battle roar, and turned to see him with the toasting fork that they had used to cook their dinner raised above his head. He smashed it into the shoulder of the hound and its grip on Leon's arm loosened. Leon grabbed at the flesh of the dog's neck, and felt under its shaggy fur the smooth touch of leather, a collar. He forced his hand under it and pulled with all his strength. The animal squirmed, but held on. With a wrenching cry, fighting the agony coursing through his arm, Leon twisted the leather band. The dog released its hold on his arm, causing a new wave of pain to shoot from his wrist to his shoulder blade. Leon's fingers lost their grip and the hound retreated into the shadows, rasping and coughing.

Tau waved the toasting fork at the two snub-nosed dogs who sent up a chorus of angry barks, but moved backwards. Leon could feel the blood running under his sleeve.

'Take this! Keep them back!'

Tau thrust the toasting fork into Leon's good hand, then, dropping to the ground, he reached through the narrow opening to shift the object which was blocking the door. Leon waved the fork around him in what he hoped was an intimidating way. He could feel the blood dripping over his hand and landing on the dusty floor in a steady stream. The dogs could smell it. The lead hound re-emerged from the shadows and stared at Leon with hatred. The other dogs' barks grew louder and more impatient, and the lead hound began to sink onto its haunches. Leon's good arm was feeling heavy. He tried to shout to Tau, but his words came in a whisper.

'The door is moving! Leon!'

Tau's enthusiasm gave Leon hope.

Tau gave a yell of triumph and forced the door open another few inches as Leon fell against it. The fork slipped from his hand and clattered to the floor.

The hound bounded forward again. Leon grabbed at the toasting fork and managed to lift it as the dog jumped. The dull prongs caught the beast below the breastbone and with a yelp it fell, then turned and shrank down on its haunches to pounce again.

Leon felt icy cold. He could not move, he was losing blood too fast.

'Good doggy,' he said with a slight slur.

Then Tau's arm was around his chest and he was being dragged somewhere. He found himself pulled and pushed out into the night air where he sprawled awkwardly onto his hands. A great roar of agony ran up his injured arm and it collapsed; his face stung as it hit the gravel, and he tasted dust and rock. Behind him he heard Tau shouting as his friend pushed the door closed and kicked loose stones against it. A black muzzle snuffled at the edge, licking saliva from its jaws, struggling to make the gap wider.

Tau tried to pull Leon to his feet.

'Leon, come. We must get away. They will find another door.'

The world seemed far away and fuzzy to Leon, like a dream he was trying to remember rather than real life, and the darkness seemed to ripple and shift in front of him.

'I'll stay here,' he said. It was fascinating watching the blood drip from his arm into the dust.

He felt Tau's shoulders under his arm and thought it was comfortable to be held up.

'Come, Leon, we must walk.'

Leon didn't see the need, but Tau seemed insistent. Walking was much more laborious than he remembered, his feet were heavy and he could not feel where he was stepping.

'Come, Leon, I see a light! Come on, Leon, you can do it. Last push, my friend. We came this far. Let's move!'

Leon lifted his head and thought that the light Tau had seen was too far away. They should rather sit down and rest for a bit. He wasn't cold anymore, so why did they need to hurry inside – it made no sense.

'Come now, or your father will catch you and make you do sums!' Tau shouted in his ear.

That didn't seem fair, but it did make Leon move faster through the swimming darkness and over the rough rising ground. He heard barking behind them and it did not sound like it was coming from inside the building anymore. Tau was dragging him along and calling out to someone else. Leon wondered if his father had found them and how furious he would be, then he heard the dogs again, their paws scrabbling on loose stone, and the memory of the dog's stinking breath made him want to vomit. He was being pushed upwards and found his feet were on the rungs of a ladder, someone else was pulling him, and Tau was shouting. The barking and growling was closer now. He felt someone grab his good arm and he fell upwards, his feet slow and clumsy on the rungs, Tau pushing him ferociously. Leon was aware of a barking dog close to him, the stink of rotten meat, then a sharp clatter of a trapdoor being dropped into place. He was somewhere warm and light, so he decided he would sleep, let Tau call his father if he wanted.

• • •

The pain in his arm woke Leon eventually; he felt weak and sick. Tau had covered him with his blanket and he peered out from under it at what seemed to be a wooden hut. He lifted himself onto his uninjured elbow and saw the back of the chamber was full of metal levers and dials, like the inside of a steam ship. It must be one of the rooms from which the great water pumps were operated, which made the mines safe to use for the men who dug the gold. An unglazed window, the shutters swung back, flooded the room with light and it was already hot. Leon steeled himself to look at his injured arm – nausea rising inside him at the thought of what he might see – but when he finally gathered his courage and looked down, he found that his shirtsleeve had been torn away and although his arm was rusty with dried blood and filth, the wound had been bandaged, and the bandage looked reasonably clean.

'Tau?' he said. His voice sounded cracked and worn.

'I am here, Leon Courtney.' Tau was sitting on a packing case in the far corner of the room. He put down his book and picked up a canteen, approached and held it so that Leon could drink.

'Where are we?'

'Still at the mine,' Tau answered. 'We washed the bite and held a hot knife to it, then bound it up. You bled a lot. Today you must eat and rest and we must hope the wound does not go bad. Does it hurt?'

'Like anything. Hot knife? I do not remember that.'

'Good. You were not very happy about it.'

'I think that dog was part lion or something. What will happen if it goes bad?' Leon asked, his voice wary. 'How will we know?'

'I think it will smell like the dog's breath, and if it does we shall have to cut off your arm with your penknife.'

Leon carefully moved his bandaged arm under his blanket.

'Who else is here? You said "we", and I think I remember you talking to someone last night.'

'A girl. She says her name is Flora, and she is not English. I do not like her.'

Leon thought he could remember her now, a thin girl with long hair and grey eyes. Leon hoped he had not cried or made any fuss while she was watching.

'Some girls are nice, Tau. And she let us in and helped wash my arm.'

'She calls me "boy", even though I have a blanket and a knife and she has nothing, and she did not want to let us in, and she didn't help very much. She said you were probably dead, so it was a waste of water to wash your wound.'

'Where is she now?'

'I told her about the tinned meat shed. She has gone to fetch more food. She is a very stupid girl not to have found the shed herself.'

'What about the dogs?'

'They are gone, I think you hurt the leader.' He mimed a choking action with his hands.

'And why is she here?' Leon said, dismissing the dogs and thinking about the girl again.

'How am I to know?' Tau's smile disappeared. 'She will not tell a "boy" anything. She will wait until Master Leon Courtney is awake, and then she will tell him her sad story.'

'Why do you think it is a sad story?'

Tau lowered his chin and cast Leon a sceptical glance. 'She is hungry and dirty and living by herself in a mine hut. I do not think it will be a *happy* story.'

Before Leon could reply the hatch slammed open and the girl's head appeared. Leon remembered the short ladder now and how it had saved them from the dogs. The girl thrust some more of the cans they had found the day before into the room then looked at Leon.

'I see you have woken.'

'Yes.' Her eyes were grey and her hair was blonde, but stringy and greasy. She smoothed it back over her ears, tucking it under the faded bonnet she wore.

'Thank you for letting us stay here,' Leon said. He felt sick still, and terribly cold despite the heat of the day.

'Your boy did not give me much choice,' she said, and Leon felt Tau's glow of disapproval.

'He is not "my boy". He is Tau.'

'Tau Modisa,' Tau added.

The girl shrugged.

Leon pulled himself onto his elbow and the room lurched and span for a moment. The girl pushed one of the cans towards them and Tau snatched it up and opened it with his knife. He pushed it back towards the girl and she ate with an appetite which precluded conversation, pulling out the meat with her fingers and hardly chewing, before swallowing the greasy pink lumps.

Leon looked away, embarrassed. Tau opened another tin and the boys shared the contents.

When they had finished their food, Tau stood up and picked up their canteens before disappearing through the hatch. Leon cleared his throat.

'I am Leon Courtney, what's your name?'

'Flora,' she said quietly.

'Why are you staying here, Flora?' Leon asked.

He found himself speaking with a strange formality as if he was talking in a foreign language. The girl was a bit older than him, he thought. She was thin, but her shape was more like a woman's than a child's. She smoothed her hair under her bonnet again, and brushed down her dirty dress.

'I have run away.' Her voice was hoarse, like someone who had not spoken for a while, or who had been crying. 'I took money, but then it was stolen from me. I came here to hide from the men who . . . stole it. I was told once, it was a good place to hide.'

'I ran away, too,' Leon said. 'From my father, and now I am going to stay with my uncle in Mafeking.'

'Mafeking!' Flora breathed it as if the word was a magic spell. 'But that is where I am going! I thought God had forgotten me when those men . . . But He has sent you to help me get there.'

'The dogs chased us in here, actually,' Leon replied.

'I was praying when your boy saw my light. I said, "God, please, if what I am doing is right, then send me a sign," and he did. You, Leon, you are His sign.'

She reached forward and touched him on the shoulder. She was pretty when she smiled.

'You must rest now. You are not well. We shall look after you.'

She clasped her hands and began to murmur – praying, Leon presumed. He shivered and felt her adjust the blanket round his shoulders.

Tau would not be pleased at the idea of taking her with them. But they were so close to Mafeking. Tau could put up with her for a few days. He wondered what her business in Mafeking might be, but he dozed off before he could ask her.

• • •

When Tau returned with water he had found in a cistern near the mine offices, he listened to the news that Flora was coming with them to Mafeking quietly and accepted the decision. He even remarked that she might be helpful as she could talk to the Boers patrolling the area. Tau put his hand on Leon's forehead.

'But we stay here for now, Leon Courtney. You are sick.'

Leon didn't have the strength to argue. By mid-afternoon the hut was sweltering. Tau decided they needed the other sleeve of Leon's shirt to make a fresh bandage and went hunting for firewood to heat water and wash the old one outside the hut. Flora disappeared to search for healing plants from the area around the mines. Leon tried to sleep.

Flora came back at a run while Tau was tending his fire. She was carrying something in her pinafore, a jar of ointment and clean bandages.

'Where did you find them?' asked Tau.

'In the offices. I thought they might have a cupboard for things like this and they did.' She was too pleased with herself to even call him 'boy'.

'This is very good,' Tau said. 'Leon is ill. You have saved him, I think. Thank you.'

She beamed at Tau and seemed to be about to say something else, then stopped herself and gave him her usual look of prim disdain. Tau followed her back into their refuge, carrying his hot water.

• • •

R yder heard his wife choke back a gasp and turned in the saddle.

'Saffy?'

She shook her head. 'It's nothing, Ryder. I think I fell asleep for a second and almost fell out of the saddle, that's all.'

Ryder reined in his pony and dismounted. They had left Estcourt with the best horses money could buy, good rifles, enough food for a month on the road and light camping equipment, but the going had been harder than he had expected – the Drakensberg lay between them and Pretoria, a great wall of stone thrown up to keep them out of the highveld.

'We'll camp here tonight. We've ridden almost fifteen miles today. That is enough, my darling.'

'No, I can go on!' she protested, feeling a new rush of energy surge through her body. 'We shouldn't stop while there's still light.'

'I am sure you can, but even these ponies have to rest sometime. We will be no use to Leon if we exhaust the horses.' He put up his arms and she let him lift her from the horse, he felt her narrow waist under his fingers and smiled at her. For a brief moment, out there in the late-afternoon warmth, he couldn't remember why he had ever been angry with her.

She lifted her hand, running her fingers over the thick growth of stubble on his cheek then as he moved in to kiss her, she froze.

'What is it?'

She pointed over his shoulder. Three men had appeared from behind the low flank of the nearest hill, and they were carrying rifles.

• • •

I t was almost a week before Leon was well enough to travel again, but at least they had time to work out how to get to Mafeking. Tau roamed the mines during daylight, looking for books and newspapers, and in one he found an advert for a bicycle shop. Leon saw it and was ecstatic. That was how they would get to Mafeking. Bicycles! They just needed to go to Johannesburg and find the bicycle shop.

Flora agreed to stand guard, but she hardly needed to – Johannesburg was a ghost town. All the light and frivolity of the city seemed to have shrunk down into a hotel on the corner of Commissioner Street – two streets away, in front of the boarded-up bicycle shop, there was nothing but darkness and silence.

They discovered a window at the back of the shop, and Tau climbed in. He unlocked the back door to let Leon inside. Twenty minutes later they wheeled out three smallish machines into the quiet streets.

Leon had ridden a bicycle a few times in Cairo, so took it upon himself to teach the others. They had returned to the abandoned mine buildings, and, after a meagre breakfast, he began his instruction. Tau mastered the machine quickly, but Flora fell off, and after the third tumble sent her sideways into a spoil heap and Tau laughed, she flew into a rage.

'Why should I ride on your stupid machine? It is stolen anyway. I think God does not want me to ride it.'

Leon was becoming bored of the number of times God worked His way into their arguments. She always claimed to know what He was thinking and, Leon noticed, He always seemed to side with Flora, no matter what the issue at hand.

'We did not steal them!' Leon said indignantly. 'The sign on the door said he had closed his shop for the duration of hostilities, so we couldn't *buy* them. I left a note, giving him our address in Cape Town.'

'It is stealing!'

'So is taking the food from the store, but you don't seem to mind eating it!' Leon shouted.

'I shall make myself sick and you can have the food back!'

'What good would that do?' Leon said, temporarily baffled.

Tau rode a circle around them both, then came to a jerky halt. 'God must want us to have the food and the bicycles,' he said, staring at some point above their heads. 'He led us to the food shed as soon as we arrived here, then He made the shop owner leave his back window open just enough for me to get in and fetch the machines.'

'See?' Leon said.

Flora muttered something unintelligible, but she seemed to concede the points. She mounted Tau's machine again and managed a slow, wobbly, but successful, run across the yard and back.

They set off towards their destination the following morning and if any Boer patrols saw them and their unsteady progress through the growing heat, they shook their heads and let them pass.

The roads in places had been turned into quagmires by the rain and the mud stuck to the wheels, weighing them down till they had to stop and clean it off. The uneven ground rattled their bones, and they had to rest through the worst of the heat and the rain, huddled together under Tau's blanket. They were exhausted after each day of riding, their buttocks raw from the hard saddles, and Mafeking seemed just as far away as it had in Cape Town.

It was the decision to bring Flora along on their journey that saved them. As evening came on, on the fourth day, just when Leon was ready to give up hope of ever reaching Mafeking, she insisted they turn off the main road onto a farm track, spotting the smoke of a cooking fire, and knowing that the stands of trees in the distance would shelter a homestead. While Leon and Tau waited, she marched up to the front door and begged for a place to rest, some fresh milk and a little food from a Boer housewife. She told her that Leon was her deaf-mute brother and Tau their servant. After that night they turned off the road at least once a day when they spotted farmland or a homestead. If it was near to the end of the day, they would ask for a place to sleep. In return, Flora offered to clean the kitchen or wash the dishes.

From that moment on, Leon played his part with some enthusiasm, while Tau kept his distance, but their story was never questioned and the rigours of the ride were eased by having good food to eat and a place to sleep.

After a little over a week of boneshaking rides from dawn to dusk, of seeking shelter from the afternoon rain, Flora returned from a farmhouse with the news they were only thirty miles from Mafeking. It seemed to make her serious, but the boys were delighted. After weeks of travel, facing enemy troops, leaping trains, trekking through the veld and fending off dogs, they were just a day or two away from their goal. Mafeking seemed to them a promised land and Leon was certain they would be greeted as heroes for their bravery and resilience.

'I will tell Uncle Penrod everything we have encountered and our adventures will be talked of for years to come,' Leon said.

'He will say: "Well done, young Courtney! That is vital information that will help us win the war." And I will say: "Just doing my duty, Colonel Ballantyne."'

Flora's canteen fell to the floor with a thud, interrupting Leon. He glanced over his shoulder and watched her scoop it up again before too much water was lost.

'Your uncle is Penrod Ballantyne?' she said.

'Yes,' Leon replied. 'Have you heard of him?'

'They wrote about him in the paper in Pretoria,' she said. 'Everybody read it.'

'What vital information will you give him?' Tau asked.

Leon opened his mouth to reply, but found he did not have an answer. Instead, he waved his hand in the air. 'Oh, Uncle Penrod is a very famous and brilliant intelligence officer. I am sure we have seen all sorts of things that it would be very useful for him to know about, even if we don't understand what they mean yet.'

Tau accepted this willingly. 'I shall help Mrs Amber Ballantyne write her stories. I think she would find all my tales very interesting. I am like Huckleberry Finn, but of Africa,' boasted Tau.

Leon shrugged, happy to let Tau have that honour, given his own vital work for British intelligence. Tau got to his feet and picked up Leon's empty plate.

'I shall take these back to the lady in the house.'

Flora grabbed them from his hand.

'I shall take them,' she said with unusual firmness.

Tau did not protest. Normally, Flora sent him back and forth, saying it was fitting to his role as servant. If she wanted to take them herself tonight he did not mind. The boys hardly noticed when Flora returned an hour later and curled up in her corner of the barn. When they were too tired to talk anymore, they made their rough beds and, in the morning, set off as soon as the darkness began to lift, eager to reach that shining city of their imagination.

The Boer housewife who had fed the strange children with such generosity did not notice that her second-best carving knife was missing until the time came to prepare the evening meal.

• • •

Ryder and Saffron travelled with quiet determination. The Boer commando they had met north of Estcourt had shared a meal with them, and told them to be careful. They would be treated as civilians away from the front lines, but they would risk imprisonment if they strayed too near to the fighting.

To avoid getting caught up in the conflict, Ryder and Saffron kept their distance from the towns that lay between them and Pretoria, striking out well to the east of Harrismith. By now they had run out of provisions and so each evening they left their horses to graze, and tracked impala and bushbuck together. Ryder had forgotten what an excellent shot his wife was. Both sisters had been taught to handle firearms from an early age, loading and reloading their father's shotgun whenever he went hunting. David Benbrook believed that any woman who lived in Africa should be able to shoot, and under his tutelage Saffron and Amber quickly became experts – Saffron rarely wasted a bullet.

Ryder butchered whatever they shot and in addition to feeding themselves, Saffron sold meat to the Boer women still trying to run their farms while their men were off fighting. The women would have armed themselves if they had seen a man on a horse approaching the homestead, but a woman on her own in the veld was a different matter.

One evening, as the daylight was fading, Ryder watched his wife lying on her stomach, taking aim at a white spotted bushbuck ewe. He watched her chest rise and fall as her breathing slowed, until it was as if she was inhaling her favourite perfume, then she slowly pulled the trigger. Ryder saw the animal collapse into the grass as the rest of the herd scattered.

'Now I'm working again,' Saffron said with pride as they went to collect her kill.

Already, to the south of Pretoria, they had come across rumours of two boys, one black and one white, bringing letters from husbands and sons fighting the British in Natal. But when they reached the city, they heard stories on every street corner. The story of the boy postmen had captured Pretoria's imagination, a distraction from the worry and fear of the times.

Saffron and Ryder tried not to bring any attention to themselves in Pretoria, avoiding the authorities, hoping that they were too busy with their own concerns to pay much attention to a pair of dusty travellers.

Once they left the city, news of the boys had dried up. The white farmers had left the land to fight the British, and the natives who remained, driving livestock out to the grazing grounds and back to the farmsteads, refused to engage with the white man and his wife who approached them on horseback.

However, late one afternoon Saffron knocked at the door of a farmer's wife who told her the story of three children riding bicycles to Mafeking – they had called in at the homestead only two days earlier. Saffron didn't even take the money the woman was holding out to her for the venison that she had sold her – turning away instantly, mounting her pony and galloping out of the yard in a cloud of dust. Two days! They were only two days behind.

Ryder hardly noticed the landscape – the fertile valleys and neat orchards which punctuated the open spaces. Each hour brought them closer to Mafeking, and the fear that they would be too late to save the boys from their own stupidity started to build into a fever. Still fifty miles from Mafeking, they stopped only to rest for a couple of hours and then rode on through the night, guided by the light of a half-moon, hoping to overtake Leon and Tau. But as dawn spread across the veld, they spotted the telltale tracks of bicycle tyres in the road. Adrenaline rushed through their bodies and they forced their mounts into a gallop. They were still behind the boys, but the hope that they would see them just over the next rise, just around the next corner, drove them on.

'Ryder,' Saffron asked, her voice despondent when they finally slowed to a canter and then a walk, 'are we too late?'

He did not reply, but his conviction she was right was a stone of dread in his belly. Perhaps the boys had already reached Mafeking, but they could just as easily have run into a commando and been captured, or worse, perhaps they would find them lying dead in the road . . . or hanging from a tree as a warning.

The horses could not continue at such a pace, so Saffron and Ryder went on slowly, riding through the dry heat of the day without speaking, each with their own demons telling them that the worst was waiting ahead.

'Ryder!' Saffron shouted.

He looked up, hearing the fear in Saffron's voice. Their way was blocked – half a dozen men with rifles cradled in their arms had emerged from the bush about two hundred yards down the road. The urge to force his exhausted pony into a gallop and charge through their ranks rose up inside Ryder. Let them shoot, he thought to himself. He was not afraid. He would storm his way through their lines, seize Leon by the collar and pluck him out of the town at the very moment he set foot within the municipal boundary. He kicked his heels into the pony's flanks and the beast plunged forward. Ryder lowered his head, his back straight, and flew towards the Boers in the road. They straightened, and lifted their rifles to their shoulders.

'Ryder, please!'

Saffron's anguished cry was the one thing that could turn him back. With a curse, he hauled on the reins and, as the pony slowed with a shudder, dismounted. The startled fighters clustered round him, shouting in German and Dutch, the muzzles of their guns inches from his face, then Saffron dashed into the circle, pushing them aside as if they were children whose games had become too rowdy.

'My son!' Saffron was saying. 'Our son is trying to get into the town with his friend and a girl. We must stop them. You have to let us by!'

'Don't tell us what we have to do, you English bitch!'

Ryder took a half-step forward and, with a right hook, sent the man who had insulted Saffron sprawling in the dust.

The Boer fighters lifted their guns again and Ryder lifted his hands.

'Shoot him, Jannie,' the man on the ground groaned.

Ryder waited, staring at the nearest man, calculating his odds. Then Saffron put herself between him and the guns.

She looked into the faces of the men surrounding them and watched their eyes. One of them glanced at an older man with heavy, sunburned features and a beard flecked with grey. He was looking at her, so Saffron spoke to him directly.

'Please let me explain, sir.'

He stared at her, then lowered his rifle.

'*Ag*, enough. Speak quickly.'

'*Oom* Gysbert! He hit Ricus!' one of the other fighters protested.

'Ricus deserved it,' the man said shortly.

Saffron told her story – of how Leon had run away from his family to join the soldiers on the front line, of his mission to get to Mafeking. 'He is riding a bicycle. We've been following his tracks.'

Gysbert's mouth twisted as he listened to her and his eyes narrowed in suspicion.

'*Nee, man!* No child has been along the road here. This is a bloody siege! That means you're going no further down this road. You think you can just wander about how you like?'

'I am not a soldier. I am a trader and a father,' Ryder said calmly, then noticing the man he had punched groan and lift himself up on his elbows, added, 'and a husband, of course.'

'I don't care if you're the king of Sweden, anyone going in or out of that town is our enemy.'

'Ryder, look!' Saffron gasped.

Two fighters were crossing the veld from the direction of the river, pushing three bicycles across the uneven ground.

The Boer's leader strode towards the oncoming party, and Ryder and Saffron followed him.

'*Waar kry julle hierdie?*' he asked, seizing the handlebars of the first machine and staring into the astonished faces of the two men.

'*Ons het dit by die rivier gevind, met wiele wat steeds draai.*'

Gysbert's face became purple with rage at their answer.

'Where?' Ryder demanded.

The other man flinched away from his commander and pointed east. 'Further up, a minute ago.'

'*Los die fietse en kom terug op jul pos,*' Gysbert ordered. 'Jannie, Ricus, you come with me.'

The commander didn't try to stop Ryder and Saffron from following him towards the river. They were entering the land between Boer and British lines, but if the men who had found the bicycles were right, they might still manage to get ahead of the children. The commander plunged into a thicket of thorn trees which led to the top of a low hill – a spot that commanded a view of the whole of the low, twisting valley the Molopo had carved for itself across the veld.

'*Gryp hierdie Engelse*, you idiots,' Gysbert shouted and Ryder and Saffron were grabbed.

'There,' Saffron said with a moan. 'I see them! Leon!'

She pulled against the fighter holding her.

'Let me go! Please! I have to stop my son!'

'I'll stop him,' the commander growled and lifted his rifle. 'The boy is a spy.'

Saffron screamed, and stamped viciously on the instep of the man holding her. He yelled in pain and staggered, but held fast to her wrists.

Ryder wrenched himself free of the man holding him, and charged at Gysbert, knocking him sideways. His rifle kicked and the shot fired off into the depth of the veld. Ricus span round, striking at Ryder's neck with the rifle butt and the two men fell together against one of the square blocks of stone that littered the kopje and into the dust. Ryder struck up with his fist into the man's kidneys, but Ricus managed to get astride Ryder's chest, pressing the long barrel of the gun across Ryder's throat. 'This is war!' he panted. 'It's no fault of mine that your child has put himself in the middle of it.'

The man who had been holding Saffron swung out with his foot, catching her ankle and sending her sprawling onto the ground, then raised his rifle and pointed it at her head. 'Gysbert!' he shouted. 'Shoot the child!'

Saffron was too winded to scream again, all she could do was groan and put up her hand to Gysbert. He looked round slowly at his men, at Ryder and Saffron sprawled in the dust and spat onto the ground. '*Ag*, they've gone into the valley. No shot now,' he said. Then he turned his gun towards Ryder. 'Let him up, Ricus.'

The rifle still pressed firmly into Ryder's throat.

'Now, Ricus.'

Ricus shifted his weight off Ryder and got reluctantly to his feet.

Gysbert still had his rifle pointed at Ryder's chest. 'Get up. Both of you.'

Ryder stood, then put out his hand to Saffron. She was trembling, but she would not weep in front of these men.

'How long have you been chasing those children?' Gysbert asked.

'A month,' Ryder replied and the older man nodded.

'Hard to come so close,' he said. 'But these are the facts. You're out, they're in. And there's one rule in this siege. Anyone we catch crossing the lines is fair game. You and your wife try and get across, we'll shoot you.'

Ryder could not trust himself to speak.

'This is my offer,' Gysbert continued. 'You can have your rifles back.' He held up his hand as Ricus whined with disappointment. 'But we'll take your ponies.'

Ryder's rage threatened to bubble to the surface again. Saffron looked between the men. In a moment the commander would decide it would be easier to murder them – and damn the consequences – than let them go.

'Ryder,' Saffron said, her voice quiet but determined, 'you and I can travel anywhere in Africa with a pair of rifles.' She took his hand, winding her fingers through his. 'Leon will find Amber. He will be safe. Let's go.'

Jannie handed over their rifles, and they were allowed to take their packs from the ponies. Then they turned their backs on the men and clambered down from the rocky promontory. Saffron heard the click of rifle bolts being drawn back and turned. Ricus and Jannie had their rifles raised.

'Stay away from Mafeking,' the commander shouted down to them. 'Head south-west, away from our lines. There is nothing you can do to help your boy now.'

· · ·

After leaving their bicycles in the bush, Leon, Tau and Flora approached the town along the riverbed. The sun was less fierce now, but it had been a long, hot ride and the waters of the Molopo were cool and appealing. Leon and Tau splashed each other and trotted along with increasing excitement, but Flora grew quieter with each minute that passed, keeping slightly away from the two boys. Only once did she lift her head to stare at Leon with such intensity that he stopped laughing and waited for her to speak.

'Leon, will your uncle come and meet us when we get into town?'

'Oh yes, I should think so. I am his favourite nephew.'

'And I have a photograph from him,' Tau said, forgetting his dislike of the girl in his eagerness to boast. 'It says I am his friend.'

Flora started walking again and the boys resumed their games. The sound of a shot in the distance made them turn their heads, but they could not see where it came from, so they continued blithely along the stream until a man in khaki hailed them from the banks.

'Hold there!' he called, and the three waited obediently until he reached them. He examined them closely and then shook his head.

'And who the bloody hell are you?'

'Hello,' Leon said brightly. 'I'm Leon Courtney, Colonel Ballantyne's nephew. We've come to visit him.'

Tau fished in the pocket of his jacket and produced his treasured picture of the Ballantyne family. It was a bit travel-stained, but Penrod's flowing handwriting on the back was still legible.

'I have a note,' he said and smiled.

'Well, I'll be . . .' The trooper turned round and shouted up the bank: 'Sergeant! You'd best come down here. We've got visitors!'

• • •

T hey say that they're with you, sir,' the sergeant said loudly some twenty minutes later as Penrod approached across the town square from headquarters.

'Leon?'

Leon grinned.

Penrod Ballantyne was rarely surprised, but the discovery that one of the three dirty-looking children in front of him was his oldest nephew came as a distinct shock.

'How did these children get through the lines?' Penrod asked. 'Who let them by?'

The sergeant looked anxious. 'That's my fault, sir. They came through my section of the line. The light was striking off the river. I thought my eyes were playing tricks on me.'

'Punishment duty for a week.'

The sergeant looked miserable, but saluted.

'Don't blame him, Uncle Penrod,' Leon said. 'We were very clever about it and we don't really look like Boer fighters, do we?'

'But what are you doing here, Leon?'

'We came from Cape Town . . . Well, we had to go through Durban and past Ladysmith and through Pretoria, and mostly it was fun because we were on the trains. We would have got here ages ago, but we were trapped in Estcourt for days and then there were the dogs . . .'

'Dear God.' Penrod grabbed the boy by his shoulders, then hugged him roughly.

Stepping back, Penrod looked more closely at the other boy. 'Tau?'

Tau nodded and smiled, pleased that he had been recognised and named.

'I am Tau Modisa now, Colonel Ballantyne.'

'Tau Modisa,' Penrod repeated, shaking his head.

Leon was still trying to describe, with large hand gestures, the route of his journey to his baffled uncle and an astonished knot of spectators, when Amber came running towards them, kissed both boys then launched into a coruscating attack on Leon, beginning with the trouble and worry he must have given his parents.

Baden-Powell, making his way across the square, approached and listened a while before leaning towards Penrod.

'Just interested, Ballantyne, but do you think any more of your family are likely to be breaking into Mafeking? Simply, we should inform the quartermaster.'

Penrod heard the dry amusement in his voice. He thought of Ryder and Saffron Courtney and considered how likely it was that they would have remained in Cape Town until they received word that Leon had been found.

'I think, sir, I'd better not commit myself one way or another on that.'

'Very well.'

Amber stopped her scolding of Leon to shake hands with Tau.

'How is your baby, Mrs Ballantyne?' Tau asked.

She smiled at him warmly. 'Well, I hope, Tau. He is with our friend Greta in Mosita. I shall always be grateful to you, for looking after him.'

'And this is Flora, Aunt Amber,' Leon said, pointing at the girl, keen to prolong the pause in his scolding. 'She is Dutch but she helped us a lot, and wanted to come to Mafeking, too.'

'Why would you want to do that?' Amber asked the girl, and Leon realised that he had never thought to ask her. 'Do you have family here, Flora?'

From the lookout tower to the west a bell rang twice, paused then rang again, a warning that one of the Boer artillery positions was readying itself to fire.

'We have drawn a crowd and created a target,' Baden-Powell said. 'To your shelters everyone – quickly, now.'

For the first time Penrod looked at the girl. While all the others had been talking and arguing she had not said a word. She was a little taller than Leon, and showed signs of a developing figure under her light-blue dress. She wore a bonnet and her head was lowered so that her face was covered.

'We must find shelter now, a shell is coming,' Amber said, 'but I'm sure we can find your people, Flora, as soon as it is clear.' She was thinking of the various Dutch families still in town. None had mentioned a child named Flora.

The girl lifted her head and stared at Penrod. It was as if no one else in the world existed other than him and her.

'I have no family. My mother died, my home was taken and my father, Gerrit Vintner, was found dead in the river here in Mafeking. You murdered my parents with your treachery, Penrod Ballantyne.'

The realisation of who the girl really was struck Penrod like a blow.

'Hester?' he said. 'Good God . . .!'

He stared at her, trying to discover in that pinched and hate-filled face the young girl he had met the previous summer, the quiet child whom he had watched sitting at the kitchen table, studying the Bible with her mother every day for hours. He put out his hand to her, and she flew towards him, crossing the ground between them in an instant.

Flora pressed herself against Penrod, her head against his chest. He put his arm around her thin shoulders and she lifted her head to look into his eyes. He saw only rage, and then he felt a sudden shock of pain, deep and sickening, in his stomach. The world went white. He gasped and shuddered.

'Knife! Knife!' Baden-Powell shouted. He grabbed the girl by her shoulders, twisting her away from Penrod. The Boer wife's second-best carving knife was in her hand, and bloody to the hilt. She began to scream and struggle in Baden-Powell's grip. The sergeant grabbed her wrist and wrenched it till the blade fell free, then pulled her hands firmly behind her back.

Baden-Powell stepped away, staring at her with disgust. 'For God's sake, lock her up!' he said. 'Penrod, are you hurt?'

Penrod could not speak. The world was becoming fogged and distant.

A shell hissed through the air over their heads and exploded against the side of one of the houses on the other side of the square. They ducked as brick and plaster cascaded outwards.

'Penrod!' Amber screamed over the blast and dust. 'Someone help him!'

Penrod's hands were pressed over his abdomen. He staggered and fell forward onto his knees, blood beginning to seep between his fingers and out onto the dusty ground.

'Penrod!' Amber cried again. She thrust Leon away from her.

'What's happening?' Leon asked, his voice breaking. 'I don't understand.'

Penrod spread his palms. A glut of blood soaked his hands. The world lurched and brightened as Amber's skirts appeared by his side. He looked up at her as the pain became a cascade, a waterfall between him and the world.

'Stretcher!' Baden-Powell shouted as Penrod collapsed against his wife.

• • •

Penrod's life hung in the balance. Anderson operated on him for an hour in the town hospital, assisted by his two senior nurses, and when he emerged his expression was grim.

The stab wound was deep, nicking Penrod's liver and the hepatic artery, and causing near catastrophic blood loss, but the bleeding had been stopped, he assured Amber, and the wound was clean. Now it was a question of waiting.

Amber took her place by Penrod's bed in the recovery ward. She knew Penrod was strong, in will and body, but he had been pushing himself to the limits for many weeks. No one could know if he could survive this shock.

Penrod's fever increased during the hours that followed and when he regained consciousness, he was confused and delirious. Amber never left his side, convincing herself that on the few occasions he opened his eyes, she saw some spark of recognition in them.

Ned Cecil took immediate charge of Leon and Tau while Hester was locked in the town gaol.

On the second night after Hester's attack on Penrod, a runner managed to slip across the lines with more grim news from the front lines in the Cape, and a message from Ryder Courtney addressed to Baden-Powell. Ryder wrote that he would not place any further strain on the garrison, or risk causing the defenders harm by attempting to enter the town, but he was behind the Boer lines and intended to stay as close to Mafeking as he could. He asked that any news of his son and Tau be sent to him and his wife care of the Frasers at the Setlagole trading post, and promised to assist the garrison if it was within his power to do so.

'Sensible man,' Baden-Powell said, handing the note to Ned and waiting until he, too, had read it. 'Ask the Barolong to get word out that the children are safe, and will be well-cared for. No need to mention the attack on Colonel Ballantyne until we know if he'll survive.'

Both boys were distraught about the attack on Penrod, and Leon begged to be allowed to visit his aunt and uncle, but Ned, after visiting Amber himself, denied them entry.

'You'll have to wait, Leon,' Ned said to the boy. He and Tau had mounted a vigil under the eaves of the hospital building and would not be moved. 'Penrod is very ill, and you must let Amber care for him. She doesn't want to see you yet.'

Leon put his head into his hands and burst into tears. Ned sighed and sat down beside him on the step.

'I didn't know!' Leon cried. 'I thought they would be glad to see me and then Aunt Amber was angry, and I could have borne that, but I came into help . . . and I brought an assassin with me!'

'She did not look like an assassin,' Tau said.

'Uncle Penrod and Colonel Baden-Powell and you, sir, are heroes all over the Empire,' Leon said, 'and we, I, just wanted to be part of it . . . and we've ruined everything.'

'Heroes, are we?' Ned lit a cheroot and blew a cloud of smoke out into the darkness. 'You wanted a taste of glory?'

Leon nodded.

'Son, there's not much glory in a siege. Just want, and boredom, and frustration, I'm afraid. But your uncle isn't dead, yet. Man has more lives than a cat. Tell you the honest truth, that's what scares me most about this attack. Penrod has survived the desert, the Dervish, battles and enemies that should have killed him a dozen times. If he is killed by violence, I think it will be something like this. A man who is impervious to warriors and guns will most likely be brought down by a child armed with a kitchen knife.'

Leon began to sob more steadily.

'I do not think, Lord Edward, that you are making him feel better,' Tau said.

'Good evening,' said a voice in the shadows and Tau looked up to see a native man approaching them. He was carrying a thin folder of papers in his hand. 'These are the young adventurers, I take it? I came to enquire after Penrod.'

Ned smiled. 'Good evening, Sol. Boys, this is Mr Plaatje. Sol, may I present Leon Courtney and Tau Modisa. Sol, join us for a moment.' He moved aside on the step to make room for the new arrival, and Sol brushed the dust away with his handkerchief, then sat down and accepted a cheroot from Ned.

'It is still touch and go with Penrod,' he said as he lit Sol's cheroot for him. 'We'll know in a day or two.'

Sol nodded. 'Two of our people tried to cross the lines tonight and were driven back. We may have more luck tomorrow reaching this young man's parents with news of him.'

'What?' Leon wiped his eyes. 'My parents are in Cape Town!'

Sol shook his head. 'No, young man, they followed you here.' He removed a typewritten sheet from the folder he was carrying and handed it to Ned. 'I have been speaking to the runner who came in with Ryder Courtney's note. This is the latest information that we have been able to gather, Lord Edward. I do not know what he said in his note, but Ryder and Saffron Courtney are asking the Barolong at Setlogole if Leon and Tau might be smuggled out of town.'

Ned scanned the report. 'Thank you, Sol. Might it be possible to get them out?'

'No!' Leon's heart beat in a wild panic. 'No! I shall not go. I will scream and fight. There are other boys here, why can't I stay?'

The two men exchanged glances. 'Every other boy has family here,' Sol replied, then addressed Ned. 'Getting anyone across the lines is a terrible risk. Our people have told Mr and Mrs Courtney as much.' Then he said something in Setswana to Tau which Leon could not understand.

Tau glanced at Leon and replied in English. 'Thank you, sir. I will stay with Leon, if that is permitted. But I thank you for your offer of hospitality.'

Sol raised one eyebrow. 'Tau speaks English as well as I do. He will take my job as translator for the town.'

Tau suddenly grinned. 'I should like that! Though I am just learning to read.'

Sol finished his cheroot, blowing out the last of the smoke with a sigh of satisfaction. 'Come to the residence when you are free, we could always do with someone to run messages, and I will help you with your reading.'

Tau beamed at him.

'Can I be of use?' Leon asked.

Ned sighed. 'Baden-Powell has gathered together some of the children into a cadet force, delivering messages. You may join them.' Leon looked pleased.

Sol got up, wished them all goodnight and, asking Ned to pass on his best wishes and prayers to Mrs Ballantyne, he left them. Tau stared after him.

'Lord Edward,' Leon said after a minute of silence. 'Why did Flora want to kill Colonel Ballantyne?'

'Some business to do with her father and Penrod before hostilities broke out, I think.' Ned dropped the butt of his cheroot to the ground, stood and extinguished it under his boot. 'Whatever work we offer you, I assume you two will not be moving from this spot until you have news of Penrod?'

They nodded in agreement.

'I would do the same. Boys, you could not have realised that girl's intentions. Amber knows that, and she is not angry with you. She just doesn't want to look you both in the face and reassure you that everything is fine until it is.'

'What will happen to Flora, I mean, Hester?' Tau asked.

'I do not know. Her case will be heard by the mayor and town council, and they will make a decision. She is a civilian, so it is a civilian matter, even if the man she tried to murder is a colonel.'

• • •

Ned brought the boys food and blankets from the HQ storeroom, which allowed Leon and Tau to continue to keep their vigil outside the hospital, begging the nurses for scraps of news. The mayor came and sat with them to hear the story of how they had met Hester for himself, and later so did a man who said he'd been appointed as Hester's lawyer. The newspaper men came, too, but Leon became cautious and said he would tell his story only to the officials, and his aunt when she was ready to hear it. Tau read to Leon from his copy of *Huckleberry Finn*. He did so quite fluently now. The news of the boys and their limited library must have got around the town, because when they woke the following morning, Tau found a note from Sol and a copy of a fat novel by Charles Dickens by his blanket. The note also said Hester's trial would be held the following day.

The trial was not what Leon was expecting. He and Tau were summoned to the town hall, but on arrival were told the building was too badly damaged by shellfire to be used for any official business, so the hearing was held outside under the shade of half a dozen broad-leafed sycamores. The man who had told them he was Hester's lawyer told them where to stand, and then Hester was brought from the gaol by a trooper. Another man walked behind her, but she was not bound in any way and Leon noticed that someone had given her a different, and cleaner, dress to wear. The mayor sat at the table with Ned Cecil and another, older man with a huge white moustache. They asked Hester her name, then asked if she was guilty of stabbing Colonel Ballantyne. She said yes, and the men at the table spoke to each other for a minute in hushed voices. The mayor said the decision of the court was that Hester be kept in the town gaol until the siege was over and the incident could be more fully investigated. Hester was led away again and the three men left without looking at Leon and Tau.

Sol walked past them, and Leon put out a hand.

'I thought we were to give evidence, Mr Plaatje?' he said.

Sol shook his head. 'She is guilty of a capital crime, Leon, but no one wishes to hang a child. They will keep her out of the way for the time being. I'll make sure that she's well treated.'

Hester had lied to them, and turned his victorious arrival into Mafeking into a tragedy, but somehow Leon was glad that she would not be harmed.

When they returned to their camp at the hospital, they found Amber waiting for them. Leon approached her slowly with his head lowered. Amber was pale from the sleepless nights that she had spent beside Penrod's bed, but when Leon was within a few paces of her, she opened her arms with a genuine smile. He ran into them without another thought. She held him close and put out her other hand to Tau.

'God heard our prayers,' she said. 'Penrod will live a long and happy life with me.'

The sudden relief made Leon feel lightheaded.

'He is asking for both of you. He wants to know how you managed to get here. You shall have to tell him in instalments; I don't want him to get tired out. Off you go now.'

The two boys dashed into the hospital, but Amber remained outside, drinking in the clean air of the morning. For three days Penrod had twisted his head from side to side on the pillow, murmuring his secrets and cursing his demons in half a dozen languages, as Amber watched and kept the flies from his face. Sometimes she had recognised scraps of his history in his words – his time in the Sudan and Ethiopia, his childhood and remnants of what sounded like poetry in Italian. She had not realised how many ghosts travelled with them in their marriage.

Then, a little while ago – while she half-dozed, exhausted, next to him – she had become aware of some change in the air and opened her eyes to find him looking at her, not with a distracted, unfocused gaze as he tried to see through a veil of fever, but clear and present.

'Amber,' he said, and squeezed her fingers. 'You look tired.'

She returned the pressure of his touch.

Amber was not alone on the hospital veranda for long. Ned, Sol and the magistrate, Charles Bell, had followed the boys over from the trial to let her know the result. She listened to them, then told them that she believed that Penrod was out of danger. Ned's long, narrow face opened into a broad smile.

'I am pleased,' Charles said. 'And I hope you understand why we have acted as we have done as regards the girl.'

She nodded. 'Sol, have any runners made it out of Mafeking since the children arrived?'

'Not yet,' he said. 'We have been cursed with clear skies at night. But we think perhaps this evening. If the rains last past sunset.'

The light falling through the pepper trees dappled Amber with shifting shadows, she looked ghost-like, insubstantial, but her voice was still clear and firm.

'Ned tells me that Leon refuses to leave, and I am sure that my sister and her husband will not move from the area around Mafeking until the siege is raised. Might Chief Wessels make use of them out on the veld? They are both excellent shots and riders.'

Sol frowned. 'To help steal the Boer cattle?'

Amber nodded.

'I shall speak to Mathakgong Kepadisa,' he said. 'He is the best of our men, and he, too, will cross the lines tonight if he can.'

'Thank you,' Amber said, then drew herself up very straight and looked at Ned Cecil. 'Penrod told me about Vintner's death and the reasons behind it. Neither of us wish for his daughter's death, but Ned . . . I should like to see her.'

'Today?'

'At once, if you please.'

Charles Bell nodded his assent, and he and Sol watched as Ned and Amber made their way towards the railway line. The gaol lay just on the other side of it.

'Sol, if you wish to return to the Stadt now, I can manage for the rest of the day. I'll have my notes for you to type up in the morning.'

'Thank you, Mr Bell,' Sol replied, smiling a little at the thought of how Mathakgong would receive the offer of help from Ryder and Saffron Courtney.

· · ·

The Mafeking town gaol was a low, tin-roofed building, with walls of corrugated iron that made it indistinguishable from the workshops and offices which surrounded it. The only point of difference was the blue lamp over the office door. It was divided roughly into thirds between offices and two sets of cells. To the rear was a small, empty yard where the prisoners were allowed to exercise, and a kitchen and washhouse to care for their needs. After consulting with the gaoler, it was decided that the washhouse, bare and secure, would be the best place for Hester and Amber to meet.

'I wish to speak to Miss Vintner alone,' Amber said, after a pair of chairs had been brought in and set on the earth floor.

The gaoler frowned, he had a face like a basset hound, and his jowls wobbled uncomfortably when he spoke.

'I'm not sure about that, Mrs Ballantyne.'

'I am.'

'But she stabbed the colonel!'

'At that point, Miss Vintner had the advantage of surprise and a knife, advantages she no longer has,' Amber remarked firmly, her exhaustion giving an edge to her voice. 'I am on my guard, and quite able to defend myself. I shall call you if I need you, and you have my word I shall be careful.'

The gaoler pursed his lips for a moment, then left reluctantly. It appeared as if Ned was also going to object, but the look on Amber's face told him that her mind was set. He stalked out and closed the door behind him.

After a few minutes the gaoler brought Hester in to join Amber in the washhouse.

As soon as the latch rattled shut, Hester looked up. She was sitting neatly, her feet together and her hands clasped in her lap as if she were in church waiting for the sermon to begin.

'Have you always been able to do that? Make men do what you say? It must make life easy.'

'Yet my life has not been easy,' Amber said, examining the child's face. 'How old are you, Hester?'

'Almost fifteen. Is he dead?'

'You mean my husband, Penrod?'

She nodded, staring at Amber.

'No, Hester. He was gravely injured, but the danger is over.'

The child made no attempt to hide her disappointment – her hands tightened in her lap and began to twist over each other.

'Your surgeon must be very good. I was sure I had done it right. I thought about it and thought about it and tried to twist the knife, but that man pulled me away so quickly. Is he in much pain?'

'Yes.'

Her shoulders relaxed slightly, but her hands still moved over each other in her lap. 'He should be dead. I thought God was trying to stop me when the men took my money, but then He sent Leon. Why isn't he dead?'

'What happened to you, Hester?' Amber asked. 'I know you have suffered loss, but Penrod told me that you were once a happy, pleasant girl who found solace in her Bible.'

'What would you know of my loss?'

'I saw my father die when I was much younger than you are, so perhaps I have more idea than you think.'

'He probably died saving you. I can see it in your face. My father died *instead* of saving me. My mother died, then they came and took the farm, and a week later we had a letter to say my father was dead.'

'You couldn't punish your father for abandoning you, so you attacked my husband instead? Is that it?'

'It's John Quinn's fault! And yours! That picture in the newspaper! Everything would have been as it ever was otherwise. It's your fault!'

Amber stared at her. 'So you think God wanted you to kill Penrod because someone printed my picture in the newspaper?'

Hester stood, agitated, and began to pace back and forth over the earth floor.

'No, He did! Or if He didn't, I don't care. I hope your husband dies and you, too!' She burst into tears. 'I hate you! Don't speak to me again!'

'You will be decently treated here, Hester. You will be fed, and given work to do. I shall have a Bible sent to you.'

Hester turned to face her, her thin body still rigid with rage and frustration. 'If He didn't want me to kill John Quinn, if He was just deceiving me, then I loathe Him, too! I shall never listen to Him again!'

Amber realised that Hester was still referring to Penrod by his false name – John Quinn – and she wondered if perhaps the girl had fallen a little in love with her husband during his stay at the farm. Of course she had. Penrod was handsome and would have charmed the women in the house with his usual ease. No wonder she hated him now. Amber called the gaoler, who opened the door, an expression of relief visible on his broad face.

Amber sent the Bible and was sad, but not surprised, when she heard it had been found in Hester's necessary bucket the next day. Every one of the pages had been torn into tiny squares. It must have taken her all night to desecrate the book.

• • •

'There,' Ryder said. 'Three boys with two rifles, but they have grown complacent. Saffron says that they didn't bother posting a watch at all last night.'

Mathakgong took Ryder's field glasses from him and adjusted the focus. Perhaps a quarter of a mile away in the shade of a lone Marula tree was a single round dwelling, heavily thatched, and beyond it a temporary kraal of thorn bushes. There was space there for forty or fifty head of cattle. 'Where are they grazing?' he asked.

'To the south-west,' Ryder replied.

'And these herdboys,' Mathakgong continued, 'they have not noticed you or Mrs Courtney watching them?'

Ryder shook his head. Mathakgong handed him back the field glasses, and made his way lightly down from the low ridge, then, with Ryder following him, further down into a shallow valley cut by one of the tributaries to the Molopo. Saffron was waiting there with the ponies and two of Mathakgong's men from Mafeking.

'What do you think?' Saffron asked.

Mathakgong grinned at her. 'A good find, Mrs Courtney. We will go tonight. Till then, we rest.'

He went to speak to his men and Ryder joined Saffron in the shade of the acacia grove where their temporary camp was hidden.

Saffron handed Ryder her canteen and he drank deeply, then smiled at her.

'You look pleased with yourself, Saffy.'

'I am pleased. Words of praise from Mathakgong are hard to come by,' she said, sitting down on one of the densely woven mats that served as their floor during the day, and their cover at night. 'I suppose it will be the same as last time?'

Ryder glanced at his watch. 'We're further from the lines than we were last time, so we shall have to go an hour earlier. Mathakgong needs to drive the cattle over the lines at first light, or he and his men will be shot from their saddles.'

He felt the familiar stirring in his blood which the approach of action always brought. This would be their third raid with Mathakgong since they had arrived here and taken up this strange existence, living wild on the veld within ten miles of the besieged city which their son refused to leave. Ryder was looking forward to nightfall.

Driven away from the encircled town, they had gone first to the Frasers, where they were welcomed warmly and had the chance to buy fresh clothes and, to Saffron's delight, a pair of sketchbooks and a fist full of pencils. It was clear, however, that English visitors would draw the attention of the Boer forces in the area. They waited only till they had news from Mafeking, then they wrote to Cape Town and rode for Mosita to visit Greta and David. Both were well and flourishing. They stayed two days, and Saffron sketched the family, then spent a long afternoon on the Bauers' veranda trying to capture the shifting shadows on the veld. It was there one of Mathakgong's cousins had found them and a meeting had been arranged.

Ryder was happy to do what he could for the besieged town, and Saffron was delighted, declaring that they were like Robin Hood. Now they travelled in great loops around Mafeking, spotting where the Boer commandos were grazing their cattle, and observing the routines of the herdboys, then sharing and comparing their information with the Tshidi Barolong allied with those in the Stadt. They rode at dusk and dawn, when keeping clear of patrols was easier, and avoided the areas populated by the Barolong boo Rapulana, who were allied to the Boers. Around them the summer rains, which often fell softly during the afternoons, poured life and colour into the veld. The trees bloomed with small white flowers, and the still air became lively with birdsong. Once every week they travelled to Modimola, a Barolong village west of Mafeking, to collect any letters that had arrived for them at the trading post – the Frasers had an agreement with the headman there and he was happy to play postman.

Saffron pulled her sketchbook from her pack and began to draw. She had spent many of these long afternoons drawing scenes from their journey to Mafeking from memory – the crowded trains and boats, the soldiers around their campfires, the streets of Pretoria emptied of all men of fighting age.

She was finishing a sketch of a young man in a hospital bed – he was the one who had told her about Leon and Tau's escape from the armoured train.

'You should send these back to Cape Town,' Ryder said.

Saffron glanced up, her chin in her hand. 'For the children?'

A bundle of letters had been waiting for them on their last visit to Modimola. They contained an inventory of the Courtney family's activities in the Cape, mostly written by Penelope, with scrawled notes from Kahruba, and details of Matthew's growth, health and nutrition as dictated by Nazeera. The news from Mafeking came from Mathakgong himself, who each time they met had a letter from Amber sewn into the lining of his jacket, and his own stories of skirmishes, shortages and Penrod's recovery.

The first letter that Saffron and Ryder had received in this way – from Mathakgong's hand – had come with an enclosure from

Leon. An apology, though it seemed to Saffron forced, and she suspected that her sister had been involved in its creation. She sent her love by return, and a curt admonishment, dictated by Ryder, requesting that his son cause as little trouble as possible. They did not know it, but that letter had been delivered stained with the blood of Mathakgong's man, who had been caught by a bullet from a Boer lookout as they had charged their first twenty head of stolen long-horned cattle over the trenches at dawn.

'Yes, but we should tell Penelope to send them to the newspapers,' Ryder said. 'Or better, to your agent in London. I'm sure the *Illustrated London News* would want to print them.'

Saffron examined the page in front of her. They had published her sketches of Ethiopia in the past. 'Perhaps I should send them to the *Chronicle*,' she said. 'To go alongside Amber's accounts.'

A shadow fell over the page and she looked up to see Mathakgong watching her.

'Can I draw your portrait, Mathakgong?' she asked.

He crouched down next to them and shook his head. 'Not till this war is over, Mrs Courtney. I do not want these Boer gentlemen to see my handsome face in the newspapers. How can I pretend to be a half-stupid herdsmen, lost in my own country, if they know my portrait? Even they would know me, if you drew it.'

Ryder chuckled. 'Where do we drive the cattle across the lines tonight, Mathakgong?'

Mathakgong cleared a space in the dust with the flat of his hand and drew a sketch of Mafeking with the end of a branch, marking the east-west line of the river and the railway track.

'Here, just west of Game Tree Fort.'

Ryder considered. 'Why not nearer to the Stadt?'

Mathakgong shook his head. 'With so many cattle we need space and speed. And the Boer are growing ever more careful of that part of the line.' He scratched the back of his neck. 'I have left men here, among the rocks, to watch for our coming and let us know the way is clear. And after tonight, you should travel north, I think. The Boer's friends among our people have been seen more often in this part of the veld. I think that they may be looking for you. And me.'

'We'll be careful who we speak with,' Saffron said.

Mathakgong dusted his hands. 'Good. Ask anyone you meet about the health of Teacher Samson. If they tell you that he has a fever, they are a friend. If they say anything else, put some ground between you and them.'

. . .

The moon had begun to sink in the sky as the raiding party made their way in silence from the shadow of the ridge towards the kraal. Mathakgong and Ryder went first, the grasses seeming to part for them as they moved swiftly towards the herdboys' hut with long strides. Saffron and Mathakgong's men were leading the ponies behind them. Ryder breathed in the hot, heavy air through his nose as they reached the hut, and took his rifle off his shoulder. Saffron was right. The young men guarding the cattle had become lazy and not set a guard. On the other side of the entrance, Mathakgong lit his lantern, then nodded to Ryder, and they turned into the doorway.

'Be still!' Mathakgong shouted in Setswana, lifting his light high, so that the three boys could see Ryder's rifle pointing at them. Ryder looked at each of them in turn. All young, all scared, and he caught no whiff of fight or defiance from them.

Outside they heard the gentle lowing of the cattle as Mathakgong's men reached the kraal.

Mathakgong grabbed the oldest of the boys by the collar and hauled him to his feet. 'You – bind your two friends and then show us the leader of the herd.'

Cows were like men. Any group of them had a leader they would follow.

One of the boys had noticed Ryder's white skin and spoke in English: 'You'll leave us to starve in the hut?'

'Once we have your cattle where we want them,' Ryder replied evenly. 'We'll release your friend and he'll come back to you. Now hurry.'

Saffron saw Mathakgong leading the boy out of the hut and held the ponies while his men shifted the thorn bushes. The cows began to stir uneasily as the boy led Mathakgong to the centre of the kraal, where one dappled cow, her horns longer than most of her companions', shook her head in greeting.

'Lead her out,' Mathakgong said and pointed north. The boy did as he was told as Mathakgong mounted his pony. Saffron lifted her head and breathed in the night air as the cattle filed out behind their leader, following Mathakgong. He and his men would ride up front while Ryder and Saffron brought up the rear, ready to stampede the cattle across the lines when the moment came.

It was a long hour as they made their way towards the Boer trenches encircling Mafeking. Saffron took the right flank of the herd, and Ryder the left, both urging their horses forward if one beast or another began to wander. At the head of the herd, she could see Mathakgong silhouetted by the moon, the herdboy perched awkwardly on the pony's withers in front of him. From time to time, Mathakgong would touch his long whip to the flank of the lead cow to urge her along.

The darkness seemed almost complete, and Saffron felt as if she was a being that understood the world in sound and shadow – the scuffle and scrape of a cow veering away, the greys and blacks on the horizon. Would her son share in their spoils? Almost certainly.

Mathakgong had told them that they were to drive the cattle between the Stadt and the town. Where were the Boer lines? Saffron could see the sky beginning almost imperceptibly to lighten in the east.

She dropped back a little. 'How far now?' she asked Ryder.

'Ten minutes, maybe less. Then Mathakgong will release the herdboy and we'll drive forward.'

Already it felt as if there was too much light. Surely the Boer laagers would be waking soon.

'Saffy!'

One of the cows was heading away from the herd, lowing and trotting briskly across the grasses towards a group of mopane trees. Had the beast scented its fruits? Saffron dug her heels into her pony's flanks and chased after the errant cow, cutting it off. It turned and headed back towards the others at once, but some movement under the tree made Saffron hesitate. She turned her pony and cantered towards it. In the shadows was a man, a rifle over his shoulder. One of Mathakgong's lookouts.

'*Dumêla rra*, brother,' she said.

He stepped forward. 'Good morning, our friend Mathakgong has done a good night's work. The way into Mafeking is quiet still.'

Saffron nodded. 'That is good news.'

The herd were already two hundred yards ahead. She should rejoin them.

'Do you have any word of Teacher Samson?' she asked.

The man looked confused. 'Samson? I hear he is well.'

'Thank you.' She smiled, turned her horse and cantered up to Ryder's side.

'Mathakgong's lookouts are dead,' she said quickly. 'We're riding into an ambush.'

Their path lay between two stone outcrops. As they passed, a tall figure raised his hand in greeting against the dawn. Mathakgong, at the head of the herd, raised his hand in return.

'Mathakgong!' Ryder yelled. 'Go now!'

The figure on the outcrop raised his rifle. Mathakgong saw the danger, rolled the herdboy off his pony's withers and dealt the lead cow a mighty blow across its back. The beast lurched forward with a bellow of protest as the boy dropped into the long grass. With sickening clarity, Saffron saw the figure on the outcrop fire, his body twitching with the recoil. One of the riders at the head of the herd spasmed and fell sideways before she even heard the shot. She pulled her revolver from her waistband and fired into the air, stampeding the beats in front of her.

Ryder saw another figure appear on the other outcrop and felt more than saw the man's attention turn towards them. Riding up behind Saffron, he leaned out of his saddle, grabbed her around the waist and hauled her off her pony and onto his. The bullet sang past his head as he rolled them both off his horse and into the grass.

Ryder landed heavily and felt his bones shudder with the impact. A shot rang out behind them and Saffron's pony bucked, screamed and stumbled. Saffron rolled onto her back and fired into the air again – the bellowing of the cattle and the thunder of their hooves shaking the ground under them.

Ryder pushed himself into a crouch. 'Take out the man behind us, Saffy!'

She was already on to her knees, holstering her revolver and pulling her rifle from her shoulder. Another bullet whined past them, but she did not flinch.

Back to back among the swaying wildflowers, husband and wife picked their targets and fired. The man who had spoken to her under the mopane tree crumpled to the ground. Ryder squeezed his trigger, and the figure on the outcrop threw up his arms and fell backwards. But then the cloud of dust thrown up by the cattle became too dense for them to see anything more. Saffron ran in a low crouch towards where her pony had fallen. A ghost in the dust, he saw her stop, and bend down to comfort the beast, then she took out her revolver again and fired.

'Saffron!'

Ryder whistled through his teeth. His horse – wild-eyed, its mane flying – emerged from the red cloud like a phoenix from the flames, and shook its head.

'We have to go, Saffy,' he said, lifting her into the saddle. She was biting her lip and her eyes were bright with tears. 'Now, while there's a chance to cover our trail.'

She cast one last desperate look in the direction of Mathakgong and the herd, then nodded. He got up behind her, urged his pony forward, and rode as fast as it could carry them towards their camp as the golden sun lifted above the horizon.

• • •

The cattle that Mathakgong brought into the town cheered the population, even while the Barolong mourned their losses.

'It was bad luck,' Sol told Tau as they drank tea together on his veranda. Sol had been a teacher in his youth, and though Tau was grateful for what Leon had taught him, he realised that his education would progress far more quickly under Mr Plaatje. They spoke in English, to practise, in Sol's words, Tau's stylistic range.

'One of Mathakgong's lookouts stumbled into a Boer patrol. Which is, at least, ironic.' Tau did not know what 'ironic' meant, but did not want to divert Sol from this more interesting topic by asking him to explain.

'It was not Mr and Mrs Courtney's fault, then?'

Sol shook his head. 'Mathakgong speaks very highly of them. He says that by the time his leg is healed, the Courtneys will have found him another hundred head of cattle to drive into the town. But he grieves for the men he lost.' He sipped his tea. 'Chief Wessels is angry that the whites are taking half of what Mathakgong has brought in.'

'Why is he called Wessels?' Tau asked. 'It is a Dutch name.'

'So is mine!' Sol replied cheerfully. 'We have borrowed much from the whites who have come to Africa. Though much has also been imposed . . .'

The afternoon rains fell softly around them, and Tau inhaled the scents of earth and greenery. It was a shame one could not eat such smells.

'And they still will not let us brew our beer in the Stadt.' Sol tutted. 'Even my friend, Mr Bell, knows so little of our life in the Stadt. I have tried to explain its importance.'

Tau finished his tea and set his cup down carefully on its saucer. 'Why is their ignorance our responsibility, Mr Plaatje?'

Sol raised his eyebrows in surprise, and looked at Tau, a faint smile lifting the corner of his mouth. 'I do not know, Tau. That is an excellent question. Perhaps my only answer is that a white man educated me, so I am endeavouring to return the favour.'

• • •

In the last days of 1899, the news of a series of shocking British reverses reached Mafeking. For once they did not have to rely on runners for news – the Boers sent them the latest newspapers from Pretoria and older issues from London under a white flag. Defeats at Stormberg and Colenso, but worst of all the advance of Lord Methuen, which was supposed to relieve the sieges of Kimberley and Mafeking, had come to a halt at the Battle of Magersfontein, thanks to General Cronjé. It was clear that relief would not be arriving in Mafeking for some considerable time. Stuttaford was summoned to headquarters and emerged an hour later looking grim – he had been put in charge of stopping all private sales of grain and other provisions and imposing new penalties on hoarders. Even in the hospital, bread was replaced with hard rusks. Those townspeople fortunate enough to still own a laying hen, made sure to keep the birds inside their houses, rather than risk them running around outside in the famished town.

Leon had been formally recruited into the Mafeking Cadets and he regarded it as his duty to keep Penrod fully informed of the state of the siege. Penrod's wound was slow to heal, and his convalescence was complicated by the lack of good food. He let the boy talk to his heart's content whenever he visited. He was certain to obtain more accurate information from Ned Cecil, but what Leon lacked in hard facts, he more than made up for in superfluous detail.

Tau visited Penrod as well, and was proud of reading each edition of *The Mafeking Mail* to him as soon as it was published. Sol had introduced him to the newspaper's editor and Tau, with Bell's permission, transferred his labour from the magistrate's office to the newspaper. As the editor was also the chief writer and printer of the daily sheet of town news, Tau began to gain a thorough knowledge of printing presses and compositing.

At night, Leon and Tau slept on thick piles of blankets by the kitchen stove in Amber and Penrod's cottage, and though Amber was afraid that they were starving, losing weight by day, neither boy showed any sign of fatigue. In fact, they shone with the importance of their work.

• • •

Christmas dinner consisted of two tins of potted partridge that Amber had bought at vast expense from Mr Weil. They shared them perched on Penrod's bed in the convalescent ward. Ned joined them for a game of cards afterwards, then lingered while Amber sent the two boys back to the cottage and bed.

'We're taking the Boer fort on Game Tree Hill tomorrow,' Ned told Penrod. '"D" Squadron is getting restive again, and B-P thinks that if we are going to break the news to the populace that we might still have three months to go, then he had better give them some good news first to sweeten the pill.'

'Three months? Can we feed the people for that long?' Penrod asked, distressed.

'It will be touch and go, Penrod. Stuttaford's doing a good job and we found a couple of hoarders and requisitioned their stock, but God knows, it's little enough.'

'I wish I could be with you at Game Tree Hill tomorrow,' Penrod said.

'I know you do, old man. That girl made a proper mess of your insides, didn't she? Still, give the other officers a chance to snatch some glory while you're laid up.'

• • •

The attack was a disaster. Penrod was forced to wait in his bed for news, his frustration growing, until Amber visited him late in the afternoon.

'The fort had been reinforced,' she told him. 'They didn't have a chance. Our bombardment had no effect at all. It was a slaughter.'

'How many dead?' Penrod asked.

'Twenty-six,' Amber replied. 'I went up with the hospital wagon. The fort looked untouched, Penrod. They might as well have attacked a mountain. Another twenty-two wounded.'

Penrod lifted himself up in bed, the pain of his wound causing the muscles across his belly to shiver, but he lowered his feet to the cold floor.

'Lend me your shoulder, Amber. I've been here long enough.'

• • •

February unfolded with a series of downpours, turning the bomb shelters into mud baths. Amber's reports were published in London to great acclaim whenever a runner managed to take them through the lines, the Sunday entertainments continued to be enthusiastically received and her own days were lightened by the presence of Leon and Tau. Penrod had recovered enough to lead a number of artillery duels with the Boers, but after the losses of the Boxing Day attack on Game Tree Hill, no major offensive was attempted against the besiegers. The garrison's strategy had become one of dogged survival. Some days were worse than others – a child was killed by a shell blast in the women's laager, and councillor Dall, a popular and good-humoured man, was cut in half in front of his wife by a ninety-four-pound shell – but the townspeople still threw themselves into the war effort. The men learned to make shells for the seven-pounder in the railway yards and the women turned their skills to cooking up gunpowder.

Leon quickly gained a reputation for bravery. Some of the town boys were disposed to be jealous at first – he was nephew of Colonel Ballantyne, after all, and had wild stories of his journey from the Cape to Mafeking. Many of the other cadets had never left the town and assumed that Leon would engage only in the easiest or most interesting activities, but it became clear from the beginning that he would take his turn scrubbing floors and rolling bandages and carrying the empty ammunition cases, and whistle cheerfully while he was doing it.

One of the paths that even the most committed of the cadets avoided was the narrow track that ran from the eastern edge of the town towards the brickfields. The Boer snipers did not like to fire on children, but they would pepper the ground in front of the cadets with bullets along that route, and more than one of them had come back white with terror or bleeding from a ricochet. When Ned Cecil came into the clubroom one day in early March and asked for a messenger to go to the outer post in that direction, most of the boys affected deafness, but Leon sprang to his feet, grabbing the note and tucking it into the pouch on his belt. He ran towards the bicycles that had been requisitioned for the cadets, and within two minutes was pedalling hard over the uneven ground.

Leon kept his pace even and his head high as the bullets sent up fountains of sand and dust a yard or two in front of him. The little jerks of excitement he felt when he saw the earth explode pleased him, and though the ground was rough, he could cycle fast enough so that a cool breeze fanned over his face. In the middle of a hot summer afternoon this was a rare pleasure.

The Cape Boys were watching him and broke into applause as he arrived panting, drenched in sweat and covered in dust, his face red from the physical effort, but shining with pride. While the sergeant read the note and considered if a reply was necessary, the ten other men on duty in the fort let Leon examine the Maxim gun and explained how the mechanism worked.

The sergeant decided that Lord Cecil's message needed no immediate reply, but Leon was allowed to stay for a cup of tea and treated to an account of the attack on Canon Kopjé, and Amber's dramatic return through the lines.

'It's still light enough for even the blindest Boer to see you're a child,' the sergeant said as he ushered Leon out of the trenches again. 'But in half an hour the shadows will lengthen, so get going now.'

Leon set off at a more sedate pace towards town. His mind wandered and he only realised that he had come off the main road, and was instead following the lonely route towards the Fingo village, when a sniper's bullet buried itself close to his front wheel. Leon braked suddenly, lost his balance and stumbled to the ground, another bullet punching a hole into the earth three inches from his right ear. He heard it zip through the air, and the grit it threw up fell across his face. Jumping to his feet, Leon felt indignant. This sniper must not know the rules. Another bullet threw up earth behind him. Leon looked around. One of the Fingo huts, smaller and shabbier than those in the Barolong Stadt, was a hundred yards away. He climbed back onto his bicycle and pedalled towards it with all his strength, his heart thudding in his chest and the muscles of his thighs burning.

He reached the far side of the hut, sprang off his bike, and curled into a ball, bringing his knees up to his chest.

'So that is what it is like to be shot at,' he said to himself. He had been under fire when the armoured train was derailed, but no one was aiming *at* him then. He found it interesting how different this felt. He was scared – his rapid breathing and shaking hands proved it – but he was also aware of a deep, surging excitement, and an intense joy now that he was hidden from the sniper. Somehow, he had won, and everything – the red earth in front of him, the shifting pattern of shade from the thorn tree – seemed painfully clear and of remarkable beauty. He was alive, and the pleasure that he felt at being alive was deeper, stronger even than the delight he had felt on that first night in the railway carriage with Tau, after he had run away from the Mount Nelson. He had a slight bitter taste in his mouth but his legs, so tired before, seemed to burst with energy. He could run all the way to Pretoria without stopping if he wanted to.

Leon laughed loudly.

Then he stopped.

He had thought the huts around him were deserted, but he had heard something, a whispering groan. Getting to his feet, he looked in through the open doorway, trying to make out shapes in the darkness of the interior, then pulled away again as a rank smell struck him.

'Good afternoon,' he called into the hut.

Silence. He thought he'd try with some of the Setswana that Tau had been teaching him. *'Thapama e e monate!* Is anyone there? My name is Leon. Can I help?'

Again, he heard the whispering groan, and as his eyes adjusted to the darkness inside the hut he could see three figures lying together on the earth floor – a man, woman and child. Covering his nose with his hands, he darted into the darkness and crouched beside them, looking for wounds or signs of sickness, but all he saw were wasted, stick-thin limbs. The man turned his head towards Leon and opened his eyes, unnaturally large in his flesh-less face. His lips pulled back from his teeth and he murmured something. Leon leaned forward to try and catch the word.

'Metsi . . . water . . .'

Leon fumbled for his canteen and put it to the man's lips, but he tried to push it away, pointing to his wife and child.

'I have enough for all of you,' Leon said. 'You have some first.'

The man managed a couple of swallows, then his head fell back and he seemed to fall into a fitful sleep. Leon managed to force a little water between the lips of the woman. The child was young, younger than Penelope, with a swollen belly. Leon lifted him up a little so he could put the canteen to his lips, feeling the weight of him, the thin bones under his papery skin. He waited patiently for a few minutes and then wet the boy's lips again.

Leon had no thought for the sniper when he exited the hut and mounted his bike. He rode like the wind, angry and determined to reach the camp as quickly as possible. Stopping outside head-quarters he paused to catch his breath, then ignoring the raised eyebrows and frowns of the senior officers in the outer room, he stormed into Ned Cecil's office without knocking.

'They are starving!' he shouted.

Ned was sitting behind his desk, his hands behind his head. He turned towards Leon, looking confused and angry.

'In the Fingo village! I just found them. We must send nurses at once and food, and I didn't even look in the other huts . . .' The realisation of his negligence hit Leon as the words came out of his mouth.

'Oh! I still have some water left in my flask! I must go back and give it to them. Why do we still have food when they are dying?'

Then suddenly, unstoppably, he began to cry.

Ned was still staring at him, his face haggard. Leon felt a hand on his shoulder. He found Penrod standing behind him, and with him was Baden-Powell.

'Pull yourself together, Courtney,' Penrod said, 'and make your report.'

Leon drew in a long and shuddering breath.

'I was coming back from delivering a message to the Cape Boys, sir, and a sniper chased me into the Fingo village. While taking cover, I heard a sound and discovered a man with his wife and child in one of the huts. I believe they are in the last stage of starvation, sir, and I came back here to make my report.'

He felt Penrod squeeze his shoulder.

'Came back here to tear my head off and feed it to them more like,' Ned said.

'Damn!' Baden-Powell said. 'Master Courtney, it seems that we have not done our duty in this case. We've set up soup kitchens, but some don't trust them, especially the Fingo refugees who have no ties to the Barolong here. Thank you for making your report. Ned, will you see someone is sent out now, the doctor, too, to supervise. Tell them to check the other huts as well. Gentlemen, we will finish our discussions this evening.'

Baden-Powell clasped his hands behind his back and left the room without further remark, and Leon felt his face grow hot with fury and frustration.

'Major Cecil, I am very sorry I shouted,' Leon said. 'Please let me join the party that is taking the food and the doctor?'

Leon saw Ned lift his gaze. He was checking to see what Penrod thought. Penrod must have nodded, because Ned straightened up his long frame.

'Very well, Courtney. You may go along, but listen to the doctor. You know that people who have been starving need to be fed just a little at first, don't you?'

'Yes, sir,' Leon said.

'Fetch Amber and take her along,' Penrod said.

Ned raised his eyebrows. 'A member of the press, Penrod? Do you think that wise?'

'Amber saw starvation when she was besieged in Khartoum. It will distress her, but not bring on a fainting fit. Also, Ned, she volunteers at the feeding station, so she will discover soon enough that these people have been found in this state. Better she reports on the humane actions of the British Army, trying to clear up the mess, than writes a story about how in a town of fewer than ten thousand souls we managed to miss the fact some of them are dying of want in the first place, don't you think?'

Leon heard a slight edge to Penrod's voice as he said this.

'Very well.'

Ned wrote something on one of the pages in front of him, tore off the sheet and handed it to Leon.

'Take that to Major Anderson at the hospital, please, Courtney, then help him gather whatever emergency supplies he needs. I'll have two men and your aunt waiting for you and the doctor when you come back.'

Leon hesitated, the note still in his hand.

'Sir, the nurses at the hospital are so busy. I would like to ask my friend Tau to help. And also Flora – I mean, Hester. They looked after me when I was sick and she is doing no good in prison.'

'For God's sake, Courtney, she tried to kill Penrod!' Ned replied, exasperated.

'I remember,' Penrod said in his dry drawl. 'Leon, you are to make sure she doesn't try again. Lord knows, I do not fear a child, but I do not have eyes in the back of my head.'

Ned shook his head. 'Very well, so ordered.'

Penrod watched the boy leave, the note clasped in his hand. The thought of the girl in the town gaol had troubled him more than he had thought it would as he recovered. He felt no responsibility for her. It was not his fault that her mother had taken to her bed and died, nor that Vintner had orphaned his child by pursuing his revenge. But to see hate move between generations disturbed Penrod. He thought of Amber's nephew in Cairo, writing his cruel letters, the way Leon hero-worshipped him and yet despised his own father. What would his own son, that child growing up in Mosita without his father or mother, think of Penrod Ballantyne when he reached the age of reason?

.   .   .

L eon would never forget the slow unfolding horror of that evening. The sniper who had been so active when he had returned from the Cape Boys' outpost earlier in the day had gone quiet, so they reached the Fingo village quickly and discovered eight men, six women and six children in the last stages of starvation.

Two carts were brought across from the Barolong Stadt, and the sick men, women and children were loaded onto them. Most had to be carried – only one old man thrust away the hands that tried to help him and tottered unsteadily out of his hut before proudly lifting himself onto the cart.

The soup kitchen had been set up on the northern edge of the Barolong Stadt and they carried the Fingo towards it. A neighbouring pair of huts had been requisitioned and lined with camp beds, covered with blankets that had been collected from the army stores. The sick were led or carried into the makeshift hospital.

Tau translated for the doctor. He was brisk and efficient, though Leon noticed his lips were pale with shock at the starving bodies in front of him – the spectacle was not for the faint-hearted. Major Anderson gave the refugees a mixture of meat, mealie meal and milk, prepared as a sort of porridge, and Leon helped to spoon small portions of the strange mess into the mouths of the children. Hester declared at first that she would not help, until Leon shouted at her and reminded her that she, too, had been starving when they found her in the mines.

Sethunya, one of the women from the Barolong Stadt, placed an infant in Hester's arms and thrust a beaker of mealie porridge into her hand. It was obvious that Hester's help was needed and when Leon looked back over to her a short while later, she was talking to the baby in Dutch and trying to feed the tiny creature.

An hour later, Leon heard Hester crying. She was holding the baby close to her chest and sobbing. Sethunya sat beside her and looked at the child, then put her slim arm around Hester.

'The baby was too sick,' Sethunya said, squeezing Hester's shoulder. 'I am sorry. But he died hearing you singing and in friendly arms.'

Hester continued crying, and Leon thought perhaps it was not just the baby she was crying for. At last, Sethunya took the baby from her, placed it on her own lap and covered its face.

'That boy over there on the cot has eaten all he is allowed,' Sethunya said to Hester. 'Go and sit by him, hold his hand and sing him your songs. I shall take this child to be buried with his mother.'

Sethunya left the lean-to without looking back. As she passed him, Leon heard her whisper to the dead child: 'No one brought you peaches, did they, sweet child?'

Leon managed to get the boy he was feeding to take another mouthful, and, when he looked again, Hester was sitting by the cot Sethunya had indicated, holding the boy's hand and singing softly.

• • •

Amber walked behind Leon and Tau, following at a distance, watching Hester being escorted back to the gaol. As soon as Hester had been handed over to the guards, Amber called the boys and they all went to their cottage, where she prepared their own meagre supper.

'Aunt Amber,' Leon said, as she was washing the dishes. 'Do we have peaches?'

'I'm afraid not, Leon. Why do you ask?'

He told her what he had heard Sethunya say, but Amber was too busy with her chores to interrogate him further and anyway, it wasn't long before he and Tau were snoring.

Amber returned to a halo of light thrown by a hurricane lamp with her pen in her hand and tried to write about what she had seen that day. At last the words found a rhythm. She detailed the weakness of the starving, their numb, ghostly hunger and her own rage. She wrote of the irresponsibility of the officers who had these refugees dig their bomb shelters and then forgot about them; of the Barolong leaders who had not helped their neighbours; she wrote of her own guilt that in a small town her fellow humans could be in such dire want, and yet she knew nothing about it. She wrote about some of the Barolong people she had known, who had been killed, the empty houses and motherless children they had left behind them. She wrote of her anger that the siege was being treated like a game by the British newspapers, who had no conception of the daily hardships all those behind the lines faced – the nerve-shattering bombardments, the snipers, the constant hunger. She wrote about their attempts to keep the worst of it from the children, to keep them fed and occupied. Finally, she described how no one would leave Mafeking without carrying the wounds of the siege with them.

Penrod arrived and she handed the pages to him. He read them through and set them down on the table, then Amber picked them up and tore them in half.

'I needed to write it, Penrod. That does not mean I need anyone other than you to read it.'

. . .

When Amber woke up the next day, Tau was making breakfast with Leon, such as it was, and Penrod had already left for his duties. The boys went to fetch Hester and returned to the feeding station, and as Amber cleaned the plates and put them away, Leon's question about the peaches came back to her.

Later, when she asked for Sethunya at the feeding station, Amber was told that she was spending some time at her home, so she went to find her in the Barolong Stadt.

The hunger was as apparent here as in the European Quarter. When Amber had first visited the Stadt, she would be greeted by everyone she passed. The women and infants would wave, and the men touch their foreheads as if they were saluting or doffing their caps to her like gallants in the London streets. Now, no one wasted their energy on smiling, and conversations were conducted in whispers. The pathways between the huts were mostly deserted and were slowly becoming overgrown. Children and women with health or strength left in them were out working in the few fields that lay within the defensive perimeter. Other homes were deserted, and Amber hoped their former residents had made it through the lines, though she knew many had not.

Amber was guided to Sethunya's hut by a child who could not have been older than four years of age. Sethunya was sitting outside in the sun with two other women. After they had exchanged the proper greetings, Amber was invited to take a seat on a low stool, and the woman who had been sitting there, the most junior of the three, crossed her legs and sat on the ground.

They were sorry about the starving Fingo, but none of them seemed surprised.

'Why did they not come to us? To the town council or my husband?' Amber asked.

'When we tell Baden-Powell we are hungry, he says to go through the lines, you will be fed there,' the woman sitting on the ground said. 'Then one of every two is shot by a Boer, like animals.'

Amber was silent. She knew that the woman spoke the truth – the Barolong were caught in between the British and the Boers, no matter what Baden-Powell said. They had defended the Stadt, so the Boers saw them as the enemy, but the British couldn't feed all of them, not anymore, they would only give them guns and ammunition. It was an impossible situation.

'And the people you found in the village – they are proud,' the woman went on. 'They would rather die than eat horse meat, or feed it to their children, and we will not give them beef because they were too proud to eat what we eat when there is no beef. It was offered in charity.'

'They spent everything they earned labouring on the special food,' Sethunya said. 'Then, when they had no more money, they sold whatever they had.'

'What special food is that?' Amber asked.

'The peaches,' the woman seated on the stool said. 'The peaches the whites take every day, which is why they do not get fever and still have flesh on their bones. You serve no peaches in the soup kitchen.'

'But the whites do not each peaches every day,' Amber said.

'So you say,' the woman sitting on the floor replied.

Sethunya said something sharp, too quickly for Amber to understand, and the girl looked at the ground. Standing up, Sethunya offered Amber her arm and Amber realised that she was being politely escorted away.

'Sethunya, you must *know* that we are not eating peaches every day?'

Sethunya patted Amber's hand. 'Someone from the garrison is telling these stories about the peaches and the whites, and some people believe them. And some believe them enough to pay a great price to possess what is offered. Me, I do not believe, but when my son was sick before Christmas, I sold my best cooking pot to get a can of peaches. Ah, what we do for our children!' She paused, a sad smile on her face. 'And my son recovered.'

'Then someone is stealing supplies, Sethunya,' Amber said. 'You must know who it is. You have to tell me.'

She shook her head. 'You wish me to go and tell stories in the town about your friends? No, Mrs Ballantyne. Look for your own bad man.'

'Does Mr Plaatje know?'

She shook her head, half-smiling. 'Ah, Sol. He is a clever man, but he lives half of the time among the white people of the town. He knows more than you about us, but not everything.'

When they reached the path to town, Sethunya immediately turned back to the Stadt without bidding Amber farewell. Amber watched her go. The Barolong didn't trust them, and they had given them no reason to do so. She marched back towards the European Quarter and straight into Stuttaford's office.

• • •

Stuttaford received Amber's report with genuine concern and swore to look into the matter. As soon as his military assessments were completed for the evening, he took a lantern and a sheaf of inventory reports and went to the storehouses.

The trooper on watch greeted him with casual friendliness – they never had managed to instil much military discipline into their irregulars – as Stuttaford let himself into the half-empty barn.

If these tins of fruit were finding their way into the Stadt, it suggested that one of his own staff was stealing them, and that could lead to a lynching. The latest meeting he'd had with Baden-Powell and the senior officers had been sobering. Supplies that Stuttaford believed inadequate to feed the town for six weeks would have to be stretched out for two and a half months, and he was certain the last of the food hoarders among the townspeople had been rooted out. It was impossible for them to hide anymore in a population that was growing so thin; already any man or woman who did not look swamped by their clothing had been questioned, and sacks of corn and dried beans hauled from the attics of weeping housewives. The cattle-rustling exploits of Mathakgong, his men and Mr and Mrs Courtney were all that stood between them and surrender.

Stuttaford set his lamp in the middle of the floor and began his stocktake. At first the numbers tallied, but peering around a stack of crates, to check his count, he rested his hand on one box in the pile and it shifted. The weight was wrong.

He lifted one of the other cases piled on top of it. The lid was not fastened down and when he opened it up, he found it empty. He sat down on one of the other crates, breathing heavily, then brought his lamp close to the empty one. A chalk mark, hardly noticeable unless you were looking for it, was visible on the bottom corner.

Stuttaford began another slow tour of the dwindling supplies and found another mark, another empty crate. By the fourth one, he didn't even bother opening the crate. He knew they would hold nothing but packing straw. There were so many of them. Not just peaches, but crates that had held meat and biscuits, too.

He sat down again and put his head in his hands. They would need to cut the rations again.

The door swung open and Cressy sauntered towards him through the shadows. He paused briefly on the edge of the lantern's dull yellow light and looked around. 'You've made a right mess, here, Stuttaford! It'll take an hour for us to neaten this up again.'

Stuttaford stared at him. 'What are you doing here? Get out.'

'Heard Mrs Bloody Ballantyne had been to see you, talking about peaches.' He craned his neck to examine the remaining piles of crates.

'This was you, Cressy? It's you who's been selling lies to the Fingo and Barolong?'

Cressy sat down casually on a crate at the far edge of the lamp-light, his knees wide apart and a grin on his face. 'I wouldn't have taken you for a prejudiced man, Stuttaford. I've been selling just as much to the white women. They take the meat. Darkies can't stand the tinned stuff, but they'll pay anything for peaches. Funny, isn't it?'

Stuttaford was shocked, then disgusted. Cressy seemed proud, looking at Stuttaford as if he expected to be admired.

'Funny? You should be shot.'

'Shot?' Cressy laughed. 'I am a man of free enterprise. Men like me pay for your uniforms.'

Stuttaford stared at him.

'If they are stupid enough to believe a tin of peaches will save them and their wretched brats, well, that's just a tax on their ignorance, and should prove educational for them.'

'The tinned fruit is reserved for the hospital and the children of the town,' Stuttaford spluttered. 'You are robbing the sick and the needy and you expect me to turn a blind eye?'

'See, I'm not even lying to the darkies, you do give the little white kids peaches!' Cressy leaned forward. 'And you will turn a blind eye. You've been doing nicely out of it yourself. We both know that. You think Lesedi is keeping you warm at night because of your charm and handsome face? Girl has a big family and none of them rich. Now, all of them are looking much more comfort-able. They help me sell to the others and them looking all sleek and well means I get more customers.'

Stuttaford blinked. 'Lesedi is paid by the garrison to act as my . . . housekeeper.'

'What? That's a little tip for her! Her real wages are paid on your behalf, by *me*.'

Cressy appeared to be pleased with Stuttaford's confusion. His heavily lidded eyes shone and, shaking his head, he got to his feet and patted Stuttaford on the shoulder. 'God, you're a sorry excuse for a man, aren't you? Keep your mouth shut, Captain. We've done nicely out of this siege. In a few more weeks Colonel French or some other bugger will come and relieve us, and we can all be heroes of the Empire. It means a nice career for you, and some happy memories of your time in Mafeking, and I'll have means enough to set up again in Cape Town. You tell anyone who needs to hear it that one of the bearers stole a crate or two of peaches in the early days of the siege and has been selling them off. All over, nothing more to see. Tell 'em it was one of those runners who got shot last week.'

Cressy strolled out of the store without waiting for a reply, his hands thrust in his pockets.

Stuttaford didn't move. He would go at once to Penrod and make a full confession. Cressy had stolen from the town and must be punished. Yet somehow he didn't go and make his report. He imagined Penrod's steady gaze, Baden-Powell's disappointment. He thought of what Cressy had said. Stuttaford could spare himself humiliation and keep his comforts with a small lie. Cressy would be more careful in future, and Stuttaford would remain, in the eyes of his fellow officers, a man to be relied on. In the middle of a war, while death skulked round every corner in Mafeking, what did it matter? Baden-Powell didn't care for the natives – they had let the Fingo starve, after all, and the Barolong were shot in the back and no one mentioned it. Messengers were killed crossing the lines; herdboys were caught in the crossfire. Death was greeted with a shrug. Stuttaford clenched his fists. It would be better for the garrison to avoid the scandal, discretion was important in times like these.

Stuttaford locked the stores behind him and nodded to the guard on duty before heading back to his home through the dark streets, passing the hulking shadows thrown by the railway sheds. If Lesedi found his lovemaking a little rough that night, she made no complaint.

The next morning Stuttaford visited Amber to explain about the theft of a crate of peaches early on in the siege and she seemed to accept the story, along with his assertion that no further action needed to be taken. On the way back to his offices he stopped at Dixon's to buy a bottle of whisky and tried to ignore the surprise and concern flickering across the new barman's face as he took his money.

• • •

Amber didn't believe a word of Stuttaford's report, but she made sure that he couldn't see her suspicions on her face. As soon as Stuttaford had left she went to the Barolong Stadt and to Sethunya.

'Is it Cressy who is selling you peaches?'

'Good day to you, Mrs Ballantyne,' Sethunya said, leaving her grinding bowl and joining Amber at the fence.

'Yes, I'm sorry. Good day. But is it Cressy? You said something about "my friends". I thought you meant all the whites, but it was Cressy who helped me with the entertainments. Why in God's name is Stuttaford lying for him?'

Sethunya leaned forward on the fence. 'Trooper Cressy sent a girl to be Captain Stuttaford's housekeeper.'

Amber nodded with the knowledge of what Sethunya meant and understood the bargain that Stuttaford had made.

Sethunya shrugged. 'What will be done?'

Amber folded her arms across her body. 'If you will give evidence, Stuttaford and Cressy will be court-martialled. Will you?'

Sethunya considered before she spoke. 'Yes. As you have come to me. What of the money he has taken?'

Amber was thinking about the sentences Cressy and Stuttaford were likely to receive and answered absently. 'It will be confiscated and given to the widows' and orphans' fund, I imagine. He shan't be allowed to keep it.'

Sethunya's silence brought Amber back to reality and she looked at the older woman, realising what she had said. The widows' and orphans' fund distributed payments to the white population. Sethunya's expression was cold.

'I'll ask Baden-Powell to see it is shared with the Barolong.'

Sethunya nodded. 'Will you need other women to testify? How many native women does it need to prove a charge against a white man?'

'When my husband is in charge, only one. But if you can bring one or two others, that would help. Can you come to the feeding station in an hour? I'll make sure that Penrod and the mayor will be there as well.'

· · ·

The evidence was damning. With Sol translating from his place next to Ned, and his wife sitting on a low metal bench with the witnesses, Penrod heard a full and distasteful account of Cressy's manoeuvrings and influence in the Stadt. Chief Wessels did not attend, but Silas and some of the other headmen from the Stadt did. Their shock and disgust seemed equal to his own. Sometimes Cressy had used the food he stole to take his pick of the women and girls who caught his fancy. He told others that the tins of peaches were a special medicine the whites used to save themselves from fever and sickness. He demanded prices which drove desperate mothers to sell whatever possessions the family had, even to steal from their neighbours. Cressy took every shilling, and told them to be grateful when they gave it to him. Penrod began to understand why some of the men employed as diggers of bomb shelters and trenches, who should have had the money to keep their families fed, were gaunt and weak. They had spent everything they had on the luxuries Cressy assured them would cure their sick, or serve as a talisman against the Boer bullets when they risked their lives to smuggle news across the lines.

· · ·

The court martial that followed raised morale in Mafeking rather than lowered it. The white townspeople took great pleasure in the fall of Cressy, even those who had been buying extra food from him, and were united in their support of the Barolong, even if they had thought little about their black neighbours in the past.

Baden-Powell announced the sentences on Sunday afternoon, the only day when the crowd gathered to hear him that would not create an easy target for a Boer shell.

Stuttaford was to be stripped of his rank and confined. For the rest of the siege he would remain in the small town gaol, allowed an hour of exercise a day in the yard, and water to wash only once a week.

Stuttaford – standing solemnly, back straight, staring ahead, between his gaolers and under the contemptuous stares of the townspeople – said nothing. Amber was in the front row of the crowd with Tau and Leon, and, watching Stuttaford, remembered his manic laughter on the night Mrs Peters had died. What was it, she wondered, that meant some men lived a life convinced that their strength would fail if they were tested, while others, like her husband, believed that they would come out the other side of any test stronger than before? It seemed, looking at Stuttaford, that life was a cruel thing.

Perhaps Cressy thought he would receive the same sentence as Stuttaford. He smirked and winked his way through Stuttaford's sentence, and listened to Baden-Powell's preamble before his own with apparent nonchalance.

'The money discovered in Cressy's strongbox,' Baden-Powell continued, 'will be shared between the town rebuilding fund and the leaders of the Barolong, for distribution in the Stadt . . .'

'No! That's my money!' Cressy roared, lurching forward, the men on either side of him grabbing his arms.

Baden-Powell ignored him. 'In accordance with the military code, Cressy is also reduced in the ranks, and sentenced to twenty lashes. Sentence to be carried out immediately in the town gaol yard by Sergeant Picard of the British South African Police.'

Cressy gaped as he saw Sergeant Picard step forward, saw the colour of his skin. He pulled forward against the men who held him, his face scarlet. 'Never! I'm a trader! It's on the back of men like me that the British Empire was built, you hypocrites! Pretending to care about the kaffirs. Liars! They are nothing to you – just a way of keeping this idiotic siege going. Will you think of them when you are finished playing soldier-soldier? You will not.

They will be left here to mourn their dead and wonder why they died – for what?'

Baden-Powell made no move.

'Why am I here, accused by you po-faced bastards,' Cressy screamed, flecks of spittle flying from his lips, 'while that boy's father is called a hero?'

Leon felt the heat of the man's gaze on him.

'Ryder Courtney rustles cattle with the kaffirs! Why does he get his picture in the paper while you bang me up in the town gaol? He made a fortune during the siege of the Khartoum and then another stealing silver from the savages in Ethiopia. Now he helps to send you the occasional cow and he's a god!'

Leon clenched his fists. Amber put her hand on his shoulder to hold him back, but he shook her off and stepped forward across the dusty ground until he was face to face with Cressy. The whole town was watching him now, military men and civilians alike.

'My father is nothing like you!' Leon shouted. 'My father is an honourable man. He *lost* a fortune in Khartoum, saving my mother and feeding people, just like he's feeding us now. And he worked that mine in Ethiopia with Emperor Menelik's blessing. They were friends! He's what the Empire is built on! You're just a greedy thief.'

Amber couldn't tell if Cressy had heard Leon through his rage and humiliation, but she had. She felt a flare of hope in her chest. Leon must have heard some of the stories of Saffron and Ryder's exploits from Mathakgong. She knew he had visited him in the Stadt with Tau. The stories, coming from Mathakgong, must have had more weight than if they had come from her. Some day she would sit with her sister and Ryder and tell them this story, of Leon defending his father's honour with such passion in front of the whole town and every man of rank in Mafeking.

'Take him away,' Baden-Powell said.

The gaolers had to drag Cressy back into the prison block, his boots scrabbling at the earth.

'I want my money back! You lying, cheating bastards! I'll have you! I swear it!'

Leon remained where he was, his chin high.

The sentencing complete, Baden-Powell nodded to Penrod and Silas, who had come with a deputation from the Stadt, and returned to headquarters without further comment.

Cressy recovered from his lashing in the town gaol, and as soon as his wounds had healed enough to allow him to put on a uniform again, he was sent to the forward trenches in the brickfields. Penrod received the news that he had gone missing in the middle of April. He assumed that he had fled, but hoped that one of the Cape Boys had put a bullet in his head and buried him in the veld.

• • •

Ryder Courtney lay in the long grass by the campfire, his hands behind his head, and watched the sky darken gradually as the African night fell across the veld. Saffron was sitting by his side, reading the latest letters carried to them via the Frasers. They had not slept in a bed for weeks, nor changed their clothes. Twice they had visited Greta and David in Mosita. The rest of the time they moved quietly across the veld, ready to help Mathakgong with his raiding, providing help for the runners when they could.

Saffron had received two precious letters from Leon – smuggled out of Mafeking in the lining of Mathakgong's jacket. He had assured them that he was well and thanked them both for the beef. She longed to see him, but had accepted, as had Ryder, that they were of more use to Mafeking here than dodging shells in the town square. Tonight they were encamped with a party of Chief Saane's men from Modimola. The chief had been seized by the Rapulana – allies of the Boers – and his cattle taken. Now his people helped with the trickle of information going into the town, and coming out of it. Ryder paid them five shillings for every message taken and received, and saw the letters passed on. He felt like himself again, he realised. The work pleased him – being on horseback all day, scouting for cattle with which to keep the town in meat, shooting for the pot in the evening. His body had changed, too – his muscles hardening, the weight he had gained at the endless carousel of dinner parties in Cairo falling away – and his knowledge of Setswana was improving.

Suddenly, Ryder heard soft footsteps and a whistle. Peter, one of their scouts, appeared in the circle of firelight.

'What news, Peter?' Ryder asked, handing him his water flask.

Peter sat down beside him and drank as the other members of the party gathered closer.

'The relief column is close, *rra*,' he said, handing back the flask. 'A week, maybe two. The Boer men know it.'

'Do you think they will run, Ryder?' Saffron asked.

Ryder shook his head. 'They may in the end, but they won't go without staging a final attack.'

Peter nodded. 'Ryder is right, and the soldiers in the town, the people – they are weak and sick. They know a battle is coming.' He glanced at Ryder. 'Good words are spoken of Leon Courtney.'

Ryder ran his hand through his hair.

'My son is a fool.'

Peter shook his head. 'I would be proud to be a father to Leon Courtney.'

'When you have sons, Peter, you will learn that you can be proud of their bravery and angry at their foolishness in the same heartbeat,' Ryder growled.

One of the other men laughed, the ironic laugh of a man who had children of his own.

Saffron folded her letters and stood up. 'The Boer will be distracted. Let's see if we can get the town a decent meal before they have to fight.'

Ryder nodded. 'Peter, see if you can get word to Mathakgong tonight. There is a kraal a mile east of the waterworks. Saffron and I will draw off the guards.'

'I shall drive the beasts through the lines to Mathakgong,' Peter agreed. 'Do well, my friends. All our people are hungry.'

Saffron had taken a step into the darkness beyond the circle of firelight. Ryder went to her, and put his arm around her waist. She was shaking.

'We should have got him out, Ryder! They are going to attack and our boy is in there.'

He pulled her close. 'Even if he had been willing, Saffy, it would have been a hell of a risk. You know how many runners have been wounded or killed carrying a letter. You think anyone could have made the trip with a struggling boy?'

She put her hand to her head. 'I know, I know! But, Ryder, they will attack.'

'He is a survivor, Saffron. I do not know what fate awaits my son, but I am sure it is not to die in Mafeking.' He put his hand under her chin and lifted it towards him, her dark eyes shone in the starlight. 'Do you believe me?'

'I believe you,' she whispered.

• • •

Penrod knew an assault was inevitable and imminent. Every day he went from one trench to another, talking to the exhausted and hungry men who remained committed to the defence of the town. The bullets and shells had thinned their ranks, and lack of food and sleep had made them weak. Now sickness seemed to rise up out of the soil and consume them – malaria, dysentery and smallpox were eating up the soldiers who had avoided the Boer snipers for six long months. Penrod tallied their numbers each evening, and at the start of May 1900, he saw the garrison no longer had enough healthy men to provide an adequate defence of the town. On every inspection Penrod found another half-dozen men too shaken with fever to hold their rifles steady or to keep watch, and he was forced to send them to join the rest in the crowded hospital. He gave orders for most of the fresh meat coming into the town to be diverted to the soldiers who were still healthy, in the hope of keeping them that way.

In the early evening of 11 May, Penrod visited Ned at head-quarters. In the gathering dark, Ned pulled the cork on a decent brandy and poured them both a measure. Ned had aged since they had arrived in southern Africa. The news of his mother's death in England had rocked him in a way Penrod, so long an orphan, could barely understand, then a shell exploding down the chimney of Dixon's Hotel, within five feet of him, had deafened him. He remained an effective officer, kind and careful in his dealings with his men and the civilians of the town, but the vitality and vigour which had distinguished him in the past had drained away, leaving him hollowed out and ghostly.

'When will the Boer come, Penrod?' Ned asked. 'The latest reports put the relief column three days away. Have your boys seen any movement in the laagers? What does Sol say?'

Penrod studied the amber liquid in his glass. He had drunk this particular vintage last in Cape Town, just before the mysterious fire which had destroyed the Central Hotel. It tasted different this evening, darker and sharper on an empty stomach.

'The Boer know that we have them under close observation. From what Sol and the headmen can gather, for the last week they have been moving men back and forth between their camps.'

'Why?' Ned asked.

'To keep us guessing about when an attack will come, and from which direction. It's a good tactic. Our men are exhausted from remaining on high alert.'

'What can we do?'

Penrod drained his glass.

'Survive, Ned. That is all.'

He stood up to leave.

'Are you going home, Penrod?' Ned asked in a vaguely hopeful voice.

'Not yet. Do go and share the meal with Amber and the boys, though. They would welcome the company. Tell Amber I will be late.'

As Penrod stepped out into the evening, he looked right and left along the street and remembered what Mafeking had been when they had first arrived. He recalled the neat, whitewashed houses with glass in the windows, the flower-edged verandas, the shops and hotels, and smart, confident citizens going back and forth about their business. Now, in the brief dusk, Penrod noted that not a single building was without its battle scars – every window in town was shattered, every house had had sections of its walls destroyed by shellfire. The wooden verandas had been torn up for fuel, the roads were pitted with craters, and the people, their faces narrow with hunger and ghostly after days spent sheltering underground, no longer greeted each other as they passed, or stopped to exchange news in front of their doors. Even the children had been turned into warriors of a sort, carrying messages to and fro. It had happened slowly, in such small increments – the damage, the restrictions, the daily hardships, the steady tick of the death toll as one acquaintance after another was taken by a sniper bullet or shell – that they had hardly noticed it happening, or realised what they had come, day after day, to accept as normal.

Penrod walked towards the Barolong Stadt, thinking about the devastation that the two armies had caused. Crossing the half-mile of open ground which separated it from the European Quarter, Penrod moved with easy assurance through the maze of huts, trees and the strange altar-like piles of rock which punctuated the Stadt, to Jabu's home. The family made a place for him by the fire without fuss or surprise and Penrod accepted a horn beaker of traditional beer and drank it with as much relish as he had Ned's brandy.

● ● ●

When Ned arrived at the Ballantynes' cottage with Penrod's message and his rusk and horse sausage ration under his arm, wrapped in an old copy of *The Mafeking Mail*, Amber welcomed him and Ned felt his spirits lift a little.

'And by "late" he means that he will not be home at all tonight,' Amber said, taking the package and handing it to Tau, who had appointed himself head chef in their small household.

'You don't mind?' Ned said.

Amber shook her head. 'No. He will spend the night in the Stadt. He is perfecting his Setswana and learning everything he can about the Barolong, their history and customs. Sometimes he spends the evening with Sol at Silas Molema's house near the church, sometimes he stays with Jabu and his family. He knows the war will not end when the siege is lifted, and the friends he makes now, he may rely on in the future. He has his duties, but more than that, being an intelligence officer is not just what he does, you know, it's what he is.'

'I don't often imagine myself in the role of a wife, Amber,' Ned said, 'but doesn't that singleness of purpose make him a rather difficult husband?'

Her face softened as she thought of Penrod, giving her fine features a warmth of their own in the lamplight of the small room. 'Yes. He's hellish at times, but I have known no other husband, Ned, and I could not love him half so well if he were any other sort of man.'

• • •

After Penrod had greeted Jabu's immediate family, the evening meal was cleared away and the women began to usher the children to bed. Jabu and Penrod left the hut and made their way to the shallow rocky shore of the Molopo, to sit on the low bank as the moon began to set.

In a short while, dawn would begin to stain the horizon citron and mauve, and Penrod would return to inspecting the defensive outposts, the pickets and sandbagged forts. In the meantime, he was content to smoke his cheroot by the edge of the river and consider what Jabu was telling him of the history and heritage of the Barolong, the fierce rivalry between the Rapulana and Tshidi, comparing it with what Sol and Silas had told him, storing the facts and phrasing in his mind, as a careful farmer stores his grain against the coming winter.

Penrod became aware of a sense of unease; something in the fabric of the night was wrong. He leaned forward and let his fingers slip into the cold waters of the river. It was gritty. Something was stirring the silt into the flow upstream, and as the remaining cattle were closed into their kraals for the night, that could mean only one thing.

Penrod reached into the pocket of his tunic, drew out his leather-covered notebook, and pulled the pencil from where it was tucked into its spine.

'Jabu,' he said as he wrote, 'this is for Captain Godley at the Limestone Fort. I need his Maxim machine gun at the northwest Molopo picket with men to fire it, and I need it at once.'

Jabu did not ask questions, but Penrod sensed his sudden alertness.

'Motswane lives on the north edge of the Stadt, does he not?'
'Yes, *rra*.'

Motswane was not one of the headmen, but he had led an attack against a sniper's nest the previous month. Penrod had marked him out as a leader of men, even if Chief Wessels had not.

'Wake him on your way to Godley and tell him to gather a dozen men, armed, as quickly as he can, and meet me on the north bank at the edge of the town. Tell Sol and Silas to spread the word – the attack is coming.'

Penrod signed his name on the note, folded it, and handed it to Jabu. 'Go swiftly, my friend.'

Jabu slipped the note into his pocket and without a word ran lightly through the shallow river and up the gentle slope of the opposite bank. Penrod listened again – just the silence of the night, dry and chill. But something was alerting him. He concentrated, staring along the river to the west, listening intently, discarding the noises of the remaining goats and sheep shuffling in the dark, a man's snore, a woman murmuring half-asleep to an infant . . . Then he heard it. A boot sliding sideways on a stone, the sound of a leather strap pulled more securely over a shoulder, a splash in the shallows. Before he was aware of his actions he took his revolver from its holster on his hip and pulled back the hammer.

He stood and strode into the middle of the stream, feeling the chill of the water through the polished leather of his boots, and waited. The darkness was absolute, but Penrod knew with certainty a body of men were making their way along the river towards him. He lifted his gun and let the passing seconds bring them closer.

'*Ons is in!*' called a voice in Dutch. '*Fakkels!*'

Sudden flames erupted into life some fifty yards in front of him and Penrod smelled the pitch as each fire caught, casting shifting red and orange light over a solid mass of Boer fighters. Penrod could see at least sixty men, and torches were still flickering alight behind them until the bend of the river hid them from view.

'*Komaan!*'

A flash flood of fire and violence, the fighters rose up one by one along the banks into the Stadt, whooping and shouting as they went to torch the village.

Penrod fired and the first torchbearer to the north fell back into the river with a heavy splash. The next man took a bullet in his chest, so that for a second he remained standing, his torch flickering over his expression of sudden confusion, before he crumpled onto the bank and his torch rolled back into the waters and was extinguished. Penrod swung his gun to the left and at a steady pace emptied his revolver, then sprinted up the north bank, reloading as he went. The Boers were setting fire to each hut they passed, thrusting their torches into the thatch until the flames caught. Penrod fired again and the man he shot span sideways as he fell. His torch yanked free a clump of the blazing thatch which engulfed his body, providing him with his own funeral pyre. A woman stumbled out of the hut and screamed as she fell across his burning body.

Penrod turned to his right, his gun still raised, but now the men and women of the Stadt were awake, dragging their children from their burning homes. Penrod could not fire without risking catching one of the Barolong as they struggled between the flaming shadows. The smoke was thickening, the hungry crackle of the fires had become a sucking roar and the whoops of the invaders were overlaid with screams and the wailing cries of the children.

Penrod heard a crackle of gunfire.

'Don't shoot the children!' a woman's voice screamed in Setswana. 'Let the children run!'

He loped between two huts, their dry thatch already alight, towards the edge of the Stadt and the direction of the scream. Three Boer fighters, rifles raised, were visible through the smoke. The woman screamed again and Penrod saw her throw herself onto the middle Boer, dragging at his gun arm. He turned and dealt her a vicious blow on the forehead with the butt of his rifle, then kicked her aside and raised his rifle again. He fired into the shadows ahead of him, and his two companions cheered. They were shooting the fleeing Barolong.

A woman, leading a child with one hand, and cradling a baby against her chest, stumbled out from one of the houses between Penrod and the fighters, then turned back to stare, distraught, at the leaping flames lifting into the night sky above her home. The dense reed porch of the hut behind her exploded and collapsed, sending bundles of living flame over her and her two children. The twisted trunk which had held up the porch fell, striking the woman. She fell in an awkward twist onto the hard earth while the fire rained down around her. Penrod turned to help her, but felt a hand on his arm.

'I will look after her. Please, see to those butchers, Penrod.'

Sol, half-dressed and coughing from the smoke, was beside him. Penrod nodded and Sol sprinted towards the woman, beating out the flames on her dress with his bare hands.

The three Boers were still shooting. Penrod lifted his revolver and fired as he ran towards them. One of his bullets struck the middle rifleman in his back, casting him forward, his arms thrown up. His two companions started back with alarm. Penrod lunged at the right-hand gunman, grabbing the heavily webbed bandolier across his chest and jerking him round so that the muzzle of his rifle pointed towards the third man. Penrod closed his hand over the Boer's trigger finger and squeezed, the man screaming as the rifle kicked. The bullet struck the third Boer in the belly, knocking him backwards into the shadows. The man he was holding roared and fought to stab the butt of his rifle into Penrod's side, but Penrod twisted around him, tripping him over his polished boot. As he fell, Penrod wrapped his arm around the Boer's neck, his elbow braced on his chest, and twisted hard. He felt the man's neck snap and let the body fall in a heap onto the dust.

Two young Barolong men raced forward and scooped up the Boer rifles. While the one unbuckled the bandolier of ammunition from the warm body at Penrod's feet, the other disappeared into the shadows where the wounded fighter lay. Penrod heard the crack of a rifle and the young man returned with another gun, another bandolier over his shoulder.

'Penrod?'

Sol was leading the woman and her children towards him.

'Get the women and children out this way, Sol. When you get to town, tell Benjamin Weil to open up his gun shop. I will personally buy a rifle for any Barolong – man or woman – who wants one today, and whatever ammunition they can carry. Where are Silas and Chief Wessels?'

'Rallying by the church.'

'I have to seal this breach, Sol,' Penrod said. 'Get word to Silas that I shall do so, then I'll be glad to see him at the picket on the south bank when he has a moment of leisure.'

'I shall. Good luck, Penrod.'

'And to you.'

Penrod stalked back into the Stadt, working his way to the river through the smoking houses and the flames. The Stadt had become a slaughterhouse, and the Boer fighters, ranging gleefully through it with rifle and torch, were like demons, their shadows made monstrous by the light of the fire.

As soon as he had seen their torches, Penrod had understood the Boer plan as clearly as if he had made it himself. Someone who knew the land well had guided them into town, of that he was sure – they could not have got through Chief Wessels' defences undetected otherwise. They must have taken the pickets along the river before the torches were even lit, widening the gap in the town's defences so more fighters could pour into the confusion of the Stadt. Setting fire to the Barolongs' homes would make it clear to the Boers watching from their trenches that the first party of fighters had got through the lines. So now those fresh fighters would be massing for a second assault. If Mafeking was to survive another hour, the breach in the defences must be sealed.

Motswane and a dozen other young men were waiting by the river. Their eyes were red from the thick smoke, their faces showed a fiery rage. Most carried a rifle; four held only spears.

The night was falling away and the first sliver of daylight appeared on the smooth curve of the horizon.

'We need to retake the pickets on the banks,' Penrod said. 'Motswane, you and I will approach the northern picket, the rest of you gentlemen take the southern bank. Do it quietly. Go now before it becomes light enough for the Boer to see the danger.'

It was all the instruction any of the men needed. Motswane and Penrod ran along the northern bank while the others turned south and disappeared into the shadows.

The picket was two hundred yards beyond the Stadt, a rough horseshoe of limestone rubble and sandbags looking down into the low river valley. Penrod guessed that the Boers would have sent at least five men to overwhelm the three sentries usually posted there. If Jabu had got the message Penrod had sent to Godley, a Maxim machine gun was on its way. Penrod's plan was simple. Retake the position and meet the fresh fighters with a storm of unexpected machine-gun fire which would push them back, and give the defenders of the Stadt vital minutes to regroup. To succeed they must reclaim the picket silently.

'Do you have your knife?' he asked Motswane as he ran.

'Yes, *rra*.'

'Use it. Fight to your right.'

It was still too dark to see much more than shadows, but Penrod could make out the outlines of the Boer slouch hats above the sandbag walls of the picket. On the north foot of the horseshoe a body was sprawled – the corpse of the British sergeant charged with watching this spot. The Boers were craning forward over the sandbags and peering into the valley. Penrod made almost no noise as he ran, covering the ground in long, fluid strides. His lungs filled and emptied, and for the first time since Hester Vintner slipped her knife into his belly, he felt his animal self again – his muscles seasoned and his instincts honed to a glittering sharpness. As he crossed the final ten yards he put his hand to his belt and pulled his knife free, and, without slackening his pace, made his attack on the Boer in the centre of the group.

Throwing his arm around the man's head, he sliced his knife across the fighter's throat. On the edge of his vision, he saw Motswane leap onto the sandbag parapet and kick away sideways, using his momentum to thrust his own spear-shaped knife between the third and fourth ribs of the fighter on the far right of the group, then spring upwards, his blade raised, catching the next man in the middle of his abdomen.

Penrod let the body fall, as the Boer on his left span round, his mouth open with surprise and sudden horror. The man lifted his rifle and with a heavy grunt drove the polished wooden butt towards Penrod's face. Penrod turned the blow with his left arm and pushed his knife into the man's chest, striking upwards. The man collapsed backwards and slid down the limestone wall as Penrod turned his attention to the last Boer. He was young – no older than twenty – and as he stared at Penrod, his rifle slipped from his grip and he lifted his hands in surrender. Penrod wondered what he must look like to the boy; he could smell the soot on his clothes and feel the blood of other men drying on his face and hands.

He returned his knife to its sheath and glanced at Motswane, who was wiping his own knife on the sandbag parapet.

'Motswane, bind this man and gag him.'

The light was trickling across the veld like quicksilver. Penrod reached round to the small of his back and took his field glasses from the case hanging from his polished leather belt. He lifted them to his eyes with a steady hand and looked into the shadows of the Molopo River. He could see them, a great phalanx of fighters, moving towards them. He swung his glasses to the right and in the soft morning light saw a Marolong fighter standing in the south picket, his spear raised above his head, and in the distance, to the north, he spotted a kicking spray of dust. Major Godley's Maxim crew riding like devils towards them. He could only wait. From the middle of Mafeking he heard the heavy tolling of the bell of the Catholic church, the signal that the town was waking to its final battle. If this gap could be sealed, the men approaching along the river held back, they might have a chance. Penrod counted under his breath, marking each second as the machine-gun crew and the fighters in the valley got closer. The Boers would be launching other attacks on the perimeter, over the rugged ground of the brickfields to the east. He thought of the men in the trenches, weary and sick, lifting their rifles and willed them on. One hundred and ten, one hundred eleven.

The Maxim crew dismounted as they reached the pickets, the men beginning work immediately on assembling the tripod. Penrod stepped back as the gun was checked, lifted and secured. The number one gunner passed the end of the ammunition belt through the feed block, turned the crank and pulled the belt straight. The bullets shone in the first light.

'Ready!' the gunner said, aiming into the valley.

The Boers were approaching at an easy walk; they thought they had already won.

'Wait for it,' Penrod said. Boots splashed in the water and they could hear individual voices in the ranks.

'Traversing fire, bank to bank.'

The gunner raised the safety catch with his left thumb.

'Rapid fire!'

• • •

Amber woke to the patter and crack of gunfire. She stretched her arm across the bed and found Penrod's side cold. No shred of moonlight showed through the shutters. She heard a rap at the door and Tau shouldered it open awkwardly, already dressed and holding a candle in one hand, a mug of coffee in the other with a shallow bowl of bran mash balanced on top of it.

'Tau, thank you,' Amber said, reaching for the mug.

'Leon has gone already, Mrs Ballantyne. I think I shall go to the newspaper office and see if I am needed.'

Amber gulped down the thin black liquid.

'Be careful, Tau. It's lively out there.'

As she spoke the heavy tolling of the bell of the Catholic church began. Amber had known this was coming, their enemy's final attack, a last attempt to overwhelm the town when help was so painfully close.

'You be careful, too,' Tau said, and padded off into the darkness.

Amber dressed and fetched her notebook and the little first aid kit she always carried with her, then blew out the candle and opened the shutters to peer into the darkness. For a moment it looked as if the square was lit with fireflies, then she realised with a shock that she was seeing bullets sparking where they hit stone or metal. She had never seen such intense rifle fire in the town and so close to her home.

Amber bound her hair up, slipped on her boots and left the house. As soon as she was outside, she smelled the smoke. The magistrate hurried past her, still pulling on his coat over his nightshirt.

'Mr Bell, what news?'

'They've come up along the river and set fire to the Stadt, Mrs Ballantyne,' he shouted. 'Shot the women as they fled. Hospital is already half-full of the wounded.'

Amber saw the flames reaching up from the thatch roofs of the huts. The tall sycamore trees which grew among them were now flaming silhouettes against the horizon. She could go at once to the hospital, but half the women in Mafeking were trained nurses and only a few newspaper correspondents remained. Amber felt her pulse quicken as she considered where she might go to best observe the action. Colonel Hore would be at the British South

African Police fort, part of the inner ring of defences between the Stadt and the European Quarter. From that elevated position Amber would be able to see the fighting, observe the defence of the town, and record it for the readers of *The Chronicle*. She ran, bullets hissing by her, wild, unaimed fire from the Boers pulsing in from the brickfields. A large group of Barolong men were gathered outside Weil's store, protected from the gunfire by the ruins of the houses to the east. As Amber ran by she glimpsed Weil himself bending over a packing crate, pulling rifles out and handing them to the men.

Officers on the few remaining horses in town thundered past Amber, and she saw small groups of Protectorate troopers jogging alongside their officers towards the eastern trenches. Everywhere she turned, Amber saw haggard and determined faces – the people of Mafeking were ready to fight the last fight.

As Amber approached the inner fort the number of men seemed to thin. She was sprinting up the rise and into the yard, when there was a crack and a flash of light exploded in front of her.

'*Moenie skiet nie!*' a voice shouted in Dutch.

Amber could see men on the veranda of the building, men in heavy corduroy with their slouch hats pulled low on their heads and heavy bandoliers of ammunition crossing their chests. Boers! They had got through the Stadt and overwhelmed the fort while the rest of the town was sleeping. Amber was so shocked that she did not even turn to run back into the darkness of the town.

One of the men picked up a lantern and came towards her, lifting it high, and when he saw her face, his thin features were transformed by a grim smile of recognition. She knew him. It was the man who had been shot in the arm and then acted as an orderly when she was helping in the Boer field hospital all those weeks earlier.

'Well, if it isn't my dear old nurse!'

Amber gasped. 'What are *you* doing here?'

He laughed, a cruel cackle. 'We've come to take Mafeking, and about time. There'll be nothing left of this place when your relief column get here. We came through the Stadt, and we were in before your boys knew what was happening. If we'd known you were this weak a month ago . . . Damn it, we could have wiped you off the map and been in time to save Cronjé at Padders.'

He peered past her into the town.

'Looks busy down there! Won't be long until the whole place is ours.'

Amber heard the crack of rifle fire and caught the smell of smoke on the air. She threw herself forward, pushing the man in the chest. He staggered back.

'Just go! Just leave!' Amber shouted. 'Why do you need to kill anyone else? It's over. You've lost the war, you've lost Mafeking. Just go!'

The man regained his balance and lifted a clenched fist, but did not strike.

'What?' he yelled. 'After all these months of waiting and misery? You expect us to roll over like dogs? Win or lose, me and mine will be revenged.'

'Blood and hate,' Amber said more quietly. 'That's all you've got.'

He dropped his fist. 'It's all I need. Now put up your hands, your town is taken and we have your colonel prisoner here.'

For a sickening moment Amber thought the man meant Baden-Powell, and looked towards Dixon's Hotel. But the hotel was all lights and activity. The Boers might have taken the fort but the town was not beaten yet. Amber raised her hands, and another man came forward to search her. Her notebook and her first aid kit were taken and handed to the man with the lantern. He flipped through her notebook then handed both back to her.

'One of your lads inside got a scratch as we came in. Come with me – you can see to him.'

The Boer fighters on the veranda stepped aside as he led her into the building, a rough structure of wood with a corrugated steel roof, combined offices and stores. The men and their officers were seated in a line along the back wall, their hands tied behind their backs, their uniforms were scuffed and torn and several of them were bruised and bloodied around the face. Colonel Hore lifted his gaze and started at the sight of her. Blood had darkened the shoulder of his jacket. Amber crouched down beside him.

'Let me see to your wound, Colonel,' she said.

'It is nothing.'

'Let me see.' She turned to the nearest fighter. 'Untie him, and get the rest of these men water.'

The man she addressed looked at the fighter who had brought her in. He nodded. Hore's hands were unbound and the man offered his water bottle in turn to the other men.

Hore pulled his jacket off, flinching as he did. The bullet had passed through the flesh of his arm – what was left of it after the months of short rations. A Boer fighter was sitting in one of the high-backed chairs by Hore's desk, his feet up and sipping from a bottle of whisky. She put out her hand. 'Give that to me,' she commanded.

With an expression of surprise he did so, which made one of his fellow fighters laugh. Amber splashed some of the alcohol onto her handkerchief and used it to clean the wound. The colonel hissed through his teeth. Amber was struck by his haggard features. It was a part of life in Mafeking now – if you did not see someone for a week or two, when you did catch sight of them they were almost impossible to recognise. Amber, already naturally slim, had taken in the waists of her skirts by two inches since March. She looked like a ghost.

'What happened, Colonel?' she asked under her breath.

'We heard firing in the Stadt and we could see the huts burning. Then these Boers came running out of the smoke. We thought they were our own boys in retreat so we held our fire and they overwhelmed us before we knew they were the enemy. How is the rest of the town? We heard the general alarm.'

'Everyone is awake and anyone who can carry a gun has been armed.'

Amber finished cleaning the colonel's wound and began to dress it.

'Is anyone else injured?' she asked.

'No. One of my men refused to put his hands up and they shot him where he stood. He was just too shocked to know what was happening.'

'How did they get past the pickets?'

'They had help, someone led them here.'

The telephone on Hore's desk suddenly rang, making Amber start. The young fighter who had handed over his whisky picked up the receiver and answered in heavily accented English.

'No, Colonel Hore cannot speak to you . . . he is busy being a prisoner of Commandant Eloff and his men. Yes, jolly good show! Bye, bye!'

He hung up and laughed as one of his friends clapped him on the shoulder. Amber looked at Colonel Hore.

'That was stupid,' Hore said. 'Baden-Powell knows we are taken now. At bloody last. That means he can rain down merry hell on us with the seven-pounders. If the Boer had any sense they'd have forced me to speak to headquarters and say all was in order or cut the wire themselves, then turned our guns on the town. It is confusion that kills in a situation like this, and now B-P has solid information to work from.' He frowned at Amber and shook his head. 'I wish to God you weren't here, Mrs Ballantyne. It's going to be rough.'

'Do not worry about me. You said they had help getting into the Stadt, Colonel?'

'You'll see the chap in a minute. Familiar face. He's in the stores, what's left of them. Drink and camping gear. We wanted to keep the drink from the townsfolk, and we haven't been able to get far enough from town to use the camping stuff.'

The door opened and a man, an open bottle in one hand, came into the room. Amber turned to him. Hore's sword dangled from his belt next to the colonel's gold pocket watch. As he lifted the bottle and tilted back his head, the shadows drifted from his face.

'Cressy!' Amber said.

He pushed his hat back on his head and grinned.

'Well, if it isn't the clever Mrs Ballantyne! Bitch! You stole my fucking money and now I'm coming to take it back.'

Approaching, he brought his face close to hers, so close that she could smell his rotten breath, and shoved the wine bottle at her. 'Have a drink, my girl. Celebrate our victory and my future. I'm going to show you bastards. All I need is the money I earned. Couple of years and I'll be sending champagne to your table in Cape Town or Cairo.'

'You're a lazy, vicious fool, Cressy,' Amber replied. 'You'll never be able to buy me a drink, and even if you could, I'd rather die of thirst.'

He grabbed the back of her head, trying to force the neck of the bottle between her lips.

Standing, Colonel Hore thrust out his left hand, catching Cressy in the chest and sending him stumbling backwards.

One of the Boers stood up. 'Leave the prisoners alone, Cressy,' he shouted.

Hore continued to look at to look at Cressy with steady contempt. Cressy spat into the dust at Hore's feet, rage burning in his face. The Boer fighters looked away. They know he is a coward, Amber thought. She could sense their embarrassment at his behaviour.

A younger man entered the room from the back stores. The other fighters did not salute or stand to attention, the Boers had no use for that sort of formality, but it was clear that this man had authority over them. The youth who had answered the phone swung his legs off the table and sat up straight in his chair.

'*Kom die ander nou Eloff?*' he said. '*Is die dorp al hulle s'n?*'

So this was Sarel Eloff. Grandson of President Paul Kruger himself. Amber watched him closely.

'*Dit sal nie lank wees nie,*' Eloff replied, walking to the centre of the room. 'We tore through these great defences like they were made of straw. All Snyman has to do is follow us in and he can buy us breakfast at Dixon's Hotel.'

Amber sat down on the floor as the colonel retook his seat.

'Do we have any chance, Colonel?'

'Perhaps. If you know any prayers, Mrs Ballantyne, say them.'

• • •

Leon should have waited in the cadet house, but in the confusion it was easy to slip into headquarters itself and watch the action. Baden-Powell was rattling off his orders, scattering officers across the thinly manned perimeter. FitzClarence was sent to form a line to protect headquarters from closer attack,

Marsh to help coordinate the fightback in the Stadt, the Town Guard to keep a presence in the north and the Cape Boys to push back across the brickfields.

'Message from Godley,' Ned called out. 'Ballantyne is in the Stadt and holding off a large force on the river with one machine-gun crew and Barolong support.'

'Send "C" Squadron to support him.'

Baden-Powell noticed Leon step forward.

'No cadet is running messages today, Courtney. Do not let me see you move again.'

Leon obeyed and stood still.

'Ned, release the British prisoners in the gaol, anyone you think is loyal to the crown, and give them arms. Put them under Marsh.'

Leon watched him. Baden-Powell's face was calm, but Leon knew it hid a furious concentration, a mind constantly tallying forces and assessing defences. They had been waiting for this moment, had known it must come and must be faced, despite their enfeebled state and shattered nerves, and they were ready for it. Now was the moment when they would find out if they had the grit to hold out, to push back against their besiegers one last time.

Ned suddenly held up his hand. He was holding the telephone receiver and his face was blank with distress.

'The BSAP fort is overrun. General Hore is a prisoner. Damn Boer on the other end of the line just told me so.'

Baden-Powell barely flinched. 'Cut the line. Ned. Warn FitzClarence. Tell him to start firing on the fort. Every seven-pounder we've got. We shall keep them tightly confined until we have retaken the Stadt.'

'And our men who are prisoners in the fort?' Ned asked.

'Will understand the necessity,' Baden-Powell said, his voice clipped.

• • •

The Boer advance on the river had collapsed in disorder under the machine-gun fire, but Penrod could see them regrouping further down the valley. 'C' Squadron arrived in the nick of time, as dawn broke across the land.

'We are depending on you, men,' Penrod told them. 'Not one more damned Dutchman will get into Mafeking. Remember, I don't care where that relief column is. If we beat them back today, the siege is won. If we fail, it is lost. Either way the siege of Mafeking ends today.'

A ragged cheer came from the men, their faces haggard in the pale light of morning.

Penrod split the squadron into two and sent half across the river to join the Barolong who had taken the southern picket, keeping the rest to reinforce his own position, then turned to face the burning Stadt. Captain Marsh and Major Godley were striding towards him with Chief Wessels. The chief had his fists clenched and his shoulders hunched.

'Let me take back the Stadt!' Wessels said. 'The Boer have starved us, killed our men and boys and now they burn our homes. Now, we will send them all to hell. We have earned that right.'

'You have,' Penrod said in Setswana. 'What do you propose, chief?'

The man's eyes glittered. He answered in the same language, a rolling baritone which seemed to flow straight from his belly.

'It is simple. They must be driven like cattle. We know our home, even when they have set it to flame. We can harry them into the nooks and corners, the closed yards of the Stadt. They will not see the traps we have set until they are netted.'

'Marsh, any objections?' Penrod said, his words clipped and clear.

'The chief is right, sir,' Marsh said. 'The Boer don't know the Stadt and we do. I'll command the men on the right bank to the north. The chief will command his men south of the river.'

'Good,' Penrod said. 'Marsh, with your permission I'll join you in operations on the northern bank.' For the first time he noticed the heat of the morning sun on his neck. 'Motswane?'

Motswane was taking a bandolier of ammunition from a herdboy. 'My business is in the Stadt now. I'll go north with the chief.'

Penrod nodded and addressed 'C' squadron: 'Gentlemen, keep men along each bank. Shoot any Boer who comes to the river for water and stay in contact with each other. Dismissed, Marsh. Thank you, Chief.'

The direction of the wind had changed and the smoke from the Stadt was drifting along the riverbed.

'Godley, it's up to you to see no Boer gets along this river to reinforce the men in the Stadt. I want that Maxim in the valley itself. Where it narrows the banks are higher.' He squatted on the ground, and Godley hitched up his breeches to do the same, as with a finger Penrod sketched out the familiar curves of the Molopo in the dirt.

'They must have come through here. Get your best gun team under this curve by the sycamore tree. Send men into a forward position to make sure no one can take them from above and protect the flanks.'

Godley nodded.

'We'll be spread damn thin, Colonel. You don't intend to let the Barolong simply drive the Boer out and along the river?'

'Let Wessels corral them as he suggests. What we must do is close the gate behind them and make sure no more fighters come this way.'

'Marsh said the Cape Boys are all heading into the brickfields to stop any advance from that direction.'

'If anyone can hold them, the Cape Boys will. They must know every rabbit hole east of our position,' Penrod said.

Godley looked up at Penrod, his face creased and drawn. 'Can we do it, Ballantyne?'

'We shall do it, or die trying. There is no middle ground. Now get to it.'

•   •   •

The shelling began twenty minutes after Amber had stumbled into the fort. Sustained rifle volleys from the centre of town thudded into the stone walls like hailstones, followed by the cough and shriek of shells. Eloff left the central room and when he returned he was frowning. Dawn was upon them now. The easy, heady banter of the Boer fighters had stopped.

'It seems you will miss your appointment for breakfast at Dixon's Hotel, Commander,' Hore said, making no effort to hide the satisfaction in his voice.

'Oh, I'm sure they'll keep a plate warm for us,' Eloff answered. 'Our reinforcements will be here soon.'

'Why aren't they here now?' Cressy asked. He was nursing the dregs of his wine in a corner of the room. 'They should be. I got you in here. That was the hard part. When am I going to get my money?'

The Boer commander looked at him with distaste. 'Guess we moved quicker than they expected, Cressy. They'll be here before Colonel Hore gets to take his sword back from you, I promise. Now shut your mouth.'

'I *am* going to claim my sword, Cressy,' Hore said. 'Then I'm going to kill you with it, because you are a thieving, treacherous dog. You don't deserve to call yourself British.'

Cressy bared his teeth at Hore, as another round of rifle fire crackled around the walls.

'Damn it!' Eloff shouted. '*Kan julle dalk eerden ophou an die voorade te plunder en terug skiet?*'

'Put *them* outside,' Cressy shouted hysterically. He strode over to the prisoners and pulled Amber to her feet, shoving her into the middle of the room. 'If the British see their colonel and the lovely Mrs Ballantyne out front, they'll stop firing at us.'

'You are a disgusting little man, aren't you?' Amber said.

Cressy pushed her towards Eloff. 'It's her fault I'm here! Everything was fine until she started sticking her nose into my business, the evil bitch. You're going to get what's coming to you now. I'll take you to Pretoria myself and it's a long way between here and there. Who knows what might happen to you in the dark?'

Eloff moved quickly, slapping Cressy across the face. Cressy put his hand to his cheek, his eyes wide with shock, and glanced around the room. Every man, Boer or British, was staring at him with contempt.

Eloff offered his arm to Amber and led her to her place next to Colonel Hore, then turned to the Boer who had answered the phone earlier.

330

'Boonzaaier maak die agterste stoorkamer skoon. Ons sal ons gaste daar hou.'

'Untie their hands,' Amber said.

Eloff frowned at her.

'You've kept them tied like this for hours already. It's torture. If you are going to lock us in the storage room, untie their hands.'

Eloff ran his eyes up and down the line of troopers.

'You have permission to do so, as soon as the doors shut behind you.'

• • •

The bombardment from the town was steady and unceasing. Amber felt each explosion shaking her bones. Once the men were untied, there was nothing to be done, nowhere to run, no way to fight back. They had to sit in the storeroom counting the seconds until the next explosion.

It was a relief when Eloff appeared. He handed canteens of water to the men and they drank greedily. Fear had parched their throats. He turned to leave again, then swung back towards them, looking at Colonel Hore.

'What is happening, Colonel? I've smashed open the gates! I tore up your lines like scrap metal and Snyman has two thousand men sitting on their arses and watching. What are they waiting for? Don't they *want* to take this damn town?'

He didn't wait for his answer, but stalked away with his spurs clinking.

Hore gave the canteen to Amber and she drank, slowly, and not too much. She passed it back and he did the same.

'What *is* happening, Colonel?' Amber asked in a whisper.

Hore shook his head. 'Mrs Ballantyne, if I weren't the man's captive, I'd almost feel sorry for him. He delivered us a hell of a shock thanks to that yapping Cressy, and any commander worth his salt would have followed up with a massed attack. We'd have been done for. But something has put Snyman off his game and made him think better of it.' He closed his eyes for a moment as if praying. 'It would be a miracle, but I think somehow our boys must have sealed the gap in the lines through the Barolong Stadt, and the Cape Boys must be holding their advance at the brickfields.'

Amber could feel a current of air, saw something shift in the shadows.

'There must be a window behind these stacks somewhere. We might see for ourselves.'

'I'll help you,' Hore said, getting to his feet.

She put her hand on his arm. 'You've been shot, Colonel. I'm sure the others will help. You supervise.'

He smiled. His skin was grey; Amber hoped he hadn't lost too much blood.

'Very well, it's got to be better than waiting to be blown to smithereens.' He looked round the other troopers, slowly getting to their feet. 'Move quietly, lads.'

. . .

They found it quickly enough, a small hole left in the wall for ventilation rather than a window, barred with iron rods that were rusting in the remorseless sun, high up on the side wall. The troopers used the packing crates to build a sort of ladder.

'Mrs Ballantyne, you have sharp eyes and a flair for description. Get up there and tell us what you see,' Hore said. 'Hopkins, give her a hand up.'

Amber clambered nimbly up the stack, and Hopkins climbed onto the level below her to make sure that she didn't fall. The storeroom was keeping them cool as well as insulating them from the rocks and shrapnel thrown up by the shells – Amber could feel the sun's power through the ventilation grille. The heat was a physical burden to be carried on days like these, it dragged at you, held you down. So bright was the glare from outside that Amber had to blink repeatedly before she saw anything but a dazzling whiteness. Then she realised that if she turned her head to the side and pushed up against the bars, she could see down into the Stadt. She began to whisper her descriptions to Hopkins. Every word she said, he passed on.

The Stadt was a confusion of smoking ruins, alive with the rattle of gunfire. Amber could just see the edge of the European

Quarter and the trenches of the inner perimeter. Figures moved back and forth along them, among the guns.

She heard a man's voice, raised in anger. It was Eloff. She shifted to her right and pressed firmly up against the wall.

'Careful!' Hopkins said sharply.

Amber lifted herself onto the tips of her toes.

'What do you see, Mrs Ballantyne?'

Three Boer fighters were clambering over a partially destroyed part of the parapet and Eloff was calling them back. 'Three fighters, Eloff's men. They are deserting, escaping over the back parapet.'

'Over the parapet?' Hopkins asked, his face crumpled with confusion.

'Shell fire has brought most of it down,' she said.

Hopkins relayed the message and the storage room filled with murmurs of relief.

'Quietly now, men,' Hore warned.

Eloff shouted again, but the men ignored him. Taking a rifle out of the hands of one of the men standing next to him, Eloff covered the distance to the tumbled section of wall in three short strides. He raised the gun and, as Amber watched, scarcely daring to breathe, he fired, once and then again. Below them, on the open ground under the fort, the first fleeing man was hit squarely in the back – he threw his arms up in the air and went down. The man closest to him turned sideways as he stumbled forward, staring in disbelief as his comrade fell. Eloff's second shot caught him in the temple, his head snapped sideways with a sickening jerk and he went down, sprawled on his side.

'He shot two of them!' Amber said.

Eloff handed the rifle back to the man beside him and stalked into the office building.

'Come down now, Mrs Ballantyne,' Hore said, and Amber – sensing the urgency in his voice – obeyed. 'Rebuild the stacks, men. It is almost over and Eloff has been robbed of his victory. Even the most reasonable man might crack in his position. Be calm.'

A shell exploded on the far side of the fort, shaking dust over them, and they looked to Hore.

'Listen, men. The rifle fire in the distance, east and west of us? There's hardly any of it. Hasn't been for half an hour. That means the fight is almost over and they are mopping up.'

Amber felt a sudden surge of panic.

'But might that mean that the Boer have won?'

He shook his head. 'They would not be shelling *us* and Commander Eloff up here then, would they? Mafeking is still in British hands.' The men looked relieved. 'Now we wait, and hope that Eloff thinks enough of his reputation as an honourable soldier not to kill us in revenge.'

• • •

Two hours later they had their answer. Eloff pushed open the door and stood on the threshold, Hore's sword in his left hand. His face was puce with rage. Hore got to his feet and walked towards him, placing himself between Eloff and his troopers. Hopkins took a step forward, too, making sure Amber was behind him.

They waited to see if Eloff would reach for his revolver, but instead he held out the sword, balanced on the palms of both hands, for Hore to accept.

'I'm sorry, Colonel, Cressy has made a run for it, and taken your watch with him, but at least I can return this.'

The colonel did not take the sword at once. 'Am I to understand this as your surrender, Commander?'

The young man's rage seemed to ebb like a tide, leaving his face bleak with disappointment. '*Ja*, I think it must be so.'

Hore took the sword and fastened it at his waist.

'Hopkins,' he commanded, 'get the Union Jack flying over this fort before they shell us to destruction.'

• • •

Marsh was supervising the surrender of the last of the Boers in the Stadt when the Union Jack was seen flying from the roof of the British South African Police fort. Penrod pulled out his field glass – Hore was walking down towards the town with a Boer commander at his side, followed by some fifty fighters, his own men bringing up the rear.

Penrod left Marsh to it and jogged back towards the town on the familiar path along the river. As he approached the column, he noticed the tear in Hore's sleeve and the blood that stained the older man's jacket.

'They didn't clip you too badly, I hope?' Penrod said.

'No, your wife did an excellent job cleaning it for me,' Hore said, turning aside from the procession.

'My wife?'

'Yes, she's been with us all day. And now she's writing up her report for the newspapers at my desk. Will you come into town to see the prisoners confined?'

Penrod shook his head. 'I want the pickets strengthened, and to reassure myself that all the units in this quarter have a decent officer left to lead them.'

Hore looked out across the smoking ruins of the Stadt. 'Do you think the Barolong exacted some measure of revenge when our backs were turned?' he said quietly.

'I would imagine so. And I cannot blame men who saw their wives shot in the back as they fled the fire, can you?'

'Less said the better in my opinion,' Hore said. 'As long as they have sense enough to hide the bodies.'

With that he turned away and once again took up his position at the head of the column, leading the prisoners and his men into the market square. Penrod strolled up the slope and into the fort offices. He saw, amid the wreckage of smashed filing cabinets and overturned chairs, his wife sitting at Hore's desk, her head bent over her notebook, furiously at work.

'Hello, darling,' she said brightly, looking up and smiling. 'All secure?'

She gave no sign that she was sorry for thrusting herself into the middle of the action again. Her belief was that as long as she did not interfere with Penrod or his men, she was at liberty, as a correspondent of *The Daily Chronicle*, to go where she wished. Penrod lifted her chin in his hand before kissing her hard.

'Monstrous woman. You never will stay where I put you, will you?'

Her voice was throaty. 'I must get out of bed sometimes, Penrod.'

He wound her hair in his fingers, making her gasp. 'I should tie you to it,' he whispered as he ran his lips down her smooth white throat. The temptation to lift her up onto the desk was almost too much for him. He released her, pushing her back into her chair.

'Finish your report, then, and don't try and get it out of town before Ned has read it.'

Her skin was flushed and her eyes glittered. 'As you command, Colonel.'

The corner of his mouth twitched into a smile as he left her.

• • •

Penrod made his way across the open ground and along the river to the positions on the northern bank. Half a dozen men remained in the shattered fort, keeping a lookout east and west. It was a thin deployment, but Hore would reinforce them as soon as his prisoners were secured. On this side of the river, Major Panzera had come up to take command, and Penrod was happy with his arrangements. Only the men who had seen the fiercest action had been sent into town to eat and sleep.

'What about him?' Panzera said, nodding his head towards a man sitting on a rock in the thin shade provided by a sycamore some fifty yards to their rear. Penrod recognised Stuttaford, his rifle propped up next to him and his head in his hands. He had been released from gaol to take part in the defence of the town.

'He did well, I heard,' Panzera added.

'Yes, I heard the same. I shall speak to him,' Penrod said.

Stuttaford got to his feet as Penrod approached, picking up his rifle.

'Good work today, Stuttaford,' Penrod said. 'I will make sure Baden-Powell knows about it.'

Stuttaford's face twisted with a half-smile. 'So I might be allowed to live, then? Some time in a prison hulk, then disgraced and abandoned in England. It is something when your best hope for the future is a cheap boarding house and a bottle.'

'That is your decision,' Penrod said. 'Or take your punishment and then try and make something of your life. Every man must make his own choices.'

Penrod noticed Leon racing along the riverbank towards them. The boy hesitated when he saw Stuttaford and Penrod speaking. Penrod held up his hand briefly and Leon came to a halt.

'Choices? I've been in the army for twenty years, Ballantyne. I can't remember the last time I made a choice of my own.'

'You decided to cover up for Cressy,' Penrod replied. 'That was your choice.'

Stuttaford clenched his jaw and lifted his rifle to his hip, the fingers of his right hand curling around the trigger and the barrel rising to Penrod's abdomen.

'And you judge me for that? You? Yes, I thought I could get away with it. The damage had been done, so why not keep quiet? Why not just enjoy a little comfort for a change, a little love? It's not as if you've ever gone without either for long.'

'You have failed to make best use of your advantages, Stuttaford. Only you are to blame for that.'

'No!' Stuttaford said, his face blazing red, his rifle still raised. 'That is not true! Do you know why I never progressed? Because of *you*, Penrod Ballantyne! Because when you got engaged to Amber Benbrook in Cairo all those years ago, I made a stupid remark. I said you'd seduced a pretty, rich girl to make another fortune and I said it within earshot of that bastard Sam Adams, and he packed me off to the Sudan to rot in a hell-hole for the next ten years, and any chance I had, any chance of advancement, was lost. I had no connections to speak for me, no rich relatives and no chance to demonstrate what I could do, because Sam Adams thought the sun shone out of your arse and he thought he should defend your honour by destroying me!'

Sam Adams had been Penrod's superior for some years. Penrod had saved his life once, carrying him from the battlefield of Abu Klea, and though their friendship had been tested at times, they had remained loyal to each other. And Penrod knew that Sam hated officers who gossiped. Then Penrod remembered, the memory like a cool breeze down the back of his neck. Sam had told him the

story himself, in those brief sunny days before his first engagement
to Amber was broken. Sam had told Penrod the story then, and
Penrod had laughed.

'I've had to watch your entire career,' Stuttaford went on.
'What is it now? Two VCs? Youngest colonel in the British
Army? And now you're a bloody hero of Mafeking, and your
wife can't write out her shopping list without making a fortune.
And I made my peace with it. Even when I had to watch my
men dying around me on Canon Kopjé, even when I woke up
every night screaming because I saw it happen again and again.
I said nothing! I obeyed orders and never said a word against
you. But you don't feel it, do you? You don't see the faces of the
men you've killed or led to their deaths floating around you,
following you? Well, I do!' Stuttaford said, his voice strangled
with emotion. 'And it never gets any easier. Then your wife saw
me, what, behaving improperly by laughing when that woman
was killed in the bar, but even then I said nothing. You took me
away from my men, but I still served. I obeyed orders. I saved
this town. If I hadn't been in charge of the rationing, you'd have
starved to death months ago! I organised the soup kitchens for
the Barolong while you bastards held lotteries for the pick of
Weil's stock or handed out tins of salmon and jam to the townsfolk who made the best flower arrangements. I met a woman and
I snatched a few moments of happiness, just a few, the only ones
I've ever managed to catch in my pathetic life and what happens?
Your bloody wife again, doing good among the natives! Who
cares if Cressy slept with a few native women and took their
bangles for a tin or two of peaches? What the hell does it matter
in the middle of this stinking sideshow of a siege? But no, Amber
Ballantyne has to make a scene about it and drag you and Baden-
Powell into the Stadt to see justice done. You are self-righteous
bastards, the pair of you! You want everyone to be without fault,
and if you drive us mad, or lead us to our deaths, or to suicide, or
murder, then that's on us.'

He took a step forward and Penrod's left hand shot out, grabbing the barrel of the rifle and holding it aside from his stomach,
but he did not try to rip it from Stuttaford's hands or make any
other move against the man.

'You know what my wife has done in the service of this town,' Penrod said, calmly. 'And yes, she has become a dedicated journalist. She's writing up her account of the attack at Colonel Hore's desk now, and no doubt making heroes of us all. And you know what Cressy did mattered, Stuttaford, you know it, otherwise you wouldn't have crawled back to the bottle as soon you learned of his crimes. What he did mattered to the women he robbed, and raped, and you will never be able to look me in the eye and tell me otherwise. I don't care if you've had bad luck. If you stopped pitying yourself in a stew of booze, you might have done more at any stage of your life. Did you drink in the Sudan? Did you do as little as possible and brood over the cruelty of fate instead of making some effort to change it?'

He saw the doubt in Stuttaford's eye and had his answer.

'You've spent years telling yourself these tragic little stories, and it's destroyed you. So, do something else. If you want to spend your life in a boarding house and a gin shop, that is your choice, but do not fool yourself. It is, has been, and always will be, *your* choice. If you want to ask someone about blighted opportunities and the unfairness of the world, I can show you fifty men worse off than you within a hundred yards of us now.'

Penrod released his grip on the barrel of the rifle. Stuttaford slumped forward slightly as if his rage had been the only thing holding him together. He uncurled his finger from the trigger and handed the rifle to Penrod. Penrod took it without speaking.

'Might I request, as a particular favour, an hour of freedom to go and find news of Lesedi in the Stadt?' Stuttaford asked. 'I was very fond of her, even if she was in the pay of Cressy, and I think she liked me a little. I would be glad to have word of her.'

'You may, Stuttaford.' Penrod pulled out his half-hunter watch and realised with a slight shock that Amber had given it to him that same evening Stuttaford had made the comment which had led to his exile. 'Report back to the gaol before the curfew hour.'

Stuttaford nodded and walked away.

Penrod removed the bullet from the rifle's chamber and span it between his long fingers as Leon jogged up to him.

'Yes, cadet,' Penrod said, with a smile. 'Anything to report?'

'No, sir. That is, I just wanted to see you and Aunt Amber and make sure that you didn't need me for anything and I wanted to tell you . . .'

'Yes, Leon?'

'I wanted to tell you what I've been doing today, but now that sounds stupid, because you are busy.'

Penrod rested a hand on the boy's shoulder. 'I am, my boy. But you may take a message back to headquarters for me.' He took his notebook from his pocket and jotted down a couple of lines. 'This is to tell them that the Stadt is secure and there's no movement in the Boer lines. I should imagine Snyman will want to send a team in to collect the bodies at dawn. The ones they can find, at any rate,' he added under his breath.

Leon hesitated. 'Uncle Penrod, that man Stuttaford was going to shoot you. Why did you let him go?'

'Many men have wanted to kill me at times, your father among them. I've learned not to hold it against them. Besides, he had a point. My actions have killed some people, hurt others. Some deserved their fates, perhaps. Others did not.'

Leon looked troubled.

'Leon, you will have men under your command one day. You should demand the best from them, but you will discover every man has periods of darkness in his life. You shall have them, too. They should not condemn a man forever. I have been too harsh at times with men like Stuttaford, and we have all suffered for it. Discipline is vital, but never cruelty. Now take that message.'

'Yes, sir,' Leon said, though his face was still troubled. He turned and ran towards the European Quarter.

• • •

Stuttaford was greeted warily in the Stadt. Most of the Baralong men had left to escort the Boer prisoners into town, and the boys had gone with them to revel in the humbling of the hated Boer, but some of the women remained among the ruins. Some wept, others were looking for friends and relatives, while others still were beginning the work of salvaging what they could from their broken homes. Stuttaford wandered deeper into the Stadt, asking after Lesedi. The people he met shook their heads, but he wasn't sure if they understood his questions. He almost ran into a young man as he rounded a corner, and was about to apologise and turn away when he recognised him - the translator from the court. They had talked once or twice before Stuttaford's disgrace, and Stuttaford knew that he had a reputation as a clever young man. He racked his brain for the man's name.

'Mr Plaatje!' Stuttaford remembered.

'Captain.' Sol smiled at him. 'I am told you did brave work today in the Stadt. How may I help you?'

'The girl who Cressy bribed to . . . to care for me. Her name was Lesedi. I was hoping that someone might have news of her.'

A look of concern flickered across Sol's features.

'I mean her no harm,' Stuttaford said hurriedly. 'She was kind to me and I wish to see if there's anything I can do to be of assistance to her.'

'She and her family left the Stadt, Captain,' Sol replied. 'Shortly after the trial, I heard that they had passed through the lines.'

'And where is she now?'

'She had said that she might go to Vryburg and look for work. You taught her English and she knows how to keep a European house.'

Stuttaford put out his hand and Sol shook it.

'Thank you, Mr Plaatje. I . . .'

There was a gasp, and the crash of something being knocked over in one of the burnt-out huts.

'Did you hear that?'

Stuttaford released Sol's hand and they approached the doorway. Neither of them were armed, and they knew that some of the injured Boer fighters had taken shelter in the smoking ruins.

'Who is there?' Sol called out, first in English, then in Dutch and Setswana.

They heard a low moan.

'That is a woman's voice,' Stuttaford said.

The interior of the hut was gloomy, but as he ducked over the threshold Stuttaford saw a woman curled in the centre of the floor, her hands clasped over her stomach.

Stuttaford knelt beside her. 'Are you injured?'

He realised the ground around her body was wet and the air had a thick coppery smell. He lifted her and her head fell back.

'Sethunya!'

He could see nothing in the shadows, so he picked her up - she was as light as a bird - and carried her into the daylight. Her clothing was drenched with blood. It pulsed from her abdomen. Stuttaford pulled off his jacket and folded it into a pad to support her head, then lifted the trailing edge of her blouse, expecting to find a bullet wound, caused by some stray round which had found her during the attack on the Stadt or its defence. But her belly had been torn with a blade. Five, six separate wounds - red open mouths across her stomach.

Other women were gathering around, asking questions. Sol spoke quickly and someone brought water and a clean cloth.

'Sethunya, who did this? Who harmed you?' Sol asked in Setswana.

Stuttaford found himself being moved away by some of the women as they took control of her care. 'Who did this?' he called out.

Sethunya opened her eyes. 'Cressy,' she whispered, and her eyes closed again.

Stuttaford stumbled backwards. He had heard that Cressy had guided the Boer fighters into the Stadt, then disappeared from the fort. The news had travelled through the men like wildfire. Had Cressy taken the chance during the initial attack on the Stadt to find the woman who had testified against him and attack her? No, the wounds were fresh, Sethunya had been stabbed within the last hour, not early this morning. Cressy had risked coming back to the Stadt, where everyone knew him as a traitor, to attack this woman and leave her to bleed to death. But he had picked his moment well, waiting until almost all of the men were busy taking the captured Boers into town. Stuttaford realised his hands were shaking. In front of him the women began to wail, a deep mourning cry which seemed to shake the air.

Cressy must have counted on gaining his revenge by betraying the town, but when Eloff's attack failed, he had decided to take his own bloody vengeance on this woman. Would this satisfy him? Stuttaford wondered. Cressy was a coward. He would not attack Penrod or Baden-Powell, who were safe in the European Quarter and surrounded by armed men. Cressy would not risk his life. He thought of Mrs Ballantyne, but Amber would be safe in the European Quarter too, surely. Some words of Penrod's returned to him, his cool precise tones telling him that Amber was still in the recaptured headquarters of the BSAP, writing up her report of the attack. After the events of the day, Stuttaford was certain that the fort would be as deserted as the Stadt. She must be warned. Stuttaford turned and ran.

• • •

Amber barely noticed the door to the office opening. She finished the last line of her report, then looked up and saw Cressy. His strange, almost handsome face, was slashed with a sneer and his tunic was stiff with dark stains. He was standing between her and the door.

'Whose blood is that?' she asked.

'I wish it belonged to your husband,' he said. He was holding a knife, the blade was black with gore. 'Or that Leon Courtney brat you keep so close. But no, this blood is from that darkie you got to speak against me in court.'

He mimed stabbing downwards with the knife.

'I don't like women who talk. And you talk all the fucking time, Mrs Ballantyne.'

He strode towards her, pushing the broken furniture out of his way.

Amber had no weapon. Her hand swept the surface of the desk and touched a heavy glass paperweight. She snatched it off the table and hurled it at Cressy's head. Her aim was perfect, but she was weak – weeks without a proper meal had taken their toll. Cressy batted the paperweight aside and sprang to block her before she could make a run for the door that led to the back corridor and the backyard of the fort, to freedom.

He caught her as she tried to dodge past him, grabbing her around the waist and pulling her towards him. She couldn't reach Cressy's eyes – her back was to his chest – so she drove her heel into his foot.

Cressy shouted, but his grip on her tightened, leaving her gasping as he lifted her off the ground.

With adrenaline coursing through her veins, Amber tried to kick back at his groin, scratching like an angry cat until Cressy threw her violently to the floor. Her head struck the corner of a desk – she felt the sharpness of the pain and her vision blurred – then he launched himself on top of her, holding her tight, pinning her to the ground, his rotten breath hot and rasping in her ear.

Amber turned her face away, feeling the bile rising in her throat. She had to find something – a bottle, a glass, a piece of wood, anything she could use as a weapon.

'I gutted that native girl,' Cressy murmured in her ear, pressing down on her, the smell of his sweat rank. 'And you need to be taught a lesson, too, don't you, Mrs Ballantyne? Friend of the African, of the poor kaffirs. I've read your books. Always making every darkie you meet the equal of a true-born Englishman. You're a poison, telling such lies to the world. At least those Dutch farmers have got that right. They don't try and tell us that we're like those apes. I shall cut your throat, Mrs Ballantyne, but first I shall cut out your lying tongue.'

Cressy grabbed her chin and twisted it so he could see her eyes, so she had no choice but to meet his gaze. His breath was coming in raw and jagged pants. He forced the tip of the blade between her lips and began pressing downwards. Amber could feel the metal against her teeth, taste the thick, clotted blood that caked Cressy's knife. She clenched her jaw.

'Come on now, darling, open wide for me.'

She thrashed with her legs, trying to buck him off her. The knife slipped and she felt it slice her lip open.

Cressy put his other hand over her face, pinching her nose. She bared her teeth, trying to breathe through her mouth without unclenching her jaw, choking as her own blood drained into the back of her throat.

Cressy saw her suffering and smiled.

The door splintered open with a shuddering crash. Cressy sprang to his feet and Amber rolled away, dragging herself upright, her limbs shaking and unsteady. Captain Stuttaford was in the doorway, his chest heaving, blood smeared across his shirt and hands. He stared wildly about him, taking in Amber's bloodied mouth and Cressy's fighting stance.

'You! Little man!' Cressy said.

Stuttaford grabbed the whisky bottle from the table next to the door – the whisky that Amber had used to clean Hore's wound. He smashed it and charged head down at Cressy. Cressy fell back – Stuttaford's wildness taking him by surprise.

'For God's sake, someone help us!' Amber screamed.

There had to be troopers outside somewhere – they must be back from delivering the Eloff and his men to the gaol.

Stuttaford thrust the bottle at Cressy's face. Cressy dodged, catching a glancing blow to his cheek, and slashed at Stuttaford's arm. The bottle fell from the captain's hands and Cressy stepped forward, punching the blade into Stuttaford's side.

Stuttaford fell to his knees as one of the Cape Boys appeared at the door with his rifle raised. Cressy turned and ran for the corridor that led to the back of the fort – leaping over a desk and sending bottles and papers flying around him in a storm.

'Shoot him!' Amber shouted at the man where he hesitated in the doorway.

'Which one?'

Amber staggered around the desk. 'The one running away!'

Grabbing the rifle out of the man's hands, Amber turned and stumbled painfully after Cressy. The rifle was heavy in her hands as she made her way down the back corridor, her head pounding and her ribs too bruised to breathe properly.

There was no sign of Cressy in the backyard.

Amber staggered over the half-ruined rampart and saw him.

Cressy had made good use of his head start, but he was still on the open veld and out of reach of cover. Amber leaned against the parapet, too weak and bruised to stand unaided, then lifted the rifle. She thought of Sethunya, putting her arm through hers, guiding her away from the Stadt as she asked her naive questions, of her quiet dignity as she gave her evidence, the glitter in her eye when she smiled. The magazine was full, one bullet in the chamber. Time seemed to narrow and slow and for a moment the pain disappeared. Amber could taste her own salty blood on her lips, feel the heat of the sun in her whole body, hear the beat of her heart. She focused on Cressy's diminishing frame. Distant though he was, it was as if she could hear his footsteps on the ground, smell his stinking breath. Sethunya smiled at her one more time, her eyes sad and knowing, as Amber squeezed the trigger.

Cressy lurched forward, thrown into the stiff veld grass by the impact of the bullet, ochre dust filling the air around him. Amber reloaded – the spent cartridge springing from the chamber – breathed in and took aim. One more shot to finish him. She thought of Cressy screaming bile in the town square, the group from the Stadt listening as his punishment was pronounced, of Sethunya singing songs to the children at the feeding station. She watched Cressy trying to stand, watched him fall and try to stand again. Then – just as she was beginning to squeeze the trigger – her view was blocked. Amber blinked, her focus dissolving in confusion. Someone had run out of the low scrub between the river and the Boer trenches to join Cressy. Long hair and a light blue dress, slight and small. It was Hester Vintner, not in gaol where she should have been but standing with her arms outstretched, blocking Amber's shot.

'Damn . . .' Amber said quietly. She could still take her shot, kill Hester, then finish Cressy. After all, this was the girl who had tried to murder her husband. But though she willed herself to do it, Amber knew she could not fire. Hester was backing away, her arms spread wide, looking over her shoulder to check that she was still putting her small body between Cressy and the fort.

Amber lowered the rifle, slumped against the parapet and wiped the blood from her mouth. Her lip would need to be stitched.

The trooper whose rifle she had taken approached her cautiously across the yard. 'That was one hell of a shot, missus.'

'I only winged him, then that girl got in the way.'

The trooper passed her his canteen and reclaimed his weapon. Amber drank hastily before wiping the blood off it with the sleeve of her silk blouse and handing it back.

'How is Stuttaford?'

The trooper shrugged. 'Being carried into town, but he don't look good.'

'How did the girl get out of gaol?'

The trooper pushed back his slouch hat. 'Guards were out fighting, I guess. They'd have locked the other prisoners in, but I was on guard duty once or twice and she always played it meek and mild. They probably didn't bother that she wasn't in a cell.'

'That girl almost murdered my husband,' Amber said.

'And even you couldn't shoot her dead,' the trooper replied.

Amber did not reply at once.

'She'd become special friends with that Cressy fella,' the trooper continued. 'She helped nurse him after his flogging. But then they let him out and he disappeared. Maybe he came back for her?'

'You saw, didn't you, that Stuttaford was unarmed?' Amber said at last, pushing aside her thoughts of Cressy and Hester Vintner. 'Cressy would have cut out my tongue and murdered me if Stuttaford hadn't charged in. I must go and make sure that they know the truth in town.'

Amber stumbled as she stood up, and the trooper hurried to her side. She pushed him away.

'I'll be fine. Let me go and wash. And if you abandon your post to see me into town, I'll report you myself.'

• • •

Penrod was on his way to find Amber. He looked concerned when he saw her, but she shook her head, then took his arm.

'Anderson will put a stitch in it when he's got a moment,' she said, trying to keep her voice steady. 'Is the butcher's bill steep?'

'It is. Baden-Powell has ordered the burials for tonight, and is visiting the injured now. But we did it, Amber. We survived. It is so nearly over.'

It was good to have Penrod to lean on, to feel the strength of his arm under his jacket, and Amber felt her cheeks wet with tears as they began to walk back towards the town.

'Will they attack again before the relief column gets here?'

'We have their commander in our gaol,' he replied. 'I believe we are safe.'

'How is Stuttaford? You realise he saved my life?' Amber said, leaning her aching head against his arm.

'I was told. Did Cressy escape?'

'Yes. I took him down, but then Hester Vintner blocked my shot.'

'Hester?'

'Yes. Perhaps it's foolish, but even after what she did to you, I look at her and see only a little girl, lost and unhappy.'

'She is a child, Amber. I have no interest in revenging myself on her. Cressy, though, I intend to hunt down and flay alive the moment the siege is lifted.' The tone of Penrod's voice told her that he meant every word. 'But first I want to get you to Anderson. I left Stuttaford with him, having his side sewn up. Anderson is hopeful that he will heal and make old bones.'

They reached the hospital to find Anderson himself looking for them. Like every adult in Mafeking, he would have been unrecognisable to the friends who had known him before the siege, when his uniform strained at the seams and his large, cheerful face was round as a full moon. Now his jacket was loose, his face careworn, the siege revealing high cheekbones which had been hidden under layers of flesh for years. His hands and apron were spattered with blood.

'Colonel, Mrs Ballantyne? Would you come and see Stuttaford for a moment? Man needs to rest, and he won't until he has seen you. Agitated. Not good for him. I've told the fellow half a dozen times that we know he saved Mrs B's life, but he won't be still.'

Anderson led them down a corridor into a small room next to the operating theatre. Stuttaford opened his eyes as they approached and tried to sit up, until Anderson pushed him back on to the bed.

'By all that's holy, Stuttaford, if you tear those stitches I shall let you bleed out! I've brought the colonel and his wife, now say what you have to say and then let me give you the damn laudanum.'

Amber stood by the bed and took Stuttaford's hand.

'Thank you.'

He shook his head, though Amber felt his fingers tighten around her own.

'Your child . . .'

'What of him, Captain? David is safe on the farm.'

Stuttaford closed his eyes and tried to slow his breathing.

'Cressy . . . murdered Sethunya. He tried to kill you, but he failed. He wants his money, and his revenge. He can't get it here.

He will go to the farm where your baby is. He will kill all of them, the girl, too, if she gets in his way.'

'But he doesn't know where the farm is . . .' Penrod said. 'Everyone knows that David is with Greta but they do not know the farm.'

Amber felt her stomach give a sickening lurch.

'Penrod! Oh, forgive me . . . I told him! I told Cressy the name of the farm while he helped me with the entertainment.'

Stuttaford started to cough and turned his head, a thin splatter of blood flashed across the pillow.

'Enough!' Anderson said. 'The warning is given. I hope the child is safe, but now I have to look after the captain.'

• • •

The Boer prisoners had been confined, marched through the town square to the gaol, and now the crowd that had gathered to cheer the victorious defenders was beginning to disperse into the evening. Leon and Tau had been among the most enthusiastic, and were still discussing the victory when Leon saw Penrod leading his wife towards headquarters.

'I must go and help at the newspaper,' Tau said.

'You don't need that alphabet in the book anymore, do you?'

'No, now I can read upside down and backwards, which you cannot.' Then Tau added more thoughtfully: 'I thank you for being my teacher, Leon Courtney.'

'It's all right. I'd have never escaped Cape Town without you.' Leon cleared his throat. 'I'm going to see if Uncle Penrod needs me.'

Leon jogged across the square. Tau watched him go, then stuck his hands in his pockets and headed to the newspaper offices.

• • •

Leon found his aunt and uncle deep in discussion with Baden-Powell.

'But this is a suspicion, is it not?' Baden-Powell said. 'Stuttaford *thinks* Cressy and the girl *might* attack the family at the farm, but that is all? He heard no definitive plan?'

'He did not,' Penrod said calmly.

'And Cressy is wounded,' Baden-Powell continued. 'Surely he will simply return to the Boer with the girl. He betrayed our positions to them, so they must give him safe harbour, and the girl is a Boer. She will most likely want to be with her people.'

'The Boer dislike Cressy. The girl has no love of her people,' Penrod said. 'Her attack on me was personal.'

Baden-Powell leaned forward, his palms spread wide on the desk in front of him. 'I cannot spare the men to check, Penrod. You know this better than anyone. We lost too many today. If Snyman decides to attack again in the morning, we will need every man to defend the town, we cannot do without them.'

Ned Cecil slammed his fist on the table.

'Snyman won't attack! And this is Penrod's son! How can you possibly not give him leave to go, after everything he has done to defend the town?'

Penrod turned towards him, his eyes flashing.

'And if I left and the town was taken, all that I . . .' He took a deep breath and continued more gently: 'All that *we* have done would have been for nothing. It would be a betrayal of the officers and men, and with Methuen's relief column only hours away. I cannot go, nor can we spare any man from the town.'

'Penrod . . .' Amber spoke in a whisper, leaning against her husband as if she could no longer stand.

'But I can get a message out,' Penrod continued, addressing Baden-Powell as if they were the only two people in the room. 'The Boer camp must be checked to see if Cressy is there. They have made use of him, but they will not hide a murderer from us. If Cressy and the girl are not in the laager then the danger is real, but I know one man outside the town whom I would trust with my life and the life of my child.'

'Who?' Baden-Powell demanded.

'Ryder Courtney,' Penrod said. 'If David is in danger, Ryder will not rest until he is safe. I know that. If Cressy is not in the Boer laager, we must get a message to Ryder.'

'But who will take it?' Ned asked. 'Whoever goes must cross the lines, make the case to the Boer and then reach Mr Courtney. I hope you are not thinking of sending Leon? He is too young.'

'No, we cannot send Leon!' Amber said in a rush. 'He almost died reaching us here.'

'One of the prisoners,' Penrod said. 'The Boer have a code. I believe there will be men in the gaol willing to carry a message with the same urgency as if it was their own child in danger.'

'Of course,' Baden-Powell said. 'Ned, my compliments to Eloff. Ask if he can recommend someone. They will be given safe passage in return for delivering the message.'

'Sir,' it was one of the cluster of cadets gathered around the door.

'What is it, Cadet Stanley?' Ned asked gruffly.

'Sir, Leon Courtney's already gone.'

'What?' Ned exploded.

'He left just after you said about checking the Boer camp and fetching his father.'

• • •

R yder stared up into the night sky, his head in Saffron's lap, counting the stars and considering what he had lost and gained in these last months. He had felt more himself than he ever had in Cairo or Cape Town. It was good to spend a week or two in luxury, but any more than that and he felt the soft beds and good food sapping his energy. If he took up residence in one of the great cities of the world, counting his vast fortune, he would become fat and irascible, the caricature of some industrialist. He needed space, wilderness, to be himself, the threat and promise of pitching himself against wild men and raw nature.

'Ryder? Saffron?' Peter crouched down beside them.

'What is it?'

'Two riders coming, man and boy. Fast. The man is a Boer but he has a white flag.'

Ryder got to his feet and checked his revolver. Saffron did the same. The rest of the raiding party readied their weapons.

In the moonlight, Ryder spotted them easily – one slim, the other more thickset, both of them travelling at pace. The younger one was standing up in his stirrups, waving his cap in the air. Saffron was already running towards them before Ryder had even recognised his own son.

Leon swung himself down from the saddle and Saffron folded him in her arms, the tears streaming down her face, saying his name again and again.

'Mama, please! I must speak to Father.'

The boy had grown a foot, Ryder would have sworn it. A man was emerging from the body of the child.

Ryder had hardly noticed the Boer, but now he spoke.

'The boy comes to you from Penrod Ballantyne in Mafeking,' he said. 'And the matter is the baby son of Colonel and Mrs Ballantyne, who is being cared for on a farm near Mosita.'

'Yes, Papa,' Leon said. 'Trooper Cressy is a dirty traitor and a liar. He has murdered one woman, and he tried to kill Aunt Amber. He is with the girl we met who wanted to kill Uncle Penrod. Aunt Amber shot him but only wounded him. We think he may be trying to reach the farm and David. He hates Amber and Penrod so much . . .'

Saffron struggled to her feet. 'Peter,' she said. She still held on to Leon's hand. 'Would you fetch our ponies and rifles?'

He went at once.

'I went to the Boer camp and they checked for me and found Cressy was not in the laager but two ponies were missing. This man here is a Boer who showed me the way to you and lent me a very good horse.' Leon turned to the fighter. 'Thank you very much, by the way. Papa, we must hurry.'

'We shall go at once, Leon, but you will stay here with Peter.'

'But Mama!'

Her voice, when she spoke, was in a tone of absolute command: 'Leon, you will stay here with Peter. You will wait until we come back.'

Peter had returned with their rifles and heard her.

'I will guard you, Leon Courtney.'

Leon looked between his parents and some sense of his shame at what he had done returned. 'I will wait.'

'The horses are ready,' Peter said, then looked at the Boer. 'You can rest your horses and share our fire. You have my word we will not harm you.'

The Boer lowered his eyes. 'I'll make my own fire, but I'll do no harm to you neither. I've sworn to take the boy back to Mafeking when this is played out.'

• • •

The moon was high as Saffron and Ryder set out for the Bauer farm. The raider's horses were built for endurance rather than speed, but they surged forward along the road into the darkness. The dry season was coming and the grasses were brittle and golden, the trees closing up on themselves as the earth became loose and dusty.

'How far is it, Ryder?' Saffron asked.

'Two, three hours at this pace,' Ryder replied. 'Leon has grown.'

'He's too thin. The girl with this Cressy man,' Saffron replied, 'Amber wrote to me about her. She sounds half-crazed.'

'I imagine so.'

Ryder thought of his son back at the camp, the young man he had become, the thin muscled body under the khaki uniform of the Mafeking cadets, and knew that the chasm between them was still as huge and unmappable as the plains over which they travelled. He and Saffron rode on in silence. Cressy. The name was unusual, but surely it had to be some coincidence.

• • •

The light from the oil lamp inside the farmhouse spread into the yard. Ryder and Saffron kept to the shadows along the rough fence. Ryder held up his hand as they came level with the house, and turned to his wife.

'Stay here, Saffron. Cover me.'

For a moment it seemed that she was going to argue, then she nodded. Ryder took his rifle from his shoulder, loaded it, and crept forward towards the veranda.

'What was that?' He heard a man's voice ask sharply inside.

'It is an old house, sometimes it creaks,' a woman answered. Her voice sounded jagged and torn, impatient, full of tears.

The male voice did not say any more, but Ryder heard the scrape of a spoon in a bowl. He reached the veranda, crossed it quickly and pressed his back against the wall.

Glancing through the window, he could see Greta's uncle on the floor, his wife crouched over him. He was lying on his back, his face blueish-grey. Beneath him a dark stain marked where his blood had soaked into the rug. Mrs Bauer, her long hair loose around her shoulders, was packing a wound in his shoulder with rags. Ryder thought it must have been her voice he had heard. The front of her night dress was red with blood and he watched as she wiped tears from her face with the back of her hand.

To the left of the older couple was the rough dining table made from long planks of acacia wood, with half a dozen chairs set around it. Ryder had eaten there on their visits to the family. A younger man was seated at right angles to the window, hunched over his bowl. He had taken off his coat and Ryder could see the shirt around his shoulders was heavily stained with blood and a rough bandage had been tied around it. The wound did not seem to impede his movements much, judging by the enthusiasm with which he was plying his spoon. On the table in front of him lay the blue-grey hulk of a German service revolver, its fat barrel was pointing towards Greta. She was sitting in her chair, her hands clasped in her lap and staring at the man eating his supper with a mixture of fear and loathing.

From the back kitchen a young girl walked into the room. She was holding David in her arms, swaying him from side to side.

'Maybe I'll take you with us, Greta,' the man said, smacking his lips. 'Maybe I'll keep you, maybe I'll sell you into a whorehouse in Johannesburg.'

Greta didn't flinch.

'I'd rather die,' she said.

'Happy to oblige.' His hand hovered over the revolver for a moment. 'No, I think I'd like to see your face when I spit that little brat on my knife. And then I'll leave you alive to tell his mother all about it.' He swallowed another mouthful.

The girl holding David stared at Cressy.

'But . . . why would we hurt the baby? You said we were coming to get your money and then we'd leave. Then you shot that man, and you stole the money. It was not yours, at all. You lied to me.'

Cressy stood up, knocking his chair over. 'It is my money! They can get it back from Amber bloody Ballantyne. But do you think I'll leave here without revenging myself on those people? You hate Penrod Ballantyne as much as I hate his wife. They killed your parents, what better revenge than killing their brat?'

The girl took a step back. 'It is a baby.'

Cressy put his hand over the gun.

'He is only a baby. And he is Leon Courtney's cousin. Leon has been kind to me, and he would not want the baby hurt!'

'Courtney, Courtney, Courtney!' He slammed the gun against the table and both women flinched. 'I would have killed Leon Courtney in a heartbeat if he wasn't surrounded by soldiers every second of the day.' He leaned forward. 'You know, Hester, it was his father who started all this! His father who sent me out into the wilderness. I found out something very important in Cape Town before I left. Listen, you'll like this. They leave death and destruction behind them everywhere, but the precious Courtneys and Ballantynes won't burn!'

He turned sideways and pointed the revolver at the girl. Ryder saw his face for the first time. The corrupt manager of the factory he had bought. The man Penrod had told him not to prosecute. His blood ran cold.

'So I thought, fine, I'll *be* Ryder Courtney, then. I'll let his brother-in-law recruit me and I'll make some money out of a siege just like he did back in the day. And it was all going beautifully till Amber fucking Ballantyne stuck her nose in, so I *will* kill that child. Even if they won't burn, they can suffer! Now, put the brat down or I'll kill you, too, I swear it.'

Greta sprang up from her seat, her arms wide, putting herself between Cressy and the girl holding baby David.

'You . . . you set fire to the hotel.'

Cressy nodded.

'Ryder Courtney took away my work, my dignity. I wanted to take something back.'

'People died in that fire.' Greta gasped. 'Good people, innocent people!'

Cressy shrugged. 'But not the *right* people.' He waved the muzzle of the revolver. 'Get out of the way. It's over! I can kill all three of you with one bullet at this range.'

At that moment, Ryder kicked the door, his rifle raised.

Cressy span round, then seeing Ryder's face, staggered backwards.

'You!' Then he smiled. 'I'm glad you are here to see this.' He pointed his gun back at Greta, the girl and the baby.

'Give up, Cressy,' Ryder said. 'Or I will kill you. Put down the gun.'

'You stole my factory. The Ballantynes stole my money. I will make you all pay . . .'

But before either man could move the room was filled with the sound of a gunshot, the window exploding into shards of glass and a wound flowering on Cressy's temple. His expression seemed to freeze and he fell against the wall, his body bouncing off the edge of the table and tumbling into the corner.

Saffron appeared in the doorway, her rifle in her hands.

'I asked you to wait outside,' Ryder said.

'I did for a bit,' she replied.

Greta helped Hester to stand from where she had fallen in shock at the sound of the gunshot. Hester's whole body was shaking, but she still was holding David tightly. David's screams were deafening, his small fists fighting the air.

'Oh, you little angel, you are safe now,' Greta said, taking David from Hester and trying to soothe him. 'We are all safe now, thank God.'

Hester sat down at the table. Saffron approached, dragging another chair close to hers and sitting beside her, then cautiously she put her arm around her shoulder. The girl started crying.

'Thank you, Hester,' Saffron said. 'I am Leon's mother. That was very brave. He will be very grateful to you for saving little David.'

Ryder watched the weeping girl. If there had to be soldiers in the world, he thought, perhaps it would be a good thing if more of them were like Leon, who could drag such loyalty out of someone as strange and damaged as this child. He laid his rifle on the table and went to help Greta's aunt. Mr Bauer's wound was serious. Mrs Bauer went to fetch hot water and bandages while Ryder examined it.

'I can sew you up, Bauer,' he said. 'You've lost a lot of blood, but if it's kept clean, I think you'll heal.'

Bauer nodded, and closed his eyes.

'Thank you, Mr Ryder,' said Greta, the tears still running down her face. 'How did you know we needed help?'

He smiled. 'Leon finally left Mafeking to bring us the message.'

'I shouldn't have listened to him,' Hester said. 'I should have known he wanted more than money here.'

Saffron cleared her throat. 'We all listen to people we shouldn't sometimes, Hester.'

Ryder glanced at her, and their eyes met. She winked at him, and he knew she was thinking of Leon and the letters from his cousin in Cairo.

'You didn't need to take the shot, Saffron,' he said in a conversational tone. 'I would have killed him before he harmed the baby or the girls.'

'I know,' she said, her eyes dancing. 'But patience was never my strong suit, Ryder.'

• • •

When they left some hours later, Mr Bauer was sleeping and the bleeding had stopped. Ryder and Saffron had dug a grave for Cressy in the paddock on the far side of the house, while Greta scrubbed the blood from the floorboards.

'What do we do with Hester?' Saffron asked Greta in a whisper when Cressy was confined to the earth. 'She should be in the gaol in Mafeking for her attack on Penrod.'

'Leave her with us, Saffron. She can help nurse my uncle.'

Saffron looked doubtful.

'Trust me,' Greta said, patting her hand.

And Saffron did.

When the work was done Ryder and Saffron rode back to their camp, where they found Leon and the Boer rider waiting for them. Leon insisted on returning to Mafeking with the news that Cressy was dead and David was unharmed. Saffron could hardly bear to let him go – only knowing the agony her sister must be in waiting for word made it possible for her to agree to let him cross the lines again.

• • •

The Boer commandos left Mafeking in great disorder two days later. The reports came in from each corner of town. The besiegers had gone, and the guns were silenced. Cautiously at first, and then with hoots of joy, the townsfolk swept out over the abandoned trenches and returned weighed down with abandoned supplies, enough to offer fresh rolls and coffee to the first of the relief column who rode into the town square at midnight.

Saffron rode in with them. Swinging herself down from her exhausted horse, she fell into the embrace of her sister Amber and her son. Leon buried his face in her neck, comforted by her touch and the dusty smell of her hair. Their meeting the night of the final attack seemed almost a dream to them both, but this, the warmth and joy of her here in the shattered town was real.

'Leon!' She laughed. 'I shall never let you out of my sight again. Keep hold of my hand for an hour at least, or I shall turn mad.'

He laughed, and wrapped his fingers through hers.

'And is this Tau?'

'Yes, Mama,' Leon said, grateful and confused by the strength of the love he felt for her. 'Tau Modisa.'

Saffron put out her free hand and Tau shook it.

'I am very glad to see you again, Tau,' she said.

Her voice sounded like honey, so sweet and warm, Tau decided.

'Welcome to Mafeking, Mrs Courtney,' he said. 'Leon taught me to read. Now I am going to be a newspaper man.'

Saffron hugged her son to her side again and ruffled his hair.

'Oh, if I am to call you Tau still, you must call me Saffron. A teacher now, are you, Leon? Your old governess would have a heart attack if she heard that. Good for you, Tau. I bet you were a great student.'

Tau looked pleased.

She put out her arms to her sister and Amber embraced her.

'Amber, Ryder went to fetch Greta and David. He'll be here in two hours.'

'I owe you both my life,' Amber said. 'Again.'

Saffron shrugged. 'Oh, who can keep count? But, Lord, you are thinner than Leon!'

Amber laughed. 'And you look happier than I've seen you in months.'

'I am. Now, who should I meet? Leon, I mean it, keep hold of my hand. Tau, take the other, do.'

Tau took it gladly, then waved at Sol. He approached and bowed to her in a courtly fashion.

'Mrs Courtney, I have heard a great deal about you from your son.'

'Oh, do call me Saffron, and I have heard a great deal about you from Mathakgong. Is it true you are translating Shakespeare into Setswana?'

Sol looked pleased. 'That is my intention.'

Amber watched her sister and sighed with relief, but it was only later that morning, when Ryder arrived, riding an ox cart loaded with sacks of flour, Greta perched beside him with David in her arms, that she felt the war was over.

David clasped his hands behind her neck and she held him tight against her skin. Saffron saw the moment, and her drawing of Mrs Ballantyne reunited with her son was published in the centre pages of the *London Illustrated News* the following month.

Ryder received the enthusiastic embrace of his wife. 'Leon and Tau are going to take me on a tour of the scenes of their victories, then we are going to pay a visit to Sol and Mathakgong in the Stadt.'

'I'll join you there,' he said.

Saffron was illuminated with joy at being reunited with her son. He saw her hand in Leon's, and the way his son glanced at her, smiling, from time to time. The boy could not be beyond hope if he loved his mother that much.

Ryder was watching her walk away, admiring the sway of her hips, when Penrod came across to him with his hand extended.

'Hello, brother,' he said. 'Leon told us what happened at the Bauer farm. You have my thanks. I'll be forever in your debt. How is Mr Bauer?'

Ryder shook his hand and looked at his brother-in-law narrowly. He was painfully thin and his skin was grey, but Ryder could see that Penrod's whipcord strength remained despite his skeletal appearance.

'I saw no sign of infection today. They have offered Hester a home there. They need the help, and I saw no reason to object.'

'Neither do I.'

Penrod offered him a cigar and Ryder took it.

'Did Leon tell you that it was Cressy who started the fire at the hotel?'

Penrod nodded. 'Leon almost tried to turn it into a reason to blame you for everything, naturally. But I informed him that I had asked you not to prosecute.'

Ryder laughed bitterly. 'I bet he didn't know what to say to that.'

'He was uncharacteristically quiet for a moment,' Penrod replied.

Ryder noticed the populace of the town had hung bunting over the square and as each new squadron of British troops marched into the town, a fresh rendition of 'Rule Britannia' began. Baden-Powell had taken a position near headquarters at the head of an informal reception committee and shook hands with each man as they arrived. However, the good cheer could not mask the condition of the people or their town.

'You did well to hang on here,' Ryder said.

'It was a close-run thing,' Penrod replied. 'And I do not believe the war is over yet. The Boer fighters have simply retreated into the bush. It will take months to harry them out.'

Ryder agreed with him. The war might be over in Mafeking, but he was certain it was not won. Not even close.

'Penrod, it is time to send Leon to school in England. I would be glad of your recommendation – he needs somewhere that will fit him for a military career.'

'I will think about it,' Penrod said, trying to keep his surprise from his voice. 'He is a brave lad, you know, Ryder.'

'I know . . . he is my son.'

Penrod blew a cloud of blue smoke into the air. 'And I know Amber is going to give you the whole story later, but he also defended your honour in front of the entire town.'

Ryder looked at him, shocked. 'This is a place of miracles.'

Penrod laughed. 'And something else. I have a man I would like you to see, currently in hospital, but recovering well. His name is Stuttaford, and I suspect you might be able to make use of him in one or other of your businesses. He is conscientious and flexible in his thinking. And courageous.'

'I'm happy to talk to him before we go back to Cape Town. What of Tau?'

'I understand he is going to be a newspaper man. We'll make sure he has the resources to do whatever he wants in the future, but I think Tau will become a protégé of Sol Plaatje. Have you heard of him?'

'I have. Enough to know Tau is lucky to know him.'

The two men lapsed into silence and watched their wives. Leon was introducing Saffron to the townspeople, while David pulled at Amber's hair with fascinated curiosity. Greta stood next to them, beaming.

'Do you think our women will ever be still for long, Ryder?' Penrod asked.

'Never,' Ryder replied. 'I know that Saffron will not go back to Cairo. It almost killed her.'

'Almost killed Lady Smythe, too, I heard,' Penrod replied, prompting a bark of laughter from Ryder. 'Amber, I think, has become a newspaper woman. I have no idea where that will lead her.'

'Somewhere interesting, I'm sure of it.' Ryder nodded towards Dixon's Hotel. 'Can a man get a decent drink in there?'

'He can get several,' Penrod replied. 'I'll buy you your first.'

The two men walked off together. Behind them the crowd launched into another raucous chorus of 'Rule Britannia' under the vast and shifting African sky.

WILBUR SMITH

THE POWER OF ADVENTURE

Visit the brand-new Wilbur Smith website to find out more about all of Wilbur's books, read the latest news, and dive into Wilbur's adventure notebooks on everything from the Boer War to the Skeleton Coast.

And if you want to be the first to know about all the latest releases and announcements, make sure to **subscribe to the Readers' Club mailing list**. Sign up today and get a preview of the next epic Wilbur Smith adventure!

Join the adventure at

WWW.WILBURSMITHBOOKS.COM

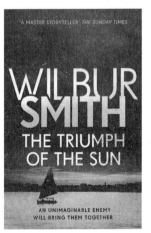

KING OF KINGS

An epic story of love, betrayal, courage and war.

Cairo, 1887. A beautiful September day. Penrod Ballantyne and his fiancée, Amber Benbrook, stroll hand in hand. The future is theirs for the taking.

But when Penrod's jealous former lover, Lady Agatha, plants doubt about his character, Amber leaves him and travels to the wilds of Abyssinia with her twin sister, Saffron, and her adventurer husband, Ryder Courtney. On a mission to establish a silver mine, they make the dangerous journey to the new capital of Addis Ababa, where they are welcomed by Menelik, the King of Kings.

Back in Cairo, a devastated Penrod seeks oblivion in the city's opium dens. He is rescued by an old friend,

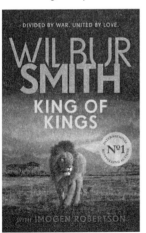

who is now in the Italian army, and offered the chance to join the military efforts. Italy has designs on Abyssinia, and there are rumours of a plan to invade . . .

With storm clouds gathering, and on opposing sides of the invasion, can Penrod and Amber find their way back to one another – against all the odds?

AVAILABLE NOW

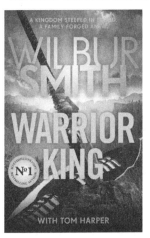

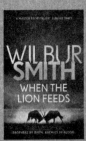

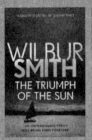

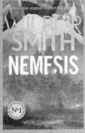

DISCOVER
THE COURTNEY SERIES

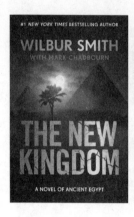